Born and raised in the was boarding-school- a career in classical m and embracing the world of computers. Happily married, with three daughters, she began writing when family commitments kept her at home. She likes to create stories that are believable, modern, fast-paced and sexy. Her interests include meaty sagas, doing word puzzles, gambling and going to the movies.

Tara Pammi can't remember a moment when she wasn't lost in a book—especially a romance, which was much more exciting than a mathematics textbook at school. Years later, Tara's wild imagination and love for the written word revealed what she really wanted to do. Now she pairs alpha males who think they know everything with strong women who knock that theory *and* them off their feet!

THE TYCOON'S SCANDALOUS PROPOSITION

MIRANDA LEE

BLACKMAILED BY THE GREEK'S VOWS

TARA PAMMI

MILLS & BOON

First Published in Great Britain 2018
by Mills & Boon, an imprint of HarperCollins*Publishers*
1 London Bridge Street, London, SE1 9GF

The Tycoon's Scandalous Proposition © 2018 by Miranda Lee

Blackmailed by the Greek's Vows © 2018 by Tara Pammi

ISBN: 978-0-263-93535-6

MIX
Paper from
responsible sources
FSC **FSC™ C007454**

This book is produced from independently certified FSC™ paper
to ensure responsible forest management.
For more information visit www.harpercollins.co.uk/green.

Printed and bound in Spain
by CPI, Barcelona

THE TYCOON'S SCANDALOUS PROPOSITION

MIRANDA LEE

CHAPTER ONE

BLAKE STOOD NEXT to the groom, wondering what the hell he was doing, being best man at this wedding. He knew this marriage wouldn't last—knew it was just a matter of time.

He'd tried to reason with Lachlan. But nothing could dissuade him. Not even Blake's argument that he himself had married at the same age—twenty-four—and the marriage hadn't lasted six months.

At least the bride wasn't an actress, Blake reasoned more positively. Also on the plus side, it wasn't as though marriage—even a temporary one—harmed a movie star's popularity these days. Gone were the days when the power-brokers of Hollywood had dictated who a star could marry. *And* when.

The rise of social media had changed all that. The public couldn't get enough of celebrity relationships. They especially enjoyed break-ups and divorces, and any whiff of scandal. Such was life in the spotlight.

Thankfully Blake's own life wasn't so much in the spotlight—though he'd gained a little more attention in the press since moving Fantasy Productions from Sydney to LA fifteen months ago. Still, movie-makers—even very successful, very wealthy ones like himself—didn't grab the headlines the way actors did. Especially those like Lachlan, with his golden boy looks, buffed body and bedroom blue eyes. Add to that buckets of boyish charm and you had a prize publicity package.

Blake had first recognised Lachlan's potential when he'd attended a performance at Australia's much lauded National Institute of Dramatic Art a few years ago. He'd instantly signed him up. And the rest, as they said, was history. Three years and four movies later Lachlan was an established star, whilst *he'd* become Australia's most successful film writer/director/producer.

Blake suspected, however, that their working relationship would not last for much longer. It was only a matter of time before something—like this marriage—would make his star move on.

'There she is,' Lachlan whispered suddenly, snapping Blake out of his cynical thoughts.

Blake followed the groom's enthralled gaze past the seated guests and up the sweeping staircase down which the bride would eventually descend, and into the large living area, which had been filled with several rows of chairs divided by a strip of red carpet.

Blake spied a froth of white up on the gallery landing. White dress, white hair, white flowers. Behind the bride, attending to the long white veil, bustled the one and only bridesmaid, wearing something long and svelte in jade-green. Blake couldn't see her properly—didn't have a clue who she was. He hadn't even met the bride, having been too busy with his latest movie, plus several other new projects, to fly back to Australia for Lachlan's engagement party, and only jetting in to Sydney late last night.

The only contribution Blake had made to this wedding had been getting billionaire Byron Maddox—who was a good friend as well as a business partner—to offer his very lovely harbour-side home as a venue for the wedding and the reception afterwards.

The original venue had rather inconveniently burnt down six weeks ago, throwing Lachlan into a panic after getting a phone call on location from his hysterical bride-to-be.

Thank heaven for rich friends, Blake thought, and threw Byron and Cleo a grateful glance.

When they smiled back at him his own face cracked open into a wide smile. God, but they were a great couple.

If ever a man and woman were made for each other it was those two. They almost made him believe in true love.

Finally some music started up. Not a traditional bridal march but a rather romantic piano rendition of 'The First Time Ever I Saw Your Face'.

It was at that moment that the bridesmaid in jade-green moved round from behind the Barbie doll bride and came into full view.

Blake's dark eyebrows lifted in surprise. She wasn't a stunner. But she was extremely attractive. Tall, with a slender figure and pale skin which suited the off-the-shoulder style of her gown. Her hair was a golden-brown colour, drawn straight back from her high forehead and falling in a softly waved curtain down her back, held in place by a simple circlet of pink and white flowers. It was her face, however, which Blake kept returning to—a face any camera would love.

Blake had a habit of looking at faces as though through a lens, especially on a first meeting. It was a long-ingrained habit, and one which didn't do any harm, really. No one knew what he was thinking at the time, so Blake didn't feel any guilt as he continued to assess the bridesmaid's looks from every camera angle.

He knew from experience that high cheekbones and a well-defined jawline photographed well in any light and from any angle. This woman's nose wasn't starlet-small, but it suited her, giving her face character. She didn't have pouting bee-stung lips either, although it was all the fad these days. Her mouth was actually rather wide, but still well formed. And expressive. So were her almond-shaped eyes.

Blake frowned as he tried to fathom the reason behind the sadness he kept glimpsing within their dark brown depths as she made her way slowly—and stiffly—down the staircase. Along with the sadness lay undeniable tension, he noted. Her knuckles were white as she clasped

the posy of pink and white flowers at her waist with unnecessary force.

At last she reached the bottom step. It was at this point
that she sucked in a deep breath, as though trying to gather
all her courage. The gesture touched him, evoking an uncharacteristic surge of compassion. Something was bothering that girl about this wedding—something much more
emotional and personal than Blake's cynical view.

'Who's the bridesmaid?' Blake muttered under his
breath, so that only Lachlan could hear.

'What? Oh, that's Kate. Maddie's sister.'

'Older sister?'

'Older? Yeah. God, doesn't Maddie look incredible?' he
exclaimed, clearly awed by the beauty of his bride, who remained standing at the top of the staircase, all eyes on her.

Not Blake's, however. He'd had his fill of Barbie doll
blondes—especially those manufactured in Hollywood
by plastic surgeons and ambitious mamas. His eyes were
all for the bridesmaid, with her natural-looking figure and
lovely but oh, so sad eyes.

Her chin lifted as she took her first step along the make-
shift aisle, her focus straight ahead during what seemed to
be a very difficult journey for her. She didn't look at him,
or at Lachlan, or at any of the guests. She seemed frozen
now—a robot with no feelings on show any more. But that
didn't mean they weren't there.

Smile, sweetheart, came the sudden wish from deep inside Blake. *Don't let the world see that you're hurting. Don't
give people the chance to hurt you further.*

And they would if she let them. People could be cruel—
especially once they'd sensed weakness. Fortunately, no one
was looking at her. All eyes were still on the beaming bride,
who was now approaching the bottom of the staircase. The
music changed to 'Isn't She Beautiful?' Which the bride
was. Even Blake had to agree that Maddie was drop-dead

gorgeous. But such beauty was often only surface-deep, he'd found, the same way Lachlan's was.

The same way Claudia's was...

The thought didn't hurt him the way it once had. But that didn't mean he'd forgotten the lessons his one and only marriage had taught him.

The main one was, *Don't, for pity's sake, believe anything that ambitious young actresses do or say to you. Sleep with them, by all means, but don't fall for their flattery or their brilliant fakery. And never marry one. Lord, no.*

In truth, marriage was not for him—even with a non-ambitious non-actress. Not yet, anyway. Aside from his scepticism over the lasting power of romantic love, he wasn't good husband material. He was way too obsessed with making movies, working seven days a week, often twenty hours a day. What time did that leave for a wife, let alone children?

Maybe when he was forty he might consider both. But he was only just thirty-two. Plenty of years left to think about such things.

Meanwhile, his attention returned to the attractive but bleak-looking bridesmaid.

Damn. She looked as if she was going to cry now. Her bottom lip was definitely quivering, accompanied by a flash of true panic in her eyes. Clearly she didn't *want* to cry. Just in time she got control of herself, her nostrils flaring as she sucked in another deep, desperate breath.

Blake wondered what on earth was going on in that girl's mind. He knew that women often cried at weddings, but they were usually tears of happiness. He could be wrong, he supposed, but he was absolutely certain that whatever she was thinking they weren't happy thoughts!

Maybe this Kate knew what sort of man her kid sister was marrying—knew that he was a player. Maybe she feared for Maddie's future happiness. Well, she had a right to be scared on *that* particular score! Not that he could be a hundred percent positive that was the reason behind her grim face. He could only guess.

In actual fact Blake often found himself speculating on the various emotions he noted on the faces of perfect strangers. He was a people-watcher—an essential talent for a writer-cum-movie-maker. After all, motivations and emotional conflicts were the backbone of all storytelling.

His gaze returned to Kate's stiffly held face and robotic walk. At last she reached the end of the aisle, flashing him a frowning glance before moving sideways to her left, where no one could see her face except the celebrant. And *he* was busy ogling the bride. Now all Blake could see was her profile. Her head and shoulders drooped for a split second, then lifted abruptly, the muscles in her throat standing out as she once again took rigid control of herself.

His heart went out to her. As did his admiration. Whatever was bothering the bride's sister, she was a brave soul. Brave, but still rather fragile.

When the posy of flowers she was holding began to shake Blake determined not to let the evening end before he found out what was upsetting her so much. He could be charming when he wanted to be. And quite good at getting people to open up. Yes, he would worm the truth out of her. Women did love to confide. And hopefully, sooner rather than later, he would bring a smile to her face.

He imagined she would be quite lovely if she smiled. Already Blake found her attractive. And intriguing. And extremely desirable.

Much more desirable than the Barbie doll bride.

CHAPTER TWO

KATE GRITTED HER TEETH, still stunned at how much she was hating this, how sick she felt to her stomach. Yet she'd known for ages that this day was coming. She'd had plenty of time to prepare herself mentally. All to no avail, it seemed.

She clasped her bouquet even tighter and willed her mind to go blank. But her mind refused to obey. It whirled on and on, tormenting her. *Torturing* her.

Because today was the end of the line, wasn't it?

The end of all her hopes and dreams where Lachlan was concerned. Today the man she loved would marry her sister. And that would be that. No more stupidly hoping that he might wake up one morning and realise Maddie wasn't right for him and that *she* was a much more suitable wife. No more fantasising—as she had during their three years studying together at NIDA—that he might finally see her as a potential girlfriend and not just as his good mate and acting buddy.

There was nothing worse, she realised, than the death of hope.

Kate sighed, stiffening when she realised just how loud that sigh had been. As much as she was wretched to her core, she'd determined earlier today not to let anyone—particularly Maddie—suspect the truth. And she'd managed—'til the moment that sickening music had started up and she'd had to step into the spotlight on those stairs. At which point she'd frozen, the sheer futility of her feelings washing through her.

She knew she should have smiled but she simply hadn't been able to. Not that it had mattered. No one had been looking at her. No one except the man standing next to Lachlan. Blake Randall, the best man.

He had kept on looking at her. And frowning at her. Wondering, probably, why she looked so forlorn.

Kate would have liked to tell him why—would have liked to scream that if it hadn't been for *him* all their lives would have taken a different course and she wouldn't be standing here today, having her heart broken.

A slight exaggeration, Kate. Your heart was broken last Christmas, when you optimistically brought Lachlan home for dinner.

They'd both just graduated from NIDA, and Lachlan's parents had gone away on a Christmas cruise. Plus he'd been between girlfriends at the time. Which hadn't happened too often. She'd thought it was her chance to snare his sexual interest. And it had seemed at first that she had. Lachlan had actually flirted with her in the car during their drive from his flat at Bondi to her parents' home at Strathfield.

But all that had changed the moment he'd met her very beautiful and very vivacious blonde sister.

Something had died in Kate when she'd seen how quickly and easily Maddie had captured Lachlan's sexual interest. By the end of Christmas dinner Maddie's almost-fiancé had been firmly dispensed with and she'd gone off with Lachlan, moving in with him the very next day.

So, in reality, Kate had had ten months to get over her broken heart. Ten long, soul-destroying months during which her own acting career had stalled and she'd been reduced to working weekends in a local deli whilst going to endless auditions during the week.

If she hadn't been living at home she wouldn't have survived. The only acting job she'd managed to snare in that time had been a part in a play. It had been quite a good part, too. But the play hadn't proved commercial or popular at the box office. Despite garnering reasonable reviews, it had closed after six weeks.

She'd tried out for various movies and television shows, but had so far been unsuccessful, usually being told that she wasn't 'quite right' for that particular part; didn't have the 'right look'—or the right height, or the right something. Sometimes she wasn't given a reason at all. Her agent said she needed to be more positive when meeting producers and directors, but any positivity she'd possessed seemed to have disintegrated.

In truth, Kate had always been on the shy side, with social skills not her strong point. The only time she felt truly confident was when she was in character, playing an outgoing role. Then she *exuded* confidence. If only she could be more like Maddie, whose social skills were second to none and whose confidence was out of this world.

A nudge at her elbow snapped her out of her thoughts, and Kate turned to see Maddie glaring at her before shoving her bouquet into her hands. The glare disappeared once she'd turned back to beam at the male celebrant. Kate felt a sudden urge to throw the bridal bouquet onto the floor and stamp on it.

She didn't, of course. But the unexpected burst of anger did achieve something, shoving aside her self-pity and replacing it with a determination to stop letting unrequited love ruin her life. It was way past time for her to get over Lachlan and move on.

Steeling herself, Kate turned her body to the right in order to watch the ceremony, seeing immediately that Blake Randall had done the same and was looking straight at her. No, he was *staring* at her, as if he was trying to work out what was going on in her head.

If she told him he would probably laugh. Whilst she'd never actually met the man, she'd seen him interviewed on television several times. Despite having made a career—

and loads of money—making movies about love and romance, he'd come across as a cynic about both, stating bluntly on one occasion that he was just giving the audience what they wanted.

Of course he had been a popular topic of conversation amongst the students at NIDA—especially after making Lachlan into a star. Kate knew Blake Randall had been married once to Claudia Jay, an Australian actress who'd starred in one of his early films. The marriage hadn't lasted long, and Claudia had claimed her new husband had neglected her shamefully once the honeymoon was over. Kate suspected there was more to their divorce than met the eye, Claudia having moved to Hollywood soon after the breakup.

She didn't feel sorry for either of them. They were both tarred with the same brush, in her opinion. Both of them ruthlessly ambitious, leaving little room to really love anyone other than themselves. Blake had gone from strength to strength after his divorce, whilst Claudia had gone on to have a successful career in Hollywood, her name linked with a succession of high-flying producers and directors.

Kate herself didn't dream of Hollywood success. Or necessarily of being in movies. She loved acting on the stage most of all. But she wouldn't knock back a decent role in a movie or a television series. *If* she was ever offered one.

Kate was about to sigh again when she remembered her agent's advice to be more positive. And a little more proactive. It occurred to her that any other aspiring actor would take advantage of being in a wedding party opposite a brilliant movie-maker like Blake Randall. She shouldn't be ignoring his interested glances. She certainly shouldn't be standing around looking like a wet weekend and sighing all the time. She should be making the most of this rather amazing opportunity by smiling and flirting and projecting Little Miss Confident and Available, not Little Miss Miserable and Vulnerable.

All she had to do was pretend. No, *act*. She *was* an actor, wasn't she?

But it was no use. She simply couldn't summon up a smile. Maybe if he'd been more pleasant and approachable-looking she might have managed it. But his looks matched his reputation as a demanding tyrant to work for. He had gleaming black hair—worn unfashionably long. Thick black brows. Deeply set piercing blue eyes. An arrogant aquiline nose. Slightly hollow cheeks. And a rather cruel-looking mouth.

The press described him as 'handsome'. Kate thought him scary-looking. And very intimidating.

She was in the process of abandoning any idea of even *talking* to him later when he smiled at her. Just a small smile, really—a slight lifting of the corners of his mouth—but it was accompanied by a wicked twinkle in his eyes. They did strange things to her, that smile and that twinkle. Made her feel more confident. And quite sexy. Which was astonishing given her libido seemed to have died ten months ago, along with her heart.

Before she could think better of it she smiled back. A small smile and possibly without any accompanying twinkle. But it was a start. His smile widened, his eyebrows lifting, taking away his scariness and making him look quite handsome. Not handsome the way Lachlan was handsome—but then, no man Kate had ever met was *that* handsome.

He mouthed something at her and she frowned, not sure what he was saying. He repeated it more slowly and she finally understood the words.

You...look...lovely.

Kate honestly didn't know how to react, blinking her surprise before looking away. She wasn't used to men of

Blake Randall's ilk coming on to her. They went for the Maddies of this world. Or for stunning actresses like Claudia Jay. Admittedly she looked the very best she could today—thanks to Maddie and her mother bullying her into hours of work at the beauty salon—but she doubted she could compete with the sort of women who usually vied for this man's attention.

Kate was still trying to work out how to respond when there was a burst of applause behind her. Kate was taken aback to realise that the ceremony was over, and Lachlan and her sister were now legally man and wife.

She waited for a jab of devastation to overwhelm her but it didn't come. Instead all she could think about was Blake Randall flirting with her.

How odd.

There was Maddie in Lachlan's arms, being kissed very thoroughly, and even whilst she couldn't bear to watch at the same time it made her wonder what it would be like to be kissed by that hard, cruel mouth which was once again smiling at her. No, *grinning* at her.

It was infectious, that grin, as was the wry gleam in his eyes as he nodded his head towards the couple who were still locked together in an exhibitionist kiss.

Without thinking this time, she grinned back, and suddenly lightness lifted her previously heavy soul, making her see that there was definitely life after Lachlan.

How silly she'd been to imagine that the world had stopped turning simply because the man she loved did not love her back. There was still plenty to live for. Her career, for starters. Kate adored acting—loved inhabiting another character's skin and making her audience believe that she really was that person. It was the ultimate high when she pulled that off. The ultimate adrenaline rush.

The besotted couple finally wrenched themselves apart, and a flushed Maddie turned to Kate to retrieve her bouquet.

'What a pity Lachlan and I can't leave right now,' her sister grumbled. 'I can hardly wait I'm so turned on. Oh, God, don't look at me like that, Katie,' she hissed impatiently. 'You know how much I like sex. And my Lachlan is just the *best* at it.'

Kate smothered a groan of despair. Or was it disgust? Whatever it was, that feeling of devastation she'd so valiantly pushed aside was back with a vengeance.

CHAPTER THREE

OH-OH.

Disappointment swamped Blake as he caught sight of Kate again, her face having been obscured by the bride turning to collect her bouquet. Gone was her lovely smile, and in its place her former bleak expression.

What the hell had happened in the last few seconds? What had the Barbie doll said to her? Something not very nice, judging by the unhappiness in Kate's eyes.

Blake knew from first-hand experience that siblings were not always the best of friends—especially those of the same sex. Rivalry and jealousy often raised their ugly heads, making true friendship impossible. His own brother was a case in point. James had always been jealous of him, despite there being absolutely no need. James was the first-born son, after all, and his parents' favourite—especially since he'd followed in his mother and father's footsteps to become a doctor, like them.

On the other hand Blake had been regarded as the black sheep of the family since he hadn't even gone to university, since he'd done something considered very left field by embracing the entertainment world—first as a DJ, then shooting music videos for a couple of years before finally plunging full-time into making low-budget independent movies.

Both his parents and his brother had given him dire warnings about his future. And Blake found it telling that now he'd made it big they were all hurtfully silent on the subject of his success. Blake had used to let it bother him, but he no longer cared. Or so he told himself. They all had small minds, in his opinion, James the smallest of them all.

Blake rarely saw his family these days, only visiting at Christmas and on special occasions. Now that he'd moved to Los Angeles to live and work he suspected he might not even do that. Just send the occasional card. He no longer kept in contact through social media or email, nor with phone calls, having resolved not to give them any further opportunity to deliver snide remarks about his lifestyle or his movies. Which they did, if given the opportunity.

Blake had no evidence that Kate's sister had just made some kind of nasty remark to her except for the look on her face. But that wasn't jealousy he was seeing in her expressive blue eyes. It was hurt. And dismay.

Why her unhappiness bothered him so much he could not fathom. He'd never been a particularly empathetic soul. Perhaps it was because he found her attractive and didn't like the idea of there being some hidden impediment which would hinder his pursuing his interest in her. Whatever the reason, Blake resolved not to rest until he'd solved the mystery of that unhappiness.

And it *was* a mystery. Because on the surface of things Kate had nothing to be unhappy about. She was gorgeous! Okay, she didn't have the in-your-face blonde beauty of her sister. But she was still highly desirable.

Of course being physically attractive was no guarantee of happiness. Maybe she was unhappy because she was still unmarried, despite being the older sister. Though not much older, surely. Blake knew Lachlan's bride was only twenty-three, which made Kate what? Twenty-five? Twenty-six, maybe? Hardly a marital use-by date in this day and age.

'Get with the programme, Blake,' Lachlan said, grabbing his nearest elbow. 'We have to sign the marriage certificate.'

As the groom ushered him over to where the paperwork had been set up on a side table Blake cast a surreptitious glance back at Kate. She seemed to have gathered herself, and her expression was not wretched any longer. It was, however, utterly devoid of emotion once more—a totally blank mask. How on earth did she manage that? When *he* was upset everyone knew about it. He didn't throw tantrums, exactly, but his face always reflected his feelings—as did his voice.

He watched her watching the happy couple sign the register, but her eyes betrayed nothing now. Which was telling in itself.

When it was their turn to step forward as witnesses, he waved for her to go first. After throwing him a closed look, she picked up one of the provided pens and signed quickly, with only the slightest tremor in her hand. He glanced at her signature before he signed his own name.

Kate Holiday, he read, and realised that until that moment he hadn't known the bride's surname. So of course he hadn't known Kate's. He'd never met the bride's parents either, or anyone else in her family. Strange, really, given he was the best man.

Blake wondered all of a sudden why Lachlan had asked *him* to be his best man. He would have thought a young Aussie male with his looks and personality would have had at least one best mate—a pal he'd gone to school with or studied at NIDA with.

Obviously not. Either that or he preferred someone famous to stand by his side at his wedding. A celebrity. Lachlan was very much into celebrity.

It hadn't occurred to Blake until that moment that he was being used—that this wedding was little more than a publicity stunt, with a trophy bride, a glamorous Sydney setting and a rich and famous best man. Lachlan was no better than Claudia, really.

Whilst the thought did bring a sour note to the proceedings Blake knew he would have the last laugh. Because in actual fact Lachlan wasn't so great an actor, and his range was decidedly limited. Once he was seduced by the big boys in Hollywood and started making movies that weren't tailored to his specific brand of looks and charm his career might very well sink like a stone. Major studios were very unforgiving once the box office results rolled in. Lachlan's past successes in Blake's movies would not carry him for ever.

A slight smirk curved his top lip as he put his signature to the marriage certificate. It was still there when he put the pen down and turned to face his intriguing partner.

'So, Kate Holiday,' he said, doing his best to hide his underlying irritation, 'we haven't been properly introduced. But I dare say you know who I am.'

'Yes, of course I do,' Kate said. 'Lachlan has spoken of you a lot.'

'Well, you have one up on me, then—because he's told me nothing about you.'

She seemed quite taken aback. 'You mean he's never mentioned that we were students together at NIDA? We were in the same class,' she went on, obviously peeved. 'We graduated together last year.'

'Sorry. He's never mentioned it,' he told her, doing his best to get his head around this news.

Kate was an *actress*! Who would have believed it? Still, it went some way to explaining her ability to hide her emotions. Though she wasn't hiding them at the moment. She was looking decidedly upset. On his part, he was just perplexed.

Why hadn't Lachlan told him that his future sister-in-law had been at NIDA with him? He knew Blake held an enormous respect for their graduates. On top of that, he was always on the lookout for fresh talent—especially actors with Kate's unique and very interesting face.

He wondered if Lachlan was jealous of her acting talent. That would be just like him. He would hate anyone to steal his thunder. Narcissistic devil!

'All I know is that you're Maddie's older sister,' he admitted. 'I don't even know how much older.'

'I'm twenty-five,' she confessed, almost as if it was a crime.

Twenty-five was a good age for an actress, he thought. And for other things...

Finding out that Kate was an actress didn't dampen his desire for her in any way. If anything, it increased it—along with his sudden resolve to help her career in any way he could. Blake suspected it might not have taken off, since he'd never heard of Kate Holiday. And he would have if she'd done anything of note. Blake had his finger on the pulse where rising stars were concerned.

Just then they were shepherded outside by the photographer—a rather officious fellow who was very full of himself.

'So, what have you been in lately?' he asked her as they trailed past the huge marquee which had been set up in the gorgeous grounds of Byron's home. 'Anything I might have seen?'

'I doubt it,' she said. 'I was in a play earlier this year, but it closed rather quickly. I was brilliant, of course,' Kate added, throwing a self-deprecating smile his way. 'But not brilliant enough, apparently. One of the reviews said I was "very decorative".'

Blake laughed. 'Which you are,' he said. 'Very.'

She looked startled, her high cheekbones pinkening a little. Acting? he wondered. Or was she genuinely taken aback by his compliment? Blake decided he didn't care either way. She enchanted him. And intrigued him. He was going to enjoy finding out more about her this evening, and at the same time putting a spoke in Lachlan's ego by giving her career a boost.

He would offer her a part in one of his upcoming movies. Nothing too large. She was an unknown, after all.

Of course Blake anticipated that his offer to help her out would come with the bonus of taking her to bed in the foreseeable future. Which he very much wanted to do. More so than he had in a long while. Whilst sex was something he enjoyed, he wasn't a sex addict. He could do without—especially when he was working long hours. Which he had been for several weeks now, finishing up Lachlan's latest movie and getting it ready for distribution.

Possibly this longish stint of celibacy was responsible for the rather urgent wave of desire he was currently experiencing. Hopefully there wasn't any extraneous reason why Kate shouldn't respond to his pursuit. The only hurdle he could think of was a boyfriend in the wings. Or, worse, a fiancé.

A swift glance at her left hand detected a total absence of rings.

Good. A boyfriend he could handle, but a fiancé was another matter entirely.

'I am *so* going to hate these photographs,' Kate muttered when the photographer started giving them orders.

'I don't know why,' he commented as they were forcefully arranged in a group in the well-lit gazebo, with the harbour and the bridge in the background. 'With your bone structure I bet you're very photogenic.'

Even if she wasn't the best actress in the world, she would look good on screen. Blake felt confident that the camera would love her.

'It's very nice of you to say so.'

'Not at all. It's the truth. I never say things just to be nice.'

Not until tonight, that is. For some weird and wonderful reason Blake felt uncharacteristically compelled to be nice to Kate. *Very* nice. And it wasn't just because he wanted to have sex with her. Right from the first moment he'd set eyes on her sad-looking self she'd brought out the gallant in him. Which was unusual. Because a white knight with women Blake was *not*—especially since Claudia's betrayal.

Quite frankly he could be a bit of a bastard where the opposite sex was concerned. Especially if the girl was an ambitious young actress who made it obvious when they met that she was his for the taking—not because of a genuine attraction but because sleeping with him would further her career.

Kate was different, though. A different sort of girl. A different sort of actress.

He'd given her every opportunity to flirt with him. And flatter him. But she'd done neither. He liked that. He liked that a lot.

'Would the bridesmaid please *smile*?' the photographer snapped impatiently. 'This is a wedding, not a funeral.'

CHAPTER FOUR

BUT IT IS a funeral, Kate wanted to wail. It was the death of her dream to marry Lachlan herself one day.

A stupid dream, really. Stupid and futile—especially once he'd met Maddie.

Of course she should never have taken him home. But she'd honestly thought it would be safe, with Maddie practically engaged. How had she been supposed to know that they would take one look at each other and fall head over heels in love?

Well, you should have known, you idiot!

Not that it would have made any difference.

Get real, you fool. Even before he met Maddie Lachlan had three years to notice you in that way. But he didn't and he never would have! You're not his type—which is blonde and beautiful, with buckets of self-esteem and a sense of self-entitlement to rival royalty. Somehow that description doesn't fit you, dear heart. Not even remotely.

A very strong male arm suddenly wound around her waist, pulling her firmly against his side and propelling Kate out of her self-pitying thoughts. Glancing up at Blake, she encountered narrowed blue eyes giving her a warning look.

'If you don't start smiling properly,' he whispered into her ear, 'I'll start thinking you can't act your way out of a paper bag.'

Kate blinked, then swallowed and straightened her spine—after which she rewarded him with a beaming smile. Because no way did she want Blake Randall thinking she couldn't act. Hadn't she resolved earlier to try to use the opportunity of meeting him to her advantage? It would be utterly foolish to ignore a man of his influence and contacts. If she couldn't have Lachlan's love, then at least she could have a career.

'That's better,' he said, smiling down at her.

Her spirits lifted again, as they had earlier when he'd smiled at her. Kate couldn't quite understand why he was as interested in her as he seemed to be—but who was she to look a gift horse in the mouth?

The photos were still a trial—especially when she and Blake mostly had to stand to one side and witness Maddie and Lachlan having endless shots taken of just the two of them in all sorts of romantic poses and clinches.

Maddie had confessed to Kate that morning that they'd already sold their wedding photos to a well-known tabloid—which wasn't surprising. Her sister was very money-hungry. Celebrity-hungry, too. They were certainly a well-matched couple in that regard; Kate was well aware of Lachlan's love of fame.

She winced as she watched him kiss his blushing bride for the umpteenth time.

If she'd been alone with Blake, Kate might have been able to distract herself by chatting about movies. But, no, fate wasn't going to be that kind. Her parents were now hurrying over to them, demanding to be introduced, and gushing like mad over the bride and groom.

After what felt like for ever, but was probably only a few minutes, Blake suddenly took her arm and said, 'You must excuse us, folks, but we really have to speak to Byron ASAP.'

He didn't explain further, just swept a relieved Kate away.

'Are they always like that?' he growled as he snatched two glasses of champagne from a passing waiter, pressing one into Kate's hand.

'Like what?'

'Raving about your sister like she's a bloody princess. They never said a word about how gorgeous *you* look. It was all about Maddie—Little Miss Perfect and oh, so clever to have snared herself a husband like Lachlan.' He snorted at that. 'They won't be saying that in a couple of years' time.'

'What do you mean?' she asked, a little flustered by his saying *she* looked gorgeous.

'Damn it,' he said, gulping his glass of champagne before giving her a slightly sheepish look. 'I probably shouldn't be saying this. Though maybe you already suspect?'

'Suspect what?'

'That where the opposite sex is concerned Lachlan is a rat. No, more of a cat. A tom cat. He can't keep it in his pants for long. Trust me when I say that being married won't stop him from sleeping around. I walked in on him having sex with a make-up girl just a few weeks ago. Long after his engagement to your sister.'

Possibly Kate shouldn't have been shocked—Lachlan had garnered quite a reputation during his years at NIDA—but she was.

'Poor Maddie,' she said, and downed half of her glass of champagne.

'I agree with you. If she truly loves Lachlan then she's in for a bumpy road.'

What an odd thing to say, Kate thought. *If she truly loves him.* Of course Maddie truly loved him. Lachlan was the sort of man who inspired love. Every time Kate looked at him she felt that tightening in her stomach, that wave of longing. So nowadays she tried not to look at him. It was easier that way.

She did go and see his movies, though. Which was the worst form of masochism since they were all love stories and always had at least one sex scene. But she simply could not resist.

'Is that why you were upset earlier?' Byron asked her. 'Because you're worried about your sister's future happiness?'

Kate stared up into his deeply set blue eyes, which held a surprisingly sympathetic expression at that moment. And there she'd been, believing he was some kind of ruthless bastard. Not so, it seemed.

'Yes,' she lied, for how could she tell him that it was her own future happiness that had been worrying her?

He reached out to touch her wrist lightly. 'No point in worrying about other people's marriages. What will be will be.'

Kate didn't know what to think. Her thoughts were somewhat scattered. How could Lachlan do something like that? It had certainly tarnished her opinion of him. Not her love, however. That didn't tarnish quite so easily.

Suddenly she frowned at Blake. 'Why did you agree to be Lachlan's best man when it's obvious you don't like him very much?'

He shrugged. 'Don't get me wrong. I don't dislike Lachlan. He's not a bad fellow. Just weak when it comes to women throwing themselves at him. Which they do. All the time. Look, he asked me to be his best man and I said yes. Call it a business move rather than a measure of close friendship. The publicity will be good for our next movie, which should be coming out in the New Year. Too late, unfortunately, to be up for any awards this year, but I couldn't get it edited and distributed any earlier.'

'I see. And is that also why you organised for the wedding to be held here? For the added publicity?'

'No. I didn't think of that at the time. When the other venue burnt down we still had a couple of weeks' shooting to complete in Hawaii, and I couldn't afford for my leading man to keep getting hysterical phone calls from his fiancée. So I stepped in and fixed things. Now, I think they're waiting for us to go into the marquee for the reception. We'll be on the same table, but I doubt we're seated side by side—worst luck. Still, there'll be a party and dancing afterwards. Then we can talk some more.'

He put a firm hand in the small of her back and gently pushed her towards the entrance to the marquee. It felt good, that hand. Very...*reassuring*. Also very intimate.

She sneaked a quick glance up into his deep blue eyes, startled when they bored back down into hers with the sort of lustful look men usually reserved for Maddie.

The realisation that Blake Randall lusted after *her* was flattering, but also very flustering. Her whole body tightened in response, which threw her. She couldn't *possibly* lust after Blake Randall in return, could she? Surely not. She was just shocked, that was all.

And yet...

She glanced over at him again, this time focusing on his mouth and recalling how she'd wondered earlier in the proceedings what it would be like to kiss him.

Exciting, she decided, her heartbeat quickening. Exciting and risky. *Very* risky. Because he wouldn't want to stop at kissing.

Kate knew in theory that love and lust didn't have to reside together. But she'd never experienced one without the other. Which was why her very limited forays into sex had been such disasters—and why, for the last four years, she hadn't had a proper boyfriend or been to bed with anyone. How could she after falling so deeply in love with Lachlan?

Yet as she stared at Blake Randall's perversely sexy mouth she could not dismiss the notion that she just might enjoy going to bed with him despite not loving him. Not that she would. She wasn't that sort of girl. She wasn't like Maddie, who'd been jumping into men's beds at the drop of a hat since she was sixteen.

Besides, you don't really want to go to bed with him,
Kate told herself firmly. *You're just flattered that he fan-*
cies you. That's what this is all about. Not true lust. Just
your poor pathetic ego, desperate for someone to show
some interest in you. Now, stop ogling the man and get
some perspective!

Just in time she wrenched her eyes away from his mouth.
But it was too late. His lips were drawing back into a knowing smile. He'd already seen her staring at him.

'First dance is mine,' he said with a devilish twinkle in
his eyes. 'Don't forget.'

Relief claimed Kate as the wedding planner bustled over
to them, interrupting what was becoming an awkward situation.

Her name was Clare. She was about fifty, a sleekly attractive blonde with an air of self-importance somewhat
like the photographer's. They were in business together,
Maddie's mother having hired them because they were supposedly 'the best'.

'*Do* come along, Kate,' the woman said, and glanced
at her watch. 'You too, Mr Randall. We are now running
behind schedule.'

Blake rolled his eyes at Kate after Clare had departed
to hurry up some of the other guests.

'Irritating woman,' he muttered as he steered Kate over
to their table. 'Do you know she had the hide to ask to see
my speech? Claimed she needed to check if it was too long.'

'How rude!'

'That's what I thought. Lord knows how people like
that stay in business. Anyway, I didn't show it to her because I haven't written one. I just assured her it would be
the shortest best man's speech in history. Which it will be.
I detest long speeches.'

Kate gnawed at her bottom lip. 'You're not going to say
anything...revealing, are you?'

'About Lachlan being a player, you mean?'

'Yes.'

'Of course not. That's not my place. My role tonight is to be complimentary and charming and funny.' Blake laughed at the doubtful look on her face. 'Don't worry. I can be all of those things when I need to be. I'm actually a very good actor myself.'

CHAPTER FIVE

BLAKE WAS AS good as his word, keeping his best man's speech very short and very witty, heaping gushing compliments on the bride and hearty praise on the groom, refraining from any of the usual tasteless *double entendres* concerning the groom's past behaviour with the opposite sex, and finishing up by toasting the happy couple with gusto.

I really am a good actor, he decided when he sat down to huge applause less than five minutes after he'd stood up. Because it had certainly gone against the grain for him to say the overly nice things he had. He hadn't lied for Lachlan's sake, of course, or for the bride, but for Kate, whom he could see had been upset by his revelation about Lachlan's lack of morals.

He regretted telling her now. It had been unnecessary. He'd achieved nothing except to increase her anxiety over the future of her sister's happiness. Clearly she was fond of her sister, despite her parents' obvious favouritism for the younger girl.

He cringed when he recalled the father of the bride's over-effusive speech about his perfect younger daughter. It had been sick-making. If he'd been Kate he would have walked out. Or thrown something at him. But she'd just sat there, sipping champagne and smiling, even laughing at some of her father's gushing stories about Maddie as a little girl.

She was an incredibly generous and sweet-natured soul. Odd, given her chosen career. Aspiring actresses were rarely sweet. Unless they were faking it. And Blake felt confident she wasn't.

He smiled when he thought of her smallish breasts and her lack of false eyelashes. No. Nothing fake about Kate Holiday.

Which was one of the reasons he found her so attractive.

She found him attractive too.

Blake was an expert in female body language, and he'd noticed her reaction to his none-too-subtle compliments. She liked them, but didn't quite know how to react to them. Didn't seem to know how to flirt.

Not like her sister. He might not have met the bride before, but he'd seen her in action tonight—both with the celebrant and the photographer and also himself, to a degree. Not that she'd actually said anything to him yet. There'd been no opportunity. But she'd fluttered her false eyelashes at him whenever she'd had a chance, her smile both sweetly coy and smoulderingly sexy at the same time.

She was a piece of work, all right. Lachlan just might have met his match with Maddie Holiday.

Finally the interminable meal and the speeches were over and the happy couple rose, leaving the table to go and cut their three-tiered wedding cake.

Blake immediately moved into the bride's vacant chair so that he could talk to Kate. 'So what did you think?' he asked her on a teasing note. 'Did my speech meet with your approval?'

She smiled at him, her expression wry. 'You're right. You're a *very* good actor. You didn't mean a single word of it, did you?'

'I meant the bit I slipped in about the beautiful bridesmaid. I didn't think the groom complimented you enough in his speech. Now, the dancing will start soon. I've been to a few weddings in my time, so I know the routine. First the bride and groom will do the bridal waltz, and then we'll all be invited to join them on the dance floor.'

'Yes, I know,' she said. 'I have been to the odd wedding or two as well. Though never as a bridesmaid.'

'Never?' That surprised him, given her age and her nice-ness. 'But you must have loads of girlfriends. Haven't any of them got married yet?'

'Actually, no,' she said.

'No, you haven't got loads of girlfriends? Or no, none of them have got married yet?'

'I do have a few girlfriends from my years at NIDA, but no one so close that they would ask me to be a bridesmaid.'

'What about from school?'

'No. I wasn't popular at school. I was considered a nerd. And not very cool.'

'I find that hard to believe,' he said, but he was lying.

He could see that she was on the reserved, rather intro-verted side. *He'd* been very popular at school—perhaps because he'd been a rebel. There was no rebel in Kate. Not a great deal of confidence, either. How on earth did she expect to succeed as an actress if she didn't exude confidence?

Still, she had *him* to help her now. She just didn't know it yet. It was probably not the right time or place to offer her a part in one of his movies tonight. Or to try to seduce her, either.

But he couldn't let the grass grow under his feet. He was flying back to LA in a few days. And Blake had no intention of going back without having some delicious sex with this delightful creature, as well as giving her career a much-needed boost.

He would invite her out to dinner tomorrow night. Some-where seriously good. After which he would take her back to the city penthouse he was staying in. It belonged to Byron, but he wasn't using it much now that he'd moved into this absolutely gorgeous harbour-side mansion.

'What about boyfriends?' he asked, wanting to know

the lie of the land before he got his hopes up too high. Not that a boyfriend would stop him now. The more time he spent with Kate the more he wanted her.

'What?' she said, blinking up at him.

God, she did have lovely eyes. And so expressive. Perfect for the camera.

'You said you don't have loads of girlfriends,' he went on, 'but you've surely had loads of boyfriends. There must be one at the moment.'

A strange cloud dulled her eyes. Strange, because he couldn't read the emotion behind it. What *was* it? Not distress. Or dismay. Sadness again? Yes, that was it. Sadness. A very deep sadness. He wondered if she'd had a serious boyfriend and something dreadful had happened to him. He couldn't imagine any man worth his salt dumping Kate, so what else could it be?

Only death, Blake decided, warranted this depth of sadness. A very recent death, possibly. That would explain everything that had puzzled him about her tonight. It might also explain why she hadn't responded all that strongly to his none-too-subtle overtures. Perhaps by finding him attractive—and he was pretty sure she did—she felt she was betraying her loved one.

Blake pulled himself up sharply before he got carried away. Which he did sometimes. Nothing worse than being a movie-maker. He found drama in every situation. The reality was probably nothing like what he was imagining.

'Actually, no,' she said, a rueful little smile hovering. 'I do not have a boyfriend at the moment. I have had boyfriends in the past, of course.'

Well of course she had. If she hadn't she wouldn't be normal.

'Then there's no one to object if I ask you out to dinner tomorrow night?' he went on.

She didn't look totally surprised, just a little wary.

'No,' she said, but there was reservation in her voice and reluctance in her eyes.

He knew then that she wasn't going to be easily seduced. One part of him admired her for it, but that other part—the part which was aching and hard and more conscienceless than it had ever been—refused to be deterred.

So he decided to play his trump card. Too bad if it was a bit premature. A man had to do what a man had to do.

'I want to talk to you about a part in my next movie which I think would be perfect for you,' he added, dangling what he knew would be a powerful carrot.

There was no doubting her surprise. No, her *shock*. Genuine, ingenuous shock. God, she really was irresistible.

'But why would you do that?' she asked, jerking her head back a little as she blinked up at him. 'Surely you would need me to audition for you first.'

Damn it all, why did she have to be so difficult? He respected her for it, but it was irritating.

'I don't need to see an audition from a graduate of NIDA,' he dismissed. 'Their programme produces the most talented actors.'

'Yes, but...but...'

'Kate Holiday,' he said sternly. 'Do you want to be a successful actress or not?'

'Of course I do,' she replied, looking quite offended. 'It's what I want most in the world.'

'Then stop looking a gift horse in the mouth.'

She smiled then. Which pleased him no end.

'You'll come to dinner tomorrow night?'

'Yes.'

'Good. Now, let's go and dance.'

CHAPTER SIX

HOW AMAZING, KATE thought a little breathlessly as Blake swept her onto the dance floor and into his arms. Dinner tomorrow night and a part in a Blake Randall movie.

Amazing, but also a little worrying. She'd heard casting couch stories, knew that it still happened, and wondered if Blake was of that ilk. Would he expect her to have sex with him at the end of the evening?

Kate knew he fancied her—had seen desire in his eyes. And even more worrying was the suspicion that if he made a pass at her she might just say yes to whatever he wanted. Which was not like her at all!

But this was her chance, wasn't it? she reasoned desperately. Her chance to get her career off the ground. And she did find him attractive. Very attractive. And sexy. *Very* sexy. It was that mouth of his. And the hot, hungry gleam which fired up his eyes whenever he looked down at her. Which he was doing at the moment. He made her feel sexy in return. And terribly tempted.

A thought suddenly came to her, however—one she didn't like at all.

'This part you have in mind for me,' she said as he whirled her round, thankfully at arm's length. 'It's not in one of Lachlan's movies, is it? I honestly don't want to be in one of his movies.'

'No, it's not a rom-com. More of a family drama. A character-based script which I wrote a few years ago but hadn't got round to making. But it's all systems go now, and we start shooting in late November. Look, keep this under your hat, but I think Lachlan and I will be parting company in the near future.'

'But why?' she asked, totally taken aback.

Blake glanced over at the man in question before answering. Fortunately the dance floor was big enough for them not to be too close. Nevertheless, when he spoke he kept his voice low.

'Mr Rodgers has an exalted opinion of his acting abilities. He doesn't really understand why his movies with me have been so successful. He thinks it's solely due to him. He might do one more movie with me, but he'll go with the money in the end. He recently got himself a new agent— one who's buddy-buddy with the big production companies. They've already offered him a very lucrative contract for three movies. He says he's just thinking about it, but I can see the writing on the wall.'

'That's not very loyal of him,' Kate said, feeling upset for Blake. Though he didn't seem that upset himself.

He shrugged. 'There's no such thing as loyalty in Hollywood. Just box office figures. I'll survive without him, I can assure you. I have several new projects already in the pipeline—none of which rely on Lachlan Rodgers.'

'That's good.'

Good, too, that she wouldn't have to work with him. That would have been just awful. And so would her acting have been, with her new brother-in-law's presence being both distracting and upsetting.

Still, Blake might be right about Lachlan's acting abilities being limited. When they'd been at NIDA he certainly hadn't come top of the class. He'd been good, but not as good as some of the others. She herself had been singled out by their teachers for more praise than he had.

'Let's not talk about Lachlan any more,' Blake said. 'I'd rather talk about you. So, tell me, if you've only had that one part in a play since you graduated, how have you been surviving financially?'

'Well, I do live at home, rent-free. And I've been working at a local deli at the weekends. That pays for my clothes and fares, and leaves me free to go to auditions during the week.'

'Do you have a good agent?'

Kate sighed. 'I thought I did. But I'm beginning to have my doubts.'

'You need to get yourself a new one, then.'

'I think I will.'

The music changed from a waltz to a faster, more throbbing beat. More people got up to dance, at which point Blake pulled Kate very close and told her to put her arms around his neck. After a slight hesitation she did so, and felt Blake dropping his hands down to her hips. His grip was firm, pulling her lower half against him, making Kate quickly aware of something hard pressing against her stomach. It was impossible to ignore.

Blake's eyelids grew heavy with the contact, and a tense silence enveloped them as their fused hips swayed to the music. On her part she felt mesmerised—both by the obvious evidence of his desire for her and her own shocking thoughts. She began imagining how it would feel to have his flesh buried deep inside hers, to have his mouth on hers, kissing her, only lifting to whisper hot, hungry words in her ear.

Her mouth went dry.

Not so another part of her anatomy.

Suddenly she needed to go to the bathroom. ASAP.

'I'm sorry,' she said, flustered by the urgency of that need, not to mention what was going on in her head. 'But I... I have to go to the Ladies. Too much champagne.'

A total lie. She'd only had one glass during dinner, worried that if she drank too much she might do something she'd regret, might somehow make a total fool of herself.

It had taken every ounce of her acting ability not to react to her father's speech, not to let jealousy for Maddie take her over. She loved her sister. She always had. But she did so hate it that everyone else loved her so *much*, with no love left over for her. Lachlan's speech had been total agony, and Kate hadn't been able to look at him even when he'd toasted *her*, as was his duty.

'Sorry,' she repeated, and then hurried away out of the marquee, almost running back to the house and up the staircase to the bedroom and en-suite bathroom where she'd dressed earlier.

There was probably a powder room or two downstairs, but she didn't know where they were and she simply couldn't wait. But, perversely, when she sat on the toilet she didn't do all that much, and yet the odd feeling of pressure remained.

She'd never felt anything quite like it. Not painful, exactly. No, not painful at all. Just weirdly tight and tense. Her belly was as hard as a rock, whilst elsewhere she was hot and embarrassingly wet. Once again her thoughts took flight, her fantasies definitely on the R-rated side.

'Good grief, Kate,' she groaned aloud, confused by the way she could want any man like this, when she was in love with someone else.

She certainly hadn't done so for the last four years. Never. Not once. Blake Randall, however, seemed to have broken through her frozen libido and brought it to life in a startling way. More than startling when she considered that even when she'd first fallen in love with Lachlan he hadn't evoked so violent a physical reaction.

Her feelings about him had always seemed more softly romantic than starkly sexual. She sighed over him. And dreamt about him. But she'd never been consumed by explicit sexual fantasies. Which she had been a minute ago.

Kate shuddered as she recalled that moment when she'd literally ached to have sex with Blake. She was still aching.

Oh, Lord, whatever was she going to do?

You're going to get a grip, that's what you're going to do. Then go back downstairs and...

And what?

She honestly had no idea. She'd probably leave it up to Blake to make the next move. And he would. She felt sure of it. And the prospect was sending an excited shiver down her spine.

After she'd washed her hands she stared at herself in the vanity mirror, seeing her over-bright eyes and flushed cheeks. Glancing down, she checked to see if her nipples were on show. Thankfully they weren't, courtesy of the corset-style underwear she had on. Maddie had chosen it for her, insisting that it would give her some shape. Which, right now, she was grateful it did.

Kate couldn't deny that she wanted Blake to pursue her. What she *didn't* want was for her own desire to be embarrassingly obvious, or for him to think any response of hers was because he had offered to give her a part in one of his movies. Because what she was feeling at the moment had nothing to do with her career and everything to do with herself as a woman.

It was quite thrilling to be the centre of attention for a change. To feel special, and attractive, and truly desired.

At the same time Kate still felt flustered by the strength of her own sexual response to Blake's overtures. She didn't quite know what to do next. Flirting didn't come naturally to her. She wasn't like Maddie. She didn't have her sister's sexual boldness. Or her confidence. What if she was misreading the situation?

This last thought brought a laugh to her lips. How could she possibly have misread that erection? Unless, of course—she giggled a little—Blake had a gun in his pocket.

Kate had a smile on her lips as she left the bathroom—a smile which was wiped away when she encountered Lachlan standing in the bedroom, with a dark scowl on his beautifully shaped mouth.

'Lachlan!' she exclaimed. 'What are you doing here? Where's Maddie?'

'Dancing with your father. She won't miss me for a minute or two. I told her I was going to the Gents. Look, I saw you duck out of the marquee and I followed you.'

Kate frowned. 'But why?'

'I wanted a word with you in private. I wanted to warn you.'

'Warn me? About what?'

'About Blake bloody Randall.'

Kate sucked in sharply. Why on earth was Lachlan speaking about his mentor and best man with such disrespect? 'What...what about him?'

'About his modus operandi with pretty women—especially ones who have acting in their blood.'

Kate was torn between being flattered by Lachlan calling her pretty and worrying about what this dreaded 'modus operandi' could be. Though she was beginning to suspect...

'First things first: does he know you went to NIDA with me?'

'Well, yes, he does. I told him.'

'*Damn.* That's stuffed things good and proper, then. No doubt he's already offered you a part in one of his movies? That's one of his moves when he fancies an actress. And you're looking extra-fanciable tonight, Kate. Frankly, I've never seen you looking so good. Blake only goes for the good-looking ones. So, *has* he offered you a part?'

'Well, yes,' she admitted, feeling a little bit sick. 'A small one.'

'I don't doubt it's just a small one,' Lachlan scoffed. 'Mr Perfectionist wouldn't risk spoiling one of his movies by giving an unknown a seriously *good* part. You'll probably only have a few words here and there. Just enough to make sure you have to be on location with him so that he can shag you every night. But once the movie is wrapped up you can bet that will be the end of it. He has a reputation for seducing his female stars, but once the movie is over so is the affair.'

He came forward and curved his hands over her shoulders—a gesture that shocked Kate rigid because it forced her to look up into his eyes...those beautiful blue eyes which had entranced her from the first day they'd met.

Perversely, however, neither his touch nor his proximity sent her weak at the knees, as she might have expected. All she felt was a confused wariness.

'I wouldn't like to see that happen to you, Kate,' he went on. 'You're far too nice a girl to be used by that bastard.'

Goodness. Such strong words! 'Is that why you didn't tell Blake I was in your class at NIDA?' she asked, trying to make sense of Lachlan's present attitude, not to mention his past actions. 'You were trying to protect me?'

That startled him, and his hands dropped away as he stepped back in surprise. It took him a few seconds to school his face into an expression of concern. 'Well, yes. Yes...yes, of *course* that's why,' he said, hurriedly but not convincingly.

Kate wasn't sure what to believe now—both about Blake's so-called bad reputation with actresses and Lachlan's using it as an excuse for not mentioning her to Blake at any stage. Nothing rang true.

Okay, so Blake offering her a part without auditioning her had been surprising. In all honesty, however, she couldn't see Blake having to bribe girls into his bed. He was the sort of man women would throw themselves at. She herself was already wildly attracted to him.

'I find it hard to believe Blake is as bad as you say he is,' Kate said.

Lachlan's bedroom blue eyes softened on her and he

once again reached to curve his hands around her shoulders. 'Oh, Kate, Kate... Trust me when I say you don't want to get tangled up with Blake Randall. He can be a twisted bastard. That bitch Claudia throwing him over totally screwed him up. He likes breaking hearts—especially when that heart belongs to an actress. He's bad news, sweetheart. Promise me you won't take him up on his offer—that you'll be having nothing further to do with him after tonight.'

Kate shook her head from side to side, her thoughts more muddled than ever. 'Why did you ask him to be your best man if you despise him so much?' she asked, in an echo of what she'd asked Blake earlier.

Lachlan shrugged. 'It was a good publicity move to promote our next movie. On top of that he was chuffed by my asking. Look, you can't afford to get on the wrong side of the right people in the movie-making world, so don't go telling him I said any of this. Just don't accept that part, for pity's sake. Tell him you don't want to make movies... that you'd rather act on the stage. That's what you always said you wanted to do.'

'I do. But I haven't been very successful at it, in case you haven't noticed.'

'What? Oh, yes. That's bad luck. Still, if you show up at auditions in future looking the way you look tonight you should be in like Flynn. Now, I really must go. Lord, but you *do* look delicious...'

He bent and gave her a peck on the cheek before dashing out of the room and running down the stairs back to his beautiful bride, leaving Kate's head in total turmoil. Because she simply couldn't believe in Lachlan's sudden concern for her. He'd hardly even spoken to her this past year, and had never asked her how things were going for her career-wise.

Not that she'd seen him all that often, but there had been the odd occasion. A family dinner last Easter. A Mother's

Day luncheon in May. Then his and Maddie's engagement party a few months ago...

Maybe his dislike of Blake's behaviour with women *was* a credible reason why he hadn't told his mentor about her. But she didn't buy it. She was beginning to suspect that Lachlan didn't want to share his success—that he wanted to be the only one in his class to make it big in the movies.

Kate's love for Lachlan didn't blind her to his faults. Behind his charm lay considerable arrogance, a selfish nature and a rather ruthless ambition. She was glad now that she hadn't made him any rash promises, because in all honesty she didn't *want* to turn down the part. It was a chance to show someone with lots of connections and contacts that she could act.

Okay, so Blake could be a devil with women. That didn't really surprise her, given his success and his power. But forewarned *was* forearmed. And she didn't have to sleep with him if she didn't want to. The trouble was...she *did*, actually. If Kate were strictly honest with herself, the idea of Blake Randall seducing her was not altogether an unattractive prospect. As for him sending her on her way with a broken heart... Well, that part was laughable. Impossible. Her heart had already been broken.

So to hell with being sweet and nice, plus a total failure. It was time to take a few risks. Time to be proactive, the way her agent kept telling her to be. Time to stop being lily-livered and put her best foot forward!

CHAPTER SEVEN

WHERE ON EARTH *was* she? Blake began thinking when Kate didn't return after ten minutes. How long did it take for a girl to go to the toilet?

Lifting his champagne to his lips, he took a deep swallow, thinking all the while that if she didn't show in the next thirty seconds he would go in search of her.

'Not like you to be standing alone at a party,' Byron said as he wandered up to him, looking splendid in his tux.

But then, Byron would look good in anything. The man had everything. Looks. Money. Charm. And more recently a gorgeous wife and a delightful baby girl. Blake would have been jealous of the man if he didn't like him so much. And if he wasn't such a solid investor in his movies.

'I'm waiting for my dancing partner to come back from the powder room,' he grumbled. 'She's been gone ages.'

'I presume you're talking about Kate?'

'Yes, Kate.'

'Sweet girl. Much sweeter than her sister,' Byron observed drily.

'Too true,' Blake agreed. 'I wouldn't want to be married to *that* one.'

Byron laughed. 'You wouldn't want to be married to *anyone.*'

'You know me so well. Ah, here she is. Kate, sweetheart, what took you so long?'

Kate had no intention of telling him the truth. Certainly not in front of Byron. Or ever, actually.

She grabbed a glass of champagne from a passing waiter and smiled at the two men over the rim as she took a long swallow. They were the sort of men that women must smile at a lot, she conceded. Both very attractive, though in entirely different ways. Byron was fair-haired and traditionally handsome, with clean-cut even features and a smile which might out-dazzle Lachlan's. He was a true gentleman. Whereas Blake looked more like a gypsy, with his wayward black hair, his dark beetling eyebrows and deeply set and very intense eyes.

They pierced her now, those eyes, making her quiver inside. *Lord, but he wouldn't have to try too hard to seduce me*, came the shocking thought.

'Kate's an actress—did you know?' Blake asked Byron, whilst not taking his eyes off her.

Byron's eyebrows lifted. 'No, I didn't know.'

'Neither did I until tonight. She's a graduate of NIDA. Was in the same class as Lachlan.'

'Really? How come he didn't mention it?'

'I have no idea.'

Once again Kate kept silent. After all, what could she say? She really wasn't sure what reason was behind her supposed good friend not mentioning her acting aspirations. But she suspected it had nothing to do with protecting her virtue. Or her heart.

The thought angered her. And made her all the more determined to take whatever help Blake could give her.

'Blake's offered me a part in one of his movies,' she said brightly, at which Byron's eyes widened considerably.

It crossed Kate's mind that maybe Byron knew of his friend's modus operandi with actresses as well. A momentary concern tightened her chest, but it was quickly dismissed—as quickly as she swallowed the rest of her champagne. The alcohol fizzed down into her near empty stomach—she hadn't eaten much of the formal meal—going straight to her head and giving her some much-needed Dutch courage.

She wasn't by nature a rash person. Or a reckless one.

Yet she wanted to be both tonight. She *needed* to be both tonight—needed to throw off her earlier wretchedness, needed to ignore her broken heart and surge boldly and bravely into a new future: a future in which her futile feelings for Lachlan had no role to play.

She had to move on. *Had* to. There was no alternative. Kate was tired of feeling depressed. And of being rejected both personally and professionally. It was time to tap into her acting skills. Time to channel Maddie and just go for it.

'I think, darling Blake,' she said, with a decidedly flirtatious sparkle in her eyes, 'that I am in desperate need of some more dancing.'

Blake almost did a double-take. Even Byron shot him a startled glance. This wasn't the Kate who'd dashed off to the Ladies. This was a different Kate. A saucier, sexier Kate. Maybe she had more of her sister in her than he'd realised.

In a perverse way, he wasn't sure he liked it. His body did, however, and his erection returned with a vengeance before he'd even taken her into his arms.

Without prompting she slid her own arms up around his neck and pressed herself against him. Blake swore under his breath, knowing she had to be aware of his arousal. It discomfited him, for some reason. As much as he wanted Kate, he had never been the kind of guy who shagged sozzled bridesmaids at weddings, however much they wanted it.

'Sweetheart…' he murmured, noting her over-bright eyes with their dilated pupils. 'How much have you had to drink tonight?'

She blinked up at him, then laughed. 'Not all that much. But I could do with some fresh air. It's rather warm in here. Fancy a walk in the garden? It's lovely down by the water.

Not cold at all. We could go and sit in the gazebo whilst you tell me about this wonderful part you have for me.'

Kate knew she was prattling on, but she really wasn't comfortable in the role of vamp, or seductress, or whatever it was she was trying to be. Not that it mattered. Blake already fancied her. She'd felt the evidence more than once. She didn't have to act like this. It wasn't her.

She had no doubt that once they were alone in the gazebo he would make a pass. Kiss her at least.

But what if he wanted to go further than that?

As attractive and sexy as she found him, Kate didn't really want to have sex with Blake tonight. So tacky to act like that at a wedding! Her *sister's* wedding, no less. No, she couldn't throw caution to the wind to that extent. And to go outside with him—to be alone with him in the vast, rather romantically lit grounds—was dangerous in the extreme.

Because she wasn't sure that if he started kissing her she would want him to stop. The way he kept looking at her was powerfully seductive. His hot gaze bored into her like a laser beam, searing her insides and making her want to be even more reckless than she'd vowed to be. She couldn't recall ever feeling quite so...*stirred*.

'Let's go, then,' he said firmly, a possessive hand on her elbow, steering her towards the exit of the marquee.

Fortunately—or perhaps unfortunately, as it turned out—they were interrupted before they could make their escape. It was her mother, still looking like the very proud mother of the bride, all puffed up and flushed in her very pretty and very expensive pink suit, an older version of Maddie with her bottle blonde hair, but just a little too much make-up for a woman of fifty.

'Maddie sent me to get you, Kate,' Janine Holiday said somewhat breathlessly. 'She wants you to help her change into her going-away outfit.'

'What? So soon? But it's still quite early and—'

'The poor love says she's terribly tired,' Janine cut in. 'As you know, she's been up since the crack of dawn.'

Kate *did* know. She'd been got up as well, and then dragged off to the beauty salon so that she could be plucked and primped and polished until she hardly recognised herself. But she supposed it had been worth it in the end. Blake thought she looked lovely.

Kate didn't believe for a moment that Maddie was 'terribly tired'. That girl was like one of those batteries which never ran down. She knew exactly why Maddie wanted to leave. She'd whispered the reason to Kate earlier. She wanted to have sex with her new husband.

An hour or two ago Kate would have been overwhelmed with jealousy. Now her only feeling was distaste. She might still be in love with Lachlan, but she no longer liked him or wanted him. After what Blake had told her about his cheating behaviour Maddie was welcome to him.

'You'd better go,' Blake said, a wry note in his voice. 'I'll catch you later.'

Kate threw him an apologetic glance before allowing herself to be drawn away by her mother.

'Maddie's already gone upstairs,' Janine said as they headed for the house together. 'I think, Kate, that after she and Lachlan have left your father and I will go home too. I'm pretty tired myself. It's been a long day. Marvellous, but exhausting. What about you?' she added. 'I suppose you won't want to leave that early.'

'No.'

In truth, Kate was horrified at the thought of listening to her parents rave on about Maddie's wedding all the way home. Strathfield was an inner Western Sydney suburb which was a good half-hour drive from Byron's harbourside mansion.

'That would be rather rude. The party's only just started.

We can't *all* leave early. Besides, Cleo said I could stay the night if I liked, so I think I'll take her up on that offer.'

'Cleo?'

'Byron's wife. You must have met her.'

'I suppose I must have. I've been a bit distracted today. What does she look like?'

'Brunette. Burgundy dress. Very stylish. And very nice. Look, I'll catch a taxi home in the morning. I'll bring the dresses with me when I come.'

'Oh, all right. But perhaps I'd best take Maddie's wedding dress home with me tonight. I wouldn't like anything to happen to it.'

'What on earth could possibly *happen* to it?' Kate asked, amazed and a little hurt.

Janine looked irritated. 'I don't know. I just think it's better to be safe than sorry. Now, off you go. I need to get back to your father before he gets himself into trouble.'

Kate almost laughed. Her father was not the type of man who ever got himself into trouble. An insurance assessor, he was as conservative as his job, his only passion in life a collection of rare stamps. And, of course, his second and much adored daughter, who'd played Daddy's girl to perfection from the time she was just a tot.

Whenever Maddie perched herself on her father's knee and wrapped her arms around him he could deny her nothing. And he never had. Whatever she wanted, she got. Toys. Clothes. Expensive school excursions. A boob job. And finally, when she turned twenty-one, a car. Which she had promptly wrecked, losing her driving licence as well. This hadn't overly bothered Maddie, because by then she'd always had some obsessed boyfriend very eager to drive her wherever she wanted to go.

Kate trudged up the stairs, sighing as she went. She wished she could hate Maddie. But she didn't. She just couldn't. Yes, her sister was vain, and manipulative, and terribly self-centred. But, despite all that, she was an engaging personality, irrepressible and outgoing, and very, *very* charming. Kate couldn't help admiring her, in a way. And loving her.

More was the pity.

CHAPTER EIGHT

'OH, *THERE* YOU ARE!' Maddie exclaimed as Kate walked in.

She'd already taken off her wedding dress and tossed it carelessly onto a nearby chair. She was standing by the bed in nothing but a strapless white lace corset, her double D cup boobs almost spilling over the top. Her stockings and shoes lay in an untidy heap on the floor.

'Join me?' she said as she swept up the bottle of champagne which was sitting in an ice bucket on the bedside table.

Next to it were two flutes, delivered to the room when they'd been getting dressed earlier. Neither of them had felt like drinking at the time. Maddie had been too excited and Kate too wretched.

'For pity's sake, watch what you're doing!' Kate groaned when the cork popped off and champagne started fizzing out of the bottle. Hurrying over, she rescued the precious wedding dress in time, returning it to the plastic cover where it had been residing for the last two weeks.

'Oh, don't be such a worrywart. It's not red wine. Champagne won't even stain. Besides, it's not like I'll be wearing the damned thing ever again. Mum will put it into her treasure box so that she can bring it out and drool over it every now and then. She's got all our grad dresses in there too. Even our christening dresses. Here—have some champers. You might need it.'

'What do you mean, *I* might need it?' Kate asked as she took the glass.

Maddie flashed her one of her mischievous glances. 'Blind Freddie could see that Blake Randall is very taken with you, darls. All thanks to *moi*, of course. If you'd turned up today looking like your usual drack sack he wouldn't be all over you like a rash the way he was on that dance floor a little while ago. Now, does he know you graduated from NIDA?'

'I told him.' Kate took a deep swallow of the cold champagne. 'Your dear husband never even mentioned it to him. Which I find quite odd, since we were supposedly good friends there.'

Maddie laughed. 'Never underestimate the male ego, darls. Lachlan wouldn't want any of his NIDA buddies stealing his thunder, so to speak. Especially not you, Kate. You're too good an actress. And then there was that other matter...'

'What other matter?'

'Your crush on him,' she stated with bald honesty.

'My *what*?'

Maddie rolled her eyes. 'Please don't pretend you don't know what I'm talking about. It was obvious—even at home. You never stopped talking about him from day one at NIDA. Lachlan tells me it was quite embarrassing... the way you followed him around like a puppy. He said he couldn't even go for coffee without you inviting yourself along.'

Kate could hardly believe what she was hearing. *Lachlan* was the one who had kept inviting *her* for coffee. His wanting to talk to her all the time had been very flattering. It hadn't been just his looks which had made her fall in love with him. But now she saw that he'd just been picking her brain, as most of their conversations had revolved around her acting methods.

A very real fury welled up inside her. Fury plus a degree of humiliation. How could she have been so taken in by him? But she had. Oh, yes, she *had*.

In her defence, *all* the attractive female students at NIDA had gone ga-ga over him. And most of them had become a girlfriend of Lachlan's at some stage—each of them dated for a while and then dumped, not harshly but cleverly. Lachlan had used buckets of his boyish charm to smooth over each break-up, with the result that they had never had anything bad to say about him, even after he'd moved on.

Kate had waited and waited for him to move on to *her*. She was the only one he hadn't dated, and whilst she knew she couldn't compare with Maddie, she wasn't a total dog. Lots of people said she was quite attractive. But he had never asked her out. Not once.

Just thinking about those wasted years had Kate finishing her first glass of champagne in no time and seeking a refill.

'Oh, come, now,' Kate said as she put the bottle down. 'I wasn't as bad as that. And I wasn't the only girl at NIDA to be impressed. I mean, he is so *very* good-looking. But we all got over that once we realised how up himself he is.'

Kate felt rather proud of her well-delivered lie. Studying acting had come in handy more than once today.

'I certainly don't have a crush on him any more, I can assure you,' she said with a straight face as she lifted the glass to her lips again.

'So you say,' Maddie said, putting down her own glass on a side table and standing with her hands on her hips, eyes narrowed and lips pursed. 'I guess I'd be more inclined to believe you if you had a boyfriend. Look, Lachlan is my husband now, and I don't want to go through my life thinking my sister still has the hots for him. *Do* you?'

Kate drew herself up tall, squared her shoulders and fixed Maddie with uncompromising eyes. 'Now you are being seriously silly. Okay, I admit I did have a small crush on him. Once. But trust me when I say I don't any longer.'

Maddie gave her a long hard glare before shrugging dismissively. 'Well, I'll just have to take your word for it, I suppose. But I did wonder why you seemed so uptight earlier. If I thought that—'

'Maddie, please stop! You've totally got the wrong idea. The reason I was uptight earlier was because I was nervous.'

'Nervous! What about?'

'About being a bridesmaid. I've never been one before.'

'For heaven's sake! I've never been a bride before and *I* wasn't nervous.'

'You're never nervous about anything.'

'True...' Maddie preened. 'Okay, now that's all sorted, let's get back to what I originally wanted to talk to you about. Blake Randall's obvious interest in you...'

'Oh, yes?'

'Yes. Now, I don't want you to waste this opportunity,' Maddie said as she went over to the walk-in wardrobe and came out carrying the very stylish ice-blue woollen dress which her mother had chosen and for which her father had paid a small fortune. 'That's why I said you might need to get a bit tipsy. To give you some Dutch courage,' Maddie added, unzipping the dress and laying it out across the bed. 'Because I *know* you, Kate. You let opportunities go by because you simply won't go for them. So go on—drink up.'

Kate did as she was ordered, glad that the alcohol was already hurrying through her veins and reaching her brain, bringing with it a much-needed devil-may-care attitude.

'You have to have tunnel vision in this world,' Maddie rattled on, stepping into the blue sheath and pulling it up onto her shoulders. 'You can't wait for things to just happen. You have to *make* them happen.'

This was hardly news to Kate. She'd thought exactly the same thing earlier this evening.

'Now, I have a confession to make,' her sister went on, doing up the side zipper and then slipping her bare feet into the pair of nude high heels which were sitting ready for her at the foot of the bed. 'When you brought Lachlan home last Christmas even though I'd almost decided to marry Riley I knew I didn't love him. But I liked him, and I knew he'd give me a good life money-wise. He owns his own plumbing business and everyone knows that plumbers earn heaps. But then I took one look at Lachlan and saw an opportunity for a much better life—a life which would be very exciting and very glamorous, with a husband who was gorgeous and brilliant and seriously sexy. I realised suddenly that I couldn't settle for Riley, even though he was very good in bed. I wanted more. I wanted Lachlan and what he could give me. I mean, the temptation to go for him was overwhelming.'

She hesitated briefly and sent Kate an apologetic glance.

'I know you liked him, Kate, and I'm sorry. I dare say you were hurt when we left together that day. But I simply had to try to get him to fall in love with me. And he already wanted me, don't you see? He didn't want you. You weren't his type.'

'Yes, I'd already gathered that,' Kate said, thankful now that she was becoming, if not merry, decidedly numb. Without thinking she lifted the glass to her lips and took another deep swallow.

'So...you're not in love with Lachlan either, then?' Kate said, trying not to look and sound as shocked as she was.

'Love?' Maddie scoffed, smoothing down her skirt before walking over and picking up her champagne once more. 'What's love?' she said dismissively after a sip. 'A very temporary state—especially where the male sex is concerned. Their idea of love is usually all about sex. A woman has about eighteen months at best to get what she wants from a man before he goes off the boil. If you want marriage then you have to get him to propose during the first twelve months. I'm under no illusions. I know that

Lachlan will stray. He's too handsome and sexy to stay faithful—especially in the movie world. But I'll always be his wife—or at least his very rich *ex*-wife.'

Kate was appalled. And suddenly she must have looked it.

'Don't get me wrong,' Maddie went on as she stepped over to the dressing table to attend to her make-up and hair. 'I *do* care for Lachlan. Very much. And we have great chemistry in bed. I couldn't stand to marry a man who wasn't a good lover. Makes up for a lot of things…great sex. It also makes a man amenable to doing what *you* want. Which brings me back to my advice to you about Blake Randall,' she said, turning round to look straight at Kate as she sprayed herself liberally with perfume.

'And what advice would that be?' Kate asked. Her emotions were still outwardly under control, but inside she was dissolving. Maddie didn't even *love* Lachlan. All she wanted was the good life. *Dear God…*

'Get him into the sack ASAP. Don't wait. He'll be off back to Hollywood in a few days. Strike while the iron is hot. And his iron *is* hot. For *you*, darls. Lachlan says he's a sucker when it comes to pretty young actresses. And you *do* look pretty tonight, Kate. More than pretty. I actually feel a little jealous.'

Kate had to laugh. 'Now, *that's* not true,' she said, turning to fill her glass again. How had it become empty so quickly? 'You've never been jealous of me.'

'Oh, I wouldn't say that. I envy your acting ability. It's brilliant.'

And so is yours, Kate thought with a touch of malice.

'Blake Randall is going to get a real shock once he realises how good you are,' Maddie went on. 'But he won't ever realise that unless you keep him around long enough to see it.'

'Maddie, he's already offered me a part in one of his

movies,' she stated, bypassing her distress and surrendering to irritation. 'I don't *have* to sleep with him.'

'Oh, God—don't be so naive.'

'I'm *not* naive.'

'Yes, you are. Hopelessly. It's a man's world, Kate. They have all the power. Our only power comes from sex. I found that out years ago. Now, how do I look?'

Kate sighed. 'Like you always do. Gorgeous.'

'Thanks, darls. I love you—you know that, don't you?'

Kate did know that—which was perverse. Somehow she smiled and came forward to give her sister a hug. 'I hope you'll be very happy,' she said, and tried to mean it.

'Oh, I will be. I know it. Now, where did I put my bouquet...?'

CHAPTER NINE

BLAKE WATCHED FROM the sidelines as the beaming couple said their goodbyes, the bride making a big fuss over her parents before throwing her bouquet straight at her sister.

Kate laughed, but the laughter didn't touch her eyes. Blake still wasn't sure what was going on in that girl's head. She'd come back downstairs shortly after the bride, sipping a full glass of champagne as she made her way a bit shakily down the steps, her spare hand gripping the banister for support. She'd looked lost and decidedly tipsy.

Blake would have gone to her then if Cleo hadn't suddenly appeared by his side, striking up a conversation and leaving Blake no opportunity to do anything except surreptitiously watch Kate's rather unsteady progress.

Once at the bottom of the stairs Kate had scanned the crowd of guests for a few seconds, then walked over to stand with her back against a nearby wall, her lips no longer sipping but drinking fast.

Fortunately by the time the bride threw her bouquet her glass was almost empty, otherwise champagne might have gone everywhere. Despite acting as if she was thrilled, Blake suspected she was on the verge of tears—which sent him striding over to her side, where he slid a firm arm around her waist and pulled her against him.

'I think you've had way too much to drink,' he murmured.

'*I* don't,' she said, lifting big brown eyes up to his.

They were very glassy, but still very lovely.

'I don't think I've had *nearly* enough. Let's go and find another bottle of this delicious champagne.'

'Not right now, darling heart. Let's go for that walk down to the gazebo instead. Get you some much-needed fresh air first.'

'Whatever you say,' she said, with a nonchalant shrug of her slender shoulders. 'Just wait while I give this bouquet to my mother. She might want to take it home with her... have it cast in gold.'

Blake smiled at the unexpected sarcasm. Or was it jealousy? Was *that* what her changeable moods tonight had been all about? Jealousy over her sister?

He was tempted to ask her, but then decided best not. He didn't want to start talking about Maddie. He wanted to talk about *her*. Kate. The deliciously sexy and intriguing Kate.

If only she'd realise that not every man liked the obvious. *He* certainly didn't. He couldn't wait to take her to dinner tomorrow night, and to get her by herself afterwards in a romantic setting befitting their first time together. He'd already asked Byron if he could use his city penthouse for the next few days. It was a fantastically glamorous pad and Kate would be suitably impressed.

And Blake wanted to impress her. Impress her and protect her and make her happy—which he could do by giving her career a leg-up and getting his leg over at the same time. It wasn't as though she wouldn't enjoy sex with him. It certainly wouldn't be a case of her just lying back and thinking of her career. Blake *knew* he was a good lover. Always had been.

God, you're an arrogant devil, Blake conceded inwardly. *Has it even crossed your mind that she might say no to you? The bed part, that is, not the movie part?*

It was a novel thought, but not one he took seriously. Kate wouldn't say no to him. He'd seen the desire in her eyes on the dance floor earlier—felt it in her deliciously uptight body. It was just a matter of finding the right place and the right time. And making the right moves, of course.

Blake had every confidence that nothing would come between him and success.

A wave of relief flooded Kate after they'd all left—Maddie and Lachlan first, and then her parents, her mother taking with her Maddie's wedding dress and veil. Kate certainly didn't want to be responsible for them, or even to see them ever again. Thank God she'd handed over the bouquet as well, or she just might have thrown it into the harbour.

In truth, her broken heart had lightened considerably with their departure. Out of sight was out of mind. To a degree. Of course it helped that she was just a little bit drunk. No, a long way drunk, she accepted with an uncharacteristically naughty giggle. It helped her be able to return to the seriously attractive man who clearly wanted *her*—Kate Holiday. Not her blonde bombshell sister. *Her.*

God, she adored the way Blake looked at her. So hot and so hungry. It made her feel weak at the knees, and yet perversely powerful at the same time. She smiled flirtatiously as she walked slowly back to him, unconsciously acting the vamp, swinging her hips and licking her suddenly dry lips.

Bloody hell, thought Blake, his body leaping into action. If she didn't watch it they'd be taking things a lot further down in the gazebo. Only her obviously drunken state would stop him. But, damn it all, resisting her was going to be difficult.

Keep the touching to a minimum, then, he warned himself. *And definitely no kissing. In fact it would be much better if you went back into the marquee and just danced*, he told himself.

Yes, and perhaps get her some more champagne. Give

her something to do with that mouth of hers instead of doing what she was doing.

Actually she didn't wait for him to do anything—just came up very close, slid her arms up around his neck, right then and there, and planted those tempting lips right on his.

What was a red-blooded male supposed to do? One with a hard-on the size of Nelson's column?

Without thinking it through he kissed her back for a few seconds before common sense returned. Then, taking her firmly by the hips, he eased her away and speared her with a reproachful look.

'Naughty, Kate,' he murmured, aware of other people staring at them. 'Come on—we're off to the gazebo. And we'll pick up a bottle of champagne on the way.'

Kate giggled. She liked being called naughty. Liked *being* naughty. God, but he was a good kisser. She couldn't wait for him to kiss her some more. For longer next time. She'd only briefly felt the tip of his tongue. She wanted more of it, diving in deeper, making her head swirl again. She wanted...

Oh, she didn't know what she wanted. Oblivion, she supposed. Oblivion from the horrid thoughts which kept jumping into her head.

Maddie doesn't love Lachlan...
Lachlan doesn't want you...he wants Maddie...
You're not his type...

She needed to block those thoughts out—needed to replace them with wild, wonderful thoughts; needed to have this man's arms around her again. Not just on the dance floor, or during a brief kiss, but all night. In bed.

Kate grabbed Blake's hand and squeezed it tight. 'I do *so* like you,' she said.

He smiled down at her. 'Good.'

It was cold down in the gazebo, a sea breeze having sprung up. When Kate shivered Blake took off his jacket and draped it round her shoulders.

'Such a gentleman,' she said, appreciating the warmth.

'Not always.'

'Oh. You forgot to get some more champagne.'

'You've had enough.'

'Don't be such a spoilsport.'

'I'm just protecting your virtue.'

She laughed. 'I'm not a virgin.'

'I should hope not. But what's that got to do with protecting your virtue?'

'Maybe I don't *want* you to protect me. Maybe I want you to ravage me senseless,' she said, a wild glint flashing in her eyes. 'Not here, of course. I understand we can't do it here. It's cold and uncomfortable. But I'm staying the night at Byron's house. Are you?'

'Yes...' he said.

Kate ignored his frown. 'In that case we could spend the night together. In *your* room, preferably,' she added, knowing the other bedroom would still smell of Maddie's perfume.

Blake knew they were getting into dangerous waters here. The alcohol was making her reckless. The really dangerous part was that he rather *liked* reckless. Yet he knew being reckless wasn't in Kate's true nature. She was going to regret this in the morning.

But, hell on earth... He was only human. And a long way from being a saint.

'Kate,' he said, clutching at what conscience he *did* have where women and sex were concerned. 'I can't. I'm sorry. You're drunk.'

She stared at him, shock and confusion in her eyes. 'What? You don't *ever* go to bed with a woman who's had a few glasses of champagne? I find that hard to believe. From what I've heard you're the very *devil* with women.'

'Not always,' he returned. 'It depends on the woman.'

Tears suddenly filled her eyes. Tears and a type of rage. 'The truth is you don't really want me, do you? Not enough. I thought you did. I thought… Oh, what does it matter *what* I thought?' she cried, jumping up and throwing his jacket at him. 'You're a total bastard and I hate you!'

CHAPTER TEN

BLAKE STOOD OUTSIDE the bedroom door, listening to the sound of Kate sobbing inside. Cleo crossed her arms and glared at him, having joined the chase when she'd spotted Blake racing after a fleeing Kate. Both of them had followed her back into the house and up the staircase, unable to catch her before she'd slammed the bedroom door in their faces.

'What on earth did you do to her?' Cleo demanded. 'You were both getting along fine earlier in the evening. She was glued to you when you were dancing, and then later you were kissing down in the foyer.'

'We went for a walk to the gazebo,' he said, sighing.

'And?'

'I refused to have sex with her.'

'*What?* Good Lord—that's a new one.'

'Look, she was drunk. I don't have sex with seriously intoxicated women, no matter how much I fancy them.'

'That's very commendable of you, Blake. But I'm not sure if I totally believe you. You *do* have a rather ruthless reputation where the ladies are concerned, you know.'

'No, I *don't* know,' Blake snapped. 'Just because I enjoy a bachelor lifestyle it doesn't mean I treat women badly.'

He supposed his so-called reputation was a hangover from those few months after Claudia had left him, when he had indulged in some thoughtless revenge sex. With actresses, of course. But those days were long gone. Okay, so his girlfriends were still usually actresses, or people involved in the movie industry. But that was only logical. Who else did he meet?

'Fair enough,' Cleo said. 'Don't get angry with *me*. I'm

just telling you what I've heard on the grapevine. Obviously Kate has heard something similar. Still, it was a strange reaction on her part. I would have thought she'd be impressed by your gallantry.'

'Obviously not. I don't understand her, Cleo.'

'I think you should go in there and talk to her.'

'She'll probably scream at me to get out.'

'If you really like her, you have to try. Don't wait. Waiting never works where women are concerned.'

'You're right.' He tried the doorknob and found it wasn't locked. Still, he hesitated.

'I really must get back to the party,' Cleo said. 'Byron will wonder where I've got to.'

'Tell him you had to check on the baby.'

'He won't believe that. April's at her godmother's tonight.'

'Well, say you had to call and check that she was okay.'

Cleo laughed. 'I can see you're an accomplished liar.'

'Hardly. I'm usually accused of being brutally honest.'

'That's not always a virtue, Blake—especially when it comes to women. Kindness is what we value most in a man, which might involve the occasional white lie. Anyway, I must go. I'll catch up with you later and see what you achieved.'

She was gone in a flash, leaving Blake mulling over what she'd said about kindness.

I can be kind, he told himself as he slowly turned the knob. *Can't I? Yes, of course I can.* And he pushed open the door.

Kate was lying face down on the bed, weeping into a mountain of pillows.

'Kate?' he said gently as he approached the bed.

'Go away,' she blubbered. 'Leave me alone.'

He ignored that and sat down on the side of the bed. 'Not until you tell me what I did that was so wrong.'

'You don't understand,' she cried in muffled tones.

'No, I don't. Not unless you tell me.'

She rolled over and showed him her pitiful face, her flushed cheeks stained with mascara and tears, her eyes swollen with weeping. 'I... I can't,' she blurted out. 'It's too...humiliating.'

'Kate, I like you. A lot. And I fancy you. A lot. I have every intention of making love to you tomorrow night, after I've taken you out for a suitably romantic dinner and then taken you back to a suitably romantic place, befitting what a lovely girl like you deserves. Does that sound like I don't really want you?'

She shook her head from side to side, then buried her face in her hands. 'It's nothing to do with you, really.'

'Then what's it to do with?'

'I can't tell you.'

Blake took her hands away from her face and held them, forcing her to look up into his eyes. 'It's something to do with your sister, isn't it?'

Her puffy eyes widened.

'I'm a fairly observant character,' he went on. 'I noticed that every time you had something to do with your sister today you became upset. Unhappy. Different. When you came downstairs after helping Maddie with her going-away outfit you were *very* different. I couldn't put my finger on it at the time, but in hindsight I think you were extremely upset and that you tried to hide your feelings behind a rather reckless façade. As much as I hate to admit it, I don't think you really *wanted* to have sex with me. Not me personally. You were just craving distraction. That's why you drank so much as well—to dull whatever pain it was that your sister caused you.'

He stopped talking then, and she just stared at him, her expression bewildered at first, and then just bleak. 'If I tell you, you're going to think me a fool.'

'I doubt that very much. We're all capable of foolishness. So what is it, Kate? What's been bothering you so much today?'

She blinked, then sighed, and then shook her head again. 'I can't believe I'm going to tell you this. I... I never wanted to tell anyone—never wanted anyone to know, especially my family.'

'Well, I'm not family. Sometimes it's good to tell outsiders. They can give you objective advice.'

Though, damn it all, he wasn't feeling all that objective where Kate was concerned. She touched him as he had not been touched in years.

'Just blurt it out,' he insisted. 'Stop thinking about what I might think of you and tell me this awful truth, whatever it is.'

Her face filled with anguish. 'That's very easy to say. Not so easy to do.'

'Just *do* it, Kate.'

She sighed again—a heavy but resigned sigh. 'All right, I will. The thing is...the awful truth is...that I'm in love with Lachlan.' And she hung her head in a gesture of shame. Or possibly humiliation.

Blake supposed later that he should not have been so shocked. After all, practically every female who'd seen one of Lachlan's movies was in love with him. Young. Old. Married. Single. They all adored him. That was why his romantic comedies were so successful.

'I see,' he bit out, angry with her at first, for being so stupid as to fall in love with someone so shallow, and then sympathetic—because hadn't he done exactly the same thing at her age? He'd fallen in love with Claudia, who was probably even worse than Lachlan.

'You *don't* see,' she cried, sitting up and wringing her hands together. 'And you *do* think I'm a fool.'

'No,' he returned slowly. 'I don't think that at all. I can

understand why you might have fallen in love with him. He's very good-looking, and extremely charming when he needs to be. So how long have you been in love with Lachlan?'

'What? Oh, since the first day we went to NIDA together.'

'Love at first sight, then?' Blake said, thinking it was more like lust at first sight. Even *he* hadn't fallen in love with Claudia at first sight.

Blake had always been a bit of a cynic where true love was concerned. Claudia had had to work hard on him in order to convince him of her love. And she had—convinced him, that was—which had made the speed of her betrayal after their marriage all the more devastating.

'Yes,' she said sadly. 'But he didn't ever return my feelings. He liked me okay, so I thought I was in with a chance—especially when he was between girlfriends. He was always nice to me...often seeking me out to help him with assignments. But Maddie told me tonight that he found my crush on him quite embarrassing. That's what he called it. A crush...' Her laugh was slightly hysterical, her hands still twisting in her lap.

'And when exactly did she tell you this?' Blake asked gently.

'Oh, when I came up here tonight to help her change. Though she didn't really want my help. She just wanted reassurance that I was over my crush and that I didn't still have the hots for her precious husband. Which I assured her I didn't. After that she proceeded to give me a lecture about you.'

'About *me*?'

'Yes, she advised me to sleep with you. Said it would be good for my career.'

'Which advice you followed to a T,' he said ruefully.

Her face twisted. 'No—no, you've got it all wrong. My

coming on to you wasn't about my career. It was because you seemed genuinely attracted to me and I was flattered... especially after what Maddie said about Lachlan wanting her and never wanting me. Apparently I simply wasn't his type. So I thought...well... I must be Blake's type. So when I came downstairs and saw you, waiting for me and smiling at me, it made me feel a bit better. Then, when I kissed you, I felt a lot better. Yes, I know I'm drunk, but I needed you, Blake. Needed to feel desirable. I wanted to be wanted. By someone. *Anyone!* So when you turned me down I just felt so bad. I... I couldn't handle it.'

Blake watched as her already fragile control began to shatter.

'And the worst thing is,' she added, her eyes filling with the most heartbreaking distress, 'she doesn't even love him. Not really. Of course she's sexually attracted to him. Who isn't? But the reason she married him was to live the good life—whatever that is. Oh, God...'

Kate couldn't go on, feeling a tight ball of emotion gather in her chest as all the hurt, misery and frustration of this past year overwhelmed her. A cry such as she'd never heard before punched from her lungs. It sounded like a wounded animal—a wounded *dying* animal.

She froze, her shoulders stiffening with the effort to hold on to herself, her eyes wide with shock. But it was no use. There was no stopping the avalanche of pain once it broke free. Whirling away from Blake's startled face, she threw herself back onto the pillows and let go, sobbing her heart out with even more fervour than she had earlier.

It was horrible, humiliating, but she had nothing left of control or courage. She told herself that she didn't even care that Blake was witnessing her breakdown.

It was odd, then, that underneath her almost hysterical weeping, plus her dizzy and decidedly alcohol-infused thoughts, she had enough brainpower left to worry that he probably wouldn't want her in one of his movies now—let alone anything else. It bothered her greatly that he would see her for what she was. A stupid fool and a total failure!

CHAPTER ELEVEN

BLAKE WAS USED to women's tears. Good actresses could summon them up at the drop of a hat. But these weren't just ordinary tears. Kate was sobbing like nothing he'd heard before. If she kept this up she would make herself ill.

He wondered if he should go and find Cleo and Byron—get them to call a doctor, someone who could give Kate something to calm her down. Though Lord knew the possibility of getting a doctor to make a house call at this hour on a Saturday night was highly unlikely. Perhaps they might have something in their medicine cabinet which would be useful. A tranquilliser of some sort.

Whilst he mulled over this possible solution he tried placing his hand on the back of her head and stroking her long hair, murmuring the sort of soft, soothing words which he often put into a script but had never actually said before.

'Now, now—don't cry...there, there...'

How soft her hair was. How silky and soft and sexy.

Must not think about sex now, he told himself sternly. *Time to be kind. Time to just be a good friend.* Clearly Kate needed a good friend—someone who would comfort her and then talk sense to her, when she was capable of listening. Which probably wouldn't be tonight.

But still... Fancy falling in love with Lachlan! What a total waste of time *that* was. It probably wasn't true love, either. Just an infatuation. He was the kind of guy girls got infatuated with very easily. His golden boy looks, of course, and that brilliant smile, that overpowering charm.

How ironic that Kate's sister didn't really love him—that she'd just married him for the good life. Not that she didn't put on a good act. She played the besotted bride to perfection. And she had the looks to carry off the role. She might even make the marriage a success. After all, if she didn't love him she'd probably be prepared to tolerate his infidelities. Either that or she herself might move on to someone even more successful, the way Claudia had.

Claudia...

Blake thought of Claudia as he stroked Kate's hair. What a bitch! A selfish, ambitious, cold-blooded bitch. He'd always hoped she'd fall flat on her face once she'd dumped him for that aging Hollywood producer. But she hadn't. Her career—whilst not top drawer—had been very successful.

She was now married to one of the executives at Unicorn Pictures. Blake had run into her at a party not that long ago, and she'd been sickeningly nice to him. Admittedly, he'd been sickeningly nice back—even chatting away very amicably with her reasonably handsome and annoyingly clever husband. No point in making enemies in Hollywood. Not good for business.

Quite frankly, he was well and truly over her. A good feeling, that, after spending years being bitter and somewhat cynical—especially where aspiring young actresses were concerned.

The fact that Kate was an aspiring young actress did not escape Blake, but she wasn't like any aspiring young actress he'd ever met before. Besides, he was *glad* she was exactly that. It gave him the opportunity to get to know her better and to do what he'd been aching to do all night.

Stop thinking about sex!

Blake gritted his teeth and continued stroking her hair, valiantly ignoring his very active hormones and concentrating on giving Kate what she needed at that moment. Which was gentle words and a soft touch.

Hopefully by tomorrow night her needs would be different. It didn't escape Blake that she'd had a very mixed agenda when she'd offered herself to him in the gazebo.

No doubt there was some rebound and revenge in there somewhere. But he still felt confident that she was genuinely attracted to him. He knew she hadn't faked that kiss.

Finally the sobbing subsided into the occasional shudder, and Blake's hand fell away when Kate abruptly rolled over.

'I... I have to go to the bathroom,' she choked out, scrambling off the bed and dashing for the nearby en-suite.

Blake groaned when he heard the sound of Kate throwing up, torn between offering further help and keeping a compassionate distance. In the end he decided on compassionate distance. He heard her flush the toilet a couple of times, then turn on a tap. Possibly to rinse out her mouth. He heard the tap snapped off but she didn't emerge. He heard her mutter something under her breath, followed by a sigh and some rustling sounds.

When a few minutes had passed and all had fallen ominously silent in the bathroom he made his way reluctantly over to the shut door. His hand had actually lifted to knock when the door opened.

Blake sucked in a breath sharply. *Bloody hell!*

She wasn't naked. But she'd removed her bridesmaid's dress and was standing there dressed in a strapless black satin corset which was so sexy it was criminal—especially when worn with flesh-coloured stay-up stockings and high heels.

'I had to take my dress off,' she explained shakily, looking both sheepish and embarrassed. 'I got some vomit on it. Mum's going to be furious with me,' she added, wincing. 'I... I would have had a shower, but I didn't know I was going to stay here overnight and I didn't bring any nightwear with me. I'm not trying to be provocative. Truly.'

She swayed on her high heels, grabbing the doorknob as if her life depended on it.

'Oh, God, will someone please stop the room from spinning around?'

Blake took a firm hold of her and led her back over to the bed, sitting her down and doing his level best to keep his male mind from corrupting his good intentions.

Kate didn't need him ogling her. But her body was exactly the kind of body he admired on a woman—tall and slender, but with enough curves to be unmistakably feminine. Still, he already knew that—had thought it when he'd first seen her walking down the staircase. She had great skin too. Clear and almost translucent, indicating that her honey-gold hair was probably natural and not the result of hours of painstaking dyeing.

'What you need,' he said gently as he removed her shoes and then her stockings, without once looking at the V between her thighs or her tiny waist...or her very nice cleavage, 'is a big drink of water followed by a good night's sleep.'

'I did drink some water in the bathroom,' she told him.

'And you kept it down?'

'Yes.'

'Good. Now, into bed with you.'

Again without really looking at her, he pulled the bedclothes back and angled her in between the sheets before swiftly covering her, right up to her neck.

But just when he thought he could safely make his escape her head lifted from the pillow, the bedcovers slipping a little—*darn it*.

Her puffy eyes sought his, their expression plaintive. 'Please don't go. Not 'til I've fallen asleep.'

'Oh, but I...um...'

'I won't jump on you, I promise.'

His smile was wry. *What a shame.* He wouldn't mind one bit if she did. Like they said, the road to hell was paved with good intentions.

'Very well,' he agreed, and lay down next to her. On top of the quilt, not under it.

She rolled over and stared at him with wonder in her sleepy eyes. 'You're really a very nice man,' she murmured. 'Very…kind.'

'There are a lot of people who would disagree with you.'

'Then they don't know the real you.' She yawned. 'They say men should be judged by their actions, not their words. You're a gentleman, no matter what other people might think.'

Blake wondered exactly what 'other people' she was talking about. Was his reputation with women really that bad? Then he wondered what she'd think of him tomorrow night, when he took her to dinner and set out to seduce her with every weapon he had in his considerable arsenal.

He rolled over and looked her straight in her heavy-lidded eyes. 'You should go to sleep now,' he advised. 'You're going to have a seriously late night tomorrow.'

'Am I?'

Was that a quiver of excitement in her voice?

Blake gave in to temptation and bent forward to kiss her—not on the lips, but on her slightly clammy forehead. 'You'd better believe it, sweetheart. We have a dinner date, remember?'

'Oh, yes,' was all she said, with what sounded like a satisfied sigh.

'Roll over the other way,' he advised thickly. 'I'll stroke your hair until you drop off.'

She obeyed him, sighing again when he started stroking.

Touching her—even her hair—was agony. But he did it, thinking all the while that she was worth the effort.

It was a relief when she fell asleep and he could creep out of the room, telling himself all the while that he wouldn't have to wait too long before he could satisfy the lust she kept on evoking in him. Less than twenty-four hours.

But as he stood in the doorway and glanced back at her it crossed Blake's testosterone-fired brain that once the alcohol was out of Kate's system and she didn't have to watch the man she loved marry her sister she might not be quite the same person who'd thrown herself at him tonight. Tomorrow morning she might be filled with shame and embarrassment. She might actually say no to him.

What a horrific thought!

Blake closed the door and walked slowly towards the staircase, pondering such a possibility. Not for long, however. Confidence in his own abilities had never been a problem for Blake. He had always achieved what he'd set his sights on. And he'd set his sights on getting Kate into his bed.

She wouldn't say no to him. He'd make sure of that!

CHAPTER TWELVE

'IT'S GOOD OF you to drive me home,' Kate said with stiff politeness once they were out of Byron's driveway.

Blake glanced over at her from behind the wheel of his borrowed Lexus. She looked vastly different from the glamorous bridesmaid of last night. Just a simple girl this morning, wearing dark jeans, trainers, and a grey sweatshirt which had a picture of the Opera House on it. No make-up, and her damp and very straight hair pulled back into a ponytail, not a curl or a wave in sight. Not a hint of perfume, either.

Blake wondered if this was some ploy to get him to lose interest in her. Fat chance of that happening. He'd thought of little else all night. Besides, he adored the way she looked. So natural, yet still so sexy.

'My pleasure,' he replied warmly.

She didn't say anything further, gazing out of the passenger window like some tourist taking in the sights. Blake doubted it was anything like that. He suspected, as he'd feared, that she'd woken this morning feeling pretty bad about what had happened the night before.

Cleo had taken a breakfast tray up to her room around ten, reporting back that Kate seemed somewhat subdued.

'There's no need to feel embarrassed,' he said at last.

Her head whipped round and her expression was totally devoid of embarrassment. Or distress. 'I'm not,' she denied. 'I was for a short while this morning. But not any longer.'

'Good.'

'I know I made a fool of myself last night, but that's all in the past now. I have to move on.'

'You definitely do.'

'I dare say that sooner or later I'll get over being in love with Lachlan, but until that happens I'm not going to waste any more of my life mooning over him or wishing things were different. I'm going to concentrate on my career—one hundred and ten percent.'

'Atta girl.'

She threw him a droll glance. 'That doesn't mean I'm going to jump into bed with *you*, just because you've offered me a part in one of your movies.'

Blake almost ran into the back of the car in front of him, braking just in time. He hadn't noticed that the lights ahead had turned red, bringing the traffic to an abrupt halt. As, it seemed, were his plans for tonight.

'Are you saying that your being attracted to me last night was all about the drink, then?' he asked casually. Oh, *so* casually. If there was one thing Blake had learned about the female sex since the debacle with Claudia, it was never to let a girl know you wanted her like crazy.

Kate scrunched up her face. 'I didn't think so at the time. But in hindsight I suppose it did play a part. Look, I want to be strictly honest with you, Blake. I was in a pathetic state last light. Your attention flattered my rather fragile self-esteem. You're a good-looking man. You're also powerful and successful. I'm not used to men like you coming on to me.'

'Then more fool them,' he said, and smiled over at her.

She didn't smile back. 'Please don't,' she bit out.

'Don't what?'

'Don't keep flattering me. I don't appreciate it. Now, I have a couple of questions to ask you about this part you've offered me. Unless, of course, you've changed your mind about that now you've seen how I usually look,' she added with a steely glance his way.

Brother, that 'fragile self-esteem' of hers seemed to have taken a back seat. There was not a hint of vulnerability in her eyes at this moment. Kate had suddenly turned into one tough cookie. Blake suppressed a smile. He liked her tough almost as much as he liked her tipsy.

The lights turned green and he drove on. More slowly this time.

'I actually like the way you look today,' he told her. 'I'm not into Barbie dolls. So the offer still stands. It would be a wonderful addition to your résumé and will get you more work. Not here in Australia, however. You'd have to move to LA and get yourself an American agent.'

'Move to LA!' she exclaimed, her eyes widening for a split second before she got control of herself again. 'I didn't realise— I...um...forgot you'd moved over there.'

'I'll probably make the occasional movie back here in Australia, but not the one I'm offering you. Look, we don't actually start shooting until late November, so you've got plenty of time to get yourself organised and over there. We're still in pre-production and I've a few more minor characters to cast.'

'I see,' she said thoughtfully. 'And how will you go about doing that?'

Blake shrugged. 'I'll have a couple of the casting agencies I use send me some likely candidates and I'll give them all an audition. Then I'll choose.'

'In that case that's what I want to do too,' Kate said firmly. 'Go for a proper audition up against other people.'

Blake suppressed his frustration and kept his voice calm. 'But, Kate, there's no need. The role's yours.'

'Why? It doesn't make sense. Unless what Lachlan said was true. That you give the girls you fancy small roles in your movies just so you can shag them every night.'

'Lachlan said *what*?'

'You heard me.'

'Bastard.'

'Is it true?' she demanded. '*Do* you do that?'

Bloody hell. What did he say to that?

'I have done,' he admitted reluctantly. 'Once or twice. In the long-distant past when I was hurting after Claudia divorced me. I'm not proud of it, but I haven't done anything like that for many years. I can't understand why Lachlan would say such a thing. These days I would never risk the success of one of my movies by offering actresses roles on the strength of how much I fancy them.'

'That's what Lachlan said too. That's why you only ever offer the girls you fancy really *small* roles.'

Blake's temper rose. 'So when did Lachlan say all this to you?' he demanded through clenched teeth.

'Last night.'

'Yes, of course. It *would* have been last night. *When*, exactly, last night?'

'When I left you briefly to go to the Ladies. He followed me. He said he cared about me and was worried about me getting tangled up with you.'

'Yeah. Right. And you believed him?'

'I believed what he said about *you*. After all, you'd already offered me a small part in one of your movies without knowing if I could act or not.'

'Firstly, madam, I *do* know you can act. You're a graduate of NIDA, for heaven's sake! Secondly, it is *not* a small role. It's a very good supporting role. Thirdly, I didn't offer you the role because I wanted to "shag" you,' he insisted. 'God, I hate that term. It sounds disgusting. I much prefer to say "have sex", or "sleep with", or even "make love". Anyway, wanting to have sex with you isn't the reason I offered you that job.'

'Oh? What was, then?' Both her question and her eyes were full of scepticism.

Blake sighed. 'I just wanted to make you happy. To make you smile.'

She stared at him for a long moment. 'So you offered me a job out of pity?' she bit out, angry now.

'Absolutely not! I'm not into pity—especially where my movies are concerned.'

'What *are* you into, then?' she asked, a challenging note in her voice.

'Success. And satisfaction.'

'What kind of satisfaction?'

His smile was rueful. 'What do you want me to say, Kate? Okay, so I want to have sex with you. That's hardly a hanging offence. I'm single. You're single. You haven't got a boyfriend and you're not a virgin. I assume you *do* have a sex life? I honestly thought you might enjoy going to bed with me. I'd certainly enjoy going to bed with you. But, aside from all that, I wasn't lying when I said my main motivation for all the things I did last night was to put a smile on your face. That was God's honest truth and it still is. I'm sorry if I've offended you. That was the last thing I wanted to do. Look, if it makes you happy I'll give you a proper screen test for the role. We can do it tonight. I'm sure I've already told you that I'm staying in Byron's city penthouse for the next couple of days. We could go there early this evening, before I take you out to dinner. Or are you reneging on that as well?'

'I'm not reneging on anything. I just need to get some things sorted in my head.'

'Such as what?'

'Such as if my audition's all right, and you still offer me the role, does the offer come with strings attached? Will you expect me to sleep with you at some stage?'

He looked at her long and hard. 'Only if you want to,' he said.

She didn't answer straight away, just turned her head to stare out through the passenger window for a while before glancing back at him.

'Fair enough,' she said, and rewarded him with a small, rather enigmatic smile.

He wondered what it meant, that smile. Whatever, he took some comfort from it. And some confidence. Which was strange, given that confidence was never usually a problem with him—especially with members of the opposite sex.

But Kate rattled him in ways he had yet to fully understand. Blake knew he was very attracted to her, but she stirred other emotions in him besides lust—emotions that were both uncharacteristic and unfamiliar.

In the past few years his relationships with women had basically been selfish ones, his only concern what pleasure they could bring to his life. Sex. Companionship. Compliments.

Oh, yes, he enjoyed the way the women in his world flirted with him, and flattered him, and, yes, were only too willing to go to bed with him. Which suited Blake just fine. He never felt he had to bend over backwards to please them. Didn't need to declare love or promise commitment to enjoy their company.

Kate, however, brought out the gentleman in him. Yes, he wanted her—but not quite so selfishly. His tendency to think only of himself was tempered by a compulsion to try to make everything right in her world. To make her... Yes... to make her *happy*. Of course that didn't mean he wouldn't try to seduce her tonight. He would. But he would stop if she made it clear that she didn't want him to. The trick was to make sure she *did* want him to...

'You might have to make a slight detour,' she said suddenly. 'I'd like to drop off my bridesmaid dress at the dry cleaner's. No way am I taking it home the way it is. Do you know your way to the big shopping centre at Burwood?'

'Not exactly.' He wasn't as familiar with the western

suburbs as he was with the eastern, having being brought up there.

'We're not far away now. I'll give you directions, if you like.'

Half an hour later they were back in the Lexus and heading for Strathfield, which was the next suburb going west.

'It will do you good to move away from home,' Blake said, after seeing how stressed Kate had been at the dry cleaner's, despite the lady there assuring her that the dress would be as good as new once cleaned properly. 'Your mother sounds like a pain. And it's perfectly obvious that Maddie is the family pet.'

Kate sighed. 'You're right on both those counts.'

'Then why are you finding excuses not to come to Hollywood and make a new life for yourself? You said you wanted to move on. So do it!'

'I'm not making excuses. I just want to make it on my own. I don't want charity.'

Lord, but she was one difficult girl. Any other actress would have jumped at the chance.

'Don't you believe in your acting ability?' he challenged.

Her chin came up and her eyes flashed. 'Yes, I do. I'm very good. *Damned* good, actually.'

'Then be "damned good" tonight and you'll be on your way to LA.'

CHAPTER THIRTEEN

'WHERE'S YOUR BRIDESMAID DRESS?' were her mother's first words when Kate walked into the family kitchen shortly after midday. 'Don't tell me it's stuffed into that silly little bag!'

Kate counted to ten, then said, 'It's at the dry cleaner's. Someone knocked into me and I spilt some wine on it.'

'Oh, for pity's sake, Kate. Couldn't you have been more careful? Just as well I brought Maddie's dress home with me or that would probably be ruined too.'

'My dress is not ruined,' Kate countered, quite calmly, hugging the hope that soon she wouldn't have to put up with this kind of thing. 'The dry cleaner said it would be as good as new.'

'I hope so. Did Maddie finally get you? She rang me from the airport and said she'd tried to ring you but your phone was turned off.'

'Yes. Yes, it was.' And would remain so for now.

The last person she wanted to talk to was Maddie. She didn't want to hear how wonderful her wedding night had been. Neither did she want to hear a blow-by-blow description of every moment of her honeymoon. Kate had told her sister yesterday not to ring her, but to put her news on social media.

Her mother rolled her eyes in exasperation. 'What's the point of having a mobile if you don't turn it on? Anyway, Maddie sent you a message via me—though I have no idea what she was on about. She said she hopes you did what she told you to last night and that everything worked out. Does that make sense to you?'

'Perfect sense,' Kate replied, and searched her mind for

a half-truthful answer which wouldn't shock the pants off her mother. 'Maddie suggested I suck up to Blake Randall and see if I could get myself a part in one of his movies.'

'Goodness. Such language. I'm sure Maddie wouldn't have said it like that. And did you do that? Er…"suck up" to the man?'

'I sure did.'

'And what happened?'

Various images flashed into Kate's head, none of which she could relate to her mother.

'Blake said that since I was a graduate of NIDA he would gladly give me a screen test.'

'Oh, my. What a clever girl your sister is.'

Kate almost lost it then. Truly, did Maddie have to get the credit for *everything*?

Another count to ten.

'So when are you having this screen test?' her mother asked eagerly.

'Blake is organising one for early this evening,' she informed her mother, thinking to herself that she really would have to turn her phone back on in case Byron wanted to ring her. 'He flies back to LA in a couple of days, so time is of the essence. Now, I'm going to go and have a lie-down. Last night has exhausted me. Oh, and don't worry about cooking me dinner tonight, Mum. I won't be coming back here after the audition. Blake's taking me out to dinner.'

'Blake Randall is taking you out to *dinner*?' she said, mouth agape.

'Yes. Do you have a problem with that?'

Her mother tossed her head, the way she did when she couldn't think of what to say for a second or two. 'Well, you're not the sort of girl men like him *usually* take to dinner,' she finally managed. 'There again, I suppose you *did* look surprisingly attractive at the wedding yesterday.'

Her eyes narrowed on Kate's outfit.

'Make sure you wear something better than what you've got on, though. And put on some make-up and do your hair properly. Truly, Kate, it's no wonder you haven't had a boyfriend for years. You simply don't try.'

Kate didn't tell her that Blake had said he liked the way she was dressed today. Her mother probably had no idea he'd driven her home. Blake hadn't come inside. No doubt she thought Kate had taken a taxi home.

'Maybe I don't *want* a boyfriend,' she fired back.

'More likely the one you want you can't have,' her mother muttered.

'Oh, not you too, Mum,' Kate said, hiding her hurt behind irritation. Did *everyone* in her family know about her infatuation with Lachlan?

Yes, of course they did. Time, then, to put things to right.

'If you're talking about Lachlan, then you're way off the mark. Yes, I did have a crush on him once—but I got over that ages ago. Frankly, I feel sorry for Maddie being married to him. He's not the type to stay faithful.'

'Oh, rubbish! Lachlan adores Maddie. And why would he look elsewhere when he has a wife as beautiful as she is to come home to? They make a brilliant couple. You're just jealous, that's all.'

'No, Mum, I'm not,' she said, with the kind of calmness which came with stating the truth.

Because, as amazing as it seemed, Kate didn't feel jealous of Maddie marrying Lachlan any longer. Not one iota. Her breakdown last night seemed to have somehow banished all the self-destructive emotions which had been affecting both her life and her career for ages. Her depression was gone this morning, along with her lack of spirit. She felt stronger, and a lot more confident.

Kate suspected that her love for Lachlan was on the wane. Her rose-tinted glasses were off where he was concerned and she was finally able to see him for what he was. Not a charming golden boy, but a selfish, arrogant and narcissistic individual, whose only aim in life was his own success. She doubted he loved Maddie any more than Maddie loved him. They were both just trophies for each other. If their marriage lasted two years she'd be surprised.

'Time will tell, I guess,' she added, and walked out of the kitchen.

By the time she reached her bedroom she'd totally dismissed her mother's annoying remarks, plus all thoughts of Lachlan and Maddie. They were not what she wanted to think about right now. She had other things on her mind. Like what *was* she going to wear tonight?

Kate wasn't all that worried about the screen test. She suspected it was just a formality. Blake had said he was going to give her the part anyway; it was only she who had insisted upon a screen test to save her dignity.

She would be wonderful tonight. Her pride demanded it. The same pride that had claimed she would not jump into bed with him just because he'd promised her a job.

His reaction to her making that stand had been very telling. Lord, he'd almost crashed into the car in front of them. Clearly he *had* expected her to sleep with him. But he'd been clever enough to pretend that he hadn't assumed as much.

'Only if you want to...'

What a devious and devilishly tempting invitation *that* was. Because she did want to. Had known it immediately he'd said those words. She hadn't dared look over at him lest he see the heat in her eyes. So she'd looked away until her reaction could be controlled and she could reply with a brilliantly nonchalant remark.

Not that he'd seemed put out by it. No doubt he still thought it was just a matter of time before she gave him what he wanted.

Which was her. In his bed.

The realisation still astounded her. Why *her*? She just didn't understand the ongoing attraction on his part—and certainly not today, when she looked anything but attractive. But she would tonight. Oh, yes, her pride wouldn't let her go for the screen test and then out to dinner with Blake looking, as Maddie would have said, 'like a drack sack'.

She did have some smart outfits—most of them bought for special occasions and nearly all of them chosen for her by Maddie, who admittedly did have good taste and was always on trend with fashion. One particular outfit came to mind. It had been in a shop window, on a tall mannequin with honey-coloured hair rather like hers. Maddie had dragged Kate out clothes shopping back in May, insisting that Kate buy something decent for her engagement party.

'That'd look good on you,' she'd pointed out.

'Maybe…' Kate had replied. 'But it's hardly a ball gown.'

It certainly hadn't been a ball gown, but a knee-length dark red satin cocktail dress, with finger-width straps, snugly fitted, and paired with elegant stiletto shoes. Hanging around the mannequin's neck had been an oval-shaped diamond pendant on a long, fine silver chain.

'No matter. We can look for a ball gown later. We've got all day. Let's go in and try that on you.'

It had suited her, and Maddie had insisted she buy the whole outfit—pendant as well. Thank God it had only been costume jewellery. As it was everything had come to over five hundred dollars. When Kate had dithered about the price Maddie had blithely used her credit card to pay for it all, telling her not to worry, that she wanted her to have it.

'Call it an early birthday present,' she'd said.

Kate had thought the gesture terribly generous of her at the time. Now she wondered if there had been some guilt involved. Whatever—it was a stylish outfit, and one in which she would feel good tonight.

Walking over to her wardrobe, she drew it out and hung

it on the door. Then she turned her phone back on—surely Maddie would be in the air by now—lay down on her bed and tried to get some rest.

But her mind wouldn't let her. She kept thinking about Blake lying next to her last night, telling her that she was going to have a very late night tonight. She wondered if he still meant to seduce her, regardless of what he'd said in the car today.

Surely he wouldn't. A *gentleman* wouldn't. A gentleman would keep his word.

But he wasn't *really* a gentleman, was he? It would be naive of her to pretend that he was. Yes, he'd been very kind to her last night. Quite the white knight. But she suspected that gallantry wasn't his true nature; more likely he was a clever and ruthless devil who wasn't beyond using bribery to get a girl into his bed.

He'd used sweet words as well.

I just want to make you happy. To make you smile...

Could she really believe that? Why should he care whether she was unhappy or not? He didn't even know her!

Lachlan had warned her about him—said he was bitter and twisted after what Claudia had done to him, that he used women and treated them badly. But that didn't ring true either. There *was* kindness in him. And compassion. Oh, Lord, she wished she could work him out. He was a conundrum, all right. Still, she really should stick to her guns and not let him seduce her tonight...even if her heart beat faster at the thought.

CHAPTER FOURTEEN

KATE COULDN'T BELIEVE her luck when her mother popped her head around her bedroom door just after four, announcing that she and her father had been invited out for dinner with some friends. They hadn't been guests at the wedding and they wanted to hear all about it.

Off she went, without another word, leaving Kate feeling both grateful and slightly miffed. Which was perverse, she thought as she rose and started getting herself ready. The last thing she wanted was her mother making critical remarks about how she looked. But she might at least have thought to wish her luck with the screen test.

Six o'clock saw her pacing up and down in the front room, watching and waiting for Blake to arrive. By five past six she was beginning to panic. By ten past six she felt sick. He wasn't coming. He'd changed his mind. But if that was so then why hadn't he rung?

It was at this critical point that she remembered he didn't have her phone number. She hadn't given it to him. She didn't have his, either. What if he'd had an accident? What if...?

And then there he was, pulling in to the kerb, jumping out from behind the wheel and striding round the front of the silver Lexus. God, he looked gorgeous, dressed all in black. Black trousers and a black silk shirt, black belt and shoes. Black as his hair. He was frowning, though, his thick dark brows drawn tightly together as he hurried through the wrought-iron gate along the path and up onto the front porch.

Kate resisted flinging open the door before he'd actually rung the bell, but it was a close call. She made him wait a few seconds before she finally turned the knob, doing her best to stay calm and composed and not act like a teenager on her first date.

Actually, it *was* her first date for some years—a fact which should have been depressing. But she had no time for depression tonight. She was having a screen test with the brilliant and wickedly sexy Blake Randall and then going out to dinner with him. How fantastic was *that*?

His deeply set blue eyes gave her one long thorough once-over. 'Good God, Kate, you make it hard on a guy, don't you?' he growled.

'What do you mean?' she asked, pretending not to understand.

'You know exactly what I mean, you bad girl. You could have at least put your hair up into a prissy bun thing instead of leaving it down. I have to tell you now that I have a thing for long hair—especially long, straight, silky honey-coloured hair. I also have a thing for silk dresses and sexy stilettos.'

His sigh was rather melodramatic.

'I thought you wanted me to keep my hands off tonight? Oh, don't bother to answer that,' he swept on, whilst rolling his eyes. 'I'll do my best but I can't promise you anything. Now, let's get going. We're already running late.'

'I have to just get my purse and lock up.'

Kate glanced in the hallway mirror as she hurried past. Her cheeks were flushed and her eyes shining. Lord, he really was a devil. Because she didn't *want* him to keep his hands off, did she?

'So, where's Mommie Dearest?' he asked as they made their way out to the car.

'Visiting some friends.'

'Does she know you're out with me tonight?'

'Oh, yes. I told her. About the screen test *and* the dinner.'

'And?'

'She was surprised at first, and then not very interested.'

'You know, she's just like *my* mother,' he said as he opened the passenger door.

'Oh? In what way?'

'I have an older brother—James. He's the apple of her eye. Can do no wrong. I'm the black sheep in a family of doctors.'

'So you understand, then?' Kate said with a sigh as she climbed in and buckled up.

'I certainly do.'

She closed the door.

'Hold on to this,' he added after getting in behind the wheel and handing her a tablet. 'I've copied the three scenes you're in and brought them up, ready for you to read. You can study them during the drive to Byron's penthouse. That way you'll be prepared by the time we get there. Your character is a secretary who's having an affair with her married boss. She's actually a bit of a closet *femme fatale*—dresses very conservatively in the office and has a witty turn of phrase. I'm sure you'll get the gist once you've read the scenes.'

It hit Kate suddenly that very soon she was actually going to audition for *the* Blake Randall—movie-maker extraordinaire. Up until now it had all seemed somewhat hypothetical. She'd just presumed she would do well. Her confidence was at an all-time high today.

But what if she *didn't* do well? What if she totally stuffed it up?

Nerves gathered in the pit of her stomach as she read through the scenes. The first one wasn't too difficult. Just an office scene with a boss and his PA, with some clever *double entendres* in the dialogue. She thought she could handle the third scene as well. Back in the same office, with the boss breaking off the affair and saying he was going to try to make his marriage work. The PA then told him she'd already got another job and quit, throwing at him the fact that she had bigger fish to fry.

Kate quite liked the idea of playing a bitch. Those sorts of roles were often remembered. But the second scene worried the life out of her.

In a hotel bedroom, it required her character to be in bed, obviously naked under the covers, watching her lover get dressed. She was described as having 'sated, heavy-lidded eyes', with 'a blistering sensuality' in all her movements. In the scene she reached for a cigarette and smoked it slowly, praising her lover's performance and claiming she'd never had better.

'So what do you think?' Blake asked, perhaps sensing her unease.

'I think,' she said slowly, 'that I am going to have difficulty pulling off this role.'

'And why is that?'

Kate knew she had to be honest with him. Or risk making a total fool of herself. But, God, it was going to be hard telling him the truth.

'Well, the thing is...when I act I can usually tap in to some personal experience to help me with the emotions involved. I'm afraid I haven't anything to tap into for this second scene.'

His forehead bunched into a frown. 'What are you saying, Kate? Spell it out for me.'

Kate sighed. 'Well, if you must know, I've never lain in bed watching my lover get dressed. I've never experienced what it is to be sexually sated. I've only ever had three serious boyfriends, and they *were* just boys, really. And I wasn't ever in a bed—just in the back of a car or on a lumpy sofa. The first time was during my last year in high school. He was a total nerd and hadn't got a clue. Same as me. My other two boyfriends were at university, where I was doing an arts degree and waiting to get into NIDA. They were a bit better than the nerd, but not much.'

'I see,' Blake said thoughtfully. 'So why didn't you have sex with anyone once you went to NIDA? Surely there were some older more experienced chaps there who asked you out?'

'Yes. But I didn't want to go out with them.'

Blake rolled his eyes at her. 'Don't tell me. By then you were madly in love with Lachlan.'

His derisive tone brought an embarrassed heat to Kate's cheeks.

'Oh, Kate, that is just *so* pathetic.'

'I know,' she said in a small voice.

An awkward silence fell, and Kate was startled when she realised they were in the middle of the CBD. Blake suddenly shot across the road and down a ramp which led to an underground car park, braking hard at the bottom so he could activate the security gate. It rose slowly, during which time he threw her a frustrated glance.

'I suppose you haven't dated anyone this year, either?' he ground out.

She shook her head, her mouth having gone dry.

'Truly?' he exclaimed, then muttered very rude words under his breath the whole time it took him to park.

He stomped around to the passenger side of the car, wrenched open the door, snatched up the tablet from her lap and threw it onto the back seat before practically dragging her out of the car and over to the bank of lifts in the corner, glaring at her all the while.

'Not another word,' he snarled when her mouth opened to protest at his caveman-like handling.

Kate backed away from him in the lift, crossing her arms in a huddle of misery when he didn't explain what was going on. Clearly she wasn't going to be doing the screen test. Maybe he was going to give her a lecture about her futile love for Lachlan. He sure as hell was angry with her.

When the lift door opened on the top floor he strode out without looking to see if she was following him or not. She did, of course. What else could she do?

Byron's penthouse was exactly what Kate had expected of a billionaire owner. The rooms were massive and lavishly furnished, and the views from the terrace almost as good as those from the Centrepoint Tower. Everything that proclaimed Sydney one of the most beautiful cities in the world lay before her.

But Kate wasn't in the mood to be impressed. Neither was she interested in being lectured.

'I think,' she said as she stood in the middle of the main living room, her arms crossed once again, but this time with stiff resolve, not misery, 'that you should just take me home. I'd call a taxi, only my purse and my phone are still in your car.'

CHAPTER FIFTEEN

BLAKE WAS TORN between seducing her and slapping her. 'Don't be ridiculous,' he snapped.

'Don't call me ridiculous,' she fired back at him. 'You wanted the truth and I told it to you. I'm sorry if you find it "pathetic" to love someone enough not to want to be with anyone else. No doubt when Claudia dumped you, you went out and shagged everything in sight. But I'm not like that. My feelings run a little deeper.'

'Should I get the violins out now?'

'Oh!' she said, stunned by his insensitive attitude.

Her fingernails dug into her upper arm whilst she struggled with the urge to actually stamp her feet. The only thing stopping her was the fact that he would think her pathetically childish if she did.

'Might I remind you that you would have been quite happy for me to shag you last night?' he threw at her.

Her arms unfolded in a flurry and she strode up close to him, her dark eyes flashing with fury. 'Trust you to bring that up. I was drunk. You *know* I was drunk.'

'Not at first, you weren't. That only came later—after you'd been screwed up by your sweet sister. You wanted me when we were dancing, sweetheart, and don't pretend you didn't. You *still* want me.'

'I do not. I definitely do not. I... I...'

He'd had enough of this—enough of wanting this girl and having to wait until she accepted the fact that she wanted him back. Without hesitation he pulled her into his arms and kissed her, his mouth quite brutal with frustration and a wild, flaring passion.

She froze at first, but then she melted into him, moaning as her arms slid up around his neck, her high, softly rounded breasts pressing hard into his chest. Her gesture of surrender calmed his fury and his mouth gentled on hers, his hands sliding up under her jumper to caress the bare flesh of her lower back. He felt her shiver, then felt himself swell to alarming proportions.

I'm going too fast, came the stern warning. *I have to slow down. Have to. Going too fast isn't going to work with this girl.*

She might not be a virgin, but she was close to it.

Kate groaned when his head lifted. She didn't want him to stop. She'd never been kissed like that in her life. And it had been mind-blowing.

'So,' he said with a wry smile, 'before I go on I have a question I must ask you.'

'What?' she asked, her voice sounding dazed.

'Do you want to?'

'Do I want to what?'

He laughed. 'Have you forgotten already the deal we had? The one where we would only have sex if you wanted to.'

'Oh. Oh, yes. No. I mean, yes. I did forget about that.'

'So *do* you want to?'

'Yes,' she said, her heart pounding in her chest.

'You won't accuse me later of taking advantage of you? Or bribing you into bed with a part in one of my movies?'

'No.'

'Good. Now, I think this is cause for celebration. I'm sure I saw a bottle of champagne in the fridge earlier. Follow me.'

Kate blinked, then followed him into one of those kitchens that often featured in house and garden magazines. All white and stainless steel, with stone benchtops and no visible drawer handles.

'What are we celebrating?' she asked breathlessly as he retrieved the champagne and found a couple of glasses.

'You discovering that love and great sex don't have to go together.'

The cork popped and he filled the glasses, handing her one before lifting the other to his lips...those cruel-looking lips which only a couple of minutes earlier had rendered her mindless.

'Have you ever had an orgasm?' he asked her, his focus unblinking.

Oh, God, how to answer that?

'Yes,' she admitted, and then swallowed. 'Just not when I'm *with* anyone.'

'Right. Okay. I can work with that. At least you know what a climax feels like.'

Kate could only shake her head at him. 'This is a very intimate conversation.'

'But a very necessary one if I'm to give you what you want. And what you obviously need. Now, let's take our champers along to the master bedroom and get this show on the road.'

'This *show*?' she echoed, appalled and excited at the same time.

'Just an expression, sweetheart. Don't take offence. Sex can be fun, you know. A form of entertainment followed by the most delicious feeling of relaxation. It doesn't have to be all serious with lots of heavy emotion. Being in love can be very disappointing, because when you're in love you try too hard. And trying too hard is the kiss of death where good sex is concerned.'

'I wouldn't know,' she choked out, her stomach suddenly in knots.

'Drink up,' he advised. 'You're looking a little green around the gills.'

'I'm nervous, I guess.' She took a deep swallow, hoping that the alcohol would do the same job as it had last night.

'You weren't nervous when I was kissing you just now. Once we get started again you'll be fine. Trust me.'

She did, letting him lead her down to the most magnificent bedroom she'd ever seen. He turned to shut the door, leaving her to wander over to the king-sized bed which was dressed all in white, with a fluffy grey throw draped across the foot of the bed.

She took another swallow of champagne as she stared at the bed and tried to imagine being naked in it with Blake by her side.

'Here, give me that,' Blake said, taking the glass from her trembling hand and putting it down with his on one of the bedside tables. 'You're thinking too much,' he said, and drew her into his arms, his eyes darkening as they roved over her probably anxious-looking face.

Just kiss me, she thought breathlessly. *Kiss me and take me again to that place where the real world recedes and there's nothing but your mouth on mine and your hands all over me.*

He kissed her, but slowly this time, tenderly, his lips roving over hers until they gasped apart. She sucked in sharply when his tongue-tip met hers, moaning for more. But he didn't ravage her mouth as she'd thought she wanted him too. Instead he made love to it, giving her pleasure and frustration in equal parts. His hands were gentle as well—not delving boldly under her top as they had before, but running up and down her spine on top of her clothes.

When he stopped, she groaned in protest.

His head lifted and he smiled down at her. 'Softly, softly, catchee monkey,' he murmured.

'What?'

'Nothing. Come on. Sit down.'

'Sit down?'

'Yes. I want to get rid of those heels for starters.'

She sank down on the side of the bed, stunned when Blake knelt at her feet and slowly removed her left shoe.

Once it was disposed of he glanced up at her, his smile wry. 'I'm always removing your footwear.' Then he bent his head and slipped off her right stiletto, easing it off and tossing it aside.

'Now,' he went on as he stood up, 'as gorgeous as your top is, I want that gone as well.'

Kate immediately thought of her simple white cotton bra—which, whilst not old, wasn't very new either. Or very sexy.

Before she could worry too much about it he'd removed her pendant, dropping it on the bedside table before slipping the thin straps of her dress over her shoulders.

'If I'd known I was going to d-do this,' she stammered, 'I would have worn some s-sexier underclothes. Not that I have any...' she muttered under her breath.

'Come now, Kate,' Blake said with laughing eyes. 'What about that black number you had on last night? That had me salivating, it was so sexy.'

'Maddie bought that for me.'

'Oh, yes—Maddie the sex kitten. Or at least she thinks she is.'

'You don't think so?'

'I already told you, Kate. She's not my type. Now, *you*...' he continued as he reached around and unhooked her bra. 'You are definitely my type.'

Kate's heartbeat stopped when he peeled off her bra and left her sitting there naked to the waist. Yet, oddly, she felt more excited than embarrassed. And totally breathless. After a few dizzying seconds she began breathing again, hard and fast, her chest expanding as she sucked in much-needed air.

Blake's eyes dropped to her breasts with their fiercely erect nipples, all tight and hard and eager for his hands, or his mouth.

'Oh, yes,' he said thickly. '*Definitely* my type.'

Just when she thought he was going to do what she craved he knelt down again, reaching up under the skirt of her dress and pulling down her white cotton panties. And then he was pushing her back onto the bed and lifting her dress, putting his mouth not to her aching nipples but to that part of her which she hadn't realised until that moment was far needier.

She gasped, then groaned. His fingers and tongue were doing things to her that had never been done before. They made her burn for him, made her incapable of stopping him. She was mindless. Tortured. Rapturous. All she knew was that she couldn't bear it if he stopped. She was so close to coming. *So* close.

He stopped.

'No, don't stop!' she cried out.

'Have to, sweetness,' he said, standing up and pulling her skirt down again.

'But I was about to...you know—' She broke off and sat up, feeling flustered and frustrated.

'Yes, I know. But so was I.'

'Oh,' she said, only then noting his ragged breathing.

'Never happened to me before,' he ground out, and stared at her as if it was *her* fault.

'I'm sorry,' she said, which was crazy. What was she saying sorry for?

'I suppose it has been several weeks since I've had sex,' he muttered, as if he was looking for a valid reason for his lack of control.

'Really?' That surprised Kate. She'd always thought powerful, good-looking men like Blake never did without sex for long. She'd imagined they always had women throwing themselves at them.

'Really and truly.' He sighed a heavy sigh, at the same time running his hands agitatedly through his hair. 'Under the circumstances, best we move on to the real thing.'

CHAPTER SIXTEEN

'I JUST NEED to go to the bathroom first,' Blake lied. 'Meanwhile, why don't you get into bed?' He made his escape, desperate for a minute or two by himself.

Blake closed the door firmly behind him, still rattled by what had just happened. He simply couldn't believe he'd almost lost it, having always prided himself on his sexual skills—especially his ability to control his body and not act like some horny teenager whose only aim was getting his rocks off.

It was especially embarrassing given Kate's sexual history. He'd been determined to give her the time of her life, and what had he done? Almost blown it—that was what he'd done.

Maybe he'd been trying too hard to please her.

That last thought bothered him. He wasn't usually a try-hard.

He glanced at himself in the bathroom mirror, shocked by what he saw. Not his usual cavalier self, but someone who was beginning to care too much. About her. That was the problem. It had been the problem from the first moment he'd seen her, walking down that staircase, looking haunted and terrified.

It annoyed the hell out of him that she was in love with Lachlan—that she probably fantasised about him when she made herself come in her lonely bed at night. He wanted to obliterate that bastard from her mind...wanted to give her something or someone better to dream about.

And that would be you, would it, Blake Randall? You—a man who doesn't even believe in love, or romance, or any of the things that seem to matter to women? What can you give Kate that would really matter to her? That would be a positive influence in her life? That would make her happy? Or at least happier.

The chance for a successful acting career, he supposed. And a healthier attitude to sex. Sex didn't *have* to be connected to love. Much better to be just about physical pleasure. And fun. That was what he had told her, and that was what he was going to deliver.

So he cared about her as well? So what? He was allowed to care, wasn't he? There was no crime in that.

'Right,' he told himself sternly, and turned to flush the toilet before heading for the bathroom door.

Kate stiffened when she heard the toilet flush. She had taken off her dress and dived naked into the bed, shivering a little at the coolness of the sheets. Not that the room was cold, the penthouse obviously had ducted air-conditioning and heating.

Her heart jumped when he emerged, but his ready smile calmed her a little.

'Sorry about that,' he said, and whipped his shirt up off over his head.

Kate hadn't really thought about what his body might look like without clothes. She'd known he was tall and slim, with nice shoulders and olive skin. But the reality was better than she could have imagined, with his well-toned arms and chest, and a smattering of dark, sexy curls arrowing down to his navel.

'You must work out a lot,' she said, just for something to say. Better than sitting there ogling him.

He shrugged as he took his wallet out of his pocket and placed it by the bed. 'I have a gym in my home. Everyone works out in Hollywood. Everyone except the really fat-cat producers. All they have to do is go to lunch and show their credit cards.'

'I jog sometimes,' she said, trying not to stare. But it was getting harder now he'd taken off his trousers. 'And I walk a lot. I don't have a car.'

'You have a great figure,' he complimented her, sitting down on the side of the bed in his black underpants and taking off his shoes and socks. 'I adore it. I like natural.'

'Well, I'm certainly that.'

Maddie had had a boob job when she was twenty, which her parents had happily paid for. But Kate didn't mind her B-cup breasts, believing they went with her more athletic shape. Her agent had once criticised her smallish bust, but she'd ignored him. Thank goodness she had. She rather suspected Blake wouldn't have fancied her if her breasts had been surgically enhanced.

Relief swamped Kate when Blake kept his back to her as he took off his underpants. Hopefully he would just dive into bed the way she had and she wouldn't have to look at his penis.

But he didn't oblige, turning to pick up his wallet and extract a condom first. He was fully erect. Impressively so. Her mouth went dry at the thought of what was to come. Her heartbeat quickened.

She looked away while he drew the condom on, not turning back to face him until she felt the mattress dip.

'Don't go shy on me,' he told her as he put his arms around her and drew her close.

She looked up into his eyes. 'I'm not shy so much as nervous. I need you to kiss me again.'

'And *I* need to kiss you again,' he replied, and did so.

It was even better with their naked bodies pressed against each other. So exciting and intimate, making her quickly hungry for more. Not just more kissing. More bodily contact. She wanted him inside her. No, *needed* him inside her. Her leg lifted to curve over his hip, giving him access to her body, urging him without words to take her. Now. *Now!*

He did her silent bidding, his body surging into hers, rolling her onto her back and going even deeper. His mouth moved away from hers, his eyes hot and hungry as he began to move. She moved with him, lifting her legs high onto his back, clinging to him and almost sobbing with pleasure. Her heart was squeezed tight in her chest, her flesh gripping his like a vice.

She was just beginning to think she might have a heart attack when she came with a rush, her release so brilliant and violent that she screamed out. 'Blake! Oh, Blake!'

His climax quickly followed hers, and his own cry of release was loud and primal, his whole body shuddering as he came. Finally he collapsed across her and buried his face in her hair.

Kate revelled in the feel of his weight, holding him tight lest he try to withdraw. She didn't feel all limp and sleepy, like she'd read in books. She felt more awake and alive than she'd ever felt before. She could hardly wait to do it again. And again. She wanted to try everything with him—every possible position—and not just in this bed.

Her fantasies were endless and wild. She was envisaging herself doing the sort of things Maddie did with Lachlan.

Lachlan...

It came as a shock to Kate that she could think of Lachlan whilst in bed with another man and not feel a single bit of regret that it wasn't him in bed with her. If anything, the thought of him vaguely repulsed her. How odd. Was she over him at last? She rather suspected she was. Whatever—she'd certainly reached a point where her feelings for her brother-in-law were not going to stop her from enjoying life. From enjoying Blake.

Kate stirred beneath him. Blake lifted his head and smiled down at her. She smiled back at him—a slow, sensual smile which echoed her satisfaction and hinted at her on-going desires.

'Methinks,' he said, with a sexy glitter in his eyes, 'that you won't have too much trouble with that movie role after all.'

CHAPTER SEVENTEEN

'YOU'RE DOING *WHAT*?'

Kate ignored her mother's horrified reaction—at least on the surface. She'd known what to expect and had steeled herself accordingly.

'You heard what I said, Mum,' she replied coolly. 'I'm going to Hollywood. My screen test went very well last night. Blake said the part is definitely mine.'

Lord, she really *was* a good actress. Not a hint of irony on her face. Nor shame. Not that she intended to feel shame over what she'd done with Blake last night. Or what she intended to do in the future. He'd opened a whole new world to her—one she wanted to explore and enjoy to the full. And she wasn't just thinking about her career.

'He's also kindly offered to let me stay at his place until I get on my feet.'

She couldn't wait to live in the same house as him, to be with him every night. Even if it only lasted a short while.

Janice Holiday's eyes narrowed on her daughter. 'Now, why would he do something like that?'

'Why not? He's a kind and generous man. Look at the way he stepped in and organised that lovely and totally free venue for Maddie's wedding, saving Maddie from a nervous breakdown and saving you and Dad an absolute fortune. He didn't have to do that.'

'We *did* pay for the marquee,' Janice huffed. '*And* the catering. Besides, it was Lachlan he was helping out—not us. *He's* the one who's making Blake Randall a small fortune.'

'I think the shoe is on the other foot, Mum. It's Blake who's making *Lachlan* a small fortune. Without him Lachlan would still be a struggling actor, trying to make ends meet.'

'Oh, rubbish! Anyone with any brains can see it's Lachlan's talent which has put Blake Randall on the map. Without him that man would be an also-ran, making boring little movies which no one would go to see.'

Kate had no intention of arguing with her mother. Experience had taught her it was a total waste of time. She always had to have the last word.

'Don't think I don't know what's going on,' her mother continued, her tone caustic. 'Men like that always want something in return for their so-called generosity. You slept with him last night, didn't you?'

Kate drew herself up to her full five foot nine inches, setting reproachful eyes on her mother. 'I did not,' she denied, quite truthfully.

They hadn't slept one bit—either before or after dinner.

'Well, it's just a matter of time. When are you seeing him next? Today, I'll bet.'

'No, I'm not.' *Worse luck.* 'He's playing golf with Byron today, and has an important business dinner tonight. Then he's booked to fly back to LA early tomorrow morning. I plan to follow as soon as I can. I checked the visa situation online and Australians can get their visa waivered—but you have to wait three days after applying. I'm allowed to stay for ninety days before reapplying.'

Her mother looked doubtful. 'Surely that would only cover tourists? Not people who are going to work in the country?'

'No, it says you can be going there for business or pleasure. And Blake said once I'm there and have a contract in my hand I can apply for some other visa which I will eventually need.'

'So you haven't signed a contract yet?'

'No. Not yet. But I will once I get over there.'

'And who's going to pay for your plane ticket to get you over there? *You* don't have that sort of money. Or is our generous Mr Randall going to pay for that as well?'

Blake had offered to do just that, but Kate had refused. She didn't mind temporarily staying in his house as a guest, but she wasn't going to let him pay for other things. That would make her feel like a kept woman. All she wanted from Blake was a helping hand with her career. Oh, yes, and lots of lovely sex.

'I was hoping that you and Dad would buy me a return ticket. After all, I've never asked you to buy me anything before.'

'We give you free board and lodging. I would have thought that was enough.'

'You gave Maddie free board and lodging too,' Kate pointed out, keeping her temper with difficulty. 'Yet she was earning good money as a receptionist. On top of which you bought her a car *and* paid for her to have a boob job. Not to mention a thousand other expensive items over the years. I have never asked you for *anything*, Mum,' she said, her voice rising a few decibels. *'Never.'*

Her father suddenly appeared in the doorway, surprising Kate. She'd thought he'd be at work by now. Possibly he had a flex day. He sometimes took one on a Monday, and he was still in his dressing gown.

'What are you two arguing about?' he asked wearily.

'Kate wants us to buy her a plane ticket to go to Hollywood. A return ticket, no less. She's had this ridiculous offer of a movie role from Blake Randall and she thinks he's doing it out of the goodness of his heart. She doesn't realise there's no such thing as a free lunch. He'll want his pound of flesh in return. And it's not as though she has a contract in her hand. On top of that, she's going to stay at his house. Well, I *ask* you. It's as plain as the nose on your face what he wants. Though Lord knows why. I mean, it's not as though Kate is a raving beauty, like our Maddie. I could understand it if Blake Randall wanted *her* for a part in one of his movies. What do you think, Neville?'

'What do I *think*, Janice?'

He answered in a tone that Kate had never heard before. It was rather cold and very firm—not what she'd expected from her hen-pecked father.

'I think we should not only support our daughter and buy her a return ticket to LA, but that we should make it business class. It's a long trip, and I wouldn't want her getting there looking all tired and drawn. Unlike you, I have every respect for Blake Randall, and I don't think he has some dastardly ulterior motive in offering Kate a part in one of his movies. Why should he when she's such a brilliant actress? Have you forgotten how wonderful she was in those plays they put on at NIDA? *She* was the star—not Lachlan. I dare say Blake Randall was already aware of her talent, even before her screen test.

'And by the way,' he added, whilst his wife's mouth was still hanging open. 'Kate might not be what *some* people call a raving beauty, but she is very attractive, with classic features which will last long after most women's faces fall apart. Now, I am going back to bed. I'm not at my best this morning. Please give Kate our credit card, Janice. And Kate? Well done. You're a hard worker and a fine actress and you deserve all the success in the world.'

'I have to confess, Blake,' Kate told him when he rang her later, as promised, 'that I didn't know whether to laugh or cry. I mean, it was amusing to see my mother stuck for words for once, but…but…' She felt suddenly choked up and couldn't go on.

'But you were touched by your father's magnificent defence of you?'

'Yes. Yes, I was.'

The things he'd said about her had meant so much. Kate hadn't realised how hurt she'd been all these years by his seeming to favour Maddie. Now she saw that it had been more her mother doing the favouring than him. He'd just gone along with what his wife and Maddie wanted to keep the peace. Of course Maddie *was* very charming—and very manipulative. It was awfully hard to say no to her. Kate also conceded that she herself had been silly to stay in the background all the time...not asking for anything, and playing the victim, in a way.

No more of that, she decided. She was done with playing second fiddle to her sister.

'How was your golf game with Byron?' she asked, lying down on her bed and stretching out. 'Did you win?'

'Did I win, she asks? Of course I won. In the end. I let him get close to me in the first nine, but I slaughtered him in the second.'

Kate smiled. He really was terribly arrogant. But she still liked him.

'Poor Byron...'

Blake laughed. 'Hardly poor. He just keeps on getting richer. That man has the Midas touch when it comes to investments. I'm always happy when he comes aboard as co-producer on one of my movies. They never bomb. Not that I *ever* make duds, of course. Anyway, I told him about the movie you're going to be in and he's agreed to put a good chunk of money in it. In the past he's only ever wanted to invest in Lachlan's movies, but he's willing to take a chance now on anything I recommend.'

'Maybe he thinks *you've* got the Midas touch?'

'There's nothing magical about *my* success. It took me years of trial and error to work out what worked in movies and what didn't. Even so, you can never be one hundred percent sure of a positive reception. Film audiences can be very fickle.'

'Speaking of movies,' Kate said, 'I've been thinking about my part and I have a suggestion to make. I hope you don't mind.'

'Good grief! Her first movie role and she's already trying to change the script,' he said, but he was laughing.

'Not at all. I just don't like the part where I reach for a cigarette. I mean, I *hate* smoking, and so do most people now. I know I'm supposed to be a bad girl in this movie, but her smoking doesn't really add anything to the role and I'd rather not do it. Couldn't I reach for a glass of champagne instead? That would be just as effective.'

'I don't see why not. Is that all?'

'Oh, yes. Absolutely.'

'Good. I'm not a man who likes it when actors try to change my scripts.'

'I wouldn't dare.'

He laughed. 'I think perhaps you would. In time. God, I wish I didn't have to go to this dinner tonight. I'd much rather be in bed with you.'

'*I'd* rather you were in bed with me too.'

'Have you booked your flight yet?'

'Yes. I fly out late Friday evening and I get into LAX around six Friday evening your time. Australia is seventeen hours ahead of you, so I found out.'

'It's a non-stop flight, then?'

'Yes.' She gave him the flight number.

'I'll just write that down,' he said. 'You'll be glad you're flying business class.'

'I still can't believe Mum and Dad forked out that much money. Maddie's going to be so jealous.'

'How will she know? She's in Europe on her honeymoon for the next month or so.'

'That won't stop her ringing Mum every day.'

'I will never understand this obsession women have for talking on the phone all the time. I can't stand it.'

'You're talking to *me* on the phone right now.'

'You're the exception to my rule. I like talking to you. Of course I'd prefer to be talking to you with your naked body next to me, but since I can't have that, then I have to settle for this. Damn—it's just occurred to me that I won't be enjoying that privilege again for over four days. You wouldn't consider catching a taxi here at around eleven tonight, would you? I should be finished with my business dinner by then. You could stay the night, perhaps?'

It was tempting. *Very.*

'I'm sorry, Blake, but I can't do that. I told my mother I didn't sleep with you last night and I couldn't stand the next few days if she found out I'd lied. Which she would if I did what you're asking.'

'Fair enough. It'll probably be better for the waiting. Anticipation is one of the best forms of foreplay.'

She could believe that. She was already turned on, just thinking about being with him again.

'Your silence betrays you, sweet Kate. Just think what we could have got up to tonight. There are so many things I want to do to you and haven't done yet. We could have had such fun.'

Kate was glad he couldn't see her red cheeks. Or hear her thudding heart. But something—a kind of pride, perhaps—demanded that she did not let him think he could do whatever he liked to her and she wouldn't object.

Last night had been amazing, sexually, showing her how good it was to move on with her life, to put Lachlan behind her and find pleasure in another man's body. But that didn't mean she was going to become Blake's mindless plaything. She did have a mind of her own and she aimed to use it.

'There are things I want to do to *you* too, Blake,' she countered coolly. 'But, as you just said, it will be all be better for the waiting.'

Now *he* was the one who was silent. But then he laughed—a low, sexily sardonic laugh.

'I'll meet you at the airport,' he said, letting the matter drop.

Kate's independent mode was not easily dropped. 'Won't that be a bother? You'll have to pay for parking, and maybe wait if the flight is late, or customs are slow. I could just as easily catch a taxi if you give me the address.'

'*Cab*, Kate. In LA they're called cabs.'

'Oh. A cab, then.'

'No, I'll meet you,' he insisted. 'Carlos can drive me and wait somewhere until we're ready to be picked up.'

'You have a chauffeur?'

She shouldn't be surprised, but she was, which showed her that she hadn't truly absorbed just yet how wealthy Blake was. The penthouse she'd spent last night in hadn't been his, after all.

'Not exactly,' Blake replied. 'Though I often use Carlos to drive me places. Carlos is my housekeeper's husband. Her name's Juanita. She does the cooking and cleaning. Carlos is handyman, gardener and sometimes chauffeur. They're from Mexico, though they've lived in the USA for over twenty years. They came with the house and I thank God every day for them both. They're a great couple. Good workers and always cheerful. I feel very blessed to have them.'

Kate was taken aback by this last statement.

'I didn't know you were religious,' she said.

'What? Oh, the "blessed" thing. No, I'm not—but most of America is. I dare say I've picked up a few phrases.'

'I rather like it. It's sweet.'

'Americans *can* be sweet. But sometimes their sweetness is only on the surface—especially in Hollywood, and especially in the movie business. Thankfully Carlos and Juanita didn't come to LA to try their hand at acting. All they wanted, they told me, was a better life for themselves and their children.'

'They have children?'

'Unfortunately, no. They weren't lucky that way. Juanita said they left it too late before they tried and then it didn't happen. But they're not bitter about it. They're thankful for what they have.'

'They sound like a great couple.'

'Yes, you'll like them.'

'I'm sure I will. And I'm sure I'll like Hollywood—no matter what dire warnings you give me. I can't wait to get there.'

'And I can't wait for you to get there too,' he said, with heavy irony in his voice.

Kate laughed. 'Will you stop that? Let's talk about something else besides sex.'

But even as she said the word it occurred to Kate that a man like Blake would rarely have to wait for the pleasure of a woman in his bed. Maybe he *wouldn't* wait. Maybe when he got back to LA he'd ring up one of his lady-friends—he was sure to have heaps—and have her fill the gap in his sex life until Kate arrived on the scene.

Jealousy jabbed at Kate. Yet it wasn't the same kind of jealousy she'd used to feel about Lachlan and Maddie. Strangely, this was more disturbing—and infinitely more confusing. Because she didn't love Blake the way she'd loved Lachlan. She didn't love Blake *at all*! She liked him a lot—found him terribly sexy and quite fascinating. But she didn't want to marry him or spend the rest of her life with him. She didn't romanticise her feelings for him in any way. She saw them for what they were.

Why the jealousy, then?

Kate decided it was just her newly found feminine ego— the ego that thought her performance in bed last night had been oh, *so* good.

Silly Kate. Don't go thinking you're anything special to Blake, because you aren't. Your mother is right. There's no such thing as a free lunch. Yes, Blake might want to help you with your career—he probably gets off on the idea of being a magnanimous mentor—but there is a price to be paid. In his bed.

Just because you'll love every minute of it, that doesn't mean sleeping with Blake is without danger. What if you do fall in love with the man? It could happen now that Lachlan seems to be history.

Never forget that Blake doesn't want a real relationship with you, came the stern warning. *There is no future with him—no prospect of you becoming a proper girlfriend. And if you can't come to terms with that before you go to LA then you're a fool and you shouldn't go.*

Kate resolved not to be a fool. Because nothing was going to stop her going to Hollywood.

'What would you like to talk about?' Blake asked.

'Movies. What else?'

CHAPTER EIGHTEEN

BLAKE STOOD IN the arrivals area, close to the gate where Kate was due to emerge. Her flight had landed a good twenty minutes ago, but still there was no sign of her. Patience was not his strong suit, and his agitation was increasing with each passing second.

And then suddenly there she was, pulling a black suitcase behind her, her eyes scanning the crowd for him. She didn't see him straight away, giving Blake a thankful few seconds to drink her in unobserved.

She was a sight for sore eyes, despite being dressed in sensible travelling clothes—stone-washed grey jeans, a white T-shirt and a black jacket. Hardly an outfit which would usually fire up his male hormones. But it did. As did everything else about her. Her hair was bundled up on top of her head in a haphazard style which he found extremely sexy, and her face was freshly made-up, bringing attention to her lovely dark eyes and wide, luscious mouth.

Blake could not wait to get her home and alone. He'd had enough of just talking to her over the past few days, having spent more time on the phone to Kate than he had with any woman in his life—including his ex.

Aside from their long discussions about movies and acting, he now knew more about Kate than he'd ever found out about Claudia. She'd told him all about her upbringing—including her not very happy days at school, when she'd been totally overshadowed by her younger's sister vibrant personality, her self-esteem plummeting until she'd discovered acting in the school's drama class. Once portraying another character, her confidence had soared. Though it had always shrunk again once she was off the stage.

There had been no boyfriends for her—not until she'd met Tom, the boy who made the sets for the drama class, who had basically been as introverted as she was. Blake already knew that sex with Tom had been ordinary, at best. But at least she'd had a boyfriend for a while.

Her meagre sexual experiences at university had been of a similar ilk. Then, of course, had come the fiasco with Lachlan. It pleased Blake that Kate could talk about Lachlan now with more pragmatism. Her rose-tinted glasses were well and truly off. Who knew? Maybe she was finally getting over the guy? He sure hoped so. She deserved better than a self-obsessed narcissist who would never love anyone as much as he loved himself.

Suddenly she spied him, her face lighting up, her expression a mixture of joy and relief.

He moved forward, all smiles, taking the case away from her. 'You made it,' he said, and bent to peck her on the cheek. Blake was not a big hugger and kisser in public.

'Only just. My shoulder bag sparked off some machine and I was taken aside like I was a criminal. They emptied out all the contents and checked it over for drugs. It came back clear, of course. I mean, I would *never* do drugs. Still, I almost wet myself with terror whilst I was waiting.'

Blake nodded in sympathy. 'That happened to me once. Puts the wind up you, doesn't it? Still, store that emotion for when you have to act a part that requires terror. Nothing is wasted when you're an actor. Or a scriptwriter, for that matter.'

Kate took the bag off her shoulder and sighed as she stared into it. 'They just threw everything back in. My make-up is all over the place. And they've squashed up the magazine I bought.'

She pulled it out. Blake recognised the beaming couple on the cover immediately. He would hardly forget *that* bride and groom in a hurry. Clearly Maddie hadn't either, no matter how pragmatic their conversation over the phone. The headline caught his eye too: *Hunky Aussie Actor Weds*.

'I couldn't resist,' she said a little sheepishly. 'I saw it on a stand at the airport in Sydney and just had to buy it.'

An emotion Blake wasn't overly familiar with grabbed at his insides. It took him a split second to recognise it as jealousy.

Blake had experienced jealousy when Claudia had dumped him for that Hollywood fat-cat—along with fury and confusion and a whole raft of other conscience-blasting emotions.

He hadn't been able to think straight, but his arrogant male ego had refused to let him cry, or get counselling for his hurt. Instead he'd behaved badly, working his pain out by indulging in revenge sex with a couple of actresses who had made a play for him.

Thankfully, neither of them had been the type to suffer from a broken heart afterwards, but one of them had told him in no uncertain terms what she thought of his callous attitude the morning after. It had been a sobering experience, and one which he'd taken to heart. After that he'd been more careful with women, always making it clear that dating him wasn't a long-term proposition. He was into flings and affairs, not relationships.

He had had what might be termed a girlfriend or two since his divorce, but nothing serious. He certainly had never invited a girl to stay at his place for more than a night.

Or he hadn't until Kate had come along.

It worried him now...what he was getting himself into with this girl. If he didn't know better he might think he was falling in love. Which would never do. If and when he was foolish enough to fall in love it wouldn't be with someone who'd spent the last four years of her life dreaming of another man. For all he knew Kate was still dreaming of him. She might talk big about moving on, but she'd bought that magazine, hadn't she? Had probably spent hours during the flight admiring photos of him and wishing she were in Maddie's place.

'Not that I really wanted the damned thing,' Kate went on. 'I was just curious. I also hoped there would be some pictures of you and me—but, no, they were all of Lachlan and Maddie. Typical.'

And without a backward glance, she tossed the magazine into a nearby bin, before throwing him a remorseful glance.

'You didn't want to look at it, did you?'

Blake could have kissed her. She wasn't pining for that fool, and the thought brought him a type of joy which might have worried him if he hadn't been so relieved.

'I've already seen the photos, Kate. As soon as that magazine came out they were all over social media.'

'Oh, yes. I imagine they are. I'm not into social media. But Maddie is.'

'And Lachlan as well. He's an incorrigible show pony. Can't say I'm overly keen on the way technology has gone. But it's the way of the world, Kate. Speaking of technology,' he went on ruefully, and whipped out his phone, 'I'll just text Carlos and tell him to make his way to the pickup point.'

'And I'll text Mum and Dad—let them know I've arrived safely.'

They both finished together, and Kate turned her phone off before dropping it back into her bag. Blake slipped his phone into his pocket, then took her elbow.

'Let's go.' Blake pulled her suitcase along behind them. 'I have a web page, of course,' he continued as they walked companionably together. 'And various other links which my PA attends to. But that's for business only. I like to keep my personal life to myself.'

'I do too. I don't understand why ordinary people—not celebrities—take photos of everything they do, even the most mundane things, then post it somewhere on the internet for people to see. I just don't get it.'

'I suppose it's a form of entertainment. And it makes them feel important. Like they're celebrities.'

'But it opens them up to criticism and bullying.'

'True. But that's become a fact of modern life, too. Social media isn't going to go away, so you might as well embrace it. You have to develop a thick skin, Kate, if you want to be a success in Hollywood. Because if and when that happens you'll be criticised to death over everything from your clothes to your weight and whoever you have by your side. You'll be stalked by the paparazzi and your life generally won't be yours.'

Kate stopped and stared at him. 'You make success sound so attractive!'

Blake shrugged. 'It's a sink-or-swim existence, being in the spotlight, but it can be very exciting. Though only if you don't let it go to your head…like someone who will remain nameless.'

'Oh, I suppose you mean Lachlan.'

'Lachlan who?' he said, with just a touch of malice. 'Ah, here's our ride.'

CHAPTER NINETEEN

KATE GAPED WHEN a white limousine braked abruptly at the kerb, next to where they were standing.

'Oh, my goodness!' she exclaimed, both impressed and slightly overawed.

Blake grinned at her. 'When in Rome, you know...'

The driver—a short, middle-aged man with black curly hair and swarthy skin—jumped out from behind the wheel, flashing Kate a welcoming smile before grabbing her suitcase.

'Better get inside, boss,' Carlos said, with only the slightest accent. 'The Indians are circling.'

'What does he mean?' Kate said as Blake yanked open the back door.

Just then a photographer stepped forward from Lord knew where and snapped a couple of shots of them both. Blake didn't say a word, just hustled Kate into the limo, throwing the photographer a big smile before climbing in after her and shutting the door. By this time Carlos was back behind the wheel and they were soon off.

'Carlos, this is Kate,' Blake introduced. 'Kate, this is Carlos.'

'Hello, Carlos.'

'Welcome to LA, Kate. Sorry I was a bit slow picking you up, boss. Friday evenings, you know... Lots of comings and goings.'

'No sweat, Carlos. If I didn't want to be photographed then I shouldn't have had you drive up in a limo.'

Carlos laughed.

'You didn't mind us being photographed?' Kate asked Blake.

'Hell, no. It's good publicity for me—and for you. Those photos will be all over the internet somewhere within the hour—with a caption something like *Blake Randall meets mystery woman at airport. A new star or a new girlfriend?*'

'Goodness!' Kate exclaimed, not sure if she was thrilled or anxious.

She didn't like the thought of her family seeing it—especially her mother. But even if she didn't see it, Maddie would. And she rang her mother every day. Being on her honeymoon wouldn't stop her. She could just imagine their conversation. Maddie might have urged Kate to make a play for Blake, but she wouldn't have dreamt that her sister would end up in LA, staying at his house.

Actually, Kate was finding it all a bit surreal herself. She could hardly believe that she was here. The last few days had seemed endless. Blake had rung her every day, which had been wonderful, but it had made her crave to be with him again. She'd almost forgotten her career for a while, her focus more on the sexual side of things. Yet they were both entwined, weren't they?

'Don't let it bother you,' Blake said, perhaps sensing her sudden unease. 'The Hollywood publicity mill runs on endless speculation. Best not to fight it or it only gets worse. Go with the flow. Have fun with it.'

'Fun?' she echoed.

He grinned over at her, then picked up her hand and kissed it like a gallant gentleman of old. *'Oui, mademoiselle,'* he said, sounding like Maurice Chevalier in *Gigi*.

Their eyes met over her hand and the air around them thickened with instant desire. How handsome he was—and very sophisticated-looking, dressed in a charcoal-grey business suit, white shirt and silver tie. Her heart had fluttered when she'd first sighted him at the airport. It had also pushed firmly aside any qualms she'd had over this trip. For she'd seen real affection in his eyes. Real caring.

Now all she saw was hunger—a raw, animal hunger which threatened to transcend her own.

A highly erotic shudder rippled down her spine and he saw it, his eyes darkening. He enfolded her hands in both of his and pulled her hard against his side. She dropped her head to his shoulder with a sigh. This would have to do. *For now.*

'If photographers are going to pop out from behind every pole or door,' she said, after a couple of minutes wallowing in the warmth of his body, 'I'll have to watch how I look when I go out.'

'You always look gorgeous,' he told her.

She smiled up at him. 'I really don't. But it's sweet of you to say so.'

'Did you bring some going out clothes with you?'

'Sort of…'

'What does that mean?'

'I suspect that my version of "going out" clothes falls a little short of the Hollywood version.'

'Maybe. Maybe not. People don't always get dressed up to the nines here. It can be a very casual city. But if you like I'll take you clothes-shopping tomorrow.'

'Will you?' she said, smiling wryly to herself as she recalled a scene from one of her favourite movies. 'In Rodeo Drive?'

'Of course.'

Her eyes slanted up to his. 'Thank you, but I think I should make do with what I have until I earn some money,' she said, knowing that that would be taking things a step too far. As it was, the balance of their relationship was a bit iffy. No way was she going to let him start buying her clothes. 'Actually, my wardrobe is not too bad at the moment. Dad forked out some more money for me—behind Mum's back, of course—and I went shopping this week.

Also, fortunately the weather here is similar to that in Sydney at the moment.'

'So it is. Your spring is much the same as our fall.'

'Fall? Oh, you mean autumn.'

'Yes.'

'You seem to have become very American in the short time you've been over here.'

'Actually, I *am* half-American.'

Kate sat up straight and stared at him, the action pulling her hand out of his grasp. 'How did that come about?'

'My mother's American. My dad met her when they were both studying medicine at Harvard. I was born over here—in Boston. They moved to Sydney just after I turned one. I have dual citizenship.'

'You still sound like an Aussie to me,' Carlos piped up. 'More so than Kate.'

'For which I am grateful,' Blake said.

Kate settled back in the seat and put her head on his shoulder again. 'The teachers at NIDA insisted that we get rid of any strong Australian accent. They said it was a negative when it came to getting work.'

'That's absolutely correct. Especially in Hollywood. They like an international-sounding voice. Not too many roles over here for Australians. By the way—did you bring all your references from NIDA?'

'What? Oh, yes—yes, of course.'

'Good. We'll need those to help get you the necessary visa for you to work here.'

Kate frowned. 'There won't be a problem with that, will there?'

'I doubt it. I've hired the best lawyer in LA to process your application. Now, no more work talk. We're almost home.'

'Already?' Kate's head swivelled to see where she was.

'West Hollywood isn't that far from the airport,' Blake explained.

The limousine wound its way up a rather steep road, with houses set back behind high security walls and often behind tall trees. Not that she could see them very well. Night had fallen, and whilst there were street lights they were few and far between. Up and up the road went, and one side of the road was now higher than the other.

Kate was craning her neck to peer up at the spectacular properties on the high side when Carlos pulled into a wide driveway in front of some tall wooden gates fixed into an equally tall stone wall. She couldn't see through that either, but she could see over it.

Up high, on a hill beyond, sat a house which took Kate's breath away. Whilst possibly not the biggest house in the world, its contemporary architecture could not help but impress. Over the wall she could see two rectangular-shaped floors, white in colour and cement rendered, the top one smaller than the one below. Both had wide covered decks which were lit up and no doubt provided splendid views of the surroundings.

Kate suspected, however, even before the gates opened, that there would be another floor out of sight. And she was right.

The bottom floor was even larger, encompassing a six-car garage, a fully equipped gym and a separate two-bedroom apartment which Carlos and his wife Juanita occupied—this information supplied by Blake as the limousine rolled into the huge garage next to a black sports car and a white sedan.

'So what do you think?' he asked her.

'I think,' she replied, 'that you are a very lucky man to live in a house as amazing as this.'

'And *I* think,' Carlos added with a cheeky smile over

his shoulder, 'that I am an even luckier man to have a boss like Señor Blake.'

Blake just laughed, but Kate could see he was pleased. Proud, too, of his house.

After meeting Juanita—who was as welcoming and cheerful as Carlos—Kate was given the grand tour by Blake. They started on the middle floor, which encompassed two large living areas, a bespoke kitchen, a home theatre, three en-suite guest bedrooms and another powder room for the use of guests, as well as a solar-heated pool which was entertainment heaven, with an indoor-outdoor barbecue and a cute cabana, complete with comfy lounge setting, a washroom and a built-in bar.

But it was the deck that led off the living area at the front of the house which took Kate's breath away.

'Oh, Blake,' she said, leaning against the wooden railing with a wondrous sigh. 'This is some view.'

That was an understatement. She could see for miles across the lightly timbered valley and over to the hill on which stood the famous HOLLYWOOD sign.

'The view upstairs is better,' he said.

'Really?' She found that hard to believe.

'I'll show you. Then we'll come down and have some dinner. Juanita's cooked something special for you. I knew you'd be too tired to go out.'

Kate actually didn't feel tired, despite not sleeping all that much on the plane. She'd been too excited. And too afraid. Not of flying. Or of Blake. But of what she had done, leaving her home and her country behind to be with Blake and pursue a career not on the stage, as she'd always intended, but in the movies—which was much more daunting to her.

Stage work was safe in Kate's eyes. Her looks weren't on display so much as they were in movies. She'd never been an overly confident or a bold person, but since meeting Blake she'd begun to change. He made her feel beautiful for starters. And now, tonight, in his company, she was changing again. No longer afraid, she felt both alive and confident. And, yes, free. Free of past failures. Free of her futile love for Lachlan. Free to really move on.

It was a delicious feeling.

'I hope you like chillies,' Blake said as he took her hand and led her up the thickly carpeted stairs to the top floor.

'I *love* chillies. I love all hot spicy food.'

'Good.'

The top floor was totally devoted to the master suite, consisting of the hugest bedroom Kate had ever seen, a bathroom which looked like a picture she'd once seen of a Roman bathhouse, and a spacious separate sitting-room-cum-study, complete with an enormous flat-screen TV on the wall.

But it was the wraparound deck which seduced and entranced Kate, with its view way beyond what she'd been picturing. She'd expected a better view of the Hollywood Hills, but when she walked round to the other side the city of Los Angeles lay before her, its many and colourful lights rivalling even those of Sydney on New Year's Eve. And beyond the city lay the ocean, dark and serene under the night sky.

'I don't know what to say,' Kate said, and smiled over at Blake. 'It's so gorgeous up here. Your whole home is splendid but, honestly, I could look at this view for ever.'

CHAPTER TWENTY

BLAKE HAD THE sudden urge to tell her that she could do that. All she had to do was marry him.

Crazy, really. Thank God he hadn't opened his mouth and said as much. Because he would have regretted it. And she would only have said no.

He told himself that it wasn't *love* compelling him to voice such idiocies. Just a temporary infatuation. And frustration. She was an enchanting creature and a highly desirable one. Give him a few weeks with her in his bed and he would come to his senses.

'So, are you going to stay with me in there?' he asked, nodding towards his bedroom.

Her eyes widened a little, but then she smiled. 'Do you want me to?'

'But of course.'

'I shouldn't…' she said, but her eyes were sparkling.

'But you will…'

'Of course.'

Of course, he thought ruefully as he swept her into his arms and kissed her, his head reminding him that she was still an actress even if she *was* different. And she was ambitious. If she hadn't been she wouldn't be here. Because she didn't love him. She probably still loved that idiot show pony, with his golden boy looks and sickeningly seductive charm.

His mouth worked hard to make her forget him—at least for now—and Blake didn't ease up until he felt her total surrender to the heat of the moment. She was a naturally sensual creature—he'd discovered that during the time they'd spent together in Sydney—and her celibacy over the past few years had made her ripe and ready for his attentions.

And attend her he would. Every day and every night. He would fill her body and her mind until she was incapable of wanting or even thinking of any other man. And he would spoil her rotten, seducing her with a lifestyle which few women would turn their backs on. And then, when the time was right, he just *might* ask her to marry him.

Okay, so it was still a crazy idea. But, crazy or not, the idea refused to be dismissed.

His mouth gentled on hers whilst his mind began working out how he could persuade her to throw her lot in with him. He reasoned that he could legitimately argue that marriage between people who liked and desired each other had a better chance of succeeding than those marriages entered into out of romantic love. He could point out that they would have a good life together. She would have *the* good life—a better one than her materialistic sister would have with lover-boy.

Blake suspected that getting one over Maddie would appeal to Kate. But his all-time winning argument might be that they didn't have to be married "til death do us part'. If it didn't work out they could divorce, and Kate could walk away with a very nice settlement.

When love wasn't involved there would be no bitterness. And no children, of course. He would never expose a child to such a marriage.

Thinking about the 'no children' aspect forced Blake to accept that Kate would never go for such a proposal. The girl was a romantic of the first order. The best he could hope for was that she would agree to live with him. At least for now.

For some reason that eluded him Blake felt somewhat disgruntled with this solution to his current obsession with Kate. But it would have to do.

He lifted his head, satisfied to find that she was breathing heavily and her eyes were glazed.

'Sorry, sweetheart,' he said, and touched a tender fingertip to her softly swollen lips. 'As much as I would like to continue, Juanita will be upset if we let her food over-cook.'

Which was a lie, Juanita having informed Blake earlier in the day that their entrée and dessert were pre-prepared and cold, with a main course that would not take long to cook. But it was better than telling Kate the truth; that he was so hard for her he might not last if he went ahead and had sex with her right at this moment.

'Well, we can't have that, can we?' Kate said, her eyes clearing. 'She's much too nice to upset.'

Blake liked it that Kate liked his housekeeper. And Juanita seemed genuinely to like Kate back. She fussed over their meal, returning often to the table to see that everything was okay. Which it was. Juanita was a brilliant cook. Her guacamole was second to none, as were all her other Mexican and Spanish-inspired dishes.

Not that Blake ate at home all that often. He networked over lunches and dinners, both at fashionable restaurants and at the various golf clubs he frequented. When working in his office he often skipped lunch entirely, living only on coffee. Today he'd been too busy to eat much, so he was appreciative of the three-course meal—especially the seafood paella which was followed by his favourite dessert: fried ice-cream, which had a delicious coconut and cinnamon flavour.

Kate, he noted, ate everything as well—a lovely change from most women in Hollywood who hardly ate at all.

'If you keep feeding me gorgeous food like this, Juanita,' Kate complimented her over coffee, 'I'm going to put on weight.'

'You are not the type to get fat,' Juanita replied. 'Not like me.'

Juanita was an attractive woman, with wavy black hair and flashing brown eyes. She was, however, pleasantly plump.

'You are *not* fat,' Kate said.

Juanita smiled. 'And you are a lovely girl. Australians are very nice people, I think. Or most of them are. I am not so keen on that fair-haired actor who comes here sometimes. You know the one I mean, Blake?'

'Indeed I do.'

'He is rude to me. He has no respect.'

Blake frowned. 'I didn't know that. What does he say or do that's rude?'

She scowled. 'He is clever, that one. He waits until you are out of the room… It is not what he says so much. It is the way he looks at me—like I am beneath him because I am Mexican.'

Blake decided then and there that Lachlan would never enter his house again. Neither would he contract him for any more movies. It was time their relationship—such as it was—was at an end. And if at the back of his mind he knew this decision was all about Kate, he steadfastly ignored it.

'I'm sorry, Juanita,' he apologised. 'You won't have to put up with that ever again. He won't be back.'

'What do you mean?' Kate asked in shocked tones once Juanita was out of earshot.

Blake shrugged, then picked up his coffee cup. 'It's time Lachlan and I parted company. Aside from the lies he told you about me at the wedding, he's become too big for his boots. And, like *I* told you at the wedding, he's not that good an actor. He suits a certain type of part but he has no versatility. I want to move on from making romantic comedies. I have a hankering for some more serious movies— like the one I've offered you.'

'Do you think that's wise?' Kate asked, frowning. 'You

made your name with those movies starring Lachlan. *The Boy from The Bush* has an enormous cult following.'

Blake tried not to react badly to her remarks, but found it impossible. 'Yes—silly female fans who think a handsome face, a good body and a dazzling smile is the be-all and end-all.'

He knew immediately that he had hurt her feelings. Her face told the story. Her face told him lots of stories—none of which he wanted to hear.

'I think you're wrong,' she defended, her cheeks flushing. 'Lachlan might not be Laurence Olivier, but he does have *some* talent. *And* star quality. I know he's vain and shallow, but I dare say lots of other movie stars are as well. Claudia Jay for one,' she added, with a curl of her top lip.

'True,' he conceded. 'Okay,' Blake went on, finding an apologetic smile with difficulty, 'he's not as bad as I'm making out. I'll admit that. But I don't like racists. Or philanderers.'

'Then perhaps you're in the wrong business,' Kate pointed out tartly. 'Hollywood is hardly renowned for treating minorities fairly. Or for its stars being faithful.'

Wow, Blake thought. *That's telling me.*

Kate might look and act quiet at times, but she knew how to voice an opinion. And, whilst it irked him that she might be defending Lachlan because she still had feelings for him, she was speaking a whole lot of truth.

His smile this time was full of admiration and respect. 'So you won't mind if I hire Lachlan for the occasional movie?' he asked, watching her closely to see how she would react.

'Why should I mind?' she shot back at him. 'If you think I'm still in love with the man, then you're dead wrong. I can see now that I was no better than those "silly female fans" you described. Who think "a handsome face, a good body and a dazzling smile is the be-all and end-all". I confess I used to watch his movies and drool with the rest of them. But I assure you I wouldn't drool now.'

Wouldn't you? Blake wasn't so sure about that. What was that saying about fearing a woman doth protest too much?

'I still won't be inviting him here to my home ever again. If and when we do business it will be at my office.'

'That's your prerogative, Blake. And your decision.'

Juanita coming in at that moment interrupted what was becoming an awkward conversation.

'More coffee?' she asked.

'No, thanks,' Kate said, and gave Juanita a warm smile.

Blake hadn't quite finished his yet, and said so.

Juanita nodded. 'Carlos wants to know what guest bedroom to put Kate's suitcase in.'

'None of them,' Blake told her. 'Tell him to put it up in my bedroom.'

Juanita smiled. *'Si,'* she said, and hurried out to tell her husband the news.

Kate glanced at Blake. 'Juanita seemed pleased.'

'She likes you.'

'Hasn't she liked any of your other women?'

'I have never had a woman stay here with me before—not even for a night.'

'Really? So where do you have sex, then? At their place?'

He had to laugh. It was a long time since he'd been with a girl who was so direct.

'Sometimes.' *And sometimes in trailers on location or in hotel rooms.* 'If you must know, my love-life has been very limited since I moved to America. In actual fact I hadn't had sex for several weeks before I met you.'

'Really? Why not?'

Why not, indeed? Maybe he was bored with the kind of women he'd been sleeping with. Maybe he was sick to death of one-night stands and ships that passed in the night.

Maybe I was waiting for someone like you, he wanted to

say, but didn't. As a very experienced scriptwriter, he instinctively knew when something was too much too soon.

Blake shrugged. 'I'd been very busy working on Lachlan's last movie. It wasn't turning out as well as I would have liked. I needed to rewrite a couple of scenes and re-shoot them. Then the editing afterwards was a nightmare. Most of it ended up on the cutting room floor. Thank God the movie's got a good score. Good music can do wonders. It won't lose money, but I doubt it will set the world on fire. Now, enough of this chit-chat, my love. I'll just finish up this coffee and then it's off to bed for us.'

CHAPTER TWENTY-ONE

'WHAT'S KEEPING YOU so long?' Blake called out to her from the bed.

Kate had insisted on having a shower first. *Alone*, this time—unlike when she and Blake had showered together during that sex-crazed night back in Sydney. She didn't want to do anything kinky with him. She just wanted to *be* with him, to have his arms around her and to have him make love to her as if she was really his love. It was silly of her, she knew, to feel like this about him. But she couldn't seem to help herself.

Was this true love at last? she wondered as she dried herself.

Her feelings were certainly different from what she'd felt for Lachlan. But she couldn't be sure yet. It was way too soon. But, oh, he made her so happy.

Kate smiled at this last thought. Because that was what he'd said he wanted to make her. Happy. Well he'd succeeded all right. And how!

'If you don't get yourself out here pronto, madam,' Blake called out, 'I'm going to come in there and ravage you on the spot.'

'You are such a beast,' she said laughingly, and emerged from the bathroom demurely covered by a huge bath sheet.

'Take that damned thing off,' he demanded testily. 'Then get yourself in here.'

Kate liked it that she didn't feel nervous or shy with him, slowly unwrapping the towel and letting him feast his eyes on her naked body. She'd returned to the beauty salon the day before her flight was due and had every scrap of hair waxed off her body. And she meant *every* scrap.

Blake's eyes smouldered with desire as they raked over her. 'How did you know I like that look?' he said thickly.

'I didn't. I just hoped you would. And it makes me feel sexy.'

'You *are* sexy—with or without clothes.'

'You say the nicest things.'

'Not always.' And he threw back the bedclothes, showing that he was not only naked but armed and ready for action.

She dived in and snuggled up to him, pretending to be shocked when he said what he wanted to do to her in rather crude terms.

'Such language,' she chided, and kissed him on the neck.

'Well, it's a much better word than *shagged*.'

'I agree with you. But I would prefer *make love*—do you mind?'

'Not at all. It's a lovely expression. Let's make love, then.'

'Yes, please.' And she lifted her face to his.

His kisses were gentle to begin with. But not for long. Kate welcomed the passion of his mouth. And his hands. Her breasts swelled in readiness for his caresses, her nipples aching to be played with. And play with them he did—sometimes tenderly, sometimes roughly. She gasped, then sighed, then gasped again.

'I love these,' he said, and pulled at them until they were even longer and harder.

When she thought she couldn't bear it any longer he moved on, one of his hands dipping down between her thighs to torture her there. But, oh, how she loved it. Loved it that he seemed to know exactly what to do. Loved it that he kissed her mouth at the same time...invading her in twin places.

He was a master magician with her body. But also with her head. For there were no bad thoughts to haunt her during his lovemaking. Nothing but the here and now, which was both blinding and blissful.

She cried out when he entered her at last, her body lifting to his, soaring higher and higher until it splintered apart. His name flew from her panting lips when she felt him come along with her. For what felt like ages she was suspended on a plateau of wild throbbing pleasure. And then she was falling, as though from a great height. But there was no fear...nothing but the sensation of freedom and, yes, love.

It was the last thought Kate had before sleep claimed her. That she loved this man who'd set her free—free to be the woman she'd always wanted to be.

Bloody hell, Blake thought as he held her sleeping body close. *If this isn't love then what is it?*

Whatever it was, it scared the living daylights out of him. Because it was almost out of his control. But only *almost*. He could still think, he supposed. Blake had always been of the belief that if he could still reason then he hadn't fallen into that particular honey trap. Not yet, anyway.

Easing her out of his arms, he withdrew, then practically staggered into the bathroom. His legs felt so weak. Yet he'd only had her once. Maybe it was the build-up of the last few days which had made his orgasm so momentous, so overwhelming. Or maybe it was just *her*. She did things to him—made him feel things and plan things which were quite alien to him.

Once he'd got over the fiasco with Claudia he'd lived a very independent lifestyle, not needing or wanting anyone in particular. He'd had the occasional girlfriend, but nothing serious. Sex for him had become nothing more than the scratching of an itch, so to speak.

Yes, his bed partners were still usually actresses, but that was only natural. In his line of work he met lots of actresses. They were invariably attractive girls, intelligent and amusing—and *very* keen to be seen with him. Sex with them was easy and satisfying, but instantly forgettable. He never made them promises he couldn't keep, never let them think there was any kind of future with him.

Blake hadn't lied to Kate when he'd said no other woman had stayed with him up here. After he'd moved into this house fifteen months ago he'd decided that it was going to be his private domain—a sanctuary where he could work and write and fantasise...not about sex, but about being lauded as the greatest movie-maker of the present day.

Success was very important to him. As it was to Kate, Blake reminded himself. He should never forget that. As wonderful as she was, she'd still had her eye on the main chance when she had accepted his offer of help plus his invitation to stay here at his house.

Yes, there was no doubt she found him attractive. Lots of women did. And, yes, she enjoyed sex with him. But she was still in the recovery phase after being in love with Lachlan. It would be foolish of him to imagine there was more to her feelings than gratitude and a whole heap of rebound lust.

Which was fine by him. He didn't really want her to fall in love with him, did he?

Did he?

Blake scowled as he flushed the toilet, washed his hands, then padded back to bed. She was still dead to the world, curled up in a foetal position under the quilt, cuddling her pillow as if it was her favourite teddy bear.

How young she looked. Young and vulnerable.

Be careful with her, Blake's conscience warned as he climbed into bed. *Don't hurt her. If you do you'll hate yourself. And you haven't hated yourself in quite a while.*

He didn't touch her again that night, despite his postcoital exhaustion quickly becoming a distant memory. He lay there next to her for ages, fiercely erect, before finally falling into a troubled sleep.

He woke before dawn and still he lay there, trying to relax—envying Kate, who hadn't moved a muscle. In the end, he rose, quietly pulled on a tracksuit and headed downstairs to the gym.

CHAPTER TWENTY-TWO

KATE WOKE SLOWLY, her eyes remaining closed whilst she wallowed in the warmth and comfort of the bed. It seemed *extra* comfortable this morning, she thought drowsily, wondering if her mother had put clean sheets on the previous day. Kate *loved* the feel of clean sheets...loved the—

Her eyelids shot up like a suddenly released blind. Kate sat up just as quickly, her rapidly clearing mind remembering everything in an instant. She was startled rather than shocked, because everything that had happened to her since she'd arrived in LA last night had been good. *Very* good. She regretted nothing. Absolutely nothing. Not even falling in love with Blake—who was, she'd already noted, no longer in bed with her.

Her eyes darted around the bedroom, which seemed even larger in the daylight, the curtainless windows and the sunshine having the effect of extending it out to the deck and the view beyond. There was no sign of Blake anywhere. He wasn't in the bathroom—its door was wide open. So was the door to his study. Perhaps he was downstairs, having breakfast.

Kate's stomach growled, but it was her full bladder which demanded immediate attention. Jumping out of bed, she headed for the bathroom, sweeping up the discarded towel from the floor on the way, planning to use it as a cover until she could unpack and find the robe she'd brought with her.

No way did she want Blake returning to find her prancing around naked. She didn't mind being without clothes when he was making love to her—that seemed perfectly all right. But an exhibitionist she wasn't. Or maybe she just didn't want to act like Maddie, who seemed to enjoy walking around in the nude—especially since she'd had her boob job.

Emerging from the bathroom with the towel wrapped around her, Kate went in search of her suitcase, which she knew was in one of the walk-in wardrobes. There were two. His and hers, presumably. One was filled with Blake's clothes, the other empty, confirming Blake's claim that he'd never had a woman stay here before her—a thought which pleased Kate no end.

She wasn't under any illusion that Blake had somehow fallen in love with her. He didn't seem a 'falling in love' kind of man. But she was obviously special to him. And he obviously trusted her to let her stay with him in his bedroom. She could see that since his disastrous marriage he'd become somewhat of a cynical loner, using women just for sex and not letting any of them get too close.

Whilst she went about the business of unpacking, Kate wondered what it was about her exactly that he liked so much. It wasn't as though she was a great beauty. Or super-smart. Or highly experienced in the erotic arts. Though maybe that in itself held some kind of attraction. Maybe Blake fancied himself in the role of sexual tutor, getting off on showing her all the different forms of foreplay as well as many and varied positions for intercourse—most of which they hadn't tried yet, but all of which Kate had read about.

She was widely read, and her choice in books was quite eclectic, from biographies to historical sagas and lots of contemporary fiction, some of which included quite explicit sex scenes. She'd always known exactly why her limited sexual experiences in the past had been disappointing, and had once upon a time hoped that Lachlan would give her what she secretly craved.

That hadn't happened, of course. And, amazingly, she couldn't care less. He meant nothing to her any more. Her only regret was that she'd wasted four whole years believing he was the love of her life. The reality was that her feelings had probably been nothing but a youthful infatuation. Puppy love, spawned by Lachlan's golden-boy looks and his blistering charm.

When she thought about it in hindsight Kate felt somewhat foolish, though she consoled herself with the fact that most of the other girls at NIDA had fallen under his spell as well. None of *them* had seen him for what he was, either. But at the same time none of them had seemed all that heartbroken when he'd dated them, then dumped them.

Obviously they hadn't deluded themselves about his character as much as she had. Or maybe, once they'd spent time with him one-on-one, they'd seen the *real* Lachlan, not the good-looking charmer. Now that her rose-tinted glasses were well and truly off, Kate appreciated just how much he'd used her to help him with his acting. It had been cruel of him to take advantage of her like that. *Very* cruel.

Maddie was welcome to him, she decided. They were well matched, those two—both vain and selfish and horribly shallow. Not worth thinking about any more. Back to unpacking.

Kate retrieved her dressing gown and toilet bag, hurrying back into the bathroom to clean her teeth before hanging up the towel and then slipping into the robe. That done, she quickly brushed her hair, put it up into a topknot, then returned to finish her unpacking.

She hadn't brought a lot of clothes with her, only the things she really liked, as well as the new clothes she'd bought this week.

Kate smiled as she drew out her favourite new jacket. It was made of black velvet, which was very 'in' this year— or so she'd been told. It was cropped at the waist, with no lapels, and had silver zips decorating the pockets. Very stylish—and rather sexy when worn with her new tight white jeans and black high heels. The salesgirl had also talked her into adding a silvery grey silk cami, which she'd said made the outfit *'pop'*.

Kate couldn't wait to wear it all for Blake.

'And what are *you* smiling at, madam?'

Kate spun round at the sound of his voice. Blake stood in the open doorway, dressed in a navy tracksuit, a dark grey towel hanging around his neck.

Her smile was enigmatic. Or so she hoped. 'That's for me to know and you to find out.'

He grinned as he dabbed at his damp forehead with one end of the towel. 'I do love a mystery. *And* a challenge.'

She laughed. 'I don't think I've ever presented you with either. I've been putty in your hands from the first.'

His own smile was wry. 'You think?'

'I *know*.'

'You know nothing, sweetheart,' he said, in an enigmatic tone of his own. 'Now, I have to have a shower. I'm hot and sweaty. Have you showered yet?'

'No.'

'Good. Stop doing that for now, then, and have one with me.'

When she hesitated—she wasn't sure why—he raised his eyebrows at her. 'Come now, Kate, you're not going to start playing games with me, are you?'

She frowned, suddenly unsure of herself. It was one thing to fall in love with this man... Another thing entirely to let him think she would jump to his command *all* the time. It was tempting to say yes, but was that the kind of woman she really wanted to be?

Definitely not. But, oh, it was difficult to say no.

Her pride struggled to her rescue—though it had a fight on its hands. Because when he went all masterful like that she wanted to obey him...wanted to do whatever he wanted her to do.

'I'm not sure what sort of games you're referring to,' she said, with only the smallest quaver in her voice. 'I'm a very straightforward kind of girl. But I don't appreciate your ordering me into the shower like that. It's not...respectful.' Even as she said the word she thought how old-fashioned and prissy it sounded.

He stared at her for a long moment, then nodded. 'You're right. I apologise. It's just that you look so deliciously sexy in that silky thing you're almost wearing. Forgive me?'

Kate glanced down at her black and white robe, which wasn't silk but polyester and had cost her all of fifteen dollars on sale. It was quite a modest garment, reaching past her knees, and it had three-quarter-length kimono-type sleeves. The sash belt, however, had come loose, and the neckline was gaping. But, since she didn't have much of a cleavage without a bra, she wouldn't have thought she looked at all sexy.

Kate yanked the lapels together and tightened the belt, aware that her nipples felt like bullets under her robe. 'Of course I forgive you,' she said, already regretting her stance. What was that she'd said about being putty in his hands?

'Would you *please* join me in the shower?' he asked politely, his dark eyes glittering with wicked intent.

She hadn't forgotten what he'd done to her the other night in Sydney when they'd showered together. The experience had been both thrilling and utterly seductive. She sighed, then shook her head at him, her own eyes glittering as well. She'd claimed she didn't play games, but this one was such fun. And wasn't that what he'd promised her from the start? That sex could be fun?

'I shouldn't,' she said. 'You will only take wicked advantage of me.'

'What if I promise not to, on the proviso that *you* take wicked advantage of *me*?'

Kate wasn't given to having lurid sexual fantasies, but

her turned-on mind was suddenly filled with a clear image of how she could do just that. She could see herself now, taking a soapy sea sponge and slowly washing Blake all over. *All* over. She would order him to turn this way and that, so that not an inch of his body was unknown to her. Only one area would be neglected.

Kate would refuse to wash him *there* until he was going crazy with need…until his erection was hard and painful and, oh, so impatient, quivering wildly for her touch. Only then would she press the hot wet sponge around its base, squeezing it tightly and sliding it up and down. He would gasp at first, then groan, and finally he would come—right there in the shower. The violence of his release would send him lurching back against the wall, his outspread palms bracing himself against the wet tiles. His breathing would be ragged and his eyes glazed as they stared at her with shocked pleasure…

Of course it didn't quite work out that way. It started well, with Blake happy for her to wash his body, and amused at first when she bypassed his penis. But he was not a man to let *any* woman take control of things indefinitely.

'I thought you didn't play games?' he growled when she turned him around and began washing his buttocks.

'When in Rome…' she quipped, echoing what he'd said the previous night.

He sucked in breath sharply when she turned him around again and brushed the sponge across the tip of his swaying erection. His eyes darkened and his right hand shot out to grab her wrist, forcibly bringing the sponge to where he wanted it to be.

'You seem to have lost your sense of direction,' he said, his voice thick and his eyelids heavy.

Using his superior strength, he forced her to do at once what she'd planned to do eventually. But he stopped her before he came—stopped her and tossed the sponge away.

Then he took her face in his hands and kissed her 'til she was lost in a haze of desire. It was Kate, then, who found herself pushed back against the wall, bracing herself whilst Blake sank to his knees before her.

'Oh, God,' she moaned when he spread her legs wide, because she knew how good he was at this. She had no hope of holding out—no hope at all. But she had to try. She didn't want to come like this.

So she lifted her eyes to the twin shower heads and watched the water gush out, trying not to think about how glorious it felt to have his lips and his fingers doing what they were doing, how her insides were twisting tighter and tighter, how she was already balancing on the edge of the abyss.

Her mouth had already fallen open in readiness for her release when Blake abruptly wrenched away from her and stood up.

'You can't stop now!' she cried out, her frustration acute.

He just smiled. 'Don't be greedy.'

He snapped off the water and bundled her out, grabbing a towel from a nearby rack and rubbing her roughly dry before doing the same to himself. Her hair was still dripping wet when he pulled her over to the double vanity unit and wrapped her hands over the edge, showing her flushed face reflected in the overhead mirror.

She could have protested...could have refused. But she did neither, just staying where he'd put her whilst he rummaged in one of the drawers and extracted a condom.

His entry was rough, but not painful—her body was supremely ready for ravaging—and their climaxes were simultaneous, their release more violent than ever.

He pulled her upright whilst their bodies were still shuddering together, holding her hard against him and nuzzling his mouth against her ear. 'God, Kate,' was all he said.

She didn't reply, her mind too dazed for her to make co-
herent conversation, her eyes tightly shut.

Never in her wildest dreams had Kate imagined sex
could be like this. Because that was all it was that they'd
just shared. It hadn't been making love. It had been just
sex. Yet she'd thrilled to it all the same.

Her eyes opened and she stared at their reflection in the
mirror, stared at his hands as they roved languidly over her
breasts, down over her stomach, then between her legs.

'No,' she groaned when he started touching her in her
most sensitive place.

He ignored her, and soon she gave up any hope of
protest...

'You're very quiet,' he said to her over breakfast.

'I was just thinking,' she replied.

'About what?' He picked up his coffee and searched her
face over the rim of the mug.

'About my screen test,' Kate lied. She'd actually been
thinking that she wanted him again. 'When will I actually
be doing it?'

'Probably Monday,' he said between sips. 'I'll organise
an actor and a studio today.'

'I wish you didn't have to go to work,' she said, quite
truthfully.

She would have loved to spend the whole day in bed with
him. Or wherever he might want to have sex with her. The
bathroom again. Or on the sofa in his study. She didn't care
where. Kate suspected that if Juanita hadn't been hovering
in the kitchen she might have tried to tempt him right here
and now. She was only wearing her robe, nothing on underneath, and it was making her hotly aware of the moist-
ness between her thighs.

She moved restlessly on the chair, desire squirming in
her stomach. And lower...

Oh, Lord!

Love had turned her into a sex addict. Or maybe it wasn't love. Maybe it was just lust. Maybe she was deluding herself.

'Have to, I'm afraid,' he replied, putting his coffee down. 'I'm juggling several projects at the moment, all of which need my personal attention. Now, speaking of work, I'll need to get my lawyer on to your visa ASAP. I hope you were able to get everything I asked you to bring? Not just your references from NIDA, but the reviews of that play as well.'

Kate blinked at him, her mind having wandered to other things. Like how gorgeous he looked in that business suit. Gorgeous and sexy and...

'Kate?' he prompted, frowning at her.

'What? Oh, yes—yes. I got everything, and more. I remembered that the director of that play actually filmed our last dress rehearsal. I contacted him and he gave me a copy of the DVD.' She'd meant to tell Blake yesterday but she'd totally forgotten.

'That's fabulous. Because seeing is believing. Much better than a letter just saying you're good. Something like that DVD could tip everything in your favour.'

'Only if my acting is good, though.'

'You know it is.'

She sighed. 'I thought so. But maybe people over here won't be impressed.'

'Now, don't start with that negative talk. Negative talk never gets you anywhere. Come on,' he went on, standing up. 'Let's go and get everything.'

After Blake had left Kate had another shower, then dressed in dark blue jeans and a lemon cotton top which suited her colouring and was not too warm, although the ducted air-conditioning was keeping all the rooms at a pleasant temperature.

It was only when she went out onto the deck or into the pool area that she felt cool. And then, not too cool. No doubt the day would warm up. There were no clouds in the blue sky. The weather reminded her of spring in Sydney.

Kate talked to Juanita for a while, offering to help her, but Juanita refused.

'No, no—you are a guest,' the housekeeper said. 'And you must be tired. Flying that far is very tiring. Or so I am told. I never fly anywhere. The thought terrifies me. Go and have a lie-down. Or watch a movie—Señor Blake has thousands.'

It was only then that Kate remembered Blake had left a printed copy of her script on the desk in his study upstairs, suggesting she read the whole thing through in order to fully understand the context of her part.

After getting herself another mug of coffee, Kate carried it upstairs and went into his study, settling herself onto a comfy leather sofa and placing her coffee on its built-in side table. She had just begun to read when the tell-tale ring of her phone infiltrated faintly, from where she'd left it on the bedside table.

Thinking it might be Blake, she hurried to answer it.

But it wasn't Blake.

It was Maddie.

CHAPTER TWENTY-THREE

'MADDIE!' KATE EXCLAIMED. 'What are you doing, ringing me? You're supposed to be on your honeymoon.'

'Honeymoon? *Huh*. Darling Lachlan spends more time on his phone than with me. His new American agent is negotiating some big movie deal for him. A franchise, apparently, all with the same hero. Rather like James Bond, only sexier. Not sure how it *could* be sexier... Anyway, he's very excited about it. Can't say *I* am. The money's fabulous, but all the films are going to be shot in Europe and he says I can't go on location with him. I'm supposed to stay home in Sydney like a good little wife.' She laughed. 'As if I'm going to do *that*. Anyway, that's not why I'm ringing you...'

Kate had an awful suspicion that she knew exactly why her sister was ringing her.

'I know all about your going to LA,' Maddie rattled on. 'Mum told me everything. And I know you're staying in Blake Randall's house.'

'Yes...' It was only one word but it carried a whole heap of meaning. Such as *It's none of your damned business, Maddie.*

'Look, I'm not against what you've done. Hell, sis, I was all *for* it. Remember? But Lachlan's appalled. Lord knows why. I moved in with *him* the day after we met. Maybe things are different in America. Anyway, he wanted me to warn you about what people will soon be saying.'

'What people, exactly?'

'Hollywood people. Lachlan says they can be very small-minded and downright malicious. He said they'll be nice to your face but they'll snigger behind your back. They don't like unknowns like you getting the star treatment just because they're sleeping with the boss. He said you haven't paid your dues and that'll get right up their noses.'

'Well, thank you for the warning, Maddie,' Kate said, sounding much cooler than she was feeling. Why couldn't Maddie be *happy* for her? *She* had everything *she* wanted. 'But I don't much care what Lachlan says. As for my getting star treatment—Blake's only offered me a supporting part in this movie. It's not like I have the main role.'

'And you won't get one, either. Lachlan says he'll screw you 'til the movie's finished and then he'll toss you out on your ear. Lachlan says that...'

'I don't give a monkey's uncle what Lachlan says,' Kate bit out. 'He's just jealous. And possibly so are you.'

'That's not true!' Maddie denied. 'I'm just worried about you. I don't want you to get hurt.'

'Oh, really? Were those your sentiments when you honed in on the one man you knew I had a crush on?'

'I've already apologised for that.'

'At the same time admitting that you don't even love him,' Kate swept on angrily. 'You just want the good life, you said. Well, I'm having a better life now—with a man I *do* love,' she threw down the line without thinking. 'And you obviously don't like it one bit!'

Kate might have said more if Maddie hadn't hung up on her. She stared down into the silent phone, swamped by a mixture of frustration and fury. Finally she turned off the phone and threw the damned thing on the bed, determined never to speak to her sister again.

It was only when she sat down in Blake's study and picked up the script again that she realised her hands were shaking. No—her whole body was shaking.

It was then that she started to cry.

Blake tried Kate's phone again but it was still turned off. *Damn it.* She'd probably turned the darned thing off and gone back to bed for that rest he'd advised. Yet he really wanted to talk to her. Excitement was still fizzing through his veins.

What to do? He couldn't go home yet. He had a meeting with the head of Fortune Films this afternoon. To cancel at this late stage would not be wise. They were the only distribution company worth having, in his opinion.

Blake glanced at his Rolex. It was twenty past one. No way could he get home and back in time for the meeting at two-thirty. A light suddenly popped on in his brain, solving his problem. *Juanita*. He would ring her and have her go in search of Kate.

If she was asleep then it was high time she woke up, otherwise she wouldn't sleep tonight. It was a thought which brought a wry smile to his face. Maybe he should let her stay asleep...

But, no, his news simply couldn't wait.

Kate was sitting out on the deck, dry-eyed, when Juanita found her a second time. She'd come up an hour ago, insisting Kate come down for some lunch. But Kate hadn't felt like eating, and had told Juanita she would be down a little later.

Now she was back, looking at Kate with concern in her dark eyes.

'Señor Blake has just rung me,' she said. 'He said he has been trying to ring you but your phone is turned off. He said he has good news and could you please ring him?'

Kate sighed, but did not move. She could not imagine any news which would make her feel better. It was silly of her to believe anything Maddie had said, but she was only human and doubts had crept in. Doubts about what she was doing. Doubts about Blake. Doubts about everything. On top of that, she hated it that Maddie had hung up on her—

hated herself for trying to hurt her sister. Revenge was *not* good for the soul.

Juanita hovered. 'Señor Blake...' the housekeeper went on. 'He...he is a good man but not always a patient one. Please... He will think I did not give you the message if you don't ring him straight away.'

Kate heard the worry in Juanita's voice and immediately stood up. Juanita's relieved smile made Kate feel guilty. It wasn't like her to be so thoughtless.

'Sorry, Juanita. Please don't worry. I'll call him now.'

'That is good,' Juanita said, and bustled off.

Kate hurried into the bedroom and retrieved her phone and turned it on. Within a few seconds Blake was on the line.

'I hope I didn't wake you,' were his first words.

'No, no. I wasn't asleep. What's up?'

'I watched that DVD of your play and I have to tell you, Kate, I was more than impressed. You were *fantastic*. In fact I was so impressed I had a copy made and had it couriered over to the agent I think will suit you best. He promised to look at it this very afternoon and get back to me.'

'Oh,' she said, somehow unable to react normally, with her old friend depression having taken hold of her. 'That is good news.'

'You don't sound very enthusiastic.'

'Sorry. I think I might be a bit jet-lagged. I tried to read through that script, like you told me, but my eyes kept glazing over.'

'Then you really should try to get some sleep. I want to take you out to dinner tonight. To celebrate. Because there's no *way* they'll knock back your working visa once they see you in that play. You're a shoe-in, sweetheart.'

Kate couldn't tell him she didn't want to go anywhere. So she said nothing.

'Kate?' he said after a few moments' awkward silence. 'What is it? Something's wrong. I can tell.'

Kate sighed. 'Maddie rang me.'

Blake swore. 'And what did your darling sister say to upset you *this* time?'

Tears suddenly swam in Kate's eyes. 'It wasn't what *she* said so much. It was what Lachlan had told her to say.'

'About what?'

'About me coming to Hollywood with you.'

Blake swore again. 'That bastard needs sorting out. Tell me what he said. And I want to hear every single word.'

Kate swallowed the lump in her throat. Then she repeated every single word of Lachlan's warnings. But she didn't tell Blake what she'd said back to Maddie about loving him.

He didn't swear this time. He just listened.

'When I accused them both of being jealous,' Kate finished, 'Maddie hung up on me. That's why I turned off the phone. So she couldn't ring me back.'

'I see. And do you believe what Lachlan said about me this time?'

'No...'

'You don't sound so sure.'

'I... I thought he had a point saying that people will believe I'm sleeping my way to success. They *will* think that, Blake.'

His sigh was heavy. 'You can't spend your life worrying about what other people think.'

'I suppose not. It's just that I want to feel I'm succeeding as an actress through my own efforts.'

'That wasn't working so well for you when we first met, was it?'

'That's because I was not in a positive frame of mind at the time. Maddie getting together with Lachlan had affected me badly. I coped whilst I was doing the play. It was the perfect escape from my melancholy, playing an upbeat girl who refused to let anything get her down. But when the play folded I lost what was left of my confidence. I was terrible at all my auditions. And I *looked* terrible. I can see that in hindsight. I wouldn't be terrible now. I *know* I wouldn't.'

'So are you saying you don't *want* this part in my movie?'

She hadn't thought that. Not until this moment. 'I think perhaps it's best I decline, Blake. I'm sorry. It was very generous of you to offer it to me, but...well...it just wouldn't feel right. Not now.'

'You mean since bloody Lachlan poisoned your mind about everything,' Blake snapped.

Kate could not deny that she'd begun having doubts about what she was doing here in Blake's house...what role she was playing. As much as she had enjoyed their interlude in the bathroom this morning, it had highlighted to her that Blake's feelings for her were probably largely sexual. His generosity and caring might not be real—just a means to an end. Falling in love with him might have blinded her to his true character.

'I wouldn't say "poisoned",' she said slowly. 'But he's given me food for thought.'

'You still love that bastard, don't you?'

'No,' she said truthfully. 'No, I don't. I told you that already.'

'I know what you *told* me, Kate.'

His scepticism shocked her.

'Love doesn't die that quickly,' he growled.

'It does when it wasn't true love in the first place.'

'If only I could believe that...'

Kate hated it that he didn't believe her. She ached to tell him that *he* was the one she truly loved, but she doubted he'd believe that, either. And if by some fluke he did, then it would just give him more power over her.

Not a good idea, Kate. She was having enough trouble sorting her head out as it was.

'I think it would be best if I went home, Blake,' she said shakily.

'No, it would *not*!' he roared down the phone. 'You hate it there.'

'I don't *hate* it.'

'Bull-dust. Your sister and your mother might not mean to, but they suck all the life out of you. Your family will make you feel like a failure if you go back now. And you're *not* a failure. You're a beautiful and talented actress who just hasn't had the right break yet.'

Blake's lovely compliments sent tears pricking at her eyes.

'You *have* to stay here, Kate. Okay, don't take the part I offered if it bothers you. Though damn it, girl, you're looking a gift horse in the mouth. I suppose that's why you don't want it? You think it's charity on my part, or something much worse. You don't realise just how fantastic an actress you are. I would *kill* to have someone like you in any of my movies. Hell, Kate, watching you in that play practically blew my mind.'

'But, Blake, you offered me that part *before* you saw me in the play,' she pointed out.

He was silent for a few fraught seconds, then he laughed. 'Okay, so you've caught me out. Yes, I wanted you, Kate—almost from the first moment I saw you—and I wasn't above using your ambition to get you into my bed. But I wasn't lying when I said I want to make you happy. I honestly do. You've touched something in me, Kate—something that is rarely ever touched. I'm not known for my empathy, or my compassion. And as for passion—the only passion I've had for years is for my movies. Until I met you. God, but I want you with *passion*, girl. And I need you. I won't let you go home—not whilst there's breath in my body. You're to stay here with me—not as a guest, but as my girlfriend. A proper live-in girlfriend. Then, once your visa comes through, you can knock yourself out going to endless auditions until you get yourself an acting job. And once you've made it on your own you will do a movie for *me*. Not some minor role but the lead, in a script I will write especially for you!'

Kate sucked in breath sharply. Lord, how did an aspiring actress in love say no to all *that*?

'And if you're worrying about how much money I'll have to spend on you until you're earning money on your own,' he charged on, 'then I'll keep a tally. You can pay me back as soon as you can. What do you say to that idea?'

'I'm pretty speechless right now.' *And brimming full of emotion.* Okay, so he hadn't said he loved her, but he did care about her. Passionately so.

'We can't let other people spoil what we have together, Kate. It's special—our connection, our chemistry. Don't you agree?'

'Yes…' she choked out.

'So you won't go home?'

'No.'

His sigh was a sound of total relief. 'Thank God.'

'But promise you won't try to change my mind about doing that part,' she said with a sudden rush of worry.

'I promise. It wasn't quite *you*, that role, anyway. You need to be the heroine of the story, not some slutty other woman. Now, I must get off this phone. I have an important meeting this afternoon. But I'll be home by six at the latest. If I'm going to be any later I'll ring you, so don't turn off your phone. And if your stupid sister rings you again *you* be the one to hang up.'

'I just might do that.'

'Good girl. I've booked dinner for us at seven. I won't be taking you to any of those celebrity restaurants—just a local steakhouse which does fabulous food. Wear something nice, but nothing over the top. The dress code at Jimmy's place is quite casual.'

'I've got just the thing.'

'Good. Have to go. Bye.'

He'd hung up by the time Kate said goodbye in return.

She sat for a long time, thinking about what he'd said. And what *she* had said.

She was proud of herself for deciding not to let Blake present her with her career on a silver platter. The temptation had been there to do just that. Face it, she'd been *well* on the way down that particular road. But, honestly, if she had she would never have felt good about any success which might have come her way.

Kate wasn't overly concerned about what perfect strangers thought of her, but she *did* care about what her family thought. Silly, really, but that was the way it was. Maybe one day she'd be able to be like Blake, not needing or caring about anyone back home. But that day hadn't come yet.

Kate already regretted being stroppy with Maddie over the phone. Maybe she should ring her back. Or text her.

And maybe not.

Best leave things for now.

Glancing at the time on her phone—it was after two—Kate decided to go in search of Juanita and that lunch she'd offered her. At the same time she aimed to find out where everything was in the main kitchen, so she could get herself her own breakfast and morning tea and lunch. She wasn't used to being waited on hand and foot and, whilst it was a deliciously pleasurable experience, Kate didn't want to become one of those spoiled rich women who wouldn't lift even one precious finger unless it was to get her nails done.

Not that she was *rich*. But she was living with a very rich man.

This was still the part which didn't sit well with Kate.

Because it made her feel like a kept woman. A mistress. Being *any* man's mistress had not been in her life plan at all. Love did make a woman weak in some ways, but hopefully not in others.

Kate reaffirmed her determination to keep that tally Blake had mentioned, of what he spent on her. And to pay him back once she got herself an acting job. She also resolved to do some research on the internet, find out what was hot now in television series. She knew that several young Australian actors had found work in LA that way. Being unknown hadn't worked against them in *that* field. It was, in fact, often seen as a plus. The television industry loved new faces and fresh new talent.

With these resolves fixed firmly in her mind, Kate stood up, slipping her phone into the pocket of her jeans before heading downstairs in search of Juanita.

CHAPTER TWENTY-FOUR

'SORRY I'M A bit late!' Blake said as he dashed in shortly after six-thirty.

When Kate had heard him running up the stairs to the top floor she'd emerged from the bathroom, where she'd been titivating for the last half-hour.

He stopped to stare, his eyes turning hungry as they raked her over from top to toe. 'God, don't *you* look gorgeous?'

'Not too casual?' she asked as she hooked silver hoop earrings into her ears. Her hair was up in a loose knot, with a few wispy bits around her face.

'Not at all. I love girls in white jeans and heels. And I *love* that jacket.'

'So do I.' She flipped it open and shut, giving him a better look at the sexy silver cami, not to mention her braless breasts.

'Damn it, girl, you *really* make it hard on a man,' he growled, his dark eyes glittering. 'I desperately want to kiss you, but if I do we'll never get to the restaurant.'

Kate's heart started racing with a hunger of her own. 'Would that be such a disaster?'

'Not a disaster. But perhaps unwise. Because I'm starving. And starving is never good if a man wants to make love to his woman all night long.'

'All night long?' she choked out as her whole chest squeezed tight.

'Absolutely. Tomorrow's Sunday. I'm not going to work and I've cancelled my morning golf game. Which—and trust me on this—is not something I do very often. I love my golf. But I love making love to *you* even more.'

'Oh...'

His eyes narrowed on hers. 'You're not going to cry, are you?'

Kate swallowed, quickly pulling herself together. But that had been so close to him saying that he loved her. So heartstoppingly close...

'No, no. Absolutely not.'

'Good. Now, I'm going to have a quick shower. *Alone*. But I don't have time to shave or we'll be late. Do you mind me with a stubbly chin?'

'Not at all. It suits you. It's sexy.'

And it was. *Very*. It made him look like a pirate. Kate loved movies with pirates in them. Their characters were always masterful. And whilst they could be wicked, it was never in a horrible way. They just dared to do what a modern man wouldn't. Like kidnap women and then force them to fall in love with them...

A bit like what Blake had done to her.

Blake rubbed his chin. 'Sexy, eh?'

'Yes. *Very*.'

He laughed. 'You're not trying to seduce me, are you?'

'Could I?'

'*Could* you?' He shook his head at her, smiling a wry smile. 'Oh, that's funny, Kate. You've no idea how funny. Now, I suggest you go downstairs and have a pre-dinner drink. There's plenty of wine in the fridge. Or champagne, if you prefer. I won't be long.'

Blake slammed the bathroom door shut, sighing as he started reefing off his clothes. Lord, but she didn't know how close he'd come to reefing off *her* clothes—her very sexy clothes.

His plan to seduce Kate with sex was really backfiring on him. *He* was the one totally seduced and obsessed, and so in love with her that he could hardly contain the words.

I love you! he wanted to shout out. *I love you and I want to marry you!*

Once again the idea of marriage had jumped into his head, and it was beginning to annoy him. He didn't need to *marry* Kate just because he'd fallen in love with her. Why marry her? It was unnecessary in this day and age. They could just live together, as he'd already suggested, which would be so much easier, and much less complicated.

But it was no use. Marriage was what he wanted—along with her love. Nothing else would do.

'Stupid bastard!' he ground out, and stepped in under a cold shower, gasping as icy shards of water beat down on his overheated brain and body, bringing him back to reality with a rush. To a reality that was as sobering as it was sensible.

Because it was still way too soon to say such things to her. He *had* to give her more time. Had to let her get over that other stupid bastard before she was capable of falling in love with him.

Meanwhile he had to be patient. *Not* his favourite activity.

CHAPTER TWENTY-FIVE

JIMMY'S STEAK HOUSE was not a large establishment. Neither was it a place whose popularity rested on celebrity patronage, like lots of other Hollywood restaurants. Or so Blake told Kate on the way there.

'You'll like it,' he said. 'The food is great and it's quiet. There are no bands playing, nor even a piano player. They have booths as well as tables, so you can get some privacy, and you can actually hear yourself talk. I hate eating in places where you have to shout to be heard.'

Kate couldn't have agreed with him more.

'This is great,' she said, once they were seated in a booth well away from the door.

Of course she would think anywhere was great if she was with Blake. But she did genuinely like the quiet ambience and the decor, which was all clean lines and simple. White walls, wooden floor and tables, no tablecloths.

They hadn't been stared at when they'd come in, though all the ladies present had given Blake a few second glances. And why not? He looked devilishly handsome in black jeans, a white silk shirt—open at the neck—and a sleek lightweight black jacket. His casually sexy clothes, combined with his five o'clock shadow and his slightly rumpled black hair, gave him that bad-boy image women found so attractive.

Kate was no exception.

'Do you like red wine?' he asked as he picked up the drinks menu.

'It's okay,' she replied. 'But I prefer white.'

'You can't drink white wine with steak,' he pronounced, with his usual arrogance.

He ordered red wine, and Kate discovered to her surprise that she did like it. Or at least she liked this particular red wine, which she suspected was hideously expensive. It had a French label, and the waiter treated the bottle as if it was made of gold.

'Well?' Blake asked after she'd had a few sips.

'Lovely,' she replied.

'I told you so. You *must* widen your horizons, Kate.'

She smiled. 'I've widened them quite enough already, don't you think?'

He frowned. 'What do you mean?'

'You *know* what I mean.'

'I suppose you're referring to throwing in your lot with me?'

'Yes. I suppose I am.'

'Best thing you ever did. You were losing your way back in Sydney.'

Kate sighed. 'Don't you *ever* have doubts, Blake?'

He looked at her hard, then laughed. 'Everyone has doubts, Kate. But you have to learn to ignore them and just go for what you want. Otherwise you'll spend your whole life regretting your lack of courage.'

'Is that what you've always done? Just gone for what you wanted?'

'In the main. I was seriously derailed once—but you don't need to hear about that.'

Kate presumed he was referring to his divorce. *Horrid* thing, divorce. Especially if there were children involved...

'How long did it take for you to get back on the rails?' she asked him.

'How long?' he mused, lifting his glass to his lips for a long sip. 'Not too long. But I was terribly bitter for a while. Which I now regret. Bitterness is as self-destructive as revenge. And it gets you nowhere. You have to learn to move on and not dwell on the past.'

'You're talking about Claudia, aren't you?'

'Partly.'

'What do you mean by that?'

'I was talking in general—not just about Claudia in particular. I harbour no animosity towards Claudia any more. I met her the other week at a party and we had quite a pleasant chat. She's not too bad when you're not in love with her.'

Kate hated to think that he'd *ever* been in love with her. Which was pathetic, really.

Their steaks arrived at that fortuitous moment—Blake's medium rare and hers well done. Both were accompanied by French fries and salad, plus a side dish of herbed bread. The steaks covered half the plate.

'My goodness,' she said. 'I wish you had a dog. Then I could take him home some of this steak. I'll never eat it all.'

'You might have done, if you'd had it medium rare like me. Goes down much easier that way.'

'No, thanks,' she said, crinkling her nose at him. 'I don't like eating meat with blood in it.'

'Have you ever tried it?'

'No...'

'Then don't knock it 'til you try it.'

'Okay. Give me a mouthful of yours, then.'

He did—and she did like it. It was very tender...more tender than hers.

'See?' he said smugly. 'You shouldn't be afraid to try new things, Kate.'

'Yes, boss.'

He laughed. 'You sounded just like Carlos, then.'

'And *you* sounded like an old schoolteacher of mine. Not one I overly liked.'

'*Ouch*. That's not good.'

'No—so cut it out with the life lessons. I'll get there, Blake. In my own good time.'

He cocked his head to one side. 'You've become quite an independent little miss during the past week, haven't you?'

'I hope so.'

'Good. I like that. Now, eat up or the food will get cold. Nothing worse than cold steak.'

They both tucked in, and Kate realised how hungry she actually was. She ate ninety percent of the steak and all of everything else—including the herb bread.

'I like to see a girl with a good appetite,' Blake said as he dabbed his mouth with a serviette. 'Rare thing in Hollywood, I can tell you.'

'I'm lucky that I can eat whatever I like and not get fat. I have a fast metabolism.'

'That *is* lucky. And good for your career. You'll stay slim and at the same time you won't get all skinny and fragile like some of the actresses I know. Speaking of your career... I was talking to Steve late this afternoon and—'

'Who's Steve?'

'Steve Kepell. The agent I think would suit you. The one I sent the DVD of your play. Anyway, he was as impressed as I was—both by your acting and your looks. Said you were very photogenic. But he *did* suggest that whilst you're waiting for your working visa to come through you have some lessons from a dialect coach. Get rid of your Australian accent entirely. Oh, and he also suggested you have a few sessions with an audition coach. He gave me the name of a good one. Anyway, I'll line up both for you on Monday so that you can get started ASAP.'

Dismay swamped Kate, and her forehead bunched up into a troubled frown.

'What?' he asked.

She shook her head at him. 'I'm sorry, Blake, but it's all getting a bit too much.'

'What is?'

'Everything you're doing for me.'

He sighed. 'You're not going to say no again, are you?'

'Coaches like that are very expensive. I'm not dumb. I know what they cost.'

'But I can afford it,' he told her, her voice tight with obvious frustration. 'My movies are raking in heaps.'

'That's not the point. People will say I'm a freeloader, or a gold-digger. I know you said I shouldn't worry about what other people think, but I do.'

Blake scowled. 'They wouldn't say either of those things if you were my wife.'

'Your *wife*?' Kate exclaimed.

CHAPTER TWENTY-SIX

BLAKE COULD HAVE cut his tongue out. He'd done it now, hadn't he? But, damn it all, he was beginning to see everything he wanted getting away from him. And he couldn't bear it.

The shock on Kate's face just about killed him. Clearly marrying him was the last thing she wanted, or would ever do. And whilst one part of him found pleasure in this undeniable proof that she was nothing like Claudia, the rest of him was plunged into the most alien despair.

True to his nature, however, Blake refused to admit defeat. With a will of iron he climbed out of the pit and put his intelligence to finding the right words to say to her, finally adopting what he hoped was the right expression. One of mild exasperation.

'Yes, yes,' he said, with a flourish of his left hand, 'I know exactly what you're going to say. We've only known each other a week. You don't marry someone you've only known for a week.'

'I… I wasn't going to say any of that at all,' Kate denied, feeling both flushed and flustered.

Because of course she would marry him in a heartbeat if he loved her. The brevity of their relationship didn't matter. She already knew more about him in a week than she'd learnt about Lachlan in four years. Kate knew down deep that Blake was a decent man. Caring and kind and above all fantastically good in bed.

'I was going to *say*,' she went on, having to force out the words, 'that I would only marry you if we were both madly in love with each other.' Blake's not loving her was a deal-breaker. Kate needed her husband to love her. 'I'm sorry, Blake, but marriage without love is not for me.'

'I see,' Blake bit out. 'Well, that's it then.' He looked at her for a long moment, his dark eyes searching hers as the corner of his mouth lifted in a strange smile. 'You wouldn't consider it even if one half of the couple was madly in love with the other?'

The truth behind his statement hit Kate with a squall of anxiety and embarrassment. 'Oh, no!' she wailed, her stomach churning. 'You rang Lachlan, didn't you? And he *told* you. Or Maddie told you. I *knew* I should never have told her. Oh, God...'

And she buried her face in her hands momentarily, before looking up at him again with anguished eyes.

Blake shook his head at her. 'Kate, I don't know what in hell you're talking about. I haven't rung Lachlan. Though I will. Soon. He needs to be sorted out. But I haven't yet. And I certainly haven't talked to your sister.'

Kate blinked in confusion, then blinked again—until suddenly she realised what this meant. If he hadn't talked to Maddie or Lachlan then he didn't *know* she loved him. So he had to have been talking about himself.

Her heart flipped right over at the enormity of her discovery.

'Are you saying that you're actually in *love* with me?'

His smile carried amusement. 'Not "actually" so much as madly. Yes, Kate, my sweet. I'm madly in love with you. Is that so surprising? Now, what on earth were you going on about just now? What was it you told Maddie that she shouldn't have told me even though she didn't?'

'Oh. Yes. Oh. No. Oh. Well...' God, she was babbling like an idiot.

'Out with it, woman. No lies, now.'

'I... I told her that I love you.'

Blake seemed stunned. 'You *love* me?'

'Yes. Yes, I love you. Very much.'

'Wow… I never dreamt…' His hands lifted to run rather shakily through his hair. His gaze searched her face with an air of wonder. 'I thought it was too soon. I thought…'

'I know what you thought, but you were wrong. Lachlan means no more to me now than Claudia does to you. The moment you came into my life I saw that he was just a cardboard cut-out hero, whereas you are the real thing.'

'I'll have to remember to use that line in one of my movies.'

'You will not!' she said. But she was smiling.

'Right. Now, can we go back to that earlier part of our conversation where I suggested you become my wife?'

'Oh, *that* part.'

'Well, what do you say?'

The temptation to just say yes was acute. But…

'You need to ask me properly first—with an engagement ring in your pocket. And the wedding won't be taking place until after I get my first independent acting job, gained by my own efforts and no help from you.'

'Done!' he agreed, grinning as he whipped out his phone.

'What are you doing?' Kate asked breathlessly. She was still in a bit of shock at the speed of everything.

'I'm calling Carlos.'

'Yes, boss?' Carlos answered. 'You ready to be picked up?'

'Yep. But we won't be going straight home. I need to do some shopping first. Oh, and bring Juanita with you.'

'Juanita?'

'Yep. I know how much your wife likes jewellery. She'll know exactly where we should go to buy an engagement ring.'

'I'm sure she will,' Carlos replied gleefully. 'See you outside in about ten minutes, boss.'

'Perfect.'

CHAPTER TWENTY-SEVEN

BLAKE LAY BACK in bed with his fiancée in his arms, feeling happier than he could ever have imagined. His original quest to make Kate happy had been achieved—she hadn't stopped smiling or admiring her engagement ring for the last hour—but his own happiness exceeded anything he'd ever experienced before.

Who would have believed that an old cynic like him could find true love—and with an actress, no less? It was the ultimate irony. But a logical one in a way. Who else would he have so much in common with? Who else would understand him the way Kate did?

Byron was going to be surprised. Or perhaps not. Since marrying Cleo and becoming a father Byron had become an old softie. He would rejoice in their news and give Blake his heartiest congratulations and best wishes. Blake vowed to ring and tell him in the morning.

He wouldn't, however, be ringing Lachlan. If the rumour mill was correct he'd soon be severing his connections with Fantasy Productions anyway. Blake didn't bother to hope that Lachlan's new venture would fail because it probably wouldn't. Action heroes didn't have to be great actors. Blake didn't really care either way, but he vowed not to have anything more to do with the man—either personally or professionally.

'Will you stop admiring that damned ring?' he said now, pretending to be angry, 'and give your new fiancé some much-needed attention.'

'Rubbish. You've had plenty of attention. I still can't believe we're engaged.' And she wiggled her left hand back and forth, the five-carat brilliant-cut solitaire diamond glittering under the light of the bedside lamp.

'Well, Carlos and Juanita believe it. They wanted to throw us a party tomorrow night, but I said no because Sunday is their day off. Instead I'm going to take my wife-to-be out for the day. I've booked lunch for us at the Polo Lounge at the Beverly Hills Hotel, and then we're going to drive down to my favourite country club and I'm going to start teaching you how to play golf.'

Kate grimaced. 'That'll be a disaster. I'm not very sporty, you know.'

'With *your* build? You'll be a natural.'

And, surprisingly, she was.

Kate smiled during the whole drive home. They hadn't gone in the limousine, instead taking Blake's Porsche.

'I *was* good, wasn't I?' Kate said smugly as they walked hand in hand up the steps into the house.

'You sure were. *Too* good. In no time you'll be beating me. Well, perhaps not. But you could probably beat Byron.'

'Darling Byron. He seemed genuinely happy for us over the phone, didn't he? And not at all shocked.'

'Men like Byron never get shocked. Not like mothers.'

Kate was taken aback. 'You told your *mother*?'

'Hell, no. That can wait until after we're safely married. Same with yours. Then they can't spoil anything, can they? Not once we're a *fait accompli*.'

Kate flashed him a questioning glance. 'How long do you think it will take me to get a job?'

'No time at all once your visa comes through.'

'I can't wait.'

'We don't *have* to wait, you know. We could fill in the marriage licence form online tonight and be in Vegas for a wedding tomorrow. What do you say?'

Kate shook her head. 'No. Let's not be silly. Let's wait. Do you want coffee?'

'Yes, but I need to go to the bathroom first. Be back in a jiff.'

Kate put on the coffee machine. after which she toddled off to the nearby guest powder room. When she returned to the kitchen Blake was there, humming as he took down two mugs.

'You know, I rather like the idea of a Vegas wedding,' Kate told him. 'Provided I have a proper wedding dress and you wear a tux. We have to have decent photos to show our children.'

'Children!' Blake exclaimed, having not thought of their having children until that moment.

'Well, of course. Don't you *want* children?'

Blake considered the idea, and then decided he did. Kate would make a wonderful mother. He wasn't so sure about his own fathering capabilities, but he would give it his best shot—like he did with everything he attempted in life.

'Yes, I'd like children. Though I don't want a big family. Two would be enough. Though perhaps one would be better,' he added drily. 'No sibling rivalry then.'

'True. Okay, we'll settle on one until we see how the land lies. Of course I have to warn you that I might change my mind and eventually want six.'

Blake laughed, then turned and drew her into his arms. 'That's a woman's privilege, I guess. Though you're not to change your mind about marrying me.'

'As if I would.'

'Tell me again that you love me,' Blake urged, and pulled her even closer.

'I love you, Blake Randall,' she said, her eyes going smoky.

'And I love *you*, Kate Holiday.'

'Perhaps you should show me how much,' she suggested saucily.

'What about the coffee?'

'It isn't going anywhere.'

Blake smiled, then bent his mouth to hers.

EPILOGUE

Four and a half years later...

KATE SAT AT her dressing table, putting the finishing touches to her make-up and doing her best to keep her nerves under control. Tonight was a big night for her. And for Blake. It was the premiere of the movie Blake had once promised to write especially for her—a romantic drama, with Kate as the heroine and not a nasty line in the whole script.

Which had come as a huge relief!

Up until now Kate hadn't done any movies at all, concentrating on the television series which had been the first job offered to her, and which had gone on to be a huge success. She had already done several seasons, with more to come.

It was part of what was called the *domestic noir* genre, and Kate's character was a black widow type who was wickedly amoral, going through a new husband each season—one murdered, one dead of natural causes and the rest divorced—whilst having countless affairs on the side.

According to the producer, she'd been chosen for the part for two reasons. She was a total unknown and she didn't look the *femme fatale* type, which added an ironic edge to her actions and made her character compellingly fascinating to watch, making the audience wonder *What next?* all the time.

Of course her character—Amanda—only ever married rich men, and she was always dressed to kill. And when Kate had fallen pregnant for real, towards the end of the first season, the writers had just written a pregnancy into the second season—though of course they'd made sure

Amanda's new husband wasn't the father. More drama that way.

The show was called *The Career Wife*, and it had already won several awards.

'When can I start wearing make-up, Mummy?'

Kate smiled at her daughter in the dressing table mirror. Charlotte—already nicknamed Charlie by Blake—was lying face down on the nearby bed, with her pretty face propped in cupped hands. She'd only turned three a few months ago, yet she seemed so much older. Though thankfully not too spoiled. Her English nanny had seen to that. And so had Juanita, who loved Charlotte dearly but refused to let her act like some pampered princess.

'Not just yet, darling,' Kate said gently. 'Perhaps when you're—'

'Eighteen,' Blake said firmly as he emerged from the bathroom, looking very suave in his black tuxedo.

'Eighteen?' Charlie squealed, sitting up and scowling at her father. 'Oh, Daddy, don't be so silly. I think seven is a good age—don't you, Mummy?'

'Er...' Kate didn't know what to say.

'Over my dead body,' Blake growled. 'Thirteen, my girl. And that's my final word!'

Kate smiled, noting how smug their daughter was looking, though she tried to hide it.

She even came up with a sulky pout. 'You *are* a meanie sometimes, Daddy.' But, having said that, she added sweetly, 'But a very *handsome* meanie.'

He laughed. 'Oh, go on—get out of here, you little minx. Your mother and I have things to talk about.'

Charlotte scrambled off the bed and ran out of the room.

'You *do* look handsome,' Kate said as she stood up and headed for her walk-in wardrobe.

Blake's hand shot out to grab her as she walked by, spinning her round into his arms.

'No, don't!' Kate squawked before he could kiss her. 'You'll ruin my make-up.'

'Bloody make-up,' he grumbled, but let her go. 'Wait 'til I get you home later,' he threw after her.

She smiled over her shoulder. 'Promises, promises...'

Kate was still smiling as she reached for her outfit. It wasn't a typical glamorous gown of the kind that most actresses wore to premieres and award nights. It was much simpler. Some would say conservative. It was a long cream crêpe skirt with a matching jacket, nipped in at the waist and then reaching down past her hips, giving her slim figure an hourglass shape. But Kate did add a touch of Hollywood glamour with a star-shaped diamond brooch and matching drop earrings, shown to advantage with her hair elegantly up.

'You look utterly gorgeous,' Blake said. 'I love that outfit. Where did you get it?'

'I had it made especially. I didn't want to wear anything like I wear on my TV show. I wanted to look classier than that.'

'Well, you certainly do. But sexy at the same time. Sometimes less is more.'

'No more compliments or I might let you kiss me.'

When he came forward with that look in his eyes she laughingly warded him off, snatched up her clutch purse and hurried towards the door.

Blake sighed and hurried after her.

'Thank you so much for minding Charlie for us tonight, Juanita,' Kate said.

Blake had give Charlotte's nanny two tickets to the premiere, and she was coming with a fellow nanny whom she'd met in a local park and who had become her best friend. Juanita and Carlos had already seen the movie, at an early screening which Blake had organised to get audience reaction. They'd loved it—and so had everyone else.

Kate still felt horribly nervous, her mouth dry and her heart racing. It was her first movie, after all. And what made her even more nervous was the fact that her parents and Blake's parents were going to be there, Blake having generously paid for the four of them to stay for a few nights in one of the hideously expensive bungalows at the Beverly Hills Hotel, only a short walk from the theatre.

'Money well spent,' he'd declared when she'd protested at the expense. 'You don't honestly think I'm going to have them all staying *here*, do you? Heaven forbid!' And he'd literally shuddered.

Both sets of parents had eventually come to terms with Blake and Kate eloping to Vegas, but none of them had exactly been happy at the time. Kate could still remember the dire warnings which had come from her mother.

'It won't last, you know. Still, I suppose you can always get a divorce and come home...'

Blake's parents had been equally negative in their prognostications.

'Not *another* actress, Blake. Oh, dear. Some people just don't learn.'

The arrival of Charlotte a little over a year later had certainly helped smooth things over—as had both Kate and Blake's ongoing success. And a visit home to Sydney last Christmas had been a big hit. Charlotte had been at her adorable best and no one had been able to resist her charm.

Even Maddie had fallen in love with her—dear, irrepressible Maddie, whose marriage to Lachlan had ended two years ago after Lachlan had been widely reported on social media as having affairs with every single one of his leading ladies. Though pretending to be heartbroken at the time, Maddie had happily taken a huge settlement— along with the house in Sydney they'd bought together— and promptly got back with Riley the plumber.

Leopards really didn't change their spots, did they?

Lachlan certainly hadn't. But his comeuppance was on the horizon. His career had faltered after his last movie, which had had some not too stellar reviews.

The movie business was a risky business—Kate knew that. And an actor's popularity could disappear overnight.

Such thinking sent a nervous shiver down her spine, made her hands twist together.

'Everything is going to be fine,' Juanita said, and clasped Kate's trembling hands in both of hers. 'You are a great actress. That is a great movie.'

Carlos said much the same on their way to the theatre. But the kind words didn't lessen Kate's escalating anxiety. They were friends, after all. And all those other people who'd come to the pre-screening had been fans of Blake's work. They might not have wanted to tell him the truth: that the movie wasn't great and Kate was simply awful as a romantic heroine as opposed to playing the conniving villain she played in *The Career Wife*!

'Are you all right?' Blake asked her as they pulled up outside the theatre.

Huge crowds had gathered on the sidewalk, along with lots of paparazzi.

Kate refused to load her anxiety onto Blake. No doubt he was feeling a little tense himself.

'No, no. I'm fine,' she said.

'Good—because there's nothing to be nervous about. Byron rang me while you were getting ready. He and Cleo had just watched the copy of the movie I sent him and they were over the moon about it. Said it was going to make us all a small fortune. The only reason they aren't here in person to celebrate is because their son is due in two weeks' time.'

'Yes, I know. But let's not forget Byron and Cleo are biased. They're friends.'

'And very canny investors. Byron doesn't wear blinkers when it comes to money. Trust me when I say you're about to become an even bigger star than you already are.'

'Promise?'

'That's not a promise. That's a fact.' And he leant over and kissed her on the cheek.

Kate's anxiety eased slightly at his confidence, and his love. Somehow she found a smiling face for the photographers, but didn't linger in the foyer, hurrying into the theatre, where she smiled some more at the already seated guests before thankfully sinking into her own seat.

Finally, after considerable delays and endless advertisements, the movie started—by which time Kate thought she was going to be sick. She tried to concentrate but her focus seemed blurred. Suddenly all she cared about was what the audience was feeling and thinking. She had to force herself not to look around and stare at people's faces.

She did sneak a few surreptitious glances at her parents, who were sitting on her left. They seemed wrapped up in the drama, and her mother's mouth was slightly agape. Was that a good sign or a bad sign?

Finally, after what felt like an eternity, the movie ended and the credits started rolling. For a few seconds there was a deathly silence. Kate didn't know what to think. And then, as one, everyone in that theatre stood up and started clapping. Clapping and shouting *Bravo!*

Even Blake seemed surprised. And touched—especially at the sight of his dad, clapping the loudest.

Kate was just stunned, and her eyes filled with tears when her mother turned to her and said, 'Oh, my dear. You were just wonderful. I'm so, *so* proud of you.'

Kate and Blake stood up to more cheers, and Kate turned to the man she knew was responsible for this moment—the man responsible for every happy moment in her life.

Reaching up, she kissed him softly on the mouth and whispered, 'Thank you, my darling. For everything.'

Blake's dark eyes were full of love and admiration as he took her hand and lifted it to his lips. 'No,' he murmured. 'Thank *you*.'

* * * * *

BLACKMAILED
BY THE
GREEK'S VOWS

TARA PAMMI

For all the readers who asked for Valentina's story.

CHAPTER ONE

SHE WAS DRESSED like a...a hooker.

No...not exactly a hooker.

No hooker he knew possessed the class, the style and the innate grace that imbued every one of his wife's movements.

More of a high-class escort.

It took Kairos Constantinou a few seconds to clear the red haze that descended in front of his eyes.

Dios...of all the stunts he had expected his impulsive, fiery wife to pull, it hadn't been this.

When his PI had informed him that he'd located Valentina and that she'd be aboard Kairos's own yacht for the party tonight, he hadn't been surprised.

Valentina had always been the life of the party scene in Milan.

Lively. Sensual. Like a beautiful butterfly that flits from flower to flower. The minute her brother Leandro had pointed her out to Kairos, standing amidst a gaggle of men, Kairos had decided he wanted her.

Three minutes into Leandro introducing them, he'd known she was going to be his wife.

She had been the best possible incentive Leandro could have offered to reel Kairos into the alliance. Kairos would gain entry into the rarefied old-world alliances that her family the Conti dynasty, swam in, and she would get a rich husband.

Not once had he questioned why Leandro had thought he needed to set up his beautiful sister like that.

All Kairos had wanted was the prize that was Valentina Conti.

Except, a week into his marriage, he had realized his wife was anything but a trophy.

She was emotionally fiery, intensely vulnerable and impulsive as hell.

The best example of which was her deserting him nine months ago without so much as a word.

And to find her here among this crowd now.

With instincts he'd honed among the street gangs of Athens, he noted three Russian investors who operated businesses barely this side of legal—the men his friend Max intended to wine and dine—another man who was a model and a friend of Valentina's, and five women to entertain them, not counting Valentina.

Women of the oldest profession known to man. Not streetwalkers, like some of his earliest friends, but undoubtedly from an escort service.

And the most provocatively dressed among them was Valentina in a flimsy gold dress.

The slinky material pooled at her chest to create a low neckline that left her shoulders and her toned arms bare. It pushed up those small breasts that he had touched and kissed and sucked while she writhed under him, like a lover's hands.

So much golden, soft, silky skin... His jaw tightened like a vise as three other men salivated over her.

But it was the smiles she bestowed on the men as she charmed them, those arms flying about in that way of hers while she narrated some escapade in her accented English, full of fire, the way she put a hand on Max's arm and thanked him when he refilled her drink...that was what caused the ice to stiffen his spine.

The wall of detachment that had always been his armor against anything was his only defense.

No, this was only want. Physical want...nothing more.

He still wanted her, desperately, because she was Valentina and even with her explosive tempers and childish tantrums, she had still snuck under his skin.

He needed her as his wife for a few months. And in those few months, he'd work her out of his blood. Out of his life.

If Valentina Conti Constantinou had indulged in some fantasy delusion that her husband Kairos had arrived on the yacht to achieve some sort of romantic reunion between them, he burned the notion to ashes within the first few minutes.

It had been disturbing enough to find that not only had her photographer friend Nikolai, at whose persuasion she had come to the party, manipulated her into wearing the tackiest outfit, but that she was surrounded by women from an escort service *and* men expected to be *entertained* by them.

She'd squared her shoulders, made Nikolai *claim* her for the evening, and had begun to charm the Russians. The one thing she knew how to do. She might have been living on nothing for months but she had class. Years of practice at playing the perfect socialite—well-versed in fashion and politics.

Until Kairos had walked in.

Barely sipping her G&T, she nodded at something Nikolai whispered in her ear, keeping her effusive smile firmly in place. Her throat was raw with the falsely pitched laughs, and her chest hurt at having to play the unruffled socialite the way she had all her life.

Every inch of her rebelled against the calm she had assumed from the moment Kairos had stepped onto the deck. Every cell in her roared to swat away the woman who was even now cozying up to him, far too pleased with herself.

She wanted to announce to the rest of them that he was hers.

But he had never belonged to her.

Her grip shook, clinking the ice in her tumbler.

Tina put her glass down, fighting for control.

Men scrambled around Max for an introduction to Kairos, and the women—hair fluffed, breasts pushed up to spill out of already plunging necklines—it was as if the rough, rugged masculinity of him was an inviting caress to every woman.

Dios mio, the strength of his sheer masculine appeal hit her like a punch now, shaking her up, turning her inside out.

His white shirt stretched tight across his broad shoulders, enhancing his raw, rugged appeal. His expansive chest tapered down to a narrow waist, over leaner hips and then he was all legs. Hard, muscular thighs followed by those runner's calves that had once driven her crazy.

His hair was cut into that short style he preferred. Her fingers twitched, remembering the rough sensation of it, and she fisted them at her side. His gaze flicked down to her hands and then back up her body, slowly, possessively.

Those silvery eyes lingered on the long stretch of her legs, her thighs, noted the short hem of the dress, up to her waist, lingered again over her breasts, moved up her neck and then settled again on her face.

If he had run those hands over her body with that rough urgency that he'd always mastered before he lost control, she couldn't have felt more owned. With one look, he plunged her into that state of mindless longing, that state of anticipation he had become used to expecting from her.

Shivering inside her skin, forgetting all the misery he had inflicted on her, Tina lifted her chin in defiance.

He had never liked her to dress provocatively. Had never liked her easy attitude with other men, that almost flirty style of talking that was her nature. They had had more than one row on the subject of her dresses, her hair, her shoes, her style, her attitude and even her body.

One of the blondes she had genuinely liked earlier— Stella of the big boobs and even bigger hips—tapped his arm. A smile curving his thin lips, he sliced his gaze away in clear, decisive dismissal.

Tears scratched up Tina's throat and she hurriedly looked away before someone could see her mortification.

Nine months ago, she'd have slapped the woman's face—she cringed at the memory of doing that to her sister-in-law Sophia, having been induced into a jealous, insecure rage. She'd have screamed and made a spectacle of herself, she'd have let her temper get the better of her and proved to everyone and Kairos how crazy she was about him.

Nine months ago, she'd have let the hot emotions spiraling through her dictate her every word, every move.

Nine months ago, she'd been under the stupid delusion that Kairos had married her because he wanted her, because he felt something for her, even if he didn't put it in words.

But no, he had married her as part of an alliance with her brother Leandro. Even after learning that bitter truth, she could have given her marriage a try.

But Kairos didn't possess a heart. Didn't know what to do with one given into his keeping.

She had humiliated herself, she had prostrated her every thought, every feeling at his feet. And it hadn't been enough.

She hadn't been enough.

* * *

"So you're truly over with him...that glowering husband of yours."

"Si," Tina said automatically. And then wished she hadn't.

When the party began winding down, she had slipped below deck with the excuse of visiting the ladies' room and hidden herself away in the lovely gray-and-blue bedroom, her nerves frayed to the hilt at the constant awareness of Kairos.

It was tiring to play the stoic, unaffected party girl. To stuff away all the longing and hurt and anger into a corner of her heart.

But Nikolai had followed her downstairs.

Although over the last couple of months she'd realized that Nikolai was harmless, he was drunk now. Her brother Luca had taught her long ago never to trust a drunken man.

"A taxi for you," she said to Nikolai, pulling her cell phone out of her clutch.

From the foot of the bed where he made an adorably pretty picture, Nikolai stretched his leg and rubbed his leather boot against her bare calf. "Or we could spend the night here, Tina, *mi amore*. Now that things are truly over between you and the Greek thug—"

Using the tip of her stiletto, Tina poked his calf until he retreated with a very unmasculine squeal.

Her head was pounding. She'd barely drunk any water. Her body and mind were engaged in a boxing match over Kairos. The last thing she needed was Nikolai hitting on her.

"Kairos and I are not divorced. Also, I'm not interested in a relationship," she added for good measure.

"I noticed him tonight, *cara mia*. He spared you not a single glance." A claw against her heart. "As if you were total strangers." A bruise over her chest. "He seemed pretty interested in that whore Stella." Bile in her throat.

Just like a man to use the woman and then call her crude names. Oh, why had she come tonight? *"Per favore,* Nik, don't call her that."

"You called Claudia Vanderbilt much worse for marrying a sixty-year-old man."

Tina cringed, shame and regret washing over her like a cold wave.

She had.

She'd been privileged and pampered and had behaved so badly. She should keep Nikolai in her life. If nothing, he'd keep reminding her what a bitch she'd once been.

While Valentina held up her phone and walked around the bedroom looking for a signal—she'd spend the night here if it meant avoiding seeing Kairos leave with one of the women, not that he'd need to pay for the pleasure—Nikolai had moved closer.

Valentina froze when his hands landed on her hips. She arrested his questing hands. "Please, Nikolai. I would like to keep the single friend I have."

"You have really changed, Tina. Transformed from a poisonous viper to a—" his alcoholic fumes invaded her nostrils while he tilted his head, seemingly in deep thought "—an innocent lamb? A lovely gazelle?"

Christo, the man was deeply drunk if he was calling her innocent.

Before Tina could shove Nikolai's hands away—she really didn't want to plant her knee in his groin like Luca had taught her—his hands were gone. Whether he skidded due to his drunken state or was pushed, Tina would never know. He landed with a soft thump against the bed, slid down it and let out a pathetic moan.

Tina whirled around, her breath hitching.

CHAPTER TWO

Kairos stood against the back door, not a single hair out of place.

There was that stillness around him again, a stillness that seemed to contain passion and violence and emotion.

And yet nothing.

Emotions surged through her, like a wave cresting. But just like a wave broken by the strongest dam, Kairos had come pretty close to breaking her.

Ignoring the fact that her dress climbed up her thighs and she was probably flashing her thong at the inebriated Nikolai, she went to her knees next to him, sliding her fingers through his gelled hair.

Nikolai's hot, alcohol-laden breath fluttered over the expanse of her chest. But it was the silver gaze drilling holes into her back that pebbled goose bumps over her skin.

A sound like a swallowed curse emanated from behind her. She ignored it, just as she tried to ignore her pounding heart.

"What are you doing?"

It had been nine months since she'd seen him. Nine months since he'd spoken to her. The hope that he would come after her had died after the first month. She swallowed to keep her voice steady. "Checking for a bump."

"Why?"

She snorted. "Because he's my friend and I care what happens to him."

Tina stared down at Nikolai's picture-pretty face and sighed. He *was* her friend.

He had gotten her the entry-level job in a fashion agency when she had returned to Milan from Paris, her tail tucked between her legs and ready to admit defeat, and found her a place with four other girls in a tiny one-bedroom hovel.

Not out of the generosity of his heart, but because he'd wanted to see her humiliated, wanted to enjoy how she'd come down in the world. Maybe even to get into her pants.

Whatever his motivations, Nikolai was the only one who'd helped her out, the only one who hadn't laughed at her pathetic attempts.

Unlike the man behind her, whose mocking laugh even now pinged over her nerves. "You have no friends. At least not true ones. Shallow women flock to you for approval of their clothes and shoes. Men flock to you because they…"

Truth—every word was truth. Humiliating, wretched truth.

But it hurt. Like something heavy was pressing down on her chest. "Don't hold back now, Kairos," she said, smarting at the stinging behind her eyes.

"Because they assume that you'll be wild and fiery in bed. That you will bring all that passion and lack of self-control and that volatility to sex. Once your *friend* here gets what he wants, he will be through with you."

If she'd had any doubt what he thought of her, he'd just decimated it.

She had fallen in love with a man who thought she was good for sex and nothing else.

A need to claw back pounded through her. "I'm shallow and vapid, *si,* but what you see is what you get. I don't make false promises, Kairos."

The silence reverberated with his shock. "I've never made a promise to you that I didn't keep. I promised your brother to keep you in style when I agreed to marry you and I did. I promised you on the night of our engagement that I would show you pleasure unlike anything you've ever known and I believe I kept that promise."

I never said I loved you.

His unsaid statement hung in the air.

No…he hadn't said it. Not once.

It had all been her.

Stupid, naive Valentina building castles of love around this hard man.

She found no bump on Nikolai's thick skull and sighed with relief. His head lolling onto her chest, he fell asleep with an undignified snore. She'd have gagged at the sweat from Nikolai's flushed head trickling down her meager cleavage if all her reactions weren't attuned to the man behind her.

The small hairs on her neck stood up before Kairos spoke. "Leave him alone."

Ignoring him, she rose to her feet, and planted her hands under Nikolai's arms.

"Move, Valentina."

Before she could blink, Kairos hefted Nikolai up onto his shoulders and raised a brow at her.

He had carried her like that once, the hard muscles of his shoulders digging into her belly, his big hands wrapped around her upper thighs, after she had jumped into the pool at a business retreat in front of his colleagues and their wives because he'd ignored her all weekend.

He'd stripped her and thrown her into the cold shower, rage simmering in his eyes. And when he'd extracted her from the shower and rubbed her down, all that rage had converted into passion.

She'd been self-destructive just to get a rise out of him.

She looked away from the memory of that night in his eyes.

Masculine arrogance filled his eyes. "Now that the poor fool has served his purpose, shall I throw him overboard?"

"His purpose?"

"You used him to make me jealous—laughing at his jokes, dancing with him, touching him, to rile my temper. It is done, so you don't need him anymore."

"I told you, Nik is my friend." She jerked her gaze to his face and flushed. "And I did nothing tonight with you on my mind. My world doesn't revolve around you, Kairos. Not anymore." She wouldn't ask whether his temper was riled.

She wouldn't.

With a shrug, he dumped Nikolai on the bed like a sack of potatoes.

Nik's soft snores punctured the silence. If she weren't so caught up in the confusing cascade of emotions Kairos evoked, the whole thing would have been hilarious.

But nothing could cut through her awareness of six feet four inches of pure muscle and utter masculinity. She pressed her fingers to her temple. "Please leave now."

"Enough, Valentina. You've got my attention now. Tell me, did you really sign up with the escort service or was that just a dramatic touch to push me over the edge?"

"Are you asking me if I've been prostituting myself all these months?" She was proud of how steady she sounded while her heart thundered away in her chest.

"I thought perhaps no first. But knowing you and your vicious tendencies, who knows how far you went to shock me, to teach me a lesson, to bring me to heel?"

She walked to the door and held it for Kairos. "Get out."

He leaned against the foot of the bed, dwarfing the room with his presence. "You're not staying here with him."

She folded her hands and tilted her head. The sheer

breadth of his shoulders sucked the air from the room. "I've been doing *what* and *who* I want since the day I left you nine months ago, since I realized what a joke our marriage is. So it's a little late to play the possessive husband."

Hadn't she promised herself that she'd never stoop to provoking him like that again?

She cringed, closed her eyes at the dirty, inflammatory insinuation in her own words.

But she saw the imperceptible lick of fire in his gaze, the tiny flinch of that cruel upper lip. At one time, the little fracture in his control would have been a minor victory to her.

Not anymore.

"It is a good thing then, is it not, Valentina—" the way he said her name sent a curl of longing through her "—that I did not believe all your passionate avowals of love, *ne*?"

Something vibrated in the smooth calmness of his tone. The presence of that anger was a physical slap. Her eyes wide, she stared as he continued, his mouth taking on a cruel tilt.

"No more pathetic displays of your jealousy. No grand declarations of love. No snarling at and slapping every woman I'm friends with. Now we both can work with each other on the same footing."

Dios, she'd always been a melodramatic fool. But Kairos, his inability to feel anything, his unwillingness to share a thought, an emotion…it had turned her into much worse. "*Non*, Kairos. No more of that," she agreed tiredly.

She didn't even have cash for a taxi, but if she'd learnt anything in the last nine months of this flailing about she'd been doing in the name of independence, it was that she could survive.

She could survive without designer clothes and shoes, she could survive without the adulation she'd taken as her due as the fashionista that Milan looked up to, she could survive without the Conti villa and the cars and the expensive lifestyle.

She picked up her clutch from the bed, her phone from the floor. "If you won't leave, I will."

He blocked the door with his shoulders. "Not dressed like a cheap hooker, strutting for business at dawn, you're not."

"I don't want—"

"I will throw you over my shoulder and lock you up in the stateroom."

It should have sounded dramatic, emotional. But Kairos didn't do drama. Didn't utter a word he didn't mean. *And if he so much as touched her...*

"Fine. Let's talk." She threw her clutch back on the bed and faced him. "Even better, why don't you call your lawyer and have him bring divorce papers? I'll sign them right now and we won't see each other ever again."

He didn't exactly startle. But again, Tina had the feeling that something in him became alert. She had...surprised him? Shocked him?

What did he think her leaving him had meant?

He stretched out his wrists, undid the cufflinks on his right hand—platinum cufflinks she'd bought him for their three-month anniversary with her brother's credit card—and pushed back the sleeve.

A shiver of anticipation curled around her spine.

He stretched his left hand toward her. Being left-handed, he'd always undone the right cuff link first. But the right hand...his fingers didn't do fine motor skills well. She'd noted it on their wedding night, how they had felt clumsy when he tried to do anything.

For a physically perfect specimen of masculinity, it had been a shock to note that the fingers of his right hand didn't work quite right. When she'd asked if he'd hurt his hand, he'd kissed her instead. The second time she'd asked, he'd just shrugged.

His usual response when he didn't want to talk.

She'd taken his left hand in hers and deftly undone the cufflink on their wedding night. And a thousand times after that.

It was one of a hundred rituals they'd had as man and wife. Such intimacy in a simple action. So much history in an everyday thing.

Tina stared at the blunt, square nails now, her breath ballooning up in her chest; the long fingers sprinkled with hair to the plain platinum band on his ring finger; the rough calluses on his palm because he didn't wear gloves when he lifted weights. It was a strong, powerful hand and yet when he touched her in the most sensitive places, it was capable of such feathery, tender movements.

A sheen of sweat coated every inch of her skin.

Dios, she couldn't bear to touch him.

Without meeting his gaze, she took a few steps away from him. "What do I have to do to make you believe that I'm done with this marriage? That my behavior is not dictated anymore by trying to get you to acknowledge my existence?"

He smirked, noting the distance she'd put between them. "Is that what you did during our marriage?"

She leaned against the opposite wall and shrugged. "I want to talk about the divorce."

"You really want one?"

"*Si.* Whatever we had was not healthy and I don't want to live like that anymore."

"So Leandro enlightened you about the fat settlement you will receive then."

"What?"

"Your brother made sure you would receive a huge chunk of everything I own should we separate. Bloody insistent, if I remember correctly." His shrug highlighted those muscle-packed shoulders. "Maybe Leandro knew how hard you would make it for any man to stay married to you."

"You think that will hurt me? Leandro…" Her voice caught, the gulf she had put between her brothers and her a physical ache. "He practically raised me, he loved me when he could have hated me for our mother deserting him and Luca. And I still cut him out of my life because he thought so little of me that he had to bribe you to marry me. In the grand scheme of things that I've lost and learned, this marriage and anything I get by dissolving it…they mean nothing to me, Kairos."

He was upon her in the blink of an eye. The scent of him—a hint of male sweat and the mild thread of his cologne—hit her first. Awareness pooled low in her belly. He didn't touch her, and yet the heat of his body was a languid caress.

"How will you afford your haute couture and your designer stilettos then?"

"I haven't touched your credit cards in months. I haven't taken a single Euro from Leandro or Luca. Even the clothes I wear belong to Nikolai."

"Ah…" His gaze raked down the length of her body. The edge of cruelty in it stole her breath even as her skin tingled at his perusal. He nodded toward the happily snoring figure behind him on the bed. "Of course, your pimp dresses you now."

"Nikolai is not a pimp and he tricked me into believing tonight was just a party."

"I have to admit, only Valentina Constantinou could make a tacky, slinky dress look stylish and sophisticated.

But that skill is not really helping, is it? Paris chewed you out and threw you back to Milan after a mere two months. Since then, you've been licking the boots of everyone at that fashion magazine. Fetching coffee for those bitchy socialites, when you had once been their queen bee, running errands in the rain for photographers and models that salivated over you for years..." His gaze swept over her in that dismissive way of his. "Have you had enough of reality? Are you ready to return to your life of luxury?"

She wasn't surprised he knew what she'd been up to in the last few months. "I don't care how long it takes, I mean to—"

"Is that why you decided to try your hand at the oldest profession in the world?"

"You're the one who bought me from Leandro, remember? If anyone made me a whore, Kairos, it was you." Every hurt she felt poured out into her words, all her promises to herself to keep it civil forgotten.

"I did not pursue you under false pretenses. I did not take you to bed, hoping that a good performance would bring me closer to the CEO position of the Conti board."

A blaze lit up in his silvery eyes, tight lines fanning around his mouth.

He tugged her and Tina fell onto him with a soft gasp. Hard muscles pushed against her breasts, sending shock waves through her. "Believe me, *pethi mou*, if there is one aspect of our marriage that both of us agree on, it is in bed."

His fingers wrapped around her nape in a possessive hold, a flicker of arousal and something else etched onto his features.

"You're the one who broke our marriage vows, Valentina. You're the one who avowed her love in passionate statements and sensational gestures, *ne*? Again and again. All I wanted was a civil marriage. Then, the fickle, spoilt brat that you are, you ran away because your little fantasy world where you rule as a queen and I fall at your feet crumbled. You leave no note. No message. You tell my security guard you're visiting your damned brothers. I imagined you kidnapped and waited for a ransom note. I imagined your body lying in some morgue because you met with an accident. I imagined one of the women or men you insulted with your cruel words may have been pushed to the limit and wrung your pretty neck."

Heart thundering, Valentina stared.

His fingers dug into her tender flesh with a grip she was sure would leave bruises. She'd never seen him like this, smoldering with a barely banked fire. "Until Leandro took pity on me and informed me that you had simply walked out on me. On our marriage."

Tina sagged against the wall, a strange twisting in her belly. He had been worried about her safety. *Terrified for her.* "I'm… I'm sorry. I didn't think…"

"Too little, too late."

He was right. If nothing else, he deserved an explanation. "I was furious with you and with Leandro. I had just learned that I was not a Conti but a bastard child my mother had with her chauffeur. That you married me as part of a bloody deal. You've had nine months to come after me." The words slipped past her tongue, desperate, pathetic.

And just like that, any emotion she had spied in his eyes was wiped away. He stared at his fingers pressing into her flesh, his other hand kneading her hip.

His eyes widened fractionally before he stepped back. Stopped touching her. "The moment Leandro informed me what you'd done, I stopped thinking of you. I had other matters—*urgent, important* matters—to deal with rather than chase my impulsive brat of a wife through Europe."

A fist to her heart would have been less painful.

But this was good, Tina reassured herself. She'd needed this talk with him. She'd needed to hear these words from Kairos's mouth. Now, she could stop wondering—in the middle of the night, alone in her bed—if she'd made a mistake.

If their marriage deserved another chance.

After tonight, she wouldn't have to see him again. Never hear those hateful words again. "*Bene*. You had important matters and I had enough time to think my decision through. I had nine months to realize what I did on impulse was right. I do not care whether you pay me alimony or not because I would not touch it. I intend to make something out of myself."

"By whoring yourself out to Russian investors? By dressing like a cheap tramp? Admit it, Valentina. You've gotten nowhere in nine months except ending up with that buffoon who wants to get in your pants. You have no talent. No skills. Your connections were the only things of value about you."

"I know that. Believe me, I have learned a lifetime's worth of lessons in these nine months. The only good thing about this is that whatever connections you thought I would bring you as the Conti heiress are now lost."

"Your brothers haven't disowned you."

"I have cut all my connections with them. With that life. I'm of no more use to you."

"Ah...so that is your petty revenge? To deny what I planned to get by cutting yourself off from your brothers temporarily?"

"You give both me and your role in my life too much credit, Kairos. I love my brothers. Every day I spend away from them tears my heart. But it is the price I have to pay to face myself in the mirror."

Finally, it seemed that she was getting through to him.

And still, ruthlessness was etched onto his every feature. "This marriage is not done until I say it is done."

"All I want is a teeny signature on a piece of paper. Ask me to sign away that alimony Leandro set up and I will. I will do anything you ask of me to be released from this marriage. You already wrote me out of your life when you decided not to come after me nine months ago, Kairos. I was nothing but a disappointment to you. So why drag this on? Is it just because your masculine pride is dented? Is it because, once again, I made you lose your rigid self-control?"

"Whether you want it or not, whether you touch it or not, half of what is mine will be yours for years to come. If I'm going to pay through the nose for the mistake of indulging you in your foolish fantasies of everlasting love, for putting up with your temper tantrums, for the pleasure of having you in my bed, I would like three more months of marriage, *agapita*. And maybe, a little more of you for that price tag."

"A little more of me for that price…" Tina whispered, his words gouging through her already battered heart.

Her hand flew at him, outrage filling her every pore.

His lightning-fast reflexes didn't let her slap land. With a gentleness that belied the hard, wiry strength of his body, he held her wrist between them, crowding her body against the wall until it kissed the line of her spine.

Hardness and heat, he was so male. Her five-inch stilettos made up for the height difference between them until she was perfectly molded against him. Muscular thighs straddled hers. His granite chest grazed the tips of her breasts, making her nipples tighten and ache. And against her belly… *Maledizione*, his arousal was lengthening and hardening.

Damp heat uncurled between Tina's thighs. A whimper

flew from her mouth—a needy and desperate plea for more. She clenched her thighs on instinct. "I do not even use my hands or my mouth. Yet you're damp and ready for me, *ne*?"

Breath shallow, she fought for control over her body, over the hunger he lit so easily. "As you said, it's why other men follow me around. I'm hot and uninhibited in bed, *si*? I could always match your sexual appetite and we both know it's insatiable. That I'm like a bitch in heat right now is not a point in your favor. You give good sex, Kairos. It was the one place where I was happy as your wife."

A lick of temper awakened in his silver eyes. "Tell me, Valentina. Do you get hot like this for any other man? For the fool lying in the bed behind us?" He twisted his hips in that way of his.

His erection rubbed against the lips of her sex and she jerked.

Pleasure was a fork in her spine, setting fire along her nerves. She could feel that thick rigidity inside her, could see the tight control etched onto his features as he moved inside her. She craved the softening of his gaze, the few moments of the real Kairos, tender and caring, that she used to glimpse after he found his release.

And she still wanted that man. Like a puppy that had been kicked but still came back for more.

His mouth was at her cheekbone and his stubble chafed her lips. A wet, open kiss at her pulse. "I have other uses for you, wife…along with a few more months in my bed." His hands moved to cup her buttocks and pulled her against his hardness.

His mouth trailed lazily along her jawline, heading for her lips—the depth of her want, the fire along her skin— and she could taste the release in her fevered muscles.

"Admit defeat, Valentina. You can pretend all you want but your best bet is to be a rich man's trophy wife. It is not a bad role for you. Accept your limitations. Adjust your expectations. Just as I did when your brother Luca stood in the way of the Conti board CEO position. I want nothing more from a wife, and who knows? You can maybe even persuade me to give this marriage another try."

He *was angry* she had walked out.

No, not angry, she realized, running shaking hands through her hair.

He was furious with an icy, cold edge to it. Every word and caress of his was meant to provoke her with its cruelty. She'd never seen him like that.

It was more temper than she'd seen of him in all of their relationship so far—and, by God, she'd done every awful thing she could think of to provoke it.

But he wasn't asking her back. He didn't want to give their marriage another chance. He didn't want to give her a chance.

No, all he wanted was a sop to his male ego. All he wanted was to punish her for daring to leave him, for calling him out on his ruthless ambition.

That pain gave her a rope with which to climb out of the sensual haze. To deny herself what she'd never been able to before—his touch.

"Please, Kairos, release me."

The moment the words were out of her mouth, he let her go. Pupils drenched with lust, he stared at her as if he couldn't believe she could put a stop to it.

Shaking but determined to hold herself up, she met his gaze. "What do I have to do to get you to agree to a divorce? To get you to leave me alone?"

He looked taken aback but recovered fast. "Three months as my wife."

"Why? Why do you need me now? Other than because you want to punish me for walking out on you?"

"I have a debt to pay to Theseus."

"The man who brought you home from the streets, the one who adopted you?"

"*Ne.*"

"And for this, you need to have a wife?"

"Yes. His daughter Helena—"

"Is causing trouble between you and him? You want me to take her on? I don't understand how your wife's presence will help..." The words trailed away from her lips as she saw his closed off expression. A mocking laugh rose. "*Non*, I've got it, I think. The daughter wants you and you want to say no without hurting anyone's feelings. How noble of you, Kairos."

His brow cleared, relief dawning in his eyes. "Theseus deserves nothing less from me."

The depth of his sincerity shook Tina. She had never seen Kairos feel that strongly about anyone or anything. Except wealth and power and the amassing of it.

"This is the only way you get your divorce, Valentina."

"You cannot drag me back into that life against my will."

"But I can fight the divorce proceedings. Make your life into the media circus that you suddenly appear to abhor. And even worse, one wrong word or move from me toward you will bring forth your brothers' fury upon me and their interference in your life...if you truly intend to make it on your own, that would be hell."

Tina stared at him, amazed despite the anger pouring through her. He was calling her bluff about all this—the new direction she wanted to take in life.

She was damned if she answered it, damned if she didn't. She didn't want to spend another moment with him and yet he had left her no choice.

She sighed. "You will release me when things are clarified?"

"When things are clarified to *my* satisfaction, yes. No sooner. I'm warning you, Valentina, I want a perfect wife. No tantrums. No reckless escapades. You could even leave with the fat settlement the divorce will award you with the satisfaction that you've truly earned it. A novel feeling, I assure you."

"And if I sleep with you to earn it, you will have truly made me a whore, *si*, Kairos? Will your dented ego be repaired then? Because, hear me out, Kairos. My body might be willing but my heart is not."

The growl he swallowed down filled her with vicious satisfaction.

Valentina smiled for the first time in nine months.

Now all she'd have to do was convince herself of what she had told him.

CHAPTER THREE

What do I have to do to get you to leave me alone?

She truly wanted out of their marriage.

The realization moved through Kairos like an earth-quake as he stared down at her sleeping form in the rear cabin of his private jet.

He'd only thought of how he would punish her when he found her. How good she would feel under him once again. How he would provoke her temper until she came at him all explosive fury and uncontained passion.

But she'd done nothing of the sort.

Oh, she'd lost control a couple of times and given him back as much as he'd deserved, but that was nothing to the Valentina he had known.

It was as if he was looking at a stranger.

If I sleep with you to earn it, you will have truly made me a whore.

Christos, only she could find such an appalling twist to what he had suggested.

But then since he was blackmailing her into his bed, was it any wonder that she had fought dirty?

He should have been impervious to her passionate, fiery declarations after ten months of living with her and her infamous tempers. Should have been unaffected by the sounds of her moans, the slide of her lithe body against his when he touched her.

That he wasn't, disconcerted him on a level he didn't understand.

His physical need for her and only her, and the fact that neither the sweet Stella nor any of the women who had readily offered him a place in their bed in the nine months since Valentina had walked out on him had remotely even tempted him, he could still somehow explain.

Like she had so crudely pointed out, Valentina was explosive in bed. He had been more than surprised when he'd discovered her virginity on their wedding night.

Valentina, as he'd quickly learned to his tremendous satisfaction, was an utterly sensual creature. Whatever he had taught her in bed, she'd not only taken to it enthusiastically but her innate curiosity for his body, her relentless eagerness to return every pleasure he had shown her. That she had remained untouched had been a shock.

She possessed a quick temper and an even quicker sexual trigger, and *Christos*, he'd reveled in making her explode to his slightest caresses. Tender and drawn-out, or explosive and fast, her passion had matched his own.

No man could be blamed for becoming obsessed like he had.

He needed Valentina with a fervor he didn't care or need to understand, and he would have her.

But the hurt in her eyes as he had dealt one cruel statement after the other, hoping to get her temper to rise, festered like an unhealed wound in the hours since he'd arranged for them to travel to Greece.

He should be grateful that the blinders were torn from her eyes. That she would not look at him anymore as if he were her knight in shining armor. Or the man who'd fulfilled all her romantic fantasies.

Whether they divorced or not, it was a good thing she had finally learned the truth.

He had no familiarity or place in his life for tender feelings or love. They demanded a price he couldn't afford, however wealthy he had become.

But the sight of her huge brown eyes as he'd torn her into shreds with his words wouldn't leave him alone. He hadn't pulled any of his punches and she had taken them as if they were her due.

He didn't believe for a second that Valentina would stick to her chosen path or that she had what it took to succeed in her career.

She was just too undisciplined, too impulsive, too spoilt for the hard work it entailed. But still, for the first time in his life, Kairos felt as if he had stood up to the title that had haunted him all his childhood.

Bastard.

He was a bastard.

For even knowing that she would end up in his bed, even acknowledging that something intrinsic had changed in Valentina and he was the one who had caused it, knowing that he would hurt her, he still couldn't walk away from her.

Neither would he keep her.

For all that she'd professed her love for him, she had proved that she was like the rest—using love as manipulation, and then breaking her word.

No one was important enough for him to risk that, to forget the lesson he had already learned.

Love was nothing but a game.

For all your avowals, you left. You proved how little your words mean.

The words and the sentiment behind them stung Tina as she lathered up in the small shower cubicle.

Had there been an infinitesimal thread of complaint in

Kairos's tone? Was she just reading too much when there was nothing again?

She had, at every available moment and opportunity, prostrated her feelings at his feet. Made a spectacle of herself.

How dare he think she'd given in too easily?

She wrapped a towel around herself, and stepped out.

Designer-label bags in every size and color covered the bed.

Mothership to Valentina... Calling now.

A soft sigh emerged from her lips.

She lasted nineteen seconds before she pulled the soft tissue out of the first bag and discovered a black cold-shoulder blouse and white capri pants. More casual pants and blouses. She counted four dresses ranging from a cocktail dress to a pale pink ball gown that would show off her tan beautifully.

Small, silky tissue bags of underwear and everything in her size. Makeup bags with her favorite lipsticks and perfumes with designer labels.

The bras were from the designer label she loved and sinfully expensive—two of them she had discovered recently would pay for her food for a month. And of the push-up kind she'd always preferred to make the most of her nonexistent boobage.

Sliding to the bed in her towel, Tina fingered the butter-soft cushioning of a push-up bra. In some throwaway remark he had made once when they'd watched an old Hollywood movie, she'd realized her husband had a thing for big breasts.

And hers were meager at best. So, like an idiot female, she'd gone on a rampage with lingerie, bras especially, and in the end there had been more cushioning and padding in her bra than flesh on her body.

One evening, she'd gone with an extreme push-up bra to a party—her boobs, exposed by a low neckline, almost kissing her chin and barely covering her nipples. Kairos had blown his top and called her entire outfit trampy—the first time in their marriage that he'd lost it.

He'd said, in clipped tones, that her need for every man's attention made her the shallowest woman he'd ever met. And then he'd walked out for the night.

She frowned.

For all his smarts, hadn't Kairos realized that she'd gone from one outrageous outfit to the next to get a rise out of him? To make up for what she thought she was lacking, for him? That from the moment Leandro had introduced her to him, she hadn't thought of another man ever again?

Why did she have to go to such extremes to please him?

Why was she even now, making such a big deal about the fact that he'd remembered the size of her underwear, of all things?

Kairos had a mind like a super computer, remembering every small detail that went in. It had no significance.

"A starved dog would look at meat scraps with less hunger," said a dry voice from the doorway.

Tina stood up and tugged the towel up.

He had also changed—a gray V-necked sweater that hugged his biceps and chest and dark jeans that caressed his muscular thighs. She had to swallow the feminine sigh of appreciation that wanted to come out.

"Old dogs can learn new tricks," she said repressively.

His laughter pervaded the small cabin. Grooves etched in his cheeks, his eyes alight with humor. "I think the saying says the opposite."

"I don't want the clothes."

"No choice. My wife, the fashionista of Milan, can't dress in trashy clothes that better suit a street walker or..."

he picked up the worn-out denim shorts and loose T-shirt that she had put out "…hand-me-downs. Wow, you have really taken this role to heart, *ne*? You would have turned your nose up at these a few months ago."

"I would have, *si*. But it is not a joke, Kairos. Those are clothes that I could afford on what I made."

He threw the shirt carelessly aside. "You have to look the part, Valentina. Believe me, you're going to need the armor."

She frowned at the thoughtful look in his eyes. Armor for what? She'd been so caught up in staying strong against his onslaught she hadn't delved too much into the details. "I want to discuss this after I dress."

A brow raised, Kairos stared at her leisurely. Water drops clinging to her skin should burn and singe for the lazy intensity of his gaze. "Still so modest, Valentina? I have seen, touched, licked, sucked every part of you, *ne*?"

She glared at him. "I was willing then. Not anymore."

"But I can see you if I close my eyes." He closed his eyes, leaning against the wall. A wicked smile dancing around his lips. "The mole on the curve of your right buttock. The mark you have on your knee from skinning it. The silky folds of—"

She pressed her palm to his mouth and whispered, "Stop, please."

Unholy humor glinted in his silver eyes. "That's not all. I have the sounds you make, the way you thrust your hips up when I'm deep inside you, I have them all in my head." He tapped his temple, his nostrils flaring. "They're the first things I recall in the morning when I wake up with—"

She drew her hand back, burned. But even beneath the sensual web around them, it was the humor in his eyes that threw her. "You're shameless."

His eyes followed a drop of water from her neck to the

tight cinch of her towel. A devilish smile glinted around his mouth. "You know how I get in the morning, *ne*? You left me with no recourse." He pulled up her left hand and frowned. "Where are your rings?"

"In my bag."

With purposeful movements, he looked through her bag. Stalking back to her, he pushed the rings on her finger. Another sleek box appeared from somewhere.

Her heart thundered as he pulled out a simple gold chain with a diamond pendant.

The pendant was a thumbnail sized V in delicately twisted platinum and gold with tiny diamonds lining up the branches. She had seen it at a jewelry store once—on one rare occasion when they'd been out shopping together to buy a gift for her niece Izzie. Buying it with her credit card—against Kairos's dictate that she stop spending Leandro's money—would have been easy.

But already…something had changed in her back then.

Clothes and shoes and jewelry had begun to lose their allure. Because none of those, she had realized, made a difference in how her reserved husband saw her.

And yet he'd noticed her watching it.

She met his eyes over the fragile chain dangling in his fingers. "I… I have a lot of funky jewelry to dress the part. I can't stand the thought of fake gifts."

"I bought it for you. We might as well use it." With one hand, he pushed the swathe of her hair aside, then his hands were gentle around her neck. His warm breath feathered over her face, his arms a languorous weight over her shoulders. "Throw it away after we're done with this for all I care."

The pendant was cold against her bare skin. Tina licked her lips, warmth pooling in her chest. "When?"

His fingers lingered over the nape of her neck, straightening the chain, but still her heart went thud against her ribcage. "When what?"

"When did you buy it?"

"When you were waiting outside, in the car. I meant to give it to you on—" he laughed, and yet beneath the mockery Tina sensed self-deprecation, even anger "—the ten-month anniversary of our wedding. I feel like a fool even saying that."

"Then why did you buy it?" Her tummy rolled at his proximity, at the revelation. "You called me a sentimental little fool when I bought you gifts on that date. A child who celebrates every little thing."

"Maybe you finally wore me down. But then you left two days after that shopping trip, so maybe it's a good thing I didn't change too much for you, *ne*?" he said, looking away.

This time, there was no doubt that he was angry, even bitter that she had left him. That she had given up on their marriage. She must have changed him a little if he had truly thought of giving her a gift on that date. Maybe just a little.

But still, he hadn't acted on that anger. He had simply written her off, like a bad asset. He had only come for her when he decided he needed her. She had to remember that.

"The clothes, the shoes, everything will stay." He walked away, a faint tension radiating from him. "I want the classy, stylish Valentina. The adoring, loving wife."

"I can't force the last part."

"Pretend then. For months, you did just that anyway. Do you need anything else?"

"Underwear. Bras, to be exact," she said the first thing that came to her lips while her mind whirled. Had he cared about her just a little? Had he bought her the necklace to make her happy?

Did his humiliating proposal that she could persuade him to try again hold a hint of what he wanted?

"The ones I have are plain cotton and will show—"

"Things I'd rather not have anyone but me see in those slinky dresses," he finished for her, possessiveness ringing in his tone. He frowned and looked at the reams of new bras. "I had my PA order those from the boutique you spend a fortune in."

She sighed—she really did like how big those push-up bras made her breasts look. No, what she liked was that they had made her feel like he would like her more. But no more of her crazy shenanigans. "Those don't...fit anymore."

His gaze moved to her chest like a laser beam. The wicked devil! "I can't tell from under that towel."

She picked up a pen and notepad and wrote down her size.

"No underwire, no padding, no lifting. All you're going to get is my tiny boobs as nature made them," she muttered to herself.

He laughed, half choking on it. She jerked her head up, realizing too late he'd been standing far too close. He stared at her as if she had grown two horns. "What?"

She pasted a fake smile to her lips. "My sanity returned nine months ago. I can't wait for the next three months to be over."

He scowled. Didn't even bother to hide it.

"Fortunately, I know you well enough not to trust a word out of your lovely mouth," said the blasted man.

If a shiver claimed her spine, she didn't let it show on her face.

A few more months in my bed...

A rich man's trophy wife...

Kairos would never see her as anything else.

She'd seen how he behaved with her sister-in-law Sophia, one of his oldest friends. A woman he'd proposed to before he'd decided on Tina herself.

Sophia was the smartest woman Tina knew. And she commanded Kairos's respect. Even Leandro's wife Alexis had Kairos's regard.

Both women, so different, and yet they had one thing in common that she did not have.

They were successful in their own right—strong, independent women who were more than enough to take on her powerful brothers Leandro and Luca.

That was what Tina wanted to be. That was what she wanted to see in his eyes when he looked at her.

If he was going to tease and torment her for three months, then she would earn his respect, his regard. She was Valentina Conti Constantinou and she would have her own form of revenge by succeeding beyond his wildest dreams.

She would rub his face in what he was giving up. And only then, only when she had brought him to his knees, would Valentina walk away. Even her Machiavellian grandfather Antonio, who'd only ever accepted her under pressure from Leandro, couldn't deny that she was any less of a scheming Conti now.

She turned around and faced Kairos. "I have been thinking of our deal since last night." Steady, flat, her voice cooperated. "I have a few conditions."

His nostrils flared. "You don't get to negotiate."

That she had shocked him snapped her spine into place.

She let a smile curve her mouth. She hadn't been born a Conti, but her proud, powerful brothers had raised her to be one. "I might be vain and vapid but I'm not *stupido*, Kairos. You came to me last night because you need me. So, *si*, I will negotiate and you will listen."

"What are your conditions?"

"You were right about the industry being a bitch. I didn't get anywhere in nine months. I want word spread that we're back together again. I want the names and numbers of everyone you do business with. And I want your backing."

"I'm a respected businessman, Valentina. I will not give the weight of my name to any harebrained scheme of yours that is sure to embarrass me and sink in a few months. If you want my money, you have to wait until the divorce is final to get your hands on it."

"*Non!* Not money. I want access to your rich friends and their wives. Or their mistresses. I don't care how you put it forward. Tell them your juvenile, impulsive bratty wife is putting together a shoot and you're indulging her. Tell them it's the way I'm whiling away my useless life. Tell them it's your way of indulging my tantrums. I don't care what you tell them. I need to put together a portfolio and a shoot. I need to get word of mouth going that I'm offering my services as a personal stylist to anyone who's got reputation, status and money."

"A personal stylist?"

"*Si.*" She raised her hand, cutting him off. "If you're going to use me, Kairos, I will use you, too. At least, we're finally speaking the same language."

"And what language is that, Valentina?"

"The language of transactions. You never do anything without some advantage to yourself. Our marriage has taught me one useful thing at least."

"You're playing a dangerous game, *pethi mou,* hurling accusations at me. You can only push me so far."

"I know you'll find it hard to believe, but I'm not doing anything to provoke you, Kairos. For the first time in my life, I'm thinking with my head. I've looked past the surface and not liked what I see in myself.

You have made me face reality. And for that, I shall always be grateful to you."

"You want a divorce because you're grateful to me?" The

stony mask of his face belied how angry he was with her again. No, not anger. But he was affected by her decision.

"Just because I've realized what was wrong with me doesn't mean you were right, does it? I will never give you power over me again."

For all her brazen confidence, she'd never stripped before him, because she had thought her body imperfect, not made to his specifications and preferences.

Or maybe because she had always wanted to be perfect to please him—perfect straight hair, perfect dress, perfect posture.

It had got her exactly nowhere with him.

Without waiting for his response, her breath suspended in her throat, she picked some underwear. Her back to him, she dropped the towel. The soft exhale behind her pulled her nerves taut. Somehow, she managed to pull her panties up the right way and hooked her bra on.

The intensity of his gaze on her body burned over her skin, as if he was stroking it with those clever fingers. But she was determined to see this through, to prove to him that he wouldn't always have the upper hand.

With barely a glance in his direction, she pulled on a pair of capri pants and a white silk top.

And then, head held high, she walked out to the main cabin, her heart a deafening roar in her chest.

She was tweaking the tiger's tail, true. But she had to do this. She had to prove to him that she was made of stronger stuff. And then, when the three months were up, she would have his respect and then she would walk away.

CHAPTER FOUR

THEY ARRIVED AT a large estate on the island of Mykonos around six in the evening in a tinted limo.

A grove of dark green olive trees beckoned as the car drove up the curving driveway.

Lush green surrounded the whitewashed villa nestled in a picturesque setting. Blue beaches stretched as far as the eye could see.

But Tina barely took it in for her gaze stuck to the myriad expressions crossing her husband's usually expressionless face.

His chest had risen and fallen with a deep breath at the first sight of the villa. His jaw clenched tight at the sight of a green sports model Beetle. Tenderness and ache and grim determination flashed across his silver eyes at the sight of the three people—an older man and woman and a young woman—waiting at the top of the steps.

Tina felt as if she was standing in a minefield. She'd never seen Kairos show so much emotion, much less such varying reactions.

"Kairos?" she said softly, loath to disturb the glimpse she was getting into a man she'd thought felt nothing, held nothing sacred.

His gaze turned to her from the opposite seat. And in the seconds it took him to focus on her, his expression became blank, as easily as if he'd donned a mask, completely shutting her out yet again.

But she couldn't scream or fight him for his usual response. "What exactly does this debt to Theseus entail, Kairos?"

Hesitation like she'd never seen flickered across his face. "There are some duties I need to fulfill. That's all you need to know."

Curiosity ate through Tina even as she told herself to stay out of it.

In ten months of marriage, all she'd learned about him was that he was an orphan who had grown up on the streets of Athens. That he had had a mentor who had given him an education. That was it, no more.

Getting her husband to talk about himself, his past, or his emotions was like getting blood out of stone. She'd honestly never met a man who talked so little.

Something about the tension wreathed in his face made her say, "You're not going to murder someone and ask me to lie for you in court, are you?"

His mouth twitched. "So you haven't stopped watching American soap operas."

"Sell me to land a business deal like that guy did in *Indecent Proposal*?"

He laughed. The warm sound enveloped her in the dark interior.

"*Oxhi*... No," he clarified. "Even if I wanted to, I don't think there's a man living who'd know how to handle you, Valentina."

"I know *oxhi* means no," she said, trying to think of his statement as a compliment. "I plan to say it quite a lot to you over the next few months. In English, Italian *and* Greek," she added for good measure.

Memories permeated the air between them, bringing a smile to her own lips.

For the first month of their marriage, they had had hilarious moments, teaching each other Italian and Greek. But they had both settled on English in the end.

Except when he made love to her. Then he slipped into Greek—guttural, pithy words that even now sent a shiver through her insides. Words she'd never hear again.

No, words she didn't want to hear, she clarified for herself.

"Cold?" he asked, his head dipping down toward her as she exited the car.

She shook her head but he draped a muscled arm around her shoulders, pulling her flush against his side. A clamor of sensation rose inside her. But still, she was aware of a pair of eyes drilling holes into her.

The younger woman, she knew instinctually.

A sliver of apprehension clamped her spine. "Kairos, this feels—"

He cut her off with the press of his lips.

It began as a soft nuzzle. A tender hold of her jaw. A warning to play along in his eyes. Barely a slide of his body against hers.

A show. He was putting on a show. For that woman, Helena.

And yet, as their lips met, as her chest grazed his, as his hand descended to her hip to keep her steady, everything changed.

Nine months of deprivation came pouring out. Desire rose—swift and spiraling.

Heat and pleasure radiated from where their lips grazed and pressed. Air left her lungs. Her knees wobbled and she clutched his arm. A whimper fell from her mouth when he licked the seam of her lips.

He cursed against her lips and Tina instantly opened up. The masterful glide of his tongue against hers made her moan and press harder into his hard body. Her hands crawled to the nape of his neck, her fingers pushing into his rough hair.

The world around them dissolved. Colors burned behind her eyelids, desire making her blood heavy. She could feel the defined contours of his body digging into hers. Images and sensations from memory drowned the little thread of her will: the cradle of his hard hips bearing her down into the mattress; his rock-hard thighs pushing against the soft flesh of hers; the utterly masculine grunt at the back of his throat when she dug her nails into his back.

Heat bloomed low in her belly as he swept over every inch of her mouth with glorious, knowing strokes. No tenderness. No holding back.

Purely carnal, he thrust in and out of her mouth with his tongue.

Pockets of heat erupted all over her, her clothes caging the sensations against her hot skin.

One hand around her neck and one encircling her hip, he held her the way he needed for his onslaught, only letting her come up for air briefly before he claimed her mouth again. He bit her lower lip with such aggressive possession that she moaned. Pleasure and pain wound around her senses.

Instantly he gentled the kiss, laving the hurt with his tongue.

Softer and slower. Ache upon ache built in her lower belly, spinning and spiraling. Tina whimpered against his mouth, craving release. Craving this closeness with him.

"Enough, Kairos! Introduce us to your little plaything."

The venom in that voice, hidden beneath a vein of sweet playfulness, was ice water over Tina's head. She pulled away, heart thundering a million miles an hour in her ears. Her lips stung, her entire body thrummed with need.

"Helena, please be…polite," came another soft voice.

His fingertips trailing lazily against her jawline, his chest rising and falling, Kairos let out a soft growl that reverberated along her trembling body. Tina sensed his shock as her own senses began to clear.

"Nine months..." he whispered against her mouth, his forehead touching hers in uncharacteristic affection. "Even if I hadn't needed you here for this day, *pethi mou*... You and I are not through."

The words were feral. Possessive. And not meant for their audience.

Tina licked her lips and tasted him there. But all he meant was for sex, she reminded her sinking senses. She frowned. "It is just one kiss."

Masculine arrogance etched into every line of his face. "You will come to me, *pethi mou*. I simply shall not allow it to be otherwise." He rubbed her lips with the pad of his thumb. "I might, however, decide not to give you what you want. As a punishment."

She saw it now. He meant to use these months to work her out of his system. He didn't like it that he still wanted her so much. And then, he would walk away.

And if the kiss had been any indication, he was right. She hadn't even mustered a token protest. "This is a game to you, isn't it? Like who will blink first, or who will draw first and shoot the other person?"

"You're the one who always plays games."

Anger and frustration pulsed through her. "No more," she said, tilting her head toward the woman waiting. She rubbed at a piece of nonexistent lint on his shirt, felt the thundering of his heart under her palm. "My days of fighting for you are over, Kairos. That woman and you are welcome to each other."

"I have never loved you, Valentina. When we were married, I could barely stand your theatrics and tantrums. But believe me when I say the only woman I have desired since I met you, the only woman that drives me insane with lust, is you. I want only you, *glykia mou*."

The truth of his declaration reverberated through Tina, leaving her shaking. His own disbelief that he still wanted her, his frustration at his inability to understand it, much less control it, saturated his words.

She barely processed it—four sentences about what he felt or didn't feel from Kairos was like a long speech from any other man—before she felt the younger woman right behind them. Her subtle floral perfume carried to them on the air.

His shoulders tensing, Kairos moved them toward the couple who had come down the stairs but who waited at a discreet distance. His arm remained at her waist in a possessive grip.

"Valentina, this is Theseus Markos and his wife Maria. They are—" his Adam's Apple bobbed as he hesitated "—friends of mine." Tension built in the older couple's faces at his label. Jaw tight, he nodded to the younger woman. "And this is their daughter Helena. My wife, Valentina Constantinou." Possession was imbued in the softly spoken words.

He addressed the greeting mainly to the man.

With a head full of thick gray hair, Theseus looked to be in his sixties. He had a heavy, beefy build but even in the afternoon sun there was an unhealthy pallor to his skin. As if he had spent the last few months away from it.

Tina shook his hand, which was warm beneath her fingers. "We have been very curious about you, Valentina," he said genuinely, the wariness melting from his gaze. Unlike Kairos, his accent was thick. "Welcome to our home. We hope you are not angry with us for taking your husband away from you for so long. Kairos has been an immense help here."

"Of course I'm not," Tina said as if she knew all about it.

This was her chance to dig in and ask questions. True to her self-centered mindset, she had simply assumed that Kairos had been away because he hadn't cared about her fleeing their marriage.

But knowing that he had been here in Greece where his presence was needed and appreciated so much, changed her view.

Maria Markos was more subdued in her welcome, though no less honest. She seemed...anxious and distracted.

Tina thanked them for their welcome.

Only then did she allow herself to look at the woman standing at the periphery. She was a striking contrast to her parents—in both health and attitude. And older than Kairos's twenty-nine.

Thick, wavy black hair was expertly styled around contrastingly waif-like features. A pale yellow sleeveless dress hugged every inch of her big breasts and tiny waist, and fell to above her knees. Familiar with the latest fashions, Valentina instantly noted the designer of that dress and the three-inch wedge platforms she wore. A simple gold necklace with a big diamond pendant shone at her neck. As did matching diamond studs at her ears.

She was short and voluptuous, almost overflowing out of her dress.

Instead of meeting Tina's eyes, Helena threw herself at Kairos. Kairos didn't let his displeasure show, but it was there all the same in the tightness of his mouth, in the way he immediately bowed his body so that only their shoulders touched.

She shouldn't have required the evidence after his statement. Yet, something in her calmed to see that he didn't want nor welcome Helena's attention.

Neither did the woman miss it. She still kissed his cheek, and squeezed his biceps, with a long-drawn sigh, as if she were welcoming a long-lost lover home.

Tina looked at Helena's parents and saw their discomfiture at their daughter's unseemly display toward Kairos in front of his wife. She cringed.

Hadn't she behaved just like Helena at one time?

Becoming jealous and irrational every time Kairos had spent one-on-one time with another woman? Hadn't she tried to stake her claim over him—just as Helena had just done—in a party full of guests, because she'd been insecure and impulsive?

Dear lord, she'd slapped her now sister-in-law because she'd learned of Kairos's regard for her. Thankfully, Sophia had been kind, seeing Tina's insecurity and had befriended her despite her awful behavior.

The outline of Helena's lipstick on Kairos's cheek called to her now, invoking her rash temper, that possessive urge to show that he belonged to her. And only her.

She trembled from the will it took to control herself.

Fortunately, before she could make a fool of herself, Theseus claimed Kairos's attention and Maria followed them up the stairs.

The silence became fraught as Helena stared at her openly. There was no overt animosity in her stare, yet it was all there.

"Valentina Conti Constantinou," Helena said her name with a flourish, ignoring the hand Tina offered. "Although the Conti is apparently not quite true, *ne*?" She didn't wait for Tina to reply. "Poor Kairos. He assumed he was getting the rich Conti heiress, and instead ended up with...a talentless, fortuneless hack. I have heard that even your powerful

Conti brothers have deserted you. I wonder why, after all these months, he brings you back into his life."

It shouldn't have hurt. She'd heard the same from countless mouths, people she'd considered friends, who had assumed the same of her situation and his actions innumerable times.

Hearing that Kairos had ended up with a talentless, poor, bastard of a wife—and that it was *her*—hurt like a piece of glass through her flesh.

Because it was all true. It was what she thought about herself in the worst moments.

She'd never taken a fight lying down but no words came. Like the little girl she'd once been, grieving for her mother, she wished her brothers were here, that she had Leandro's arms to cocoon her in safety, that Luca was at her back bucking her up, that more than anything she had the respect and trust of the man she had once loved so desperately to throw back in the spiteful woman's face.

But she had none of them around her. She had nothing but the truth to face.

Swallowing the deep ache in her belly, she considered the woman staring at her.

Again, she saw the similarities between her and Helena. The insecurity beneath the beauty, the expensive clothes and shoes, the pampered, spoilt attitude that screamed that what she wanted, she would have.

But neither did she feel sympathy for Helena. "Maybe Kairos realized that even without all the trappings of wealth and fortune, he still wants me. He needs me desperately." Just saying the false words was a punch to her middle.

As if she hadn't spewed the most hateful things to her face, Helena looped her arm through Tina's and propelled her forward. "In the end, he will discard you again, you

know. He will choose me. We have too much history between us. It would be better for you if you accept that."

"What history?" The question escaped her mouth before
Tina could bury it forever.

Helena laughed. A gentle, tinkling sound. "He hasn't
told you? Then I can't, either."

With a smile, she wandered off, leaving Tina at the entrance, wondering at the sanity of the woman. And her
own, as well.

What the hell had Kairos dropped her in the midst of?
What was it that he wanted of her? To scratch and scream
at the woman who so boldly touched her husband in front
of her? And if she did, how much would be for pretense
and how much for real?

Unless he did want to win Helena's hand in the end and
was only using Tina to make her jealous, to cement his grip
over Helena? To get a better deal?

Bile crawled up her throat.

No! She wasn't going to torture herself like this.

He was welcome to the woman, if that was what he really wanted.

Her skin prickling, she looked up.

Kairos was standing at the balcony with a wine glass in
his hand, studying her openly while Theseus talked to him
from the side. His shirt was undone at the cuffs and to his
chest, owing to the summer heat. The sun glinted off the
dial of his platinum watch—her six-month anniversary gift
to him, bought with Leandro's money.

That he had kept the watch didn't mean anything. All
the thousand tiny things didn't mean anything when he
hadn't come for her.

It was her mantra.

He raised the wine glass to her in a mocking toast, his
brows raised inquiringly.

She knew what he could see in her face—her longing for him, her distress that he might want Helena, her frustration that he still had this much power over her.

She chased away every expression from her face. Took a deep breath. Even affixed a smile to her mouth.

She pulled her phone from her clutch and texted him, then waited for him to see her text.

The shock in his gaze, the smile fighting to emerge around his mouth...it was a balm to her soul.

Shocking Kairos was her barometer in her fight for independence and if him raising his wineglass to salute her was any indication, she had won this round.

CHAPTER FIVE

Your move, Kairos...keep up your side of the bargain.

LIKE A LOVESICK teenager, Kairos stared at Valentina's text for the millionth time since the night they had arrived. Like she used to say when he had taught her chess.

True to form, he was a master at strategizing, never betraying himself with a look or gesture, laying out traps to lure her in. And she, impulsive, bloodthirsty and eager for mayhem, would charge forward with everything she had, would mount attacks without thinking them through and had always walked into his traps.

It had been a delight to teach her, to see her fight her innate nature and try to stay at least one step ahead of him.

But yesterday, the week since he had seen her on the yacht had been nothing like guessing her chess strategy. The woman he had married was nothing if not unpredictable.

He'd expected her to throw a tantrum right in front of the steps when Helena had hugged him and kissed him in a provoking display. Helena's actions had been purely for Valentina's and Theseus's benefit.

And yet Valentina had recovered. Quickly and smoothly. Had kept her composure as he'd never seen her do before.

And there had been no questions. At all. About his past. About his past relationship with Helena. About his history with Theseus and Maria.

Nothing.

He'd seen her during dinner, then kissed her cheek good-night. Like the quiet, poised wife he'd always wanted, she'd retired without a word at the appropriate time. When he had finally gone to bed around midnight, she'd been asleep.

When he'd gone outside at five the next morning for his run, he had found her running laps around the house already. When he'd quietly joined her, she'd barely blinked.

It had been the same for four days. Since he'd been gone for more than a week to fetch her, work had piled up. So he had left her mostly in Maria's care, knowing that she would treat Valentina with kindness, at least.

Even as he wondered how long this new serenity would last, he missed the Valentina he'd married. The Valentina that had given voice to every feeling that had crossed her mind, the Valentina that lived through every emotion fearlessly, the Valentina that had, again and again, vowed that she'd always love him.

The Valentina that he only realized after she had left him had brought so much color and noise to his life.

The realization unsettled him.

Designer clothes, haute couture heels and reigning over her little clique—that had been the extent of her interests. *You have made me face reality*, she had claimed.

And the weight of that statement hung around his neck. He hadn't wanted the weight of her love nine months ago and he didn't want the burden of the new direction her life had taken now, either.

Attachment and affection only brought the worst out in all people, as Theseus had taught him seven years ago. And Kairos never wanted to experience the pain that came from people letting him down. Of people taking away what they had given, when it was not convenient anymore.

But of course, all this was dependent on the fact that Valentina had changed. And *that* he still could not believe.

Just as he was about to check where she was, Valentina walked into the sunlit breakfast room.

Desire punched him anew, a sharp pulse of longing that he didn't quite understand beneath the voracious hunger.

She stilled at the buffet laid out on the side table, like a doe caught in the sights of a predator. Slowly, her breath evened out, her expression assuming that calm he was beginning to detest.

There were a lot of changes in his wife and this was the most aggravating. She'd never been able to hide her emotions before. *Christos*, there'd been moments when her open longing for him had embarrassed him, when he'd wished she had a little control over herself.

Only now, when he couldn't decipher what was running through her mind, did he appreciate how refreshingly guileless and unflinchingly honest she had been. Only now when she was scrunched up in a corner of the bed did he realize how much he'd missed her warmth in his bed.

"*Kalimera*, Valentina," he said, his tone husky.

"*Buongiorno*, Kairos," she greeted sharply, and turned away toward the food.

He didn't drop his gaze from the delectable picture she made. The tight clench of her shoulders covered in thin straps told him she was aware of his gaze.

Black trousers followed the line of her long legs lovingly—legs that she had wrapped around his shoulders more than once. An emerald green blouse showed off her toned arms.

The wide V-neck gave no hint of a cleavage—had she finally abandoned those ghastly bras that had hidden the curve of her soft flesh from his fingers but exposed the bones in her chest?

She had always been more muscled than soft or fleshy because of her runner's build but she bordered on scrawny now. Even last night, as she had cozied up to him unknowingly in sleep, he had noted she was all sharp angles and bones. Not that it had made any difference to the erection he had sported in a matter of seconds. It was as if he had no control over his lust when it came to her. Lust he needed to address soon.

She had fashioned her glorious hair into some kind of tight braid, pulling it away from her face. It only made her features sharper.

He frowned at her grapefruit and coffee. And the way she settled down at the chair farthest from his. "You have lost weight."

She shrugged, raising those bony shoulders. "I didn't eat much in the last few months."

"Or sleep much?" The dark shadows under her expressive brown eyes were still there after a week. "You missed me so much that you couldn't eat and sleep?" he said, wanting to see a smile on her lips. Wanting that wariness in her eyes gone.

"I didn't know you were capable of cracking a joke," she taunted. Then sighed. "I would think you wouldn't want to engage in a discussion about our marriage where Theseus or his family could walk in or overhear."

"Theseus took Maria and Helena out first thing in the morning for a tour of the estate as it's Saturday. To give us the privacy we've been denied for the past week."

"That was kind of him," she replied. "Is he well? He looks like my grandfather—" she shook her head, a raw glitter in her eyes "—like Antonio did after his heart attack."

A tightness gathered in his chest at the clear distress in her gaze. "Antonio said words to you about your mother?"

He knew how much importance the Conti patriarch put on his bloodline.

"He didn't dare say a thing to me. Not in front of Leandro and Luca." The flat tone in which she spoke revealed how much it really did matter to her. "But I finally realized why he'd always been reserved with me. I always wondered if it were the fact that I was a girl that he cared so little for me.

"Now I know it's because I'm not really his blood." She pushed a lock of hair behind her ear. "Tell me about Theseus."

Why did her pain reach him like a hand into his chest when nothing she'd ever done had? Because he'd never even thought her capable of this depth? Kairos cleared his throat. He didn't know how to handle her emotion. Or maybe he didn't know how to handle this new Valentina at all.

"Theseus had a heart attack nine months ago. Maria says his health had been suffering for a while. An almost successful hostile takeover at his company, I think, precipitated the attack. For a while there, we weren't sure he'd make it through."

"He sent for you then?"

"Something like that."

"You've been here all these months?"

"Yes."

"And the hostile takeover?"

"I stopped it."

"He thinks the world of you, doesn't he?"

He shrugged. "Doesn't matter what he thinks. I...have a duty to him, that's all."

Kairos waited for a question about Helena to come his way. He waited for the cloak of zen around her to disappear now that she knew they'd have no audience.

Time ticked on, seconds gathering into minutes. Only silence.

Disappointment curdled in his stomach.

She took a sip of her coffee. "I...wasn't making enough to buy nice meals and afford the rent on the flat," she said, answering his earlier comment. "Even shared four ways, it was steep."

Her guilelessness in openly admitting failure after he had taunted her shamed him. Scraped him raw, too. "Was it so awful to remain married to me that you preferred walking away from every luxury I offered? From the penthouse suite and an unlimited credit card to live in some hovel with three other women and barely enough to eat?"

"*Si,* it was."

Blunt, and without the theatrics. Everything about this... *new her* unsettled him.

"I'm to believe that neither of your overprotective brothers smothered you in money and comforts? Not even a care package from Luca?"

"Luca respects my wishes. Leandro..." Her throat moved, her knuckles tight around her coffee cup.

Longing vibrated in her voice. This—this rift with her brothers, obviously enforced by her, more than anything else made him wonder about the change in her.

Leandro, Luca and Valentina shared a bond unlike anything he'd ever seen before. Even more astonishing, for it had been revealed that Valentina only shared a mother with her brothers.

Was that why he had gravitated toward Leandro's offer when there had been so many?

No, he hadn't been looking for a ready-made family. He had been burned enough with the one he had considered his.

It was Valentina that had caught his attention from the

first moment Leandro had pointed her out to him. Valentina whom he had wanted to possess.

She rose, put away her untouched grapefruit. "I told Leandro our rift will be permanent if he interferes in my life again."

That she meant it was clear. That it tore at her was also clear.

He had wished so many times that she was more intellectual, more contained...more everything she was not. Yet now that she was like a shadow of her former self, he felt protective of her. "You barely ate anything."

"Since when do you—"

He watched, fascinated, as she shook her head, took a deep breath that made her chest rise invitingly and then met his gaze. "I want to talk about what you're going to do for me. I made a list of—"

"I can do a lot of things for you, Valentina, if only you'd quit this whole 'Independent Valentina' project."

"Wow! Jokes and innuendoes, I don't know if you're the Kairos I married or not. All I usually got were nods and sighs and grunts. And oh, that look you used to get when you wanted sex."

Seeing Kairos disconcerted was like an adrenaline shot to her body.

Dark color stole under his cheeks and for the first time in months, Valentina laughed.

He pushed his chair back and stretched his long legs. His running shorts pulled back, exposing the hard muscle of his thighs. Greedily, she drank in the hair-roughened legs, and the calves. Her breath halted in her throat. Until she'd seen Kairos's muscled calves, she hadn't thought of a man's calves as sexually arousing.

But then, every inch of him was made to be appreciated. Touched. Stroked. Licked...not that he'd ever given her a chance to do all those things. Even in that arena, he had held the strings.

"I don't know what you're talking about." His words tugged her out of the sensual haze. "In my defense, you usually talked so much, fought so much, bitched so much that all I could interject was nods and grunts."

Even his cruel remark couldn't dampen her spirits. "You would get this strange glitter in your eyes. First, you would fight it. As if wanting to sleep with your wife was an urge you had to conquer. Then a run, followed by a shower. Then you would walk into our bedroom and stare at me. For a while there, I thought you found my pajamas distasteful. Then you—"

"You thought I found those little shorts with bows on the sides and sleeveless, braless tops you wore distasteful?"

"You'd sit in the chaise, elbows on your knees, and rub your neck," Tina continued as if his words hadn't sent a shiver of pleasure down her spine. "If you ran your fingers through your hair three times, I knew I was going to get laid that night. If you swore during all this aforementioned waiting time, it meant..."

Stillness surrounded him. Dark slashes of color in his cheeks. "It meant what?"

"Never mind," she dodged.

"What did it mean, Valentina?"

"It meant you would be demanding and a little...rough. It meant you would draw it out until I had no breath left in me. Until I was begging for you to grant me release."

It meant he would punish her. For his own loss of self-control as he saw it. For pushing him to the edge, Tina realized, trembling from head to toe. *Because he couldn't even put into words how much he needed her.*

Why hadn't she realized how much of his true self Kairos had revealed during sex? The power balance in their relationship—had it been more fluid than she'd thought?

She'd never really tried to understand him, never tried to look beneath the surface. She'd expected grand gestures and sweeping statements. And like a little girl denied what she wanted, she'd made his life hell for it.

But—thinking about it now—he had been twenty-seven when they had married, had been estranged from his adoptive family. He had had a rough upbringing, and neither of them had much experience with romantic relationships.

Had she taken any of that into account? Had she ever tried to reach him in a different way?

Non. All she had wanted was a fairy tale without putting any work into the relationship.

A long, filthy curse exploded from him, polluting the sunlit breakfast room. "*Dios*, Valentina! You should've told me if hurt you."

"You didn't. You never hurt me, Kairos. Whatever we did in bed, I was a willing, enthusiastic participant. So don't...don't make it a thing you did *to* me. Instead of with me. I craved the..." *the intimacy I found with you there* "...the pleasure you gave me. I told you that enough times."

His gaze darkened, a faint tension enveloping his muscular frame. Things she didn't say swirled in that cozy glowing room.

He knew now how much she'd watched his every move, every gesture for meaning. How deprived she'd been for a single word of affection. Even a simple statement of his desire for her. For a word of praise—even if it was about those blasted pajamas she'd spent hours choosing. Or about her hair. Or her readiness for him whenever he wanted sex.

That he'd even liked her sexual appetite for him, was something she'd only realized when he'd cruelly commented on it on the yacht.

"You cannot doubt I found satisfaction with you." His gaze held hers in defiance and something else. As if only now he realized how much he had hurt her.

Legs shaking, she walked to the buffet table and poured herself another cup of coffee she didn't want. She took a sip just to force the lump in her throat down.

"I do not find relationships easy to manage."

Stunned that he would even make that concession now, she stared at him. If the consequences of that hadn't hurt her so much, she would have laughed at his mulish explanation.

"Those words would have meant a lot back then," she said sadly. "All I ever heard from you was criticisms."

"And every time I criticized you or compared you to Sophia or Alex, you fought back with an outrageous act," he said slowly, as if he was finally figuring it out.

"Si." Her cup rattled loudly when she put it down on the table. "It's all in the past anyway."

If he had forced the discussion to continue, she'd have fled the room.

He went to the buffet. The clatter of cutlery behind her calmed her nerves.

Her relief was short-lived when he reached her, clasped her wrist in his rough fingers, tugged her and pushed her into the chair. The plate he deposited in front of her overflowed with fresh strawberries, a slice of toast and scrambled eggs.

Her stomach growled.

Without thanking him, Tina dug into it. Within minutes, she had polished off most of the breakfast.

She noticed only as she swallowed the last piece of the toast. Toast *he'd* prepared for her. Almost blackened, slathered in butter.

Just the way she preferred it.

Warmth bloomed in her chest. He'd noted that much

about her. She tried to remind herself that it was too little. But the truth was there now that she wasn't in a fairy tale but real life.

Kairos had cared about her. It had been in all the little things he'd done for her. In the silences after they made love and the way he had held her as if she was precious, in the unsaid words between them after one of her escapades, in the way he had always encouraged her to come out from under her brothers' protective umbrella and make something of herself.

But how could she ever overcome the fact that she hadn't been enough? That she might never be good enough?

CHAPTER SIX

IT SEEMED IT was a day of shocks. No, a week of shocks.

From the moment he had set foot on the yacht and seen his wife dressed like a hooker to now, looking at the spreadsheet she showed him on her laptop screen.

Even the slide of her thigh against his couldn't distract his attention this time.

There were reams and reams of data in her pretty pink sketchbook and laptop.

While she pulled up different files—her lower lip caught anxiously between her teeth—he took a huge notebook and flipped it open.

Maybe two hundred pages were filled with sketches— dresses and accessories. Outfits put together from cutouts of dresses and hats and handbags. Pictures of people they had both known—Conti board members' wives and daughters and whatnot. And next to each person's photo cutout from some society pages were notes about how they were dressed wrong. Little corrections to their outfits, makeup, hair, shoes… Kairos idly flipped through the book, then picked up four more like the first one.

There were eight sketchbooks in all. It was years and years of work, he realized, shock vibrating through him.

"When did you start doing these?"

She shrugged, juxtaposing two different spreadsheets on her screen. "When I was eleven, twelve? About two years after I came to live with Leandro and Luca.

"I didn't really have a lot of clothes and accessories to play with until then. When they took me on that first shopping spree to this designer boutique..." Unadulterated joy filled her voice. She leaned back against the chair and closed her eyes, a smile playing at her lips. "It was like I was in heaven. I spent the whole day picking out dresses and shoes and hairbands and bows and belts and pins and more shoes... Leandro says I kept looking behind me every minute."

"Why?" Kairos asked automatically, even as he understood.

An uncomfortable tightness descended in his chest.

He'd forgotten that she hadn't always been this spoilt, rich Conti Heiress. It was the one time he'd wanted to go back for her after she'd walked out on him—when he'd heard the vicious rumor mill repeat the dirty truth.

Valentina Conti wasn't truly a Conti, but her mother's bastard with a chauffeur after she'd left the maniac Enzo Conti after years of abuse.

He had wondered who had leaked the news when the patriarch Antonio Conti and his grandsons Leandro and Luca Conti had hidden the truth for years; he wondered what it had cost Valentina to learn the truth.

A shimmer of doubt nagged at him.

"According to Luca, I was worried they would abandon me at the store and disappear. He says I was this little scrawny thing that would dig my nails in if he even loosened his grip around my hand." She straightened in her chair, her tone so devoid of emotion that the hair on the back of his neck prickled.

"Why?" he asked again.

He'd been married to her for nine months and he'd known nothing about her. *Christos*, he hadn't even been interested. He hadn't loved her, but he also knew firsthand what came of negligence. Of how simply holding back belief in someone could destroy one's belief in oneself.

Theseus had done that to him. And he had never recovered.

"I don't remember clearly actually. Even the bits I do, it's only because Luca would prod me softly. To make me remember. He said I would come running into his room or Leandro's in the middle of the night, crying and in panic. That for years, they would find me sleeping at the foot of his bed, one of my hands on his ankle.

"All I know is that there were months after my mom's accident before someone came looking for me. When Leandro found me and told me he was my older brother, he said I clung to him like a rabid dog."

When she seemed to be lost in the memories of the past, he tugged her hand into his. She returned the tight clasp before she opened her eyes and met his.

Such strength shimmered in her eyes that he felt singed by it. He could see why her brothers were so protective of her. Could see that little feral thing in her eyes. Could see the vulnerability that had always lurked beneath her dramatic personality.

Before he could say a word, she pulled her hand away.

"Valentina, who leaked the fact that you were not...a Conti?"

"I did," she replied instantly, her dark gaze holding his.

He sat back in his chair, reality as he knew it shifting and sliding. "Why?" It seemed to be the only word he could speak around her today. "How did you find out?"

"Sophia knew I was...miserable with you.

"Luca had told her about the circumstances of his birth, about how our mother left his father after his monstrous actions for years. About how Leandro sought to protect me from the truth. About why you married me.

"For the first time in my life, I had a friend who truly cared about me, who trusted me to have the courage to face the truth."

"What did she think it would solve?" He had always liked Sophia, but right now, he could happily wring her neck for interfering in his marriage.

"She thought the truth would free me from that downward spiral I was in because you…" Again that shrug. "She was right. When I learned I wasn't a Conti, I realized how tightly I had clung to it because it had given me an identity when I'd been so scared and alone. When I learned about the alliance between you and Leandro…everything fell apart. If I wasn't Valentina Conti Constantinou, I was nothing. Something you told me again and again. It would only be a matter of time before you learnt the truth too, before you realized you hadn't gotten quite what you wanted. So I left."

Before you left me, the unspoken words reverberated between them.

That he measured so little in her estimation burned his gut. "I didn't leave you after Luca thwarted my fight to be the Conti CEO," he said, knowing it was the utter truth, "and I wouldn't have left you for not being the Conti heiress."

Instead of pacifying her, his words just caused a flash of that old temper to glitter in her eyes. "Do you even realize how arrogant that sounds? As if you were doing me a favor by keeping me on? I wasn't willing to find out what *would* drive you to leave me."

"Valentina—"

"Kairos, please don't pretend as if my leaving—once you get over your dented ego—didn't fill you with relief. It was a circus and it is done. Let it go."

It took every ounce of his self-control to let it go. Every

inch of his pride to give in and admit failure. But her accusation that he was relieved...how dare she?

No, their marriage hadn't been great. Not even close to normal. They hadn't known each other at all.

But it was something he had begun to count on, even with her ridiculous, outrageous theatrics day after day.

She had become a constant in a life that had never known one.

The strength of the urge to punish her for disappointing him, for breaking her word to him, for thinking so little of him...the hurt driving that urge...it stunned him.

He fought the urge to swallow it away, to let it fester. If they were pulling skeletons out of the closet... "For what it's worth, I did hold our marriage sacred, Valentina. I counted on you sticking with me for the next fifty years or more. To have children with me, to build a family of our own... You showed me a glimpse of a future I'd never wanted before. And when it didn't work the way you wanted it to, you took it away, without even bothering to tell me. So don't you dare tell me what I felt when you walked away."

She had acted just as Theseus had once done. He had given Kairos everything and then snatched it away in the blink of an eye.

Maybe he should be glad that it was over with Valentina.

In nine months, he'd proved to himself—and her—that he didn't need her.

He wouldn't have seen her except for the divorce proceedings, if Theseus's situation hadn't forced him to seek her out.

And as she was so wisely reminding him, *she* had walked out. *She* had broken her promise. And that meant she wasn't worth all this thought, much less his regard.

His wife was what he had thought her initially—impulsive, immature and without loyalty.

"Let's just focus on the future like adults," he finally said.

* * *

Her throat stung as Kairos's words penetrated her defenses. For him to admit that her leaving had dented more than just his ego...

Her leaving had hurt him. So he had lashed out on the night at the yacht with cruel words. It didn't excuse it, but it explained so much.

She had been right. Kairos felt so much more than he ever let on.

What was she supposed to do with that knowledge? Why hadn't they ever talked like this before?

When she had talked about her childhood, she'd seen understanding.

Even a little flash of respect when she'd said *she'd* leaked that she wasn't a Conti. As if he hadn't thought her capable of shedding that safety blanket, that position of privilege. It was respect she craved with every cell in her body.

For a few minutes, he'd been kind. Understanding. Interested in her past and how it had shaped her. Interested in her—the person she was beneath the Conti tag—beyond what she could be for him.

But the admission about her leaving had cost him. The walls were back up, as if he had given her far too much.

Now, as she pointed to him several rows and columns, all she got was a polite stranger. The hard press of his thigh against hers, the graze of his corded forearm against the sides of her breasts as he pointed to the screen made her supremely aware of every inch of her body.

"What are all these names?" he asked pointing to the calls she'd highlighted.

"These are the names of the personnel I called at different couture houses—assistant buyers, vendors, designers' assistants and more."

He pulled the laptop to himself and browsed down.

"There are almost...one hundred entries here. With times and dates."

She tried to shake off the vulnerability that descended on her. This was almost a year's worth of work. And she had nothing to show for it. For months, she would finish working a nine-hour workday, and then settle down to make calls. Humiliating chitchat, answering gossip about herself—she'd endured everything in the hope of getting the answer she wanted.

Nothing. Nada. Zilch.

"I kept a very thorough record."

"I see that. But what is it a record of?"

"Calls I made to different people over the last few months."

"You called all these people?" Disbelief rang in his tone, making her all prickly. When she tried to take the laptop from him, he resisted. "Answer me, Valentina."

"*Si*. I called all of them."

He ran a square-nailed finger against the column of Yes/No and the paltry maybes peppered through. "And what does this column mean?"

"It means whether they agreed to let me borrow the piece of clothing, the accessory or the shoes I called about. These are people who have access to the latest designer wear. Magazines and fashion houses and distributors and vendors, etc..."

"Why do you need all these? I thought you turned your back on things you couldn't afford? To attend parties with your pimp?"

That he still thought so little of her made her want to thump him. "I need a portfolio. As a stylist, whether a personal client or a house of design, it's the first thing clients and businesses want to see.

"I roped Nikolai into helping me do the photoshoot, and

even enlisted an up-and-coming model to pose for me. But I don't have access to any clothes or shoes. Without that I have nothing."

"Weren't some of these people your friends? That one and that one...that guy?"

"Si."

"But it says no against their names."

Tina gritted her teeth. "Are you being dense on purpose?"

One look at him told her he wasn't.

She sighed and rubbed her temple. "It's because they said no. They didn't say no to my face. Half of them wouldn't return my calls. And when I showed up at their workplace anyway, they had their minions tell me they were busy."

"Why?"

"I guess because word had spread that Leandro and Luca had abandoned me and that you dumped me after learning that I wasn't the esteemed Conti heiress. Only Nikolai would even talk to me. He got me that job. It took me a month to understand that none of my so-called friends were really friends. Just as you pointed out. Sophia, of course, offered the Rossi connections but I said no."

"That was foolish. The business world is nothing without connections and networking. You think I chose to ally myself with Leandro because I lacked business acumen? That I chose to head the CLG board because of the politics? Your brothers and Antonio have connections unlike anything I've ever known. I knew that if I wanted to go further in the business world, I needed more. I needed the powerful connections Leandro brought with him. I needed the old families to accept me into their circle."

It was the first time he had mentioned the agreement he had come to with Leandro. The agreement that had led to their marriage. It didn't sound as ruthless a transaction as she'd imagined.

"Are you giving me an explanation for why you did what you did? Perhaps asking for my forgiveness?" *Dios*, she was such a fool.

"No. The agreement we entered into is not that unusual. Leandro knew me. He knew that I would treat you well. And I—"

She glared at him. "But you didn't treat me well."

"Name one thing I deprived you of during our marriage."

"Respect. Affection. Regard." *Love*.

His silence was answer enough for Tina. "If I let Sophia help, then Luca would get involved, too. And if Luca got involved, Leandro would move heaven and earth to open every door for me. And soon, I would be drowning once again in my brothers' favors. I would forget why I started all this. I would become *that* Valentina."

He closed the laptop with a soft thud. With a glare, she hugged the thing to her chest. He took the laptop back from her clenched hands with exaggerated patience and set it down on the table. "Why *did* you start all this?"

She felt like an insect being examined under an industrial microscope. "I told you. I want to make something of myself."

His silver eyes pinned her to the spot. "What I'm asking is why you want to make something of yourself? What is this sudden need to prove yourself? Why all this hardship when before you couldn't even be bothered to understand anything beyond the little circle you were queen of?"

She couldn't tell him that he was the reason.

That she wanted his respect, his regard more than anything else in the world. That she wanted him to be proud of her. That she wanted him to regret—at length and at great pain—what he had lost by letting her go. Of course, she hadn't shed her vindictiveness.

"It's high time I took responsibility for myself. For my happiness, for my life," Tina repeated the lines she'd remembered Sophia spouting at her when she had been at her lowest.

All those things had significance, yes, but not in comparison to what she wanted to see in Kairos's eyes.

"So now that you have seen what I have done so far—" she opened her notepad and drew a couple of bullet points "—tell me the different ways you can help me. I know we talked about you putting word out to different friends of yours. But even if you succeeded in letting them hire me as their personal stylist, I would still need this portfolio to impress them, to gain their business. Now, with Nikolai and Marissa, I have a photographer and model lined up. All I need—"

"You're not working with that Russian joker anymore."

"You don't get to dictate who I talk to or not. You're not my husband anymore."

He pulled her left hand into his and awareness exploded through her. Callused fingers gripped hers, the pad of his thumb wiggling her wedding ring. "Officially, I am."

She pulled her hand away. "Nikolai's talented and he's proved that he has my best—"

"He wants to get in your pants, Valentina."

"I know he does. It doesn't mean he'll get there. Or that I want him there."

"You're not attracted to him."

The statement, which was really a question, arrested the millions of neurons firing away in her brain. Like complex machinery coming to a screeching halt.

Was that doubt in his question? A minute fracture in his arrogant confidence?

She wanted to lie and say she was attracted to Nikolai, to give him a taste of that uncertainty that had been her companion all during their marriage.

No games, Tina!

"I've never been interested in Nikolai. Not even before I met you." She cringed. "But I... I don't think I was kind in my rejection of him."

"What if he had attacked you that night on the yacht?"

The flippant response that rose to her lips arrested as Tina saw the whiteness of his knuckles. "I know him, Kairos. He's all bluster, and believe me, he has punished me enough with innuendoes and insults over the last few months. He's had his petty revenge. I have confidence that he'll be here when I ask him."

"I will not tolerate his sniffing around about you. You will entertain only me."

If her outrage could have been given action, Valentina would have had smoke coming out of her ears. She picked up her laptop and stood up. "I was a fool to think you'd take me seriously."

He gripped her arm and arrested her. "Even if I let you work with him, you still have no access to all the designer clothes and accessories you need. Unless you were thinking of asking me to buy them for you. As long as you—"

She covered his mouth with her palm. And instantly realized the foolishness of the move. His breath was warm against her palm, sending a rush of heat to her breasts and lower belly. As if he was touching his sensuous mouth to those places.

"*No*," she said and then cleared her throat. "I don't want you to buy anything for me. I only agreed to have my wardrobe back because my role as your loving wife demands it."

Was she never going to solve this Catch-22? What would she show prospective clients if she didn't have a portfolio to interest them, and how would she develop a portfolio if she never had clients?

Kairos pulled her hand away from his mouth but held it against his chest. His heart thundered against her fingertips. "You could join Theseus's company and try to achieve it that way. Go at your goal in a different way."

"Theseus's company?"

"He owns an advertising agency among the group. They put together a lot of shoots here and abroad to design the catalog for the luxury boutiques the Markos group holds all over Greece. A styling internship with such a company could get you valuable experience and contracts."

"And you can get me a position at his company just like that?"

"The woman who runs that department is a friend of mine. It'll be unpaid. Chiara's a no-nonsense go-getter who will only hold it against you that I got you the position."

"I'm willing to do any kind of work if it means I'm a step closer, Kairos. Being here with you when I'd rather mop floors at the fashion agency should prove that."

He ignored her petty barb. "But… Helena is in charge of that division. The moment she figures out you're there, she'll interfere."

"*No!*" Refusal escaped her lips even before she could process his words.

One thing she'd realized in the last week in his company was that she'd always be vulnerable when it came to Kairos. This proximity was bad enough without adding a woman who wanted him. A woman who shared history with him.

A woman who provoked every one of Valentina's baser, jealous instincts to the fore.

He tilted her chin up. "You do not have to be afraid of her, Valentina. She will not harm you, not while I'm here."

"That you have to reassure me of that speaks volumes."

"It's me she's after."

"I know that," she said, her voice going to that whiny octave she hated so much. That Helena wanted Kairos had been written in every malicious smile, every cruel remark of the past few days.

The whole situation twisted her gut. "I'll ask only this one question. Please, Kairos, answer it honestly."

He scowled, his fingers inching into the hair behind her ear tightly. The pad of his thumb pressed at her lower lip roughly. "I've never lied to you."

"Is this—" she waved her hand between them "—some elaborate ploy to make her jealous or to prove your power over her? To make her want you even more?"

At least, that was what Helena had hinted at over last night's dinner. That this thing between her and Kairos was a minor lovers' tiff. That he was using Valentina for any number of purposes.

"I have never played those kinds of games. With anyone."

No, those stupid games had been her forte. Observing Helena's antics was seeing a mirror version of her worst self.

"That doesn't answer my question."

"I don't want Helena."

"You never—"

"*Oxhi!* I wouldn't dishonor Theseus and Maria like that."

The depth of relief that spread in her chest scared the hell out of Tina. This was so not the time to discover Kairos's honorable streak or any other fine qualities. *Dio mio*, he was not for her. "But Theseus and Maria...they want you for their daughter. They think of you as their son. It was clear they—"

"Thinking of me as their son and being their son is

different, Valentina. In the end, blood wins." His nostrils flared, the topic clearly hitting a nerve. "At least, that's been my experience."

Because Theseus had chosen Helena to head the company over him the last time? Tina had gathered that much from the hints Helena had dropped over the last few days. And from the obvious tension between Theseus and Kairos every time the discussion shifted to the companies.

She pushed out of his hold, needing to think clearly. "I can't work with Helena."

"Opportunities like this internship won't come your way often."

"I'll somehow—"

"You won't. If it's not this job, it will be a troublesome client. If not Helena, someone else to whom you would have to grovel. The fashion industry, whether here or in Milan, is cutthroat. Full of pitfalls and backstabbing men and women. There's no shame in knowing your shortcomings. No shame in giving up."

Tina stared at him. "Giving up?"

"Aren't you? You'll be here for at least three months, and you're turning down a position in the field you want to work in. Not that I'm surprised."

"Your pride—which is a monumental thing—got bruised because I left you. And for that, you're punishing me by making me work for her."

His mouth twitched. "Actually, I have always thought you and Helena were cast from the same mold. All glitter and no substance."

She'd thought the same, yet the laughingly delivered comment punched Tina hard. Her chest tightened. Did he think so little of her? Still?

All glitter and no substance.

No words could encompass her so well. No one had

ever stripped all pretense, all her armor, and laid her bare like that.

This intimacy, his admission that their marriage had been sacred to him, it was making her forget what kind of a man he was. Making her forget that there was no place in his life for anything but ambition.

"You know, from the moment you told me you 'needed' your wife, I've been wondering why." She stilled at the wide doors to the courtyard, the sun caressing her bare arms. The villa, the grounds, everything was paradise. Sharing a room with the man she'd given her body and soul to, pretending that they adored each other, was incredibly seductive.

A thin line of tension appeared between his brows. "I told you why."

"But not all of it."

Silence stretched. She waited, wanting him to offer to tell her. Wanting him to want her to know the truth about his present, his past. About the ruthless choices that seemed to define his life.

To want to make her understand him.

"And what did you figure out?" Pure steel in his voice.

"Maria said that you flew to Theseus's side the moment you heard of his heart attack. That you held off a hostile takeover on his board that would've wrenched control from Theseus. And Helena mentioned that you had almost been engaged. She clearly adores you still. But there's tension between all of you. It's clear that you had a falling out, something that prevented you and Helena from being together the last time around. You saved his life and his company…"

A brow rose on his face, his hip cocked out at a jaunty angle, but still he waited. Ruthlessness dripped from his very pores. "Make your point, *pethi mou*."

"I think you saw an opportunity."

Any hint of charm disappeared from his eyes. "What opportunity would that be, Valentina?"

Even as he asked the question, there was a warning in his words.

Not to voice it. Not to give form to her thoughts. But she wanted to fracture that icy control, that smooth, uncaring facade. Bloodthirsty by nature, she wanted him to tell her the whole truth. To admit that her accusations hurt.

"You want to take over Theseus's company but not his daughter, so you produced me to pretend we have a perfect marriage. I haven't quite figured out why you can't get rid of me and marry her, and then you would have everything you want. But what I know is that when you have the company in hand, you'll discard me, leash Helena and become the CEO. What else would motivate you to put your life on hold except the fact that you can gain power by this move?"

A cold smile sliced his cruel mouth upwards. "And here I worried that Helena would twist your mind with lies."

There was such a wealth of emotion in his tone that Tina's heart pounded. "Will you deny that at the end of all this you'll own Theseus's company?"

"No."

"That you brought me here to deceive that sweet couple, to avoid Helena's attentions?"

"No."

"Then where is the lie in what I said, Kairos?" She waited for him to deny her accusation, to give her another reason. Anything for her to hold onto, a chance for them.

"Everything you do, every decision you make, it's to acquire more wealth. More power. More connections." She thought she was over the worst but it only hurt to see the coldness in his eyes. "Why should this be any different, when all that ever motivates you is ambition?"

CHAPTER SEVEN

EVERYTHING YOU DO is motivated by ambition.

Valentina's words played like a broken record through his mind even after a month. Taking another sip of his throat-burning Scotch, Kairos admitted it grated still.

For years after he had walked away from Theseus, all he had been able to think of was how to advance, how to prove to Theseus—and himself—that he could make it work without his former mentor's help. And without Theseus's legacy.

In that blind drive, he had developed a reputation for ruthless deals and an expertise in getting rid of broken parts of a company. He had forgotten that there was more to life than business deals and the next takeover. A fact Leandro had pointed out when he had first met him.

He smiled. The man was a master strategist if ever there was one. But his words had sunk in. And once he had seen Valentina, he had wanted her. The idea of marriage, settling down, making a family of his own…had held appeal.

He'd seen it as another forward move in his life, not an adjustment.

Or maybe his mistake had been to let his libido choose the wrong wife. Maybe if he hadn't been so obsessed with winning Valentina, hadn't reveled in how artlessly she had fallen for him, he would have said no to Leandro's offer.

Leaning back into his seat, he swept his gaze around the nightclub. His tension deflated a little when he found

Helena dancing with one of the younger board members on Markos's board of directors.

Valentina's accusation had been correct...and yet also not correct at the same time. It rankled that she thought so little of him, that he would take advantage of Theseus in his feeble state. And yet he had balked at explaining himself.

The more she delved beneath his surface, the more he wanted to hide himself away.

Why did it feel like giving Valentina a piece of the past was giving her a part of his soul? Why didn't the damn woman revert to what he had considered her default?

Restlessness slithered in his blood. Even the brutal three-hour-a-day training he had been pushing on his body, in preparation for a triathlon, was still not enough to rid his body of that simmering energy.

And his sweet, little wife was the cause.

It was close to a month now since she had accepted that position in the ad agency. A month of waiting to receive a call from Chiara that Valentina had slapped someone, or fought with someone, or that she had stormed out because she had had to work too hard.

Not a peep from his wife's boss or Helena or Valentina about her job. Not a single complaint.

They had sort of fallen into a routine as husband and wife far too easily—they had started running together in the morning, breakfasting together, and then he gave her a lift to work and they parted ways. Most evenings, they dined with Theseus and Maria until either he or she went back to work again.

And then came the long torturous nights.

His balls, he was afraid, were permanently going to shrivel if he had to take one more cold shower, if he had to untangle Valentina from himself in the middle of one more night.

She thought him a ruthless bastard anyway. So what stopped him from taking what he wanted like he'd always done?

If he waited on some twisted notion of honor, he'd have had nothing in life. He'd have still been foraging through some dumpster in the back alleys of Athens, ended up either dead or pimping some poor prostitute to make a life. It was only by taking what he wanted he'd gotten this far in life.

He wanted sex—*Christos*, it was all he could think of— and he had a wife who matched him in his fervor for sex if nothing else. So what the hell was he feeling guilty about?

She was changing how he saw her, and she was changing him from the inside out.

Why else did his gut clench when he saw the shadows under her eyes, when he saw her weave tiredly through dinner? Why else did he want that adoration, that love back in her eyes?

Was celibacy making him sentimental?

Andaxi!

He ordered another glass of Scotch—his second, which was one more than he ever allowed himself, when he heard the soft hush around his table. The hairs on the back of his neck prickled.

Desire came at him in that same visceral punch when his gaze found her. But with that ever-present hum came a bubble of laughter bursting out of his throat. The shocked silence around the table was enough proof that he rarely laughed like that.

He should have known she would do something like that. Knew the subdued shadow she was making herself into was…unnatural for her.

Thrown into brilliance by the multicolored strobe lights from the bar, her copper-colored sheath dress with a million metallic chips contrasted dazzlingly against her golden skin tone. The material clung to her chest and waist like a lover's hands and then ended just below the thin flare of her hips.

His mouth dried. Her gaze swept through the club, landed on him.

The long, toned muscles of her thighs when she moved... it was pure sensuality in motion. Five-inch stiletto heels made her legs go on for miles. Her hair was in its usual braid.

Only he knew how the silky mass would caress a man's face or how it provided an anchor to hold on to when he was driving into her wet heat. She wore no jewelry except those plain diamond studs at her ears that were a gift from Luca, and the pendant he'd given her. A foolish piece of sentimentality he'd indulged in.

His knuckles gripped the seat as she reached their table and every man's gaze in the vicinity devoured her.

A subtle thread of her fragrance wafted over him as she bent and kissed his cheek.

"Hello, Kairos," she said, wrapping her arms around him from behind. Her breasts pressed against his neck. Sensations assaulted him, his muscles curling with the control it took not to clamp his mouth over hers.

Slowly, that initial roar of desire settled into a simmering hum. Clarity came.

For a month, she'd been so careful around him. Never touching him unless necessary and unless they had an audience. Even then, he could feel the tension in her frame every time he came near her. Could feel her flinch every time he touched her.

Now, she was all over him. And instead of leading her into one of the backrooms specifically reserved for couples who wanted private space and taking her against the wall as every instinct was riding him to, he found himself frowning.

One elbow over the back of his seat, she looked down at him. Shadows swirled in her eyes, hiding what he wanted to see.

"Are you drunk?"

"I had three glasses of white wine while I dressed in Chiara's personal suite after your high command."

He noted the jut of her collarbone, the bluish shadows under her eyes. "Did you remember to eat before the wine?"

She scrunched her forehead. "No wonder it went straight to my head. You'll have to put it down to the shock that you ordered me to meet you in a nightclub, of all places. That's like—" she frowned, her lower lip jutting out "—the old me going to a sale in a department store, or being kind to Claudia Vanderbilt. Or the new me succeeding at something." She laughed.

Beneath the low, husky sound, Kairos found something disconcerting. A hint of pain.

It wasn't just the dress. Her lips were painted a dark voluptuous red—the only feature she possessed that was plump and lush. It was a color he'd once forbidden her to wear.

Because, throughout the formal dinner with his new business partners one night, all he'd been able to think of was kissing that mouth, of wanting his innocent wife's lush mouth wrapped around his cock even as she goaded his temper by flirting outrageously with another man across the table.

Something was wrong. Because whenever something went wrong in his wife's little world, she acted like a teenage rebel.

It had taken him this long to understand the pattern. For a smart man, he lost all capability for logic and rationality when it was Valentina.

She'd slapped Sophia when he'd refused to define his relationship with her.

She'd stripped and jumped into a pool in her underwear at a venture capitalist's retreat in Napa Valley because he'd told her in no uncertain terms that they weren't there for fun but business. A fact she'd been made aware of well in advance.

When he'd forced her to return the Bugatti she'd had delivered for his birthday present—bought with her brother's money no less—she'd decided to return it recklessly and almost hit a tree in her anger.

All actions that had infuriated him.

Was this another ploy?

But what he saw this time was vulnerability in her gaze. The tremble in her fingers as she picked up his drink and took a sip. The fine lines of tension around her forehead.

Valentina never indulged in spirits at least. Something to do with her mother's accident. And yet, here she was, not completely sloshed but without the wariness and inhibition he'd spied in her eyes in the last month.

The booth was U-shaped and he was sitting at the end. "Let me see the back of your dress," he taunted, some devil in himself goading him.

She turned around obligingly, moving with an innate grace that had captured his attention the first time he'd met her. He gritted his teeth. He was right.

The fabric barely covered her buttocks. But *Christos*, his palms ached to cup them, to pull her flush against him until she felt what she did to him.

"You asked me to join you at a nightclub." Her gaze swept over the club and landed on Helena leaning against the bar and watching them with a smirk. The glitter in his wife's eyes brightened as her gaze swept over the cool blue knee-length dress Helena wore. In contrast to Valentina, he noticed now, she looked elegant, refined.

His wife's tension doubled. "I assumed it was to put on a show for Helena."

He pulled her down to sit beside him. "How has she been treating you?"

"Nothing I can't handle. Except the little snippets of your history that she keeps dropping around the team. How many favors Theseus did you. How many disappointments you've had to face in life. I think everyone on the team realized she was talking about me."

"Valentina—"

"She doesn't bother me, Kairos."

"No?"

She shrugged. "All the scenarios she desperately tries to plant in my head would have driven me crazy if…you still meant something to me." She looked up then and smiled. But the smile didn't touch her eyes. "Anyway, I came armed with the weapons I possess."

"Weapons?" he said, his mouth twitching. For all he tried, he couldn't muster disappointment or anger that she'd shown up dressed like a…delectable morsel he wanted to consume.

He felt anticipation and tenderness. For something was definitely not right and he wanted to fix it for her.

"She flaunts her breasts in your face every opportunity she gets. I don't have big breasts or flaring hips. My legs are my weapons and I decided to showcase those."

He rubbed his fingers over his face, fighting the urge, but laughed out loud anyway. He had a feeling it would hurt her feelings. And it had, if the way she gripped the table showing white knuckles was anything to go by.

"Twisted, *si*? That my insecurity about my body has finally found your sense of humor?"

Just like that, his smile disappeared. "What in God's name are you talking about now?"

"The fact that I obsessed for nine months over your fascination with my lack of melons."

"Melons?" he said, almost choking on the sip of his whiskey.

She mock-cupped her hands in front of her chest like men did when they talked about big breasts. "You know... jugs. Bazookas."

His mind roiled, came to a jarring conclusion. "*Christos*, is that why you took to wearing those obscenely ridiculous push-up bras? Because you assumed I was into big breasts?"

Color streaked along her cheekbones. "*Si*. I wanted to please you. I was naive and foolish enough to believe that the illusion of big breasts would somehow make you appreciate me more. Make your nonexistent heart beat."

"I hated those bras. When I touched you...all I could feel was padding." He muttered another oath. "Where in hell would you get the idea that I liked big breasts?"

"From things you said when we watched old Hollywood movies. From the way all your love interests were built in the front. From the way you never..." She looked away, her throat bobbing up and down.

He turned her to his side until she faced him. Strips of light caressed the high sweep of her cheekbones. The narrow blade of her nose. She licked her lips nervously. He couldn't be distracted. At least not yet.

"I never what, Valentina?"

She shuffled her legs under the table but he wouldn't let her budge. In the end, she ended up piling her legs above and around his. It was the closest he'd been to her in months. Fever took root in his muscles.

"I don't know why we're talking about this."

"Because I want to know."

"Francesca Pellegrini told me that her husband was obsessed with her breasts." Her cheeks burned. "But when we made lo—when we had sex, you never…spent a lot of time with my breasts. So I assumed you didn't like them. There? Are you happy? Or would you like more humiliating details from our marriage?"

"Did it not occur to you that I might have just been in a hurry to get to other places? That unlike Francesca Pellegrini's husband—who by the way always gawks at you, the old pervert—I might be a leg man?" he whispered, not knowing whether to laugh or groan.

She had built up so many things in her head and it was his fault. He had incessantly found fault with her.

Shame settled in his chest. He ran his knuckles over the lean line of her leg, and her breath hitched.

"You have legs that go on for miles, *glykia mou*. You're so tall that I don't get a crick in my neck when I kiss you. You fit so perfectly against me that I could hold you against the wall and be inside you in a second. When I'm inside you and you wrap your legs around me…" He cleared his throat, forgetting where he was going for a second. "But of course, forgive me for my oversight." He let his gaze rove over the deep V plunge of her neckline. His blood became sluggish, his erection an insistent ache in his trousers. "I promise to spend more time with your breasts in the near future."

A choking gasp fell from her mouth. Her eyes sparked outrage. "You're not getting anywhere near my breasts."

He raised a brow, loving the warm flush on her cheeks. "We'll see about that."

A waiter brought some appetizers he had ordered. He picked up a piece of cheese and held it to her mouth. "Eat."

She shook her head, held his gaze defiantly and took another sip of his Scotch.

"You're acting like a child. You'll be sick if you chase wine with Scotch. You don't do well with alcohol."

She pouted, leaning back against the seat. "You don't like dancing, you don't want me to drink and you don't like for me to have any fun. Why am I here then? If it's for Helena's sake, you should know she doesn't buy our reunion."

"Let Helena think whatever she pleases."

"Please, Kairos. The truth, for once. Why are you here?"

"When one of the board members suggested we check out the new club, I joined them. Georgio," he said nodding at the man standing close to Helena, his angelic features visible even from here, "is—"

"Alexio Kanapalis's son," she said, shocking him into stupefied silence. "Alexio tried to get the vote to oust Theseus from his own board. You booted him out instead. But Georgio stayed. So you wonder if Georgio's loyalty lies with his father or with Theseus. Of course, that he's so... chummy with Helena goes in its own column of uneasy matters."

He stared at her.

She laughed. "I'm not stupid. Georgio visits my department all the time. All the ladies swarm around the pretty boy cooing over his perfectly symmetric features and all that dark blond hair. Not counting his charm and wit, he reminds me a bit of Luca."

"Stay away from him, Valentina."

She sighed. "How many men will you order me to stay away from?"

He ignored her question, but didn't quite succeed at ignoring the jealousy in his gut, however, when Tina looked at the other man and his damned perfect features. "In nine months of living together, you never once had an inkling of my business affairs."

She scrunched her nose at him. "Because I didn't care. Not because I didn't lack intellect."

"And now you're interested?"

"Si."

"Why?"

"Because as soon as you figure out who's behind all this, Theseus and you will come to an agreement, and the sooner I'll be out of your life. Forever this time."

Her eagerness to be done with their charade made him grit his teeth. "It wasn't just to keep an eye on Georgio and Helena," he admitted. She was always so damned honest with him. Was he such a coward that he couldn't even admit small things to her? "You've been working far too hard. I thought you would like to have a change of pace for one night."

"Did Theseus comment that you've not shown me any sights? Has Helena poked a hole in our happily-ever-after?"

The brittleness in her smile tugged at him. "Does there have to be a reason to want to see my wife?"

"Ah...you want sex. What did you assume—you'd spend two hours being nice to me and I'd let you screw me in the back room? I'm sure there are any number of women, including Helena, who'll be happy to be your screw toys."

He gripped her chin in his hand, anger and hurt riding him hard. *Christos*, only Valentina could turn him into a little boy. "Your insults to my character are getting annoying, Valentina. Is it so hard to believe that I wanted to give you a night away from the villa? From work?"

"Si, it is. You don't do anything without a motive or a goal, Kairos."

Yes, he meant to keep an eye on Helena and Georgio, but he'd wanted to give Valentina a night out on the town, too.

But his wife was as receptive as a porcupine.

Whose fault is that? Have you ever treated her as a partner, as an equal?

He slid the small package he'd had delivered the minute he'd finished his call with her brother, and pointedly ignored the awkward silence that fell when she saw it.

Leaning toward her, he kissed her cheek. Her shoulders tensed, a sudden stillness enveloping her.

God, she had such silky soft skin. All over.

His favorites were the incredible sensitive skin of her inner thighs, the neatly delineated curve where her tiny waist flared into hips, and the skin right below her right buttock where she had another mole.

He remembered her body like it was a map to some treasure.

"Happy birthday, Valentina."

She went still. "Who reminded you?"

When he didn't answer, she turned to him. "I know you're not big on remembering or celebrating birthdays and anniversaries."

His laughter when she'd joyously given him the platinum cuff links for one month of their marriage reverberated between them. He'd thought it hilarious that she bought expensive gifts for him with her brother's money without batting an eyelid.

She'd pouted prettily, argued that he was laughing at a romantic gesture.

He remembered the crushed look in her eyes when he'd blithely stated that it had probably cost her nothing to charge her brother's card.

Dios, he'd been an uncaring jerk of the first order. If she'd been juvenile and volatile, he'd been cruel and ruthless.

When he'd realized the wife he had acquired as part of

a merger was not the elegant, refined socialite he could be proud of, not the political asset he could count on, but a living, breathing creature with feelings and wishes, he'd resented her.

When she'd avowed love for him, he'd pitied her for her grand delusions. Become indifferent to her, waited for her to grow out of it.

When she'd started acting out, he'd been infuriated.

Not once had he realized how much vulnerability she had hidden beneath the fiery temper and impertinence. How honest she'd always been.

He wouldn't have fallen in love with her, but he could have been kinder to her. He was a man who thrived and succeeded in actively hostile environments—he could have molded her to what he wanted in a wife with one kind word or a romantic gesture.

Yet, he'd rigidly shut her out. As a clever business man, his own actions didn't make sense to him. He had used her for only one thing. And he'd made up his mind to do it again before discarding her for good.

Her slender fingers fiddled with the strings on the small package. "Kairos?"

He cleared his throat. "Leandro called me last night. He said it was the first birthday in years that you were spending away from them. He asked where you were and what I had dragged you into."

She pushed the gift away from her with such force that the small package flew off the other end of the table. She pinned him with a furious gaze. "I told him to stay out of my life." Her chest fell and rose with her harsh breaths. "I told you our deal was off if you even spoke to one of them behind my back."

When he'd have calmly walked away before, he said, "I told him this was between you and me."

He tugged her wrist when she'd have walked away. "They're simply worried about you. About what you're doing back with me. About your job and even about your safety—"

"Because no one thinks I can take care of myself. That I'm capable of being anything other than a naive sister or a trophy wife. No, wait, you've made it clear that I failed at even that. Not much of a trophy, am I?"

Somehow, she loosened his grip on her and walked away. She cut a wide swathe through the crowd, her hips swaying.

It was only one of her tantrums, he told himself.

He was not going to chase her like some lovesick boyfriend.

She had lasted a month—a miracle in itself—before that cloak of serenity had been ripped. Just what he had expected.

There had been innumerable occasions when she'd lost it just like that. And Kairos had always let her stew in it. He'd always set the boundaries so she would understand that he would never indulge her juvenile temper.

She would come back to him. She always had done. She would walk back in, and he'd pretend like nothing was wrong.

Until one day, she had left. Walked out, a voice mocked.

Until now, he'd attributed it to her foolish, romantic delusions but for the first time, he had to consider the possibility that he had driven her away. That he hadn't been the man she needed.

Punishing Valentina for walking out on him, seducing her and then discarding her…the very idea felt wrong now. Without honor. Yet what was the alternative?

Running his hands through his hair, he cursed long and hard.

Did he want to keep her? Knowing now that she'd always want something he couldn't give. Something he didn't know how to do.

And even if he did, his blind confidence all these days that Valentina would come back to him smacked of arrogance.

All he knew was that he was far from done with her. And she... *Christos*, even without trying this past month, the woman still had her hooks in him. There was passion between them and if he allowed it, there could be respect and even affection maybe.

Was there a chance for them?

Right now, all he knew was that she was hurt, that she needed a friend. And for once, he wanted to be everything Valentina needed.

CHAPTER EIGHT

TINA KNEW SHE was acting childishly, just as Kairos had predicted. She knew she was letting her emotions rule her head once again.

But she couldn't just sit there, with the pity gift he'd probably had his assistant order for her, mocking her. God, she hated herself for the leap in her pulse when he'd kissed her cheek, the hope bubbling in her throat when he'd placed the present in front of her.

She couldn't face him knowing that sooner or later he was going to find out what a spectacular failure she was; couldn't pretend anymore that being around him—seeing him day in and day out—wasn't wearing her down.

She walked away from the dance floor into the interior of the nightclub.

Black marble gleamed at her feet. Slowly, the music and noise from the crowd faded. She reached a door marked VIP lounge and hesitated.

When the six-foot-tall guard let her through without raising a brow, she slipped into the room.

The silence in the room was absolute. It was properly soundproofed. Black leather sectionals lined the entire back wall. Except for soft recessed lighting, the room was all shadows. She opened the refrigerator built discreetly into the wall. More wine and champagne.

It was so tempting to have some more. To bury the sensation of sinking, the bitterness of knowing that Kairos was right about her.

Instead she took out a bottle of water. She picked up one of the remotes. The music system, built into the walls, came on. Alicia Keyes crooned out a love song.

Sighing, she turned to the wall that was completely glass and looked down to the dance floor.

She sensed Kairos's presence behind her even before she heard him. Her spine felt like it would crack in two at the rigidness she infused into it. For a man who was six foot four and built like a bouncer, he'd always moved with such economy of movement. She chanced a quick look.

He was leaning against the door. Black dress shirt and black trousers—he could have blended into the shadows if didn't have such an electric presence. Goose bumps rose over her arms, remembered sensations zigzagging over her skin.

It had been foolish to think he wouldn't follow her. Right now, she was sort of an important asset to his complex machinery. Why had she trapped herself in here with him? Especially in the reckless mood she was in.

Even though they had shared a bedroom for the last month, she had left herself no chance to be alone with him. He worked late most nights, closeted in the study with Theseus and after sixteen-hour days with barely a break for dinner, she had been falling into exhausted sleep.

Now they were enclosed in the dark room—every sound and sight of the outside world cut off, electricity charging the air. His desire was like a scent she couldn't escape and every cell in her responded to it.

He'd never given her anything as a husband—not a word of praise, not a token gift, not a gesture of affection. But the knowledge of his desire for her, and that it seemed unquenchable, was a powerful aphrodisiac. It filled her with a false feeling of power over him, over this situation between them.

She turned and faced him, the harsh beauty of his face stealing her breath away. "Go back to your…strategies. Christian will drive me back to the house."

He prowled into the dark room, picked up the bottle she had left on the table and emptied it within seconds. "You're upset. You've been upset from the minute you walked into the nightclub. What happened?"

His concern, shockingly, was genuine. And it would only make her weak. "I won't run away in the middle of the night, if that's what you are worried about."

His growl was soft yet so loud in the soundproofed room. Goose bumps broke out on her skin. "Forget about the damned company for a second, Valentina. Forget about Theseus and Maria and Helena. Forget about our godforsaken pretense of a marriage. I'm asking you to tell me what's bothering you. Whatever it is, I will solve it for you."

"I don't want your help or your damn pity gift, or your concern."

"It is not a pity gift. I feel any number of things for you, Valentina, but pity is not one of them."

"I don't want any more clothes or jewelry or shoes. Giving me those things when I insist that they don't matter to me anymore only hurts me. Deeply." She hugged her middle. "I never thought you were a particularly cruel man. Heartless, but not cruel."

"It is not any of those things." His breath hissed out. "And I don't… I don't like hurting you. I never wanted to. Well, except for that night when I found you on the yacht."

"What is it then? The gift?"

"A subscription to an American network channel that streams Westerns. All you have to do is plug in the serial number on that card and you can stream an unlimited number of shows and movies." His mouth pursed at her silence.

"I heard you and Theseus discuss them the other day. It would be a good way to pass Saturdays. He loves it when you join him to watch those movies."

Shock enveloped her, followed by a rush of such powerful joy that she felt dizzy. "I...don't know what to say." She felt vulnerable, small. The strength of what she felt for him...she shook from it.

A flash of light illuminated his face. His nostrils flared, his mouth tightened. "I was cruel and harsh toward you that night. All through our marriage, really. I don't know diplomacy with you. I don't know how to soften my words. You...you weren't what I expected. Your days were filled with shopping and parties. You dressed outrageously. You flirted with every man you met—"

"I only did that after we were married," she shouted into the dark.

"How is that better?" He spoke more and more softly, gritting the words out.

With every step he took toward her, she stepped back. "I flirted to make you jealous. I flirted to get your attention. I flirted with friends who knew why I was doing it and who pitied my pathetic efforts. Because I was married to an uncaring beast."

He stilled. And if she weren't so miserable, Valentina could have laughed at the absurdity of it all. Hadn't he realized such a small thing?

"I didn't succeed even then, did I? You had no regard for me, I knew—"

He continued as if she hadn't interrupted him. But any hint of warmth she'd seen earlier was gone. His eyes were chips of the coldest frost. His jaw set into a granite cast.

"You drove me crazy, Valentina. I couldn't concentrate in meetings for worry of which party you would show up at that night, or with whom you would flirt all evening, or what hijinks you would get up to because I refused to cut the single friend I had. I canceled my trips abroad because I was worried what scandal you'd get into behind my back. I couldn't sleep when I went to Beijing because I was so worried you'd stay out too long with those useless friends of yours in some damn club with no one to look after you. I wanted a wife—instead you were like a child, who wanted the latest, shiniest, most expensive toy.

"I didn't know when you would decide you'd had enough of me. When you would ask your bloody brothers to purchase you a new man. When you would decide that you didn't want me in your bed anymore. When you would decide to welcome another man into your body—"

Her hand flew at his cheek. The sound reverberated in the silence like the crack of thunder.

Valentina gasped, waves of pain radiating up her arm. Still, that pain was nothing compared to the hurt in her chest. His head jerked back but he didn't even touch his cheek.

Her chest heaved, her breath rattling against the outrage she felt. "I've never looked at, much less thought of, another man since the first evening I saw you. Yes, I was shallow, naive, I had no purpose in my life. But what I gave to you, I gave it with conviction, with loyalty. You wanted a robot you could screw at night, a trophy you could display to the world during the day. You don't know how to give, Kairos. But you don't know how to receive, either. That first month… God, I was deliriously happy because of the orgasms you doled out. You shouldn't have married me when you don't know how to have a simple relationship."

She made to get away from him but his arm snagged around her waist. She fell into his side, her breasts and belly pressed up against his hard body. Her breath was punched out of her, shallow and serrated. One hard thigh tangled between hers, rubbing at the center of all the ache. Wetness pooled at her sex, soaking into her flimsy thong.

A whimper fell from her mouth as she tried to move back and rubbed up a little more against him. One arm stayed tight around her waist while he lifted her chin with the other.

His silvery eyes glowed with unbanked desire. Both his hands gripped her hips now. Such large hands that his fingers could always easily span her waist. Her breath fell in soft pants, which seemed amplified in the room.

"It's been more than ten months, now, Valentina. I've been going crazy with wanting you."

Her eyes widened. "I don't believe you. You…"

"Because I'm so dishonorable that I would bed another woman while my wife is missing? Because one woman is the same as the next for an ambitious, ruthless man like me? Because I didn't miss you in bed with a longing that eats at me, a hunger that I can't control?"

"Then why didn't you come after me?"

"Because I don't need you, Valentina."

He growled the words out loud as if he could make them true and yet Tina knew that he meant them. Everything seemed to tilt and shift, the flash of hurt in his eyes when she'd called him a robot, not imagined but real.

For the first time, he felt like a flesh-and-blood man. He was determined to prove to her, and more important, to himself, that he didn't need her.

Why was he so determined to keep her out, to pretend that he didn't care? The gift, this night, his care for her when she was exhausted—everything said he did care.

Further thought was extinguished when his mouth fell onto hers with a rapacious hunger. Relief poured through her, twisting with need. She missed his body, the sense of excitement and danger as he toppled her inhibitions one by one. She missed his bruising kisses, his insatiable appetite that drew out her pleasure until she was begging him, even the epithets that flew from his lips during sex.

His tongue plunged into her mouth, sliding and stroking around her own. Power. Passion. Possession. His mouth stamped all of them over hers. His stubble rasped roughly against her jaw, her lips stinging from the torturous pleasure.

Her hands roamed all over him—the broad shoulders, the muscled arms, the defined chest. The thud of his heart filled her with a reckless urgency. Just tonight, she promised herself. Just a few kisses.

His hands sunk into her hair, pulling at it roughly as he tilted her face up. Rough and hard, he kissed her as if he meant to devour her. As if she had finally pushed him over the edge.

She reveled in the pain and the pleasure his grip forced on her. Moans and whimpers, the sounds she made filled the quiet room. Her eyelids fell, her breath was not her own. An explosion of color filled her body as his mouth left hers to trail down her jaw. Featherlight kisses alternated with hard, guttural words from him in Greek.

She tugged at his hair, desperate to be closer. She shuddered as he sank his teeth into the crook of her neck. Her pulse beat fervently against his tongue. He closed his mouth against the tender skin and sucked. Tremors raced across her skin, pooling between her legs. He swept his tongue over the tender hurt. "Look at me, *pethi mou*. Look at what you drive me to, still. Look at what you turn me into."

Raw desire glittered in his eyes. Tina gasped as cold glass pressed against her bare buttocks. And in front of her he was a cauldron of desire. Heat blasted up her neck and into her cheeks as she realized he had walked her to the back of the room. Shock and desire made her voice strange, husky. Fingers bunching into his shirt, she fought the sensual haze. "We're…they can…"

"No one can see you but me, Valentina. No one knows this body except me, *ne*? Let them be witness to what you drive me to. Let me take you here, in a public place with nothing but a flimsy piece of glass separating us from the crowd. Does this tell you how much control I have? Does that tell you what insanity you drive me to?"

His hands tugged her dress up. Madness filled her body. Rough hands pulled her leg up to wrap it around his hip. She moaned loudly. Her aching sex pressed into his pelvis like that. So close. So hard. Head thrown back into the glass, Tina let herself drown in the sensation.

Nothing else remained anyway. Nothing she was good for. She wanted to gorge on the sensations he created. One callused hand cupped her buttock while one hand roughly pushed her thong out of the way. Gaze holding hers, he simply covered her mound with his palm. All the roughness, all the urgency faded. Soft and exploring, his fingers stroked the lips of her sex.

The intimacy of it in such a public place pushed her arousal to the edge. Her heart pounded, she was past rationality.

Slowly, his fingers separated her folds and dipped inside. "You're wet. So ready for me. Always ready for me."

It was a statement that rang with masculine pride. Her palms flat against the glass, she shivered as he spread the dampness around her opening in mind-numbing circles with a thoroughness that cinched her body into a tight knot.

"Please, Kairos," she whispered, burying her mouth in his neck. Roughly, she dragged the lapels of his shirt apart, until a button popped. She was ravenous for him. For his skin, For his taste. She licked the strong column of his throat. Tasted the sweat and masculinity of him.

He growled, the sound bursting out of his chest. His hand left her buttock. Valentina moaned in protest. But he only laughed. With deft movements, he undid the knot at the back of her neck.

The silky strings fell over her chest. His silver gaze held hers, a wicked smile curving his sensuous mouth. Slowly, he pulled the strings down.

Down, down, down until the dress flopped at her waist. It bunched around her hips, leaving her breasts and her sex exposed to his devouring gaze.

He looked like a marauder from the dark ages, the stamp of desire on his hard features. His gaze moved to her breasts. They were brown tipped and tight from the cold air kissing their pert tips. His breath fell in hot strokes. Their gazes held. Breath was fire in her throat. Callused fingers cupped their meager weight. Molded and cupped. He drew maddening circles around the aching tips.

And he bent, licking one engorged tip. Again and again. This breast and then that breast. He cupped them and pushed them up, his tongue flicking around and around. "You were right. I was a selfish bastard to have ignored these. To have overlooked what pleasure I could bring you by touching you here. Never again, *pethi mou*. Never will I neglect these again." And then, as if to seal his promise, he opened his mouth and closed it over one turgid peak.

Tina shook and shuddered, coming off the wall as he suckled her deep into his mouth. Pleasure forked down from the tips of her breasts to her pelvis in deep, sharp arrows. He pressed his tongue against the tip and began the torturous pleasure all over again. Just when she thought she couldn't bear it anymore, he started on the other breast.

The tremors coursing through her were constant now. Dampness coated her skin. His mouth still at her breast, he moved his hand down to her sex and penetrated her with a finger while his thumb pressed against her clit. Her head banged against the glass pane, Tina thrust her pelvis into his hand. Release was so close now, a shimmer of heat all over her skin, building and building.

"Open your eyes, *agapita*," Kairos whispered huskily. His words vibrated against her skin, pulling that knot in her belly tighter. "I know what brings you over the edge."

Tina looked down. His mouth was at her breast, his silver eyes darkened to a dark gray that happened only when he was aroused. His fingers didn't stop their rhythm but it was the heat in his gaze that pushed her. He rubbed his cheek against the wet, glistening nipple. His thumb and forefingers pinched her clit just as he commanded, "Come for me, Valentina."

Her orgasm broke over her, rolling and rippling through her in a flurry of waves that kept coming and coming. But he didn't stop. His fingers kept her at that high, riding that swollen, sensitive bundle.

The aftershocks shook her muscles until she flopped her forehead onto his shoulder and arrested his wrist. She felt boneless, as if she were nothing but a conduit for pleasure and sensations. "Stop, please, Kairos. No more."

His big hand remained between her thighs, soothing the tremors in her muscles. The other pushed back a damp tendril from her forehead. Tenderness. He'd always shown her tenderness in bed. For the span of a few minutes.

The last flutters of her release left her body, leaving an aching void behind. She'd challenged him so boldly that she would resist him. That she would never again fall into his arms. And here she was, her dress bunched up around her waist, against a glass wall while a crowd danced beneath them.

Still, there was a physical ache inside her where she wanted him. Needed him.

His mouth moved from her temple to her cheekbones to her jaw. His mouth was warm and hard, hungrier now. She thrust her tongue into his mouth, determined to pull him into the same sinking well of pleasure. He growled, his chest vibrating with it when she dug her teeth into his lower lip. Hard. And again.

He'd always controlled their sex life—when, where, how—all of it. Enslaved by the pleasure he gave, she'd allowed him to lead, blindly following. But no more.

Her hands automatically locked at his nape, pulling him closer.

His hard chest crushed her sensitive breasts. His hands were filled with her buttocks. Lifting her against the glass, he brought her pelvis closer to his erection.

Moans erupted from their mouths as he rocked into her. Thick and long, his erection pressed against her sensitized clit, sending a quiet flutter of sensation through her again.

"Put your hands up."

A shiver went through her at the raw lust in the command. Denial whispered at her lips yet no words came out.

A rigid line to his mouth, he gripped her wrists and pulled her arms up. The arch of her spine pushed her breasts toward him. He didn't let go of her wrists. As if he didn't trust her. But his other hand, palm down, moved from her forehead to her nose, to her mouth.

When his fingers stilled at her lips, she instantly opened her mouth. She knew what he liked. He had trained her well enough. Though he had never let her take him in her mouth, even when she'd offered. But it wasn't just that he had taught her what pleased him.

She was addicted to his pleasure. Drunk on the power she felt for the few minutes when he needed her so desperately. When his control balanced on a serrated edge.

And she needed that tonight. She needed him to want her as desperately as she'd needed his touch.

His features hardened when she sucked his finger into her mouth. A shudder went through him at her caress. The raw pleasure etched on his hard, implacable features turned her on as if he had touched her again at her core.

She had lived for those moments. She took each callused finger into her mouth one after the other, knowing that it drove him crazy.

His silvery gaze devouring her, he undid the clasp of his belt buckle. The soft rip of the zipper punctured the sound of her harsh breaths. His trousers fell from his hips with a shy whisper.

She had no will left. Her gaze dipped down to his groin. Heat broke out over her skin again, instant, explosive, like lightning appearing over a dark sky in the blink of an eye. She stared, greedy for the sight of him.

Reaching out boldly, she pushed his shirt up until a patch of his ripped abdomen was visible. Dark skin stretched taut over defined musculature delineated with a line of hair. Even the V at the juncture of his groin was well defined.

His cock—she blushed at thinking the word he'd made her say in the second week of their marriage—thickened and lengthened under her hungry gaze, the soft head already glistening wet.

He hustled her back toward the glass again, his hands kneading her buttocks. His mouth buried in her neck again. Her nipples, hard once again, poked at his chest. His hands were everywhere. Even after he'd given her release, he wouldn't just take her. No, he built her body into a frenzy all over again.

If he had been a selfish lover, if he'd denied her pleasure even once, maybe she wouldn't have become such a slave to it. And to him. But no, he pushed her again and again to the edge. To release.

Rough hands pushed her dress all the way down. "I need to be inside you. Now. Valentina."

The question in his statement jerked her head up. He wouldn't assume, he wouldn't take.

"*No!*" The stillness that came over him had such restrained violence in it that she shivered.

In a fluid move, she sank to her knees.

His curse ripped the heavy silence when she wrapped her fingers around his hardness. Velvet-coated steel, he was so soft and yet so hard at the same time. His thigh muscles tensed like rocks when she braced her hands on them.

"Valentina, you don't—"

"Will you give up control for a few minutes? Will you let me in?"

She didn't wait for his answer. Bracing herself for the taste of him, she licked the soft head.

Salty and masculine. She looked up, her mouth open and ready. Tension etched onto every angle of his face. Such raw need and longing written on every hard plane of it that satisfaction pulsed through her.

Tilting her head down, she took him in her mouth this time. Another curse burst through the air. His hips jerked forward until he was filling her mouth.

Instantly, he pulled back. He was losing control. The thought spurred her on like a wild fire in the forest. *Bene,* she wanted him to lose control.

She repeated the movements of her mouth and hands. He said nothing, made no demands. When she glanced a look up at him, he growled an animalistic sound that sent shivers up and down her spine. But his body spoke for him. His hands had reached into her hair at some point. Every time she clasped him harder, he thrust a little into her mouth. Every time he hit the roof of her mouth, his thighs clenched a little more.

His body betrayed him, his need took over just as hers had done earlier. Using it, Tina sucked him harder, faster, intent on blowing his mind apart.

Her mouth felt hollow, her knees dug into the hard marble, her wrists were beginning to hurt from the repeated action but she didn't care.

Every discomfort was worth it for now her husband had no control left. His hands in her hair directed her mouth where and how he wanted it. Deeper and faster and harder.

And then suddenly, he pulled out of her mouth. Rough hands grasped her under her shoulders and pulled her up. She swayed, her knees shaky, and he held her fiercely close with one arm while he stroked himself.

His roar of pleasure vibrated around them as he came against her belly.

Tina looked up, a fever of arousal in her muscles at how completely undone he looked. Silence beat down around them, punctured only by his harsh breaths. His head bent against her shoulder, his breath hit her in warm strokes. His powerful body was still shuddering against hers.

She had no idea how long they stood like that. The scent of his release and hers cloyed the air, leaving her no escape from it. When he looked up at her, she closed her eyes. His thumb traced the line of her jaw softly, almost with reverence.

Her eyes flew open when she felt his fingers on her belly. He wiped her tummy with a napkin he produced from somewhere and then gently righted her dress. Heat swamped her cheeks.

His hands shook as he zipped up his trousers and buckled his belt. She tucked her hands to the side but the little tremors wouldn't subside.

She couldn't pretend that the whole experience hadn't shaken her. She truly was naive. Drawing satisfaction by seeing his control shatter, by bringing him to his knees like that, the raw intimacy of his actions...it had only seared him deeper into her psyche.

She looked away from him just as his gaze turned toward her. She walked over to the refrigerator on trembling legs and poured herself a glass of water. She drank the whole thing in one gulp, her mouth parched.

She felt him come to a stop right behind her. Hesitation, so uncharacteristic of him, charged the air. "Valentina—"

"Please, Kairos. Take me home."

He stared at her for what felt like an eternity before he nodded.

CHAPTER NINE

SHE HAD BARELY reached their room and changed out of the stupid dress, then come down for a cup of hot tea when he cornered her.

"I want to sleep. I'm… I can already feel the headache beginning."

He took hold of her wrist, tugging her into the study he had taken over from Theseus.

The smell of wood and cigars instantly reminded her of her grandfather Antonio. Another man who had thought she would amount to nothing.

While she stared into the empty fireplace, Kairos came back with steaming black coffee, cheese and perfectly cut apples.

"Eat."

Her stomach roiled so she took the plate from him and dutifully ate. He sat down on the step of the fireplace, his long legs bumping into hers until she shifted and the line of them grazed hers.

"Valentina, look at me."

Concern and something else glinted in his silver gaze. She forced a fake smile to her mouth. "My knees are a little the worse for wear, but, *si*, I'm perfectly fine."

He flinched then, whatever he saw in her eyes making him draw back. *As if she could hurt him!*

"I've never… I didn't ask you to do that for me."

"You did it for me." Just mentioning the day when he

had put his mouth to the most intimate part of her sent shivers through her.

He scowled. "Why today?"

She looked at him and then away, afraid of what he would see in her eyes. "I was frustrated, feeling reckless." She looked down at her locked fingers. "The release you gave me took the edge off before I did something stupid. So I returned the favor."

A dangerous glint appeared in his eyes. One brow arched on his arrogant face. "Took the edge off? Was that what I did?"

His gaze dared her to shrug, to cheapen it.

He pinned her to the spot with his penetrating stare, as if he could see into her soul.

She swallowed and looked away. The endless silence, his painful indifference—it was all gone and there was a different man watching her. A man she'd always sensed beneath his ruthlessness but could never touch.

She struggled to make her voice casual. "Compared to my history of making a spectacle of myself every time I get upset, giving my almost separated husband a blow job is probably of minor consequence, *si*?"

"You do not fool me, Valentina. What happened at the nightclub couldn't have left you untouched—" he placed a broad palm over her chest "—in here."

Her heart pounded away under his touch. "Because only you can be casual about sex? Not I?"

"I've slept only with two women in my entire life. You and one other girlfriend. It was a convenient relationship I fell into and we went our separate ways when it wasn't more. I have never been casual about sex. I told you I don't fall into relationships easily. I had Theseus's support but when I left him, I had to start all over with little to my name. Careers like that don't leave room for relationships."

"You proposed to Sophia."

"Because I thought we would suit. Because we were friends and I admired her." He blew a breath, the light from the chandelier caressing his rugged features. "She was wiser than I was, which is why she said no. I realize now she had felt like a safe choice."

Every word out of his mouth mocked the wall she had erected.

She couldn't bear his tenderness, this concern. She couldn't fight her own need for him like this. Especially not today. "If I had known a blow job was all it would take to get you to open to me, I would have gone down on my knees long ago," she said flippantly.

When she would have shuffled away from him, he clasped her arms. "Stop being so glib! Stop acting as if that didn't mean anything."

"What did it mean then, Kairos?"

He looked as if she had slapped him, not asked a simple question. But when she thought he would shut down and walk away, he looked thoughtful. "It meant that you and I are not done with each other. And not just sexually. It meant that...this is not just about Helena and Theseus and our stupid deal or the divorce anymore. It is about us."

Her breath left her, her heart thudding against her ribcage. When he opened up like that, when he let her see what he was feeling, thinking, she... *No!* She couldn't.

Tina had never been so terrified by her own vulnerability, by her own stupid hope.

She wanted to break through the barriers he had erected between them, wanted to find the sweet man who had bought her a gift he knew she would love.

She wanted that Kairos in all the moments, not just every now and then. She would always want him. But would the way he saw her ever change? Could she give herself to him completely if he didn't respect her?

No. She couldn't.

She strolled onto the veranda, trying to get a grip on herself.

He settled down next to her on the small wicker sofa. Hesitation shimmered in his eyes. "I…shouldn't have kissed you today. I shouldn't have lost control. I want you every minute of every day. But only today I realized that what I…planned for you is wrong. What I thought about you is wrong."

"What did you plan for me?"

"I thought I would work you out of my system in these three months. I was angry… I felt betrayed when you left. My ego was definitely bruised."

Laughter burst out of her. "Oh, please…don't look so guilty. I meant to bring you to your knees by rubbing your nose in my fabulous self. I was going to make you regret ever leaving me."

Elbows on his knees, he bent forward. He sighed and studied his hands. One thick lock of hair fell forward onto his forehead, his shoulders bunched into a tight line. It was a rare glimpse into his true self that she couldn't help but drink in.

Her heart clenched when he looked up and smiled.

"I knew, even that night when I couldn't find you, that it wasn't just your fault our marriage had failed. I just… my pride wouldn't let me accept it, accept that while we both have flaws, what you gave me is priceless. You didn't throw it away on a whim or an impulse."

It felt as if they had reached a crossroads. "Look at us, all grown up, *si*?" she said trying to lighten the moment. "Being adult about a breakup. Maybe we can be friends like they show in American sitcoms?"

A blaze lit up in his eyes and she looked away. Of course, it was a foolish suggestion. But the thought of having to walk away all over again, especially when she was finally getting to see beneath the rigid exterior…the very thought of it made her shiver.

"Will you please tell me what happened, Valentina?" He exhaled roughly. "I promise you I won't be cruel or mocking. I want to understand."

With one promise, he knocked all her barriers down. For Kairos never promised anything he didn't mean. "Chiara fired me. Only *I* could get fired from an unpaid internship, *si*?" The words fell over themselves to come out now.

"What? Today?"

"Right before you called me. I was…putting away my stuff. I feel like such a failure."

His arm came around her gently.

Tears pooled in her eyes and she inhaled noisily. "Don't be kind to me."

"What was the stupid thing you would have done today? Run away again?"

"Crawl back to my brothers. I miss them today." She swallowed the ache down. "I miss Leandro's tight hugs. Luca's corny jokes. I miss Alex's calm acceptance, Izzie's wet kisses. I miss Sophia's quiet support."

"They adore you, don't they?" he said softly.

"For years after Leandro brought me to live with them, every time something went wrong in my world, I would throw one hell of a tantrum." She laughed through the tears, realizing how insecure she'd been to doubt her brothers' love for her. "I'd push them to the edge as if to test them."

"To see how far you could push them before they rejected you? And if that was going to happen, you'd rather know sooner?"

The depth of his perception stunned her. "*Si.* If there's one thing I've learned through the debacle of our marriage, it's that I process everything that doesn't go my way by acting out. I think I did it at regular intervals—either when I thought Leandro was distant or when Luca disappeared for weeks. I would wreak hell and they would rush to reassure me that I was indeed loved and wanted. I was so... needy and vulnerable and they spoiled me to make up for losing my mother, for how terrified I had been when they found me after her death.

"There was nothing I wanted that couldn't be mine. Leandro even tried to protect me from the truth, *si*? And then I met you and you wouldn't dance to my tune...and all my insecurities came pouring out."

"Today, you wanted your brothers to tell you that it was okay to get fired at a job?"

"Yes. That I wasn't a useless waste of space. I wanted them to protect me from you."

He groaned and she laughed at the regret pinching his mouth. "I was such a—"

"Uptight, self-righteous ass?" she supplied. When he nodded and laughed, her heart slipped a little out of her reach. "Sophia's words."

"The last time I spoke to Chiara, she told me that your team all adore you. That you're taking them by storm."

She nodded. "I've been enjoying it. Chiara's not easy to work for but she's so talented. You were right, I was learning so much. We've been preparing for the fall collection. I've been liaising with designers and their assistants, and PR people to put a marketing campaign together. She let me put the outfits and accessories together. I even handpicked the models to showcase each different outfit. I talked to the photographers, the lighting assistants. A hundred different things have to come together perfectly for the collection to be showcased. I…honestly don't know how it happened. I double-checked and triple-checked everything. I spent most of the previous evenings calling every personal assistant and designer checking to make sure things would go smoothly. I…"

"What went wrong?"

"Honestly, I've no idea. I must have messed up something because we ended up with ten boxes of swimwear. Which is a *disaster* because it's October and the same order was shipped to about eleven different stores. Instead of Burberry coats, we have Bermuda shorts. Instead of designer pantsuits, we have sleeveless tops and shorts. Everything was wrong. The catalogs are not even ready. Chiara had a nightmare to fix on her hands and no inventory. Her phones kept going off. I tried to stem the panic from store managers waiting to figure out what to do. I… When I went into her office, one of the vice presidents was ripping into her. I told him it was my fault, not Chiara's. I… I quickly put together a letter of resignation and walked out."

"So she didn't really fire you then?"

He squeezed her fingers softly. "She was so buried that she didn't get a chance. We were alone for a moment in her office. She looked up and said she knew she shouldn't have taken me on. She knew I would only bring trouble."

"Valentina—"

"I… I had a simple job to do. And I messed it up." She rubbed the base of her palms around her eyes. "You were right. I should just accept that I'm not good for anything—"

Kairos tilted her chin up until she looked at him. "That's not true. I was a cruel bastard to say that." He'd always thought her weak-spined, a slave to suggestion, but only now could he see the strength that had always been there. "Valentina, listen to me. Making a mistake in a job is not the end of the world. What you do after is what matters.

How many times you pick yourself up after you fall...that's what matters."

"Then I failed in that, too, *si*?" She laughed and the sound couldn't hide the frustration she felt. "Don't you see, Kairos? Letting you kiss me, touch me, letting myself get physically close to you...what I did today was not cheap, *no*. Was not meaningless. Seeing you undone—" her gaze landed on his mouth, his eyes, and he felt burned by the intensity of it "—it's a high I could chase again and again. But it is self-destructive behavior. It is harmful to me. *You are harmful to me.* Every little bit of your past you give me, every small admission you make about what you feel for me...it comes at a high price. It comes with a fight, it feels like squeezing blood out of a stone. I think that's just how you're made. And if I've learned anything by watching my brothers and their wives, I know it shouldn't be this hard. You broke my heart last time and if I give you half a chance, you will do it again.

"So please...if you have ever cared for me, even a little bit, don't touch me. Don't kiss me." A ghost of a smile flitted over her face as her brown gaze moved over his. "Don't follow through on your nefarious plans."

"This...what happened between us tonight—" he moved his hand between them, a fine tension in his body "—is nothing shameful. This is not something that I would ever use against you."

"And yet this—my sexual desire for you—is what made you think I wouldn't hesitate before falling into another man's bed. That I would betray our vows."

He clasped her jaw, forcing her to look at him. "I was lashing out. I knew you wouldn't betray me. I just...on the best of days, you're like a hurricane. All I wanted was to contain you, contain the damage you did to—"

"Your reputation? Your business alliances?"

"Damn it, Valentina! *Damage to me!* To the way I wanted to live my life. I've never in my life cared about anyone. The only way I learned to survive was by being in control of myself. Even after I came to live with Theseus and Maria... I don't know how to let someone close. I don't know how to handle emotion and all that it entails. I can't bear the pain that comes from loving someone. I just...can't. And you...every day you made me insane. You mocked my rules, you teased my attention even when you weren't trying and when you got up to one of your spectacles, you threatened every ounce of my control."

"But you never lost it," she whispered, his confession searing through her.

Every time Kairos thought he had a grip on her, Valentina showed him a new side. Unraveled him anew. What they had done tonight at the nightclub had not just been physical release.

Christos, it only showed again how open she was. How much he could hurt her, if he wasn't careful.

And suddenly the idea of hurting Valentina was unconscionable.

"The more you pushed me for a reaction, I see now, the more I retreated. It became a matter of my will against yours. I couldn't...let you...have so much control over me. Being married to you—it was like asking a man who doesn't know how to walk to swim an ocean. You are right, though. It shouldn't be this hard. But I can't... I don't know if it will ever be different, either. I can't change what I am."

I won't love you.

Kairos knew she understood what he'd said because she paled and nodded. If there were tears in her eyes, she hid them by looking down at her clasped hands.

He should have felt an ease of the weight that had been cinching tight around his neck. Instead of relief that he had set the score right, that he had told her what the future could be, all he felt was an ache in his chest. An unnamed longing.

"The fault is not all yours, Kairos, I know that."

The vulnerability in her eyes, the lovely picture she made in the moonlight melted something near his heart. That she thought herself a failure because of his cruel words was unacceptable.

He knelt in front of her, took her hands in his, looked her in the eye. "I'm...sorry for making you feel like you're less than what you are. Even if Chiara fired you, you're not a failure. You're the most courageous woman I know. It took guts to walk away from your brothers, from me, from the lap of luxury. Guts to face all the people who mocked you, who treated you so horribly and to go to work at that place all these months. It took guts to try again and again to put together that blasted portfolio, guts to stand up to your blackmailing husband and make a deal of your own.

"You live your life with all your passion poured into it. You take risk after risk with yourself. And maybe there's no way forward for us, but *Christos,* I still want you. Desperately. Like I have never wanted anything else in life. But I won't touch you. Not unless your heart and mind both want me to."

Tina took a long, hot shower, took even longer to dress and finally walked back into the bedroom. She wasn't going to fall asleep anytime soon. She was too wired, too many thoughts whirling through her head. And she definitely didn't want to have the confrontation that was coming.

It was ironic since she'd always been the one that had pushed for it.

Since the nightclub a week ago, she'd been avoiding Kairos, faking sleep when he came to bed, running around the estate like the very devil was chasing her in the evening when he was home.

As always, he'd given it to her straight. Told her he would never change, never open himself up to her. Which should have sent her running for the hills.

Instead, his words seemed to have burrowed deep into her soul. She had seen the respect she'd wanted in his eyes. She'd seen the glitter of regret and pride when he had told her it had taken guts to stand up for herself.

That should have been enough. But all she wanted was more of him, more of the Kairos who saw the true her, the Kairos who kissed her as if he couldn't breathe, the Kairos who—

Dios, had she no self-preservation instinct?

"Couldn't hide any longer in the bathroom?"

Kairos's low voice halted her hand toweling her hair. She shrugged. Taking a deep breath, she finished brushing her hair, trying her hardest not to let her gaze settle on him in the mirror.

Turning to the dresser, she pulled out her running shorts, a T-shirt and a sports bra. She pulled her hair back into a high ponytail.

She barely took two steps before he was in front of her. Blocking her. Breath halted in her throat.

"Where are you going?"

She kept her gaze on his chest. The olive skin shadowed through his white dress shirt, which wasn't tucked quite neatly into his trousers. Every time she looked at him, she remembered him undone now. Heat swarmed her face again. *Dios*, what had she been thinking to be so...bold with him? That was a memory she wouldn't forget to her dying days. Nor did the image of him climaxing fail to arouse her.

"I... I'm going for a run. I'm too restless to sleep."

"It's eleven thirty at night. And if you run anymore, you will disappear into thin air."

Before she could even blink, he took the clothes from her and threw them on the bed. A finger under her chin tilted her face up. "Is it working, Valentina?"

"What?"

"Avoiding me. Is it making the ache to be with me any less? Because if it is, you have to share the secret with me."

"I don't know... *No*. It is not helping. You're like that slice of chocolate cake that you can't resist even knowing that it will go to your hips and buttocks."

He laughed, lovely crease lines fanning out near his eyes. "I talked to Chiara today."

Hurt punched through her. "I can't go back to a job where not only am I not wanted, but can't even do anything properly, Kairos. How can I face my colleagues when they all see that I returned because of my powerful husband's recommendation? I will have no more value than a mannequin."

"Fine," he said, releasing her. Something like humor shone in his eyes. "Maybe I'm wrong in assuming you would want to hear what Chiara told me involved Helena."

Having dropped the bomb, the devilish man casually strolled to the balcony attached to the bedroom.

"What do you mean Helena was involved?"

"Sit down and maybe I will tell you."

She glared at him. And sat down.

He pulled her closer to him and she went unwillingly.

His thighs pressed against hers and instantly that awareness slammed into her. But beneath that ever-present hum was something else, something new between them.

Tenderness. Rapport. The connection she had craved for so long with him. As if all the cacophony and noise in their relationship had been cleared away and they could see each other clearly for the first time.

And the more she saw of Kairos, the more Valentina liked him. Genuine like, not the I-want-to-rip-his-clothes-off kind. Although that was there, too.

"I have been thinking on what you said to me."

Instantly, he tensed. "Which part?"

Tina could literally feel his stillness. The way it contained his rumbling emotions. He thought she had made a decision about them, their future. And he was hanging on an edge just as she was any time she thought about it. "About picking myself up, planning my next move. I will find another way to achieve my goals. Working with Chiara gave me the confidence that I'm in the right field, that I can work as hard as it takes. That I have a natural talent for fashion. It's just a matter of finding the right outlet, the right opportunity."

The smile he shot her was full of joy and admiration. "I'm glad to hear that."

"So...anyway, *efharisto*, Kairos."

"You needn't thank me, I did nothing."

"Thank you for seeing me through that first hurdle. For...just being there." And since she had to fight the glittering desire she saw in his eyes, she quipped, "For showing me that when I hit the next hurdle, all I have to do is get drunk, go to a nightclub and maybe find a guy to—"

"You finish that sentence at serious threat of harm to yourself, Valentina."

His growl made laughter explode from her mouth. She leaned back into her seat, and took a deep breath of the scented air.

When Kairos had handed her a glass of red wine, she took a sip and sighed.

"No more than one glass," she added.

He smiled, slanted a teasing, hot glance her way. "I was hoping you wouldn't count. I was hoping to get you drunk and have my wicked way with you. I like you drunk."

"Ha ha…not funny. You like what I do when I'm drunk." *Dios mio*, he was even more irresistible when he teased her like that.

"Too horny for it to be a joke?" There was a flash of his white teeth and that rakish smile. Tina wondered if her panties could melt by how hot and wet she was.

"Something like that, *si*," she replied haughtily and had the pleasure of being enveloped by his deep laughter again.

"I have always loved your honesty, *agapita*." Her heart thudded against her ribcage. "Fine, no more than one glass."

As far as the eye could see, darkness blanketed the grounds. Crickets chirped. The scents of pine and ocean created a pungent yet pleasant perfume on the air. For a long while, neither of them spoke.

His arm came around her shoulders, his fingers drawing lazy circles on her bare skin. There was nothing sexual about his touch and still her breath hung on a serrated edge. The intimacy of the moment was even more raw than what they had shared at the nightclub.

"Do you realize we've never once…spent time like this? Without fighting, without ripping each other's clothes off?" The words escaped her—wistful, poignant—before she could lock them away.

Moonlight threw shadows on her hand clasped in his. His thumb passed back and forth over the veins on the back of her hand. She sensed he was as loath to disturb the moment as she was. "Hmmm. Although I always liked the ripping-clothes-off part, too."

She snorted and he snorted back.

"Today is my mother's birthday," he said suddenly into the silence.

"I…do you miss her?"

"Yes. She would have liked you. She was like you—fierce, bold."

She laced her fingers through his and brought his hand to her mouth, pressing a soft kiss to the veins on the back of his hand. Strength and willpower and vulnerability—she was only beginning to realize what a complex man he was.

"I would like to know more about her, please."

He remained quiet for so long that Tina sighed. She couldn't force him to share pieces of himself with her. She couldn't forever be the one who took that first step. Not because of pride but because she couldn't bear the hurt of it when he left her standing again.

Until he started speaking. "She was a prostitute. I know how they're forced into those choices firsthand, the wretchedness of that life. She fed me from the money she made through her…job. Until she fell sick and drifted into nothing."

Even in the slivers of moonlight, Kairos saw how pale Valentina became. She blinked until the sheen of tears dimmed. Only then did he realize he'd revealed something he'd told only one other person. Theseus.

"I'm sorry that you…"

"That I came from such a dirty past?"

"That you lost a mother you loved." Pure steel filled her voice, daring him to mock her sympathy. "No matter her choices. I know what it feels like to lose a loved one."

Why did he forget that beneath the sophistication and good humor, Valentina's childhood hadn't been smooth, either? That she, more than anyone, understood the ache that came with loving someone?

It was as if he still, willingly, refused to look beneath the impulsive, reckless woman he had initially assumed she was.

"Are you ashamed of who she was?" The question was soft, tentative.

He scowled. "No. Never. Why the hell would you think that?"

"Because," she said with a sigh, "you play your cards pretty close to your chest, Kairos. Even when they did that exposé on you for that business magazine, there was nothing about your background. Top businessman under thirty and it was as if you had sprouted from nowhere as a full-grown businessman at the age of twenty-three."

He grimaced, recognizing the truth in Valentina's summation.

The journalist who'd done that interview had been so frustrated. More than once, she'd tried to steer the conversation to his childhood and he'd bluntly steered her away, keeping his answers to his successes and the companies he had fixed.

He wasn't ashamed, but for years, he *had* hidden his roots. He'd pushed away men who could have been friends because he'd felt separate, isolated. Felt as if he hadn't belonged because of where he had come from.

His mind whirled as thoughts poured through him.

"How did you come to live with Theseus and Maria?"

He braced himself, knowing what it was building to. Knowing that Valentina wouldn't stop until all of him was stripped before her. His illusions and his control. "He and Maria came to one of the most impoverished areas of Athens and he caught me as I cut the strings to Maria's purse and started running."

He heard her soft gasp and clenched his heart—or what remained of it—against the pity. Memories came at him like swarming bees. The poverty. The filth. The fight to survive another day. As if she was losing him to the past,

Valentina tightened her fingers around his, brushed a soft kiss against the underside of his jaw.

"Do not pity me, Valentina. This is why I wouldn't reveal my background before. Because it skews people's perception of me. Instead of a powerful businessman, they see a man who's crippled by his roots."

She snuggled into him as if he hadn't just snarled at her. "Or they see a man who made something of himself even when the odds were stacked against him. You keep treating me as if I'm unfamiliar with anything in life but designer couture and privilege, Kairos. If Leandro hadn't persuaded Antonio that I belonged with them, if he hadn't found me and brought me to live with him and Luca, where do you think I would be today? You think I've forgotten the fear that no one will care about me. Just because I pretend as if that doesn't matter it doesn't mean it's not there every day within me."

He looked at her and this time only saw understanding. Again, the realization, that this understanding had always been there for him to reach for, filled him.

The realization that Valentina was more than he'd ever wanted in a wife. It was as if his subconscious had been aware of it all along.

Was that why he'd always kept her at a distance? Why he'd retreated in the face of her passionate declarations, treated her with cold indifference?

She cupped his palm tenderly, her thumb tracing his jawline back and forth. It was comfort, it was affection. And still the jolt of that contact rang through him. Neither was he unaware of the different kind of intimacy the night and their discussion had wrought on them.

She was stealing away pieces of him. He tried to fight it, a sense of dread blanketing him, but her tender touch anchored him to the here, to the now. To her.

"How old were you?"

"Eleven? Twelve?" He rubbed his free hand over his face. "I was this…feral animal that would have done anything to survive another day. I was terrified he'd turn me in to the police. Theseus was really built in those days. He restrained me for fifteen minutes while I tried to break his hold and run. I stopped fighting when he said he would not turn me in. I was shocked when he brought me to his home. That first year I was terrified he would change his mind and throw me out. By the time, I was thirteen, Theseus and Maria adopted me officially."

"Then why did you leave them?"

The question came at Kairos like a fist, smashing through the walls he hadn't even known he'd need against her. "You know the answer to that."

"*No*, I don't." Something almost akin to desperation rang in her voice. "All I have is conjecture based on the little tidbits Helena hints at. Based on what you show me and the world at large."

Jaw tight, he stared at Valentina. Felt a visceral tug at the genuine concern in her eyes. Not pity. Not disgust. But a real emotion that had always been there. That he chose not to embrace, not to want.

He still couldn't make himself want it. If he went that last step… "It was time to see the world, time to stretch my wings. To reach for bigger and greater things."

"You mean find a richer and maybe slightly less crazy heiress compared to Helena?"

He laughed. And she laughed. But they both knew he was skating over the issue. A part of him wanted her to push, like she did, relentlessly. One part of him wanted never to see her again.

It was the same torment he faced night after night.

Every cell in him wanted to tie Valentina to his side. To

seduce her, to chain her to him with his touch, to promise her whatever she wanted. To build a family with her, to fill his life with laughter and drama and everything she brought into it. He wanted to be selfish and take what he wanted, despite the aching vulnerability in her eyes.

Another part of him cringed at the very idea, his self-preservation instinct coming to the fore. His subconscious had known even back then.

Valentina was dangerous to him. She would send him down a path where only pain waited.

And soon he was going to have to make a decision. For he had no doubt that she would leave him when their deal was up if he didn't reach for her.

The idea of Valentina forever walking out on him this time…he couldn't bear it.

CHAPTER TEN

TINA HAD PLANNED on escaping the party Kairos and Helena had arranged to celebrate Theseus and Maria's fiftieth wedding anniversary by hiding behind her workaholic boss.

The truth was that she was afraid to face what was happening between her and Kairos. To face what was happening to her.

After he had told her how Helena was the one who had messed up the purchase orders—something Chiara had realized from the beginning—she had returned to work. Despite Kairos's worry that Helena's antics were escalating and against his wishes.

Of course, he hadn't let her confront Helena.

Loath to disturb the truce they seemed to have achieved, she had quietly gone back to work.

Seeing him night after night stretched her nerves to the end. They couldn't look at each other without plunging into sexual tension. It was like waiting for a rumbling volcano to erupt. She sensed his hesitation, too, the way he studied her as if he wanted to devour her, the way he barely even touched her, as if his control were hanging by a thread.

The way he talked about everything but the future.

There was a friendship of sorts between them, however much he didn't like the label. They talked about her job, his work, about mutual friends. About their livelihoods.

She wanted to hide tonight. From him, from Theseus

and Maria and Helena and from every board member that wanted to meet Valentina Constantinou.

She wanted the world to disappear and leave her alone with Kairos so that she could...

She could what? Figure out where it was that they were heading? Figure out if she wanted to take a step toward him again?

Was she willing to put herself through all that heartache again? Was she prepared to wait forever if she wanted him to take that step toward her?

Kairos had, of course, in his usual commanding tone ordered Tina's presence at the party. She was, he'd decreed this morning over breakfast, required as his wife.

Keep up your side of the bargain, Valentina, were his parting words without so much as a look in her direction. He hadn't even taken her calls the rest of the day so she couldn't offer him excuses.

In the end, she'd decided she didn't want another argument with him. She didn't want to push him for she had a feeling they were both treading a fine line.

She arrived at Markos Villa with the dress and shoes she'd purchased with his credit card on her lunch break, to find a mass of activity in the huge acreage behind the villa.

Sunset was still a couple of hours away but the orange light lent a golden glow to the white silk marquees being put up. Tables were being dressed with lanterns and orchids in little glass jars. An extensive wine bar was set up on one end while a small wooden dance floor had been erected in the middle of all the small tents.

Fifty years! Theseus and Maria were celebrating fifty years of marriage. Of being together, of knowing one another inside out. Of belonging to one another.

Something she still wanted with the Kairos she was slowly discovering.

With a sigh, she made her way up the stairs outside the villa.

An eerie calm dwelled inside the high-ceilinged walls, in contrast to the hubbub of activity outside. A line of sweat poured down between her shoulder blades. Something felt wrong. As she walked through the airy villa, poured herself a glass of water in the kitchen, the sense of unease only got stronger.

Where were Theseus and Maria and Helena?

Apprehension sitting like lead in her gut, Tina took the stairs up. Suddenly, all she wanted was to see Kairos. To reassure herself that he was okay. On the first-floor landing, she was walking past the main master suite—Theseus and Maria's rooms—when she heard the argument.

She hadn't meant to pause and overhear, but over the last month, she had only become more and more attached to the older couple. Whatever the tension between their daughter, Kairos and them, there was a bond of steel between the husband and wife. An unshakeable love that Tina wanted in her own life. A bond made of respect, humor and utter affection. She'd even wondered how such a lovely couple could have given birth to such a brittle woman like Helena. She wouldn't have dreamed of eavesdropping but it was Maria's voice raised, close to breaking, and uttering Kairos's name that halted her steps.

She had a good grasp of Greek now and yet Maria's impassioned argument was hard to follow. She was imploring Theseus not to cut their own daughter out. To give Helena one more chance to prove the truth? To come to see the proof of it with his own eyes.

Kairos's true nature? Proof?

Wait, Theseus was going to cut Helena out of the company? How could he do that to his own daughter? Had Kairos persuaded him to it finally?

Tina's thoughts whirled and collided, a cold chill sweeping over her skin. What kind of proof was Maria talking about? What did Helena mean to prove to her parents?

She had tried to fill Valentina's mind with the supposed love between Kairos and her. It hadn't worked. She had tried to get her to leave by ruining her work. It hadn't worked.

What new scheme was she cooking now?

Heart racing a thousand miles a minute, Tina reached the vast bedroom she'd been sharing with Kairos. She dropped the bags on the floor, her gaze sweeping over the furniture and contents.

Kairos's huge desk was littered with papers, as was customary, but nothing seemed out of place. She could hear the shower running. And then she saw it—a flash of blue silk from the connecting door that led to the shared veranda. The other door from the veranda, she'd discovered the first evening, led to Helena's bedroom.

When she'd laughingly inquired of Theseus, he had told her that the house had been originally designed for a husband and a wife to share different bedrooms. With a wink at Kairos, the older man had gruffly announced he'd never want Maria to sleep in a separate bedroom. Maria had charmingly blushed.

Tina knew who would walk in to their bedroom in a few seconds. She could already hear the gruff baritone of Theseus's voice and Maria's pleading one—still close to tears. She didn't wait to see who would emerge from the veranda.

Unbuttoning her dress shirt, she pushed it off her shoulders. Next her trousers. By the time she reached the huge, rectangular glass-enclosed shower, she was in matching black bra and lace panties. The shape of a muscular flank made her hesitate.

With a deep breath, she pulled off her bra, then pushed down her panties and entered the shower.

To say her husband was stunned would have been the understatement of the year. To say she had forgotten how the sight of his naked body made her feel would be the understatement of the century.

All she could do was stare at him.

Water poured down Kairos's muscular body in rivulets. His dark hair pasted to his scalp made his rugged features harsher. His nose was broken and bent. His mouth a wide, cruel line. His neck was corded and muscled. Every inch of him was a feast to her starving senses.

Sparse hair covered a broad chest. His skin was like rough velvet—a sharp contrast to her own soft skin.

A line of hair arrowed down over his ridged abdomen, becoming thicker near his hips and then his pelvis. Legs built like a gladiator's clenched at her leisurely perusal.

Then, and only then, did she let her gaze drift to his arousal. He lengthened and hardened until it was curved up toward his belly.

A soft moan flitted from her mouth as she remembered the sensation of him moving inside her. For a man who didn't dance, he made love with a sensuality that made her eyes roll.

"If you don't stop looking at me like that, I will be inside you in two seconds. I will not give a damn if it is harmful or a weakness or what promises you drew from me." He sounded ragged, at the end of his rope. "I'm but a man, Valentina."

Her skin prickling, she pulled her gaze to his. The heat she saw there blasted through her meager defenses. Her nipples tightened into painful points, her breasts ached to be cupped.

Her breath came in serrated puffs as his gaze took in the plump points of her nipples, down her midriff to the junction of her thighs where wetness suddenly rushed, the scent coating the moisture-laden air around them.

Legs trembling, Tina turned away.

One more second of his gaze traveling down her length and she would have begged him to take her.

From the moment he'd slowly peeled off her wedding dress on that night, she'd realized she loved sex. That she had an appetite to match his own voracious one. And yet today, enclosed in the glass cubicle with his hard body mere fingertips away, all she felt was a longing. To belong to him. To possess him in equal measure—mind, body and soul.

To love him for the rest of their lives.

She touched her forehead to the glass wall, hoping to cool off. Willing her body to find a thread of reason as to why this wasn't a good idea.

She felt him move in the small space. He didn't touch her yet the heat radiating from his body was like a blanket over her skin.

"Valentina?" In his husky voice, her name was both an order and a request. He touched her then, his palm around her neck, while his other hand traveled down her bare back to her spine. To her hips.

With a deep groan, he pulled her closer, until his erection settled against her buttocks. Their guttural gasps rent the air.

"Wait," she managed, the scrape of his chest against her tightening her hunger.

"Now who's punishing whom, *pethi mou*?"

"I would never tease you like that," she whispered hurriedly. "She...planned something, Kairos. I don't know what. I just couldn't... I couldn't let them think that of you."

Instantly, she felt the change in the air. He was still warm and hard but it was as if he had turned off a switch. "Who planned what?"

She didn't have to answer the question. They could hear voices just outside the bathroom—Maria urging Theseus.

The silence raging behind her had such a dangerous quality to it that she turned.

Rage filled Kairos's face, making it so harsh that Valentina instantly clasped his cheeks. What could she say? What platitude could she offer when she had willfully believed the worst of him? Wouldn't she have believed her own eyes, too, if she'd been but a few minutes late?

He pushed her palms away as if they burned him. Cold dawned into his silver eyes, making them into a winter wasteland. "Did you see her?"

Valentina shook her head. "Only a flash of her dress. That turquoise blue silk she'd chosen for tonight."

He said nothing in reply.

Valentina shut the shower off and grabbed the towel from behind her. "I will go out first," she said softly, afraid of touching him.

He wouldn't harm Helena however angry he got, but she was also aware of his struggle to control his temper. She'd never seen him like this, so ragged at the edges.

What Helena had attempted to do, what Theseus and Maria would have seen if Valentina hadn't acted quickly... it was dirty, disgusting. And it had shaken him to the core.

She could see his frustration, his anger, but also for the first time since she'd met him, the depth of his affection for Theseus. He loved that old man and his wife. It was written in the torment on his face.

Becoming the company's CEO meant nothing to him. Only Theseus's love, his good opinion of him mattered.

It would have hurt him immeasurably if Theseus and Maria had found him in the shower with Helena. Finally—a true glimpse of the man she had married. A deeply caring man beneath the hard shell, the ruthless ambition.

All she felt were his emotions—raw and bleeding in that moment. And her own answering ones—desperate and potent. Everything to do with him and not her.

It was the first time in her life Tina felt someone else's pain. The first time she felt this overwhelming urge to reach out. To do anything she could to take that pain from him.

She wanted to hold him and never let go. But she understood him now. He would reject any comfort she offered. "Don't...do not embarrass them," he said between gritted teeth.

Confused for a few seconds, she stared at him. Then nodded, another realization hurtling through her.

He would do anything to protect them from embarrassment, from hurt. Even if it was heaped upon them by their own daughter. He would go to any lengths to hide Helena's reality from Theseus, to protect Theseus.

Even pretending to love the impulsive, juvenile wife that had walked out on him without doing the courtesy of telling him face to face.

She wrapped the towel around herself, pasted a smile to her face and stepped out. The pristine marble tiles were cold beneath her feet, jerking her into this moment.

Grabbing a smaller towel, she wiped the water dripping from her hair. Took a few deep breaths to clear the lump from her throat. Forced a cheery tone into her voice and said loudly, "Wait until you see my dress, Kairos. You're not going to want to leave the bedroom."

CHAPTER ELEVEN

ALL THROUGH THE party Tina waited for the explosion of Kairos's temper to come.

Maybe not in front of Theseus and Maria. It was after all their wedding anniversary celebration.

Maybe not in front of the guests who were extended family and board members from the Markos company and even employees and their families.

But in private maybe. Just between them? Would he confront Helena at least to see if what they'd assumed was right?

No!

Her husband acted as if nothing untoward had happened.

Helena appeared a few minutes after her parents and Kairos and Valentina had started welcoming the guests together.

Like a queen finally drifting down to meet her citizens. Like she hadn't tried to spread poison among people who cared about her.

Kairos's fingers clamped tight around her bare arm. "Stay out of this, Valentina."

Her hackles rose at his whispered warning. "But she—"

His fingers drifted to her hips, his grip so tight as he turned her that she had to smother a pained gasp. Instantly, he released her, a flash of something in the silvery gaze. "It doesn't concern you."

"How can you say that? If I hadn't—"

"You played the role I brought you here for, *ne*? You went out of your way to keep up your side of the bargain. For that I thank you. But Helena is my business and mine alone."

Hurt festered like an unhealed wound but for once in her life, Tina tried to put her own hurt aside for a moment and think of him.

He was in pain and he was lashing out at her. But she wouldn't let him. She wouldn't let him shut her out again. With all the guests' gazes on them, she clasped his jaw and pulled him until his mouth was a bare inch from her. Until he was all she saw, all she felt. Until everything she felt was mirrored in her gaze.

Until there was no escape from the truth in her eyes. "I did it because I care about you, because I couldn't bear to see you hurt. Don't shut me out tonight, not after everything we have shared the last couple of months. Please, Kairos. Don't turn away from me. From us."

She didn't wait for his reply. She had said what she meant to say, what she meant to do.

Helena was dressed in an exquisite blue, knee-length cocktail dress that made her look like a voluptuous baby doll. A diamond choker glittered at her throat. She looked innocent, beautiful—a façade.

Tina smoothed a hand down her own emerald green dress that left her shoulders bare and fell to her ankles, with a slit on one side. Her hair—since she hadn't even washed it properly in that shower—was neatly tied into a French braid.

Much as she tried to separate herself from the occasion and the people, Tina was drawn into the warmth of the celebration. She danced with Theseus, another older man with a bulbous face and kind eyes, a younger man who told her in Greek she was beautiful and that Kairos didn't deserve two beautiful women drifting about him.

Kairos had danced with Maria first, and then he'd

twirled Helena around the dance floor. Which had lasted four minutes and fifty-two seconds, too.

But he hadn't asked her. He'd watched her all evening with that consuming gaze—until Tina had felt as if she were standing naked in front of him again. As if he was testing her words, as if he didn't trust them. As if he loathed believing her.

Defiant and resolved, she met his gaze every time he looked at her. Let him see that this time she wasn't backing out, let him see the decision she had already made. The awareness between them was underscored by something heavier, darker.

Soon, she was surrounded by both men and women as she regaled them with the stories of growing up around her powerful brothers.

Unlike Conti Luxury Goods, however—which was a much more powerful and bigger conglomerate than the Markos Group, thanks to Leandro—Theseus's company was smaller and possessed a close-knit community feeling. Most of the board members and employees had been with the company for over twenty or even thirty years. And intensely loyal to Theseus, which made the attempted hostile takeover that much worse.

Even after a gap of seven years—Kairos had left when he'd been twenty-one—their trust and confidence in him was absolute. That he would naturally succeed Theseus as the CEO a foregone conclusion. She heard tales of Kairos's kindness, his leadership, his work ethic as he'd learned the ropes of the business under Theseus's guidance. Something she had learned herself in the last few weeks.

As night drove away the remnants of the lovely day, small lanterns lit on the tables threw faces into shadows. Strings of lights illuminated the grounds, marking paths.

Dinner was a lavish affair, with guests calling out for speeches. Theseus made one about Maria while she looked up at him adoringly and smiled. Helena made one, though it was mostly about the legacy Theseus would leave, as if he were already gone.

When Kairos raised his glass, a palpable hush fell over the crowd. "To Theseus and Maria...you are..." His Adam's apple bobbed up and down. Clearly, he was battling with his own emotions. "To another fifty years," he finished simply.

Maria burst into tears, her arms loosely wrapped around Kairos's waist from the side. The entire party came to a silence as if the moment were frozen in time. Helena frowned. Theseus kept his hand on his wife's back, concern lighting his eyes.

But it was Kairos's reaction that made Tina's chest so tight that she could barely breathe.

He had become utterly still the moment Maria had wrapped her arms around him. His shoulders painfully rigid, his jaw so tight that he might have been cast from marble. Only his eyes glittered with such raw emotion, such depth of pain that Tina had to look away. Seconds piled on into minutes as Maria silently sobbed, her face buried in Kairos's chest.

Tina took his free hand in hers and shook him slightly. "Kairos?"

Awakening from whatever held him in its ragged grip, Kairos awkwardly patted Maria's back while Theseus pulled her to him.

Theseus stood up again, raised his wineglass and announced his retirement. A pin dropped could have sounded like thunder in the thick silence.

"It is something I should've done years ago," he said, holding Kairos's gaze, an apology and something else in his tone. "I announce Kairos Constantinou as the new CEO of the Markos group of companies."

Applause thundered around them and yet as she saw Helena's face, dread curled around Tina's spine.

Helena hated Kairos and the depth of it terrified Tina. But even beneath that fear throbbed the sinking realization that he had what he wanted.

He was the CEO.

Which meant he had no need of Tina anymore.

While she…she had only just realized how desperately she was in love with him.

Midnight had come and gone by the time Tina went upstairs. Theseus had tired soon and Tina had convinced him and Maria to retire. Since Helena had been missing in action for several hours, she had taken over as the hostess. And stayed with a smile on her face until the last guest had departed.

But now as she dragged herself up the stairs, her feet hurt and a headache was beginning to throb at her temples. The staff had already cleaned up most of the debris from the party. Utter silence reigned over the villa.

Kairos was nowhere to be seen.

She took a quick shower and dressed in pajamas. Urgency and anxiety together made a nasty cocktail in her head. But she held onto the belief that he would come to her. He had to. He felt something for her and she would make that enough. She would make it work. They belonged together.

She drifted into sleep, the same thought running circles around her head.

Tina awoke suddenly, consumed with a feverish sense of urgency.

Pure darkness blanketed the room. The curtains that would have let in the moonlight were closed. Her skin prickled with awareness. She scooted up in the bed and turned on the lamp on the night stand.

Kairos was seated in the armchair in the corner. A bottle

of whiskey lay unstoppered next to him. Half empty. And
no glass. Tall legs stretched in front of him drew her gaze
to his muscular thighs. His tie was gone. Jacket discarded.

The white shirt was unbuttoned all the way to his abdomen. Golden olive skin dotted with sparse dark hair beckoned her touch.

And yet it was his face, wreathed in shadows, that drew
her breath in serrated puffs. Dark brows winged over deep-
set silver eyes perfectly framing his face. The thin, cruel
slash that was his mouth. The strong column of his throat.
His nostrils flared as he seemed to wait for her to acknowledge him.

"Kairos?"

"Your negligee is loose."

"What?" It took her a few seconds to comprehend his
words. Heat swarming her cheeks, she tugged the strap
that had fallen off her shoulder, baring most of her breast.
"What are you doing here?"

"I'm not allowed in our bedroom?"

"Of course you are," she said, swallowing down the
panic rising through her. Something was wrong. The way
he stared at her, the stillness… He hadn't looked like that
even when she'd told him what Helena had planned. Now…
whatever had happened in the evening since, he looked unraveled. Completely undone.

And yet he had sought her out. He had been waiting for
her in the dark, pain etched on every feature.

"I meant, why are you sitting there? In the darkness.
Alone."

His tongue flicked over his lower lip. Her pulse raced.
He stared at her for a long time before he responded. "I was
wondering if I should wake you or not."

"Wake me?" she repeated, still grappling with the dangerous quality surrounding him. It seemed as if her mind

couldn't concentrate on his words. Only on the vibe that radiated from him. "Is something wrong with Theseus or Maria? She did seem off all evening, I wondered if she was ill or if…"

Her words fell away as she reached him. Something about his stillness discouraged touch. Her hands hung loosely at her sides.

Silvery eyes raked down the length of her with a thoroughly possessive intent. She hadn't brushed out her hair before falling into bed. Now her braid was half undone, thick strands falling over her shoulders.

The negligee she'd picked was one she had bought after their wedding, a soft pink silk that hung loose around her chest now. Falling several inches above her knees, however, it bared most of her thighs and legs.

A sharp laugh from him startled her and she instinctively jumped back.

Her hand shot to her chest, rising and falling heavily. "What is funny?"

"Your legs."

"My legs are funny?"

"Did you pick that negligee on purpose?"

Her cheeks heated as the memory of all the provocative nightwear she'd worn to entice him. "I…was too exhausted and honestly I didn't think you'd be coming to bed anytime soon."

"You make it hard, Tina. You always make it so damn hard," he whispered, almost to himself.

She could no more stop her gaze from moving to his crotch than she could stop breathing. The shape of his arousal spiked her heartbeat.

He laughed, again, and she hurriedly pulled up her gaze to his. "That, too, *glykia mou*." Wicked lights danced in his eyes. "I always rise to the occasion, *ne*?"

"*Si*, always."

It was impossible not to laugh, even in the fraught moment. He looked young and charming and careless then, as if the tight grip he held over himself had snapped finally. It was a stark contest to the focused, always strategizing man she'd come to know.

What had snapped it?

"Kairos, how much have you drunk?"

Without answering her, he took the heavy bottle and took a huge gulp again. "You don't drink," she said softly.

"Usually, I don't. My mother..." His words didn't quite slur, though he seemed to lose focus. "I told you about her, *ne*?"

Her throat burned at the affection in his voice. "*Si*, you did."

"She hated what she was forced to do to...feed me. So every evening, as she got ready for work, she would drink. She would drink after she came back. For years, she drank to drown out her reality. In the end, her liver was so damaged that she drifted away into nothing. I hate alcohol. How it promises to dull things down and yet it doesn't."

He stared at the bottle in his hand, and plunked it down with such force on the side table that the thick glass instantly shattered, and his hand plunged into the broken shards with the force of it.

Valentina gasped and reached for him.

"*Oxhi, Valentina!*" His hands held her hips in a bruising grip. "There are shards everywhere. Your feet are bare."

Blood from the cut on his hand painted his shirt. "Kairos?"

"Yes, *agapita*?"

"Your hand...will you please let me dress it?"

He nodded and released her.

Tina darted into the bathroom, and came back with the first-aid kit. In silence that pulled her nerves, she finished dressing the deep cut, and wound it with gauze. She put the kit away, and pushed the broken fragments under the table and stared down at him.

He was staring at her as if he meant to devour her. And didn't know where to begin.

She was arrested between his wide legs, his face scant inches from her belly. Heat from his body hit her in powerful waves, the thin silk of her negligee no barrier.

"*Christos*, you smell like heaven," he said, pulling her closer. "Like you're the only place I can land, Valentina. But that is a mirage, too, *ne*? You're dangerous, *glykia mou*. Always a threat to my sanity."

Tina sank her hands into his hair to steady herself while he buried his face in her belly. He nuzzled her, as if he meant to burrow into her, setting every nerve ending on fire.

"Kairos?"

"I need you, *agapita*. So badly… I need you tonight." There was a ragged question underneath the demand that twisted her heart. He was not sure of her and she had only herself to blame for it.

"I'm here, Kairos. I've always been here, for you."

But there was no tenderness left in the moment. No humor. Only his need. Only the pain in his eyes and the frantic urgency she felt in his breath, in his movements to escape it.

His hands circled her waist restlessly, settling on her buttocks, and pressed her harder into his face. Molten heat spread from his mouth. The wet patch stuck to her skin. A heaviness filled her breasts, pooling into damp warmth at the juncture of her legs. The tension in his frame multiplied as he held her like that.

Then his hands were teasing the backs of her legs and thighs. Sneaking under the silky hem, cupping her buttocks, dragging her higher up against him. Higher, higher, lifting her with those sinewy arms. Until she was half standing, half draped over his shoulders.

Until his face was flush with her mound.

Tina swallowed the sound that rose to her lips, her trust absolute. Willing him to take whatever he needed.

His hot breath fell in puffs against her.

She jerked at the sudden surge of sensation so sharp that she almost fell backwards. But he didn't release her. He held her as if he would never let go.

As if she were his salvation.

Her fingers crawled from his hair to his neck. When he pressed a warm, wicked kiss against the silk pooling at her sex, she dug her nails into his neck.

He growled and burrowed his mouth into her folds. Her spine arched, the knot in her lower belly so tightly wound. Her breath became fire. His fingers bit into her hips, the pain coating the pleasure with a sharp contrast that made it unbearable.

A thousand little tremors exploded when he opened his mouth, when his teeth dug into the lips of her sex. Violent shivers that she couldn't contain. Moans and whimpers that she couldn't swallow. Up, up, up went the silk. Until she was bared to him utterly and there was not even a flimsy barrier between his wicked mouth and her willing flesh.

Rough fingers dragged over her hips, her buttocks, stroking, kneading, clutching. No thoughts marred the pure lights of sensation darting up and down her body.

And then his tongue was there at the place where she ached for him. Always. Stroking, licking, laving. Pushing her higher, higher, higher onto the cliff. Driving away everything else from her body except him, and what his mouth, and his wicked tongue did to her.

Insistent. Raw. Relentless. She moaned and rocked into his mouth, clutching onto him as if he were her everything.

She was transported to that wanton place only Kairos could take her. And then the knot in her belly broke apart, her muscles clenched long and deep, pleasure splintering through her. Her thighs shook from the pressure, every inch of her trembling.

Arching into the warmth of his body, she pulled the negligee off and threw it away. His cheeks were flushed with stripes of color. Fingers trembling, she somehow undid the clasp of his belt. Unzipped his trousers. And then he was in her palm. Hard and hot. Thick. Lengthening.

"Inside you, Valentina, now." The open need in his words was a balm to her soul.

Straddling his thighs that spread her indecently wide, she pushed down. His hips jerked up, and he thrust into her with one smooth stroke, fingers holding her hips grounded against him.

A long curse ripped out from his sinful mouth.

Tina gasped. Her body felt invaded even after the release he had given her, shivers of a different kind building over her skin. He was so deep. So hard inside her. Entrenched inside her body just as he always was in her heart.

A slow panic began to build inside her. She would never be free of him now. Never come out of this intact if he pushed her away.

"Shh...*agapi mou*..." he whispered against her temple. Long fingers stroked her damp skin softly. Soothingly. Until the tremors quieted.

A soft kiss against her damp lips. A featherlight stroke against her cheek. He nuzzled his stubble into her neck as if he had all the time in the world. As if just being inside her was enough.

"I didn't forget for one second how tight you feel around me. But I didn't realize that after so many months...you would be…" He sounded so adorably puzzled that Tina laughed. "Am I hurting you?"

Arms wrapped around his shoulders, she looked at him. His hair was damp and sticking to his forehead. His mouth pinched with the control he exercised. Skin pulled taut over his hard features, the depth of his need glimmered in his eyes. "*Si*," she whispered, unable to stem the truth from falling from her lips. She'd forgotten how huge he felt inside her, but it was the panic running amok that she wanted to control. "Give me a moment."

His hands tightened around her hips. "Do you want me to stop?"

"*No!* I… I just need to get used to you again." She wriggled her hips in a small movement. The tightness was still there but something else fluttered beneath it.

A soft kiss against her breastbone. "Take all the time you need."

She hid her face in his shoulder, blinking back the tears that rose. Did they have time? Did he want forever, like she did?

Anchoring her hands on his shoulders, Valentina arched her spine, then moved up and down. The tightness eased. In its wake came little flutters of sensation. She pushed against the sensation, chasing it. Lips pulled first at one nipple and then other, sharpening the little jolts that went to her groin.

Clasping his stubbled jaw, she took his mouth, hard and possessive, letting her kiss speak what she couldn't say. "I want your skin, Kairos. All of you."

In a blink of movement, he brought her to the bed. In the next, he had stripped his shirt, boxers. And then he was prowling on to the bed and she watched him to her heart's content.

The sleek lines of his body. Velvet-rough skin stretched taut over rippling muscles. When he covered her body with his, when he thrust into her, Tina was ready this time.

The drag of their sweat-slicked bodies against each other brought familiar pleasure racing along her nerves. When he thrust, she raised her hips. His grunt of satisfaction made her growl in response.

Hands on her hips, he held her down and yet he was slow, taking his time.

Driving her out of her own skin.

"Faster, please, Kairos. Harder," she urged him on, knowing what he needed. What he desperately craved. Wanting to be everything he needed.

No, not wanting to be.

She *was* everything Kairos needed already. She understood him, she loved him so much, and there wasn't anything she wouldn't face for him. No one she wouldn't fight to be by his side.

All she needed was to make him realize that. To make him understand that she belonged with him.

The realization flew through her veins, turning the moment into so much more than pleasure. He was hers and she would do anything to keep him.

She stroked his broad shoulders, his chest, dug her fingers into his buttocks, tasted the saltiness of his skin. Bit the arch between his neck and shoulders. Possessively, she drank him in.

He pressed a kiss to her temple, his rough thighs grazing her soft ones. "I don't want to hurt you."

"You won't. I can take whatever you give me, Kairos. Don't you know that already?"

As his thrusts became rougher and faster, as his breath hitched, as he growled and his body shuddered on top of her, Tina kissed his temple, breathing the sweat and scent of him.

Whatever his ambitions, whatever had made him into what he was today, she loved all of him. And she would fight for him.

CHAPTER TWELVE

KAIROS COULDN'T HELP HIMSELF. Gathering Valentina to him, he kissed the slope of her shoulder, the skin still damp from their shower an hour ago.

He had pushed her body relentlessly tonight, craving release after release, a need for escape riding him hard. He'd barely soaped her and himself after he'd pushed her against the wall and taken her. Much less toweled them both dry before they had tumbled into bed.

He felt like he had run a triathlon, so sore was his body.

Valentina had, as usual, fallen asleep and nuzzled into him but sleep had evaded him. He'd wanted to leave the bed and her.

Intimacy was always hard on him and the more he'd been determined to limit his increasing need for Valentina to bed, the more she had undone him there.

But last night he hadn't wanted to go. He hadn't wanted to be alone. No, that wasn't right. He was not going to lie to himself now.

He hadn't wanted to leave *her*. The haven she provided against the cruelty of the world. Against the pain that had filled him.

She was warmth and fire and heaven.

He'd seen her slave hour after hour to make it up to Chiara, to find her place in the fashion world.

He'd seen her care for Theseus and Maria in the last month, responding to their kindness. Worrying about Theseus's health. Persuading a reluctant but smiling Maria into letting her redo her entire wardrobe, because she'd declared impishly to a stunned Theseus that being married to a grouchy bear like him for fifty years, Maria deserved to be dripping in diamonds.

The laughter that had boomed out of Theseus, the shock and gratitude in Maria's eyes that Valentina could make her husband laugh like that again... Theseus had ordered a stunning diamond necklace for Maria on Valentina's advice and when he'd asked Tina to pick something for herself for a present, she'd ask to be counted among his friends, no matter what.

"You like him," he'd said to her later in the privacy of their bedroom. "And he likes you."

"Most people like me, Kairos. I'm fun to be around most of the time. And who wouldn't adore Theseus? Helena is truly poor that she doesn't care for such loving parents. I never knew my father but now I know how to imagine him, at least.

"Theseus...he reminds me of you."

He'd looked at her, shocked. "What?" She couldn't have known what that meant to him.

"Or rather I see what you will be forty years from now. If you..."

He'd backed her against the wall then, something in her expression goading him. "If I what, Valentina?"

"If you learn to be more fun and communicative and a little less brooding."

Before he could punish her for such insolence, she'd slipped away from him.

And in that glimpse of longing and adoration in her eyes when she looked at Theseus, he saw the similarities between them.

Just like him, she had never left that scared, little girl

behind. And yet there was fire inside her and for a night, he had wanted what she could give him.

Words never came easily to him and this strange vulnerability she'd created in him robbed him of what little did come.

So, when morning dawned, he had woken her up with kisses and soft caresses, needing to be inside her desperately. Needing to hold her close one more time, needing that intimacy where he could show that he did appreciate her. The only place he could do so.

She had whimpered when he had filled his hands with her breasts.

Arched her behind into him sleepily and whispered, 'Si...' in that husky tone when he'd hoarsely asked if he could take her like that. So he had slowly stroked himself into her with her back pressed to his chest, her legs caught between his, played with her clit until the need for release was riding her just as hard as it did him. And when her muscles had clenched him even tighter in blissful climax, when she had clung to him, and whispered his name against his own lips again and again, only then did he claim his own release.

And every time his release rushed at him, and he was lost to the pleasure inside her, it felt as if she was stealing some other part of him. As if he was not whole anymore.

But the truth he had learned today, the renewed pain—it was a reminder. He couldn't love Valentina, and he couldn't bear it if...she did the same thing as people who claimed to love him had done.

He would rather hurt her now, keep her whole, than destroy her later, all in the name of love.

When he had woken up this time, she was sitting in the chair he had sat in last night. Freshly showered and dressed in his shirt, she looked the perfect mixture of innocent and siren, a woman capable of tenderness and guts.

Their gazes met and held, the air in the room redolent with the scent of sex and them. Poignant. So much emotion in her eyes that he felt inadequate.

"Come back to bed," he said, pulling the duvet up.

Without a word she crawled back into bed, her trust in him complete.

A faint tension shimmered over her. He kept his arm around her, unwilling to let her retreat from him. Her fingers gripped his forearm, whether asking him to release her or not, he didn't care.

He buried his face in her hair. Tugged her so close that his groin pressed into her buttocks. His chest crushed her back to him. His arm cushioned under her breasts.

"You're not going to ask me about last night?" he whispered.

She pulled his palm to her mouth and pressed a soft kiss. "You will tell me when you're ready."

He stiffened. "What does that mean?"

He felt her exhale, as if she was striving to be patient. "Are you asking to know or to annoy me?"

He swatted her buttocks and she laughed.

Just hearing that sound made his chest lighter.

"It means that whether you share your past or not, whether you continue to act like a gruff bear or a fluffy unicorn, whether you lose your temper or subject me to these heavy silences...nothing changes how I see you, how I think of you. I think, finally—" her voice wobbled and she pressed her face into his hand tightly, before releasing it "—I know the true you, Kairos. Nothing and no one will shake my belief in you. Not even you."

"And if you had seen me in that shower with her?" The question slipped from him, his tone ragged.

"Then I would have dragged her out by her lovely hair and slapped her face. Like I wanted to before you stopped me."

"Your trust in me is that absolute, Valentina?"

"*Si*, it is. Even when I taunted you that you want Theseus's company. I knew the truth, I was just too scared to acknowledge it."

And that implicit trust in her voice broke Kairos down. Words no one had ever heard from him came pouring out. "She told them that I...was the one who got her pregnant."

Valentina jerked, moved in his hold as if to turn around. But he arrested her movement, for he didn't know if he could speak if she pitied him. Slowly, the rigidness in her shoulders eased. A long exhale left her but she gripped his fingers tighter. "Helena?"

"Yes. She... I...one of her high-flying friends, he ran the moment she told him. She and I...we never were close but mostly she tolerated me. Theseus wanted her to show interest in the company and she did, as long as it allowed her extravagant lifestyle. When he learnt that she was pregnant, he became extremely angry. Helena's recklessness never knew bounds but this was too far for him. He threatened to cut her off if she didn't change her ways, if she didn't settle down. She realized that he meant to give me control of everything."

"So she told her parents that you were the one who got her pregnant?"

He could feel her heart racing. Could almost see the conclusions she was running through. He held onto her, long beyond the point where he could fool himself into thinking the comfort was for her.

"Kairos, what did Theseus do?" He felt her kiss his wrist, hold it to her face as if she were bracing herself. For him. Everything she felt—the fear, the worry—it was all for him.

He let it wash over him, let himself bask in it.

"Theseus—" he cleared his throat, wishing for her sake that he was a different man "—decided that Helena and I would marry and possess equal power over the company. He trusted me to keep her in line, I suppose."

"What did you say to his proposal?"

"I agreed. I told him I would do whatever he asked of me."

"You were willing to be a father to some other man's child?"

"Yes. I asked only that he believe that I had never even touched her."

This time, there was no stopping Valentina. She turned in his arms, her gaze peering into his, as if she meant to own everything of him. A bright shine made them glitter. "And he didn't believe you?"

"No. He wouldn't even look at me. I don't think he even cared if Helena and I had been...together. But, however many times I insisted, he wouldn't say that he believed me. By denying his trust...he...he took away everything he had ever given me.

"It felt as if I was that orphan boy again looking through a glass window into what a family looks like." His voice shook. "I don't even remember being angry with Helena's blatant lies. Only crushed by his silence. I...felt betrayed. I told him I didn't want the company if I didn't have his... respect. His trust." His love.

Theseus had chosen Helena's lies over Kairos's truth, and that was what had broken Kairos's heart, why he had left.

Unable to stay still, Tina pulled herself up on the bed and the sheet with it. Every muscle was tense in his body as if he was living through the ghastly moment again. The anguish in his eyes only showed that she had been right. There was a heart that beat under all that ruthless exterior.

She clasped his jaw and pulled him close. He became

still, too rigid, as if he could physically will himself to reject her concern. But she didn't care. All she wanted was to tell him he wasn't alone. That she understood his pain. That it was okay to have loved Theseus so much that it still hurt after all these years.

That he was a good man, one of the best she had ever met. That her brother Leandro, as always, had made the right decision, that he had chosen for her the best man she could ever have asked for.

But she felt too fragile, stretched far too thin after everything they had shared in the last few days.

So she did the only thing she could.

She crawled to him on her knees, the sheet barely covering her breasts and her legs. He watched her with glittering eyes, as if daring her to come closer. Hands on his shoulders, she bent until their noses were touching.

Softly, slowly, she took his mouth. So rigid and hard and yet capable of such tender kisses. Mouth slanted over his, licking the seam of his lips, she willed him to accept it. The sheet slithered down her body, and she heard the hitch in his breath when her nipples grazed his chest.

When he suddenly opened up for her, she plunged her tongue inside. And just like that, the tempo of the kiss changed as he took over.

Even with her body sore in so many places, pleasure inched over her like petals unfurling ever so gently. His fingers wrapped around her neck and he kissed her back hungrily. As if he needed the taste of her to get through this moment. It took but one touch, one stroke, one moment for their hunger to rise, to sweep them away. Their harsh breaths reverberated as he pulled away.

His nostrils flared as he fought for control. He got off the bed, pulled on the shorts he had thrown off some time during the night and looked out the French windows.

She swallowed the words rising through her throat. She would not beg but neither would she retreat. Limbs heavy with exhaustion, she pulled on his discarded shirt and buttoned it down.

Slowly, as if she were dealing with a wounded animal, she reached him and tucked herself into his side until he had to relent. Until he wrapped his hand around her shoulders and pulled her close.

"What happened at the party? Something…changed." It wasn't what Theseus did seven years ago that had cut him.

"I figured out why Theseus didn't believe me seven years ago. Or why he let himself be convinced that Helena was telling the truth."

Breath on a serrated edge, Valentina wrapped her hands around his waist, refusing to be pushed out. Her heart ached for him. His words, his voice reverberated with the depth of his love for Theseus. The rawness of his wound created by Theseus's refusal to trust his word.

"You still came back," she whispered. "You came back when you heard he was sick."

"How could I not? He…" His voice broke and he looked away. "He…gave me the world, Valentina. How could I not rush to his side when he had need of me? When after years of living on the streets, he had shown me compassion, affection? When he made me into everything I am today?"

"You figured out who backed the hostile takeover. That's why you were…" She didn't want him hurt anymore. The notion of him closing down the part of him that cared, it terrified her.

He ran a hand through his hair, his bare chest falling and rising. "Helena was in cahoots with Alexio all along, yes. But it was Maria's stock that tilted the whole thing."

"Maria would have gone against Theseus? But why?" Maria was devoted to her husband. The absolute love and trust between the couple...through everything, they had held together.

Whereas she had avowed love again and again to Kairos, and then run way at the first obstacle.

"I think Theseus wouldn't...didn't believe me over Helena back then because Maria had told him that she'd seen Helena and me...together. In bed."

Tina gasped. "Maria backed Helena's story knowing it was a lie?"

"Helena was desperate and Maria couldn't say no to her daughter. She's always been kind to me and I can almost see how she would think I was getting not a bad deal out of it, that I would be able to control Helena's wildness if we married."

He spoke as if it didn't matter but it was the clear lack of emotion that told Tina how much it had hurt him to realize what Maria had done.

"You are making excuses for her. And all the guilt, it has been too much for her. That's why she cried on your shoulder like that. That's why she kept saying she was sorry."

Kairos nodded.

"Why give her stock to Helena? Why deceive Theseus?"

"Theseus is stubborn to the core. He...he knew his health was deteriorating, he wouldn't slow down, the company was doing badly. Maria told me that first day she'd been begging him to ask me for help. She'd been terrified about his health. So, coupled with Helena's insistence that it was for the best, I think Maria signed over the proxy on her stock to Helena, which gave Alexio the boost, the vote of confidence to begin turning men loyal to Theseus toward him. Men who were genuinely worried about the company. Men who thought Alexio was the better of two bad choices. Instead, it precipitated Theseus's heart attack."

"But how did you stop it when Maria had already

signed it over?" She frowned and then it came to her. "They see you as Theseus's true successor. So when they saw that you had returned, they decided not to back Alexio's coup."

He smiled faintly, but it didn't reach his eyes. "Again, I'm the better choice for the company."

"You can't seriously believe that, Kairos. They treated me like I was part of a family, as if being Kairos Constantinou's wife was something in itself.

"Their trust in you, their confidence is absolute. It is you who always holds himself separate. Who isolates himself. I wish I could make you see it. I wish I could…"

He pulled up their laced fingers and kissed her knuckles. The intimate gesture sent a ray of hope through her. "What?"

"I wish I could change you, just a little."

"Valentina…your trust in me about everything after the way I treated you…it has meant a lot to me. It's a gift I never expected."

"I'm full of surprises like that," she added, trying to lighten the atmosphere. "What happened then?"

"When Maria saw me at Theseus's side within a few hours of his attack, when she saw that all Helena cared about was the company and not her father… I think she started having second thoughts."

"So Helena changed tack, told them that she truly loved you all these years. Since you will not tell Theseus the truth, you had to bring me here. Did you tell him Maria's part in all this? How she deceived him, too?"

Any hesitation she saw in him vanished. His mouth took on that stubborn, uncompromising tilt. "I will not do anything that could harm him. And I forbid you to tell him anything."

"What if Maria will forever continue to assist Helena?

Kairos, you didn't see the look in her eyes when he made the announcement. What if, even this evening, Helena had Maria's backing in that…disgusting move?"

White lines fanned around his mouth, and Tina knew that the very real possibility had struck him, too. "It will never be good for both Helena and me to be here. She will only hurt them to get to me, to cut the little trust that there still is between me and Theseus. I can't put Theseus through that. I can't face seeing disillusionment in his eyes again. I will not tell him that his wife of fifty years lied to him to protect their daughter."

"Maria was supposed to protect you, too."

"Listen to me, Valentina. You have to leave what I told you here in this room. I've already started a head hunt for another CEO. An impartial outsider will be good for the company. Helena will be terminated from her position at the company. As soon as I locate her, I will inform her that her stock options will be set up in a trust fund from which she can draw an income, a more than comfortable one. But going forward, she will have no stake in the company. Hopefully that will stop her from trying…to ruin her parents' lives. What she planned two nights ago…it would have broken Theseus. In so many ways." He became again that ruthless man she had lived with for nine months. "I will cut away everything she wants if she doesn't behave."

"And when this is all settled to your satisfaction?"

"I will remain on the board since Theseus insists on signing over his stock to me, and I will oversee things from time to time. Other than that, I'm finished here."

Finished here?

If he could have slammed a door down between them, the message couldn't have been more absolute.

Hands around her waist, Tina swayed against the wall. Even the scent of his skin, the radiating warmth of his body…it felt like they could sear her skin. Tears lumped in her throat, and she breathed deeply, trying to keep them in. "You mean you don't need me anymore in this role," she said almost absently, as if it were happening to someone else.

As if the crack of her heart was outside, not within her.

"*Ne*."

She moved her hand to point behind her toward the once-again rumpled bed. Sometime before or after he had made love to her for the third time, he had carried her to the armchair, pulled the sheets off and made the bed again with clean, crisp bedlinen. When she had looked askance at him, he had winked at her and told her he was nowhere near done.

"What was that then? The four orgasms were parting gifts to remember you by?"

He rubbed a hand over his face. "That was me being selfish, being weak. Needing escape." He looked away and then back, as if he found it hard to focus on her. His features could have been carved in granite for the emotion in them. "Dealing with Maria's lies, Helena's deceit…it has reminded me I have no stomach for this."

"Lie to yourself all you want, Kairos, but don't equate what I feel for you with them."

"Don't make this hard, Valentina. I… I have an upcoming trip to Germany in four days. I'll be gone for almost three weeks. I'm trying to tie up everything before I leave. But even then, I… I think you should return to…"

"To whatever hole I crawled out from?"

He flinched. "Like you pointed out, Helena is going to be furious. She's focused all her anger on me now. I've no idea what she's going to throw at me next and I would rather you were a thousand miles away than here when that happens."

"*Per piacere,* Kairos! Treat me with respect and give me the real reason." Pain crystallized, morphed into fury and Tina embraced it with everything she had. "Shall I send you divorce papers then? Shall I have my powerful brothers throw everything they have at you so that I can take half of everything you own? What does leaving here mean, Kairos? You will damn well spell it out for me!"

When he stayed silent, her heart slipped from her chest.

He simply stared at their clasped hands as if they were talking about the weather. "It will mean divorce. It will mean you can take me for everything I have. You can bring me to my knees."

"You're a bastard!"

"You have no idea how close to the truth you are."

"That's not what I meant. You could have left me well alone. You shouldn't have...you should have let me think you were nothing but a ruthless jerk, Kairos."

He clasped her cheeks with such reverent tenderness that her heart broke a little more. "But I am, Valentina. What I feel for Theseus is gratitude. Don't you see? You were right. It is only a transaction for me. He gave me everything so I repay as much as I can."

"That's not true." She fought against his grip even as he was kicking her out of his life.

"But you... I was wrong about you." Another hard kiss, another piece of her heart forever lost to her. "When Leandro said any intelligent man would know that you are worth more than a hundred companies, he spoke the truth. You deserve everything a man can give you, Valentina. You deserve more than I can give you."

"You're just choosing not to."

"No," Kairos repeated, steeling himself against the bright sheen in her eyes. "I don't know how to love you, Valentina. And I do not wish to learn. Go back to your brothers, *pethi mou*. Tell Leandro, for once in his life, he made a bad bet. Tell him he was wrong about me. Tell him——" Kairos ran his thumb over her lower lip, a cold void opening up inside him "—that I do not deserve the precious gift he gave me."

If only he could embrace it…*this, her.* If only he was capable of giving her what she deserved. Needed.

She felt like home. Like warmth and acceptance. Like a splash of color to his gray canvas. After years of near starving, of no companionship, that was how Maria and Theseus's home had felt. He had been so cautious at first, but eventually they had won him over. He hadn't asked for anything but they had given kindness, care and love again and again, in so many ways.

Until he had believed it all. Until he had forgotten the cautiousness he had learned on the streets. Until he had forgotten the wretchedness of being alone.

Until he had started loving them, until they had simply become a part of him.

And then everything had been taken away. In one moment, everything had been lost. Seven years ago and now again…

If he trusted Valentina, if he opened himself up to everything she made him feel and things fell apart…it would be so much worse. A million times more painful. And he would break this time. If she took it away like Theseus and Maria had done, if suddenly he found himself all alone after having had a taste of…

Oxhi!

That was a fate he couldn't even indulge in.

He was not ready for the weight of her love.

He was never going to be ready for her.

For this.

For them.

She would only starve for affection with him. He'd already trampled her spirit. If he broke her because he couldn't love her, he couldn't bear it.

"You're right." She pushed the silky mass of her hair away angrily, the innate sensuality of the gesture stealing his breath. "You don't deserve me. I always thought I was not good enough for you. That I had to earn your love somehow. But this has nothing to do with me. *You're* the coward, Kairos. You're unworthy of me, not the other way around. You want to choose a miserable existence instead of trusting me, instead of taking a chance on us, fine. Then please stay in the other bedroom until you leave for your trip."

Her words hit him hard. "I can have you flown back to Milan tonight."

She backed out of his reach, a fiery tenacity to her expression. His shirt hung on her, baring most of her sleek thighs. Curves he'd never touch or feel wrapped around himself again. "I'm not leaving, you are."

He jerked his gaze back up, the void in his gut only deepening. "Valentina—"

"I have three more weeks left with Chiara. People are counting on me to do my job. I will not let them down, I will not let myself down because you've decided you've had enough of playing marriage. I will not disappear in the middle of the night from Theseus and Maria's lives as if I had done something wrong. As if I'm responsible for this debacle."

"I don't want you here," Kairos said before he could stop himself. Her mouth pinched into a thin line. "Helena—"

"I can handle Helena. At the least, I know what to expect from her. I want to finish my work here, work the contacts I made. Maria will need someone to look after her, too." She gazed at him for a few seconds that felt like an eternity. He couldn't bear the disillusionment in her eyes. Broken hope.

He took a step toward her, but she shook her head and backed away. "Goodbye, Kairos."

CHAPTER THIRTEEN

KAIROS STARED AT the society pages of a leading online fashion magazine, his breath hurtling through his chest and throat like a hurricane.

Valentina was laughing in this picture, standing in between her friend Nikolai and Ethan King—an American textile magnate whose burgeoning alliance with Conti Luxury Goods was all the rage in the news.

He'd known Leandro had been hunting for a new CEO for the board of CLG for months now. The initial prize he had promised Kairos himself. The prize Kairos had thought important enough to take Valentina on.

Thee mou, he'd been such an arrogant fool.

Leandro had stepped down himself after he had discovered he had a child with Alexis seven years ago. When Kairos had looked askance, he'd laughed and said that he would understand one day.

Luca had married Sophia, who headed her stepfather's company Rossi's. The playboy genius still did his own thing, as he had always done. He'd never had any interest in CLG except to thwart Kairos because Luca had assumed that Kairos would only hurt their sister. He'd been right.

Ethan King was a good choice. For the CLG board.

His gaze returned to her in the picture.

She'd fashioned her silky hair to fall over one side. A pink pantsuit made everything of her long legs. A thin chain glittered at her neck and disappeared into the neckline of her blouse.

Frantically, he clicked through more pictures to see if she'd kept the pendant he had bought for her. But he couldn't spot it.

Christos! What was he doing?

Her arms around Nikolai and Ethan, her eyes glittering with laughter, she looked gorgeous.

She looked...*happy*.

Seven weeks since he'd last seen her. Since she'd told him defiantly that she'd finish her position before she left. Since he'd walked out of her life for good.

By the time he had returned from Germany, she'd been gone. Every trace of her removed from their bedroom, from the villa.

The first time she had left he'd been so angry.

This time, it felt like she had taken a part of him with her. As if she'd ripped him apart, never to be whole. Everything was so blank, so dull since he'd returned. As if all the color in the world had been leached out.

He'd been so sure that he'd done the right thing by her. For once, he'd put her happiness, her well-being before his. Before his own ambitions.

Somehow, he'd been getting through his days.

Until she'd sent him divorce papers.

Until suddenly, she'd exploded into the news again in true Valentina fashion. She'd partnered with Sophia to launch a full-service fashion boutique—for clients who had personal styling needs and a host of other services.

She had collaborated with major fashion brands to launch an online vlog in which she had models of different sizes showcase the latest creations from designer brands.

The camera loved Valentina. She was a natural.

The vlog had exploded within a week of launching,

drawing more than a million hits on the internet and her business had taken off.

She'd already hosted a fashion show on a morning talk show to advertise her services. Stylish and sophisticated, she was already adored by the media. She had appeared in numerous TV style segments.

His heart in his throat, he clicked Play on a small news clip that had been recorded on another talk show.

"I always used to think my talent was useless. But then I learned that I was wasting my potential by denying myself the connections I did have. So I partnered with my sister-in-law and launched the boutique. It was she who gave me the idea. Sophia, for example, is an exceptional businesswoman but had always had problems dressing herself because she——" a fond laugh here "——she wasn't as she says, 'a giraffe with legs that go on forever.' She's curvy and sexy, and it was my pleasure to help her find clothes that showcased her body, to make her feel confident in her own shape.

"I love dressing people and now I can put my expertise into making someone else feel comfortable in their own skin. Be confident in themselves while they go out to capture the world. Everyone needs fashion advice..." She hesitated and then laughed—that husky full-bodied sound—when her brothers walked onto the stage in matching dark gray suits. She stood up and walked to them until they were both standing on her sides. "Even my handsome, powerful brothers, the legendary Conti men."

Kairos closed his laptop hard. He had watched the same damn clip a hundred times.

Leandro and Luca had walked onto the show to give their support to their sister—a spectacular publicity move he was sure had been orchestrated by Sophia, to thrust Valentina's fashion venture into the limelight. With their backing, with Sophia's business acumen and Valentina's own talent, he had no doubt her business would reach unprecedented heights.

She had found her place in the world.

He should be happy that she had taken his advice. That she had used what was at her disposal to fuel her dream, to launch her dream career.

He should be happy that he hadn't…damaged her permanently.

But then Valentina had an unquenchable spirit, a fierce strength, a generous heart. She drew people to her wherever she went.

If not today, if not this month, if not this year, she would find that happily-ever-after that she so desperately wanted. Some man would see what a beautiful person she was, inside and out, and love her as she deserved.

Suddenly the picture of Ethan King and her laughing into the camera at some new nightclub he was launching flashed in his mind's eye.

With a curse, he strolled to the bay windows.

Would Leandro go down that path again? Would Valentina let him find her a husband again? Or had she already found someone who did appreciate what an extraordinary woman she had grown into?

Had she finished with him already?

Bile rose through his throat at the thought of the man holding his wife, touching her, kissing her. At the thought of Valentina surrendering all that passion, surrendering her heart to another man.

A breeze ruffled the papers he had left on the side table. He should just sign the divorce papers and be done with her.

Give her whatever she wanted.

Release her from this marriage. Release himself from the grip she seemed to have on his heart. Be done with it.

He'd made the safe choice, for once in his life, so why couldn't he just live with it? Why couldn't he accept it and move on?

"Kairos?"

He turned around to see Maria standing at the door, wary and hesitant.

He frowned, wondering how long she'd been standing there. He'd mostly avoided her since the night of their anniversary party and she had let him.

"Does Theseus need something?"

"*Oxhi*. He's resting." She looked at her hands and then back up again. "I... I wish to speak to you. Do you have a few minutes for me?"

"Of course," he said, forcing himself to move from his spot.

He watched her silently as she flitted around the room restlessly. As always, she was elegantly dressed in a dark sweater and neatly pressed white capri pants. Her nails had been done with that signature red color for as long as he could remember. Her hair had grayed considerably, still cut into a short bob.

Only now did he realize how much weight she had lost in the last year. She'd been tirelessly caring for Theseus for so many months now. Not to mention whatever hell Helena had put her through.

He poured out water from a jug and placed a glass for her on the side table.

"Is everything okay?" he prompted, her restlessness increasing his own anxiety.

"No. It is not."

"What can I do to help?"

"You would help, Kairos, still?"

Something in her gaze made him uncomfortable. "Of course, I would, Maria. You have but to command me."

A brittle laugh fell from her mouth. "Theseus is right. I am a foolish woman."

He hardened himself against the emotion twisting his gut. It had to be about Helena, about all the decisions he'd been making about the company.

He could take whatever she threw at him, he reminded himself. He could take it and still stay standing. After all, Helena was her daughter and he was...an outsider.

Since the minute Theseus had decided he would adopt Kairos, Maria had welcomed him unflinchingly. She had only ever shown him kindness. And he would pay it back a million times over.

"Maria, whatever it is, you can say it to me without hesitation. I understand how hard this must be for you. And whatever you request for Helena, I promise I will try to do my best to accommodate it. I just can't... I can't let her be a part of the company anymore. Not if I have to do what's best for the business. And for Theseus and you."

She flicked another wary glance at his face and then away. Then she sat down and gestured for him to do the same. Her head down, she looked at her clasped fingers. When she looked up, there were tears in her eyes.

Tears that cut through his heart.

"He's so angry with me. So angry. But it was the right thing to do," she half muttered to herself.

Any walls he had erected against her crumbled at the sight of her tears. He took her hands in his. "Maria, what are you talking about?"

"Can you believe it...in fifty years of marriage, today is the first time he wouldn't look at me. The first time he said he was disappointed in me. He is ashamed of me, and I deserve it."

He sat back, shocked. "You and Theseus never fight."

"I told him everything. Everything Helena ever did. Everything I shielded from him. Everything she...lied about. About the pregnancy. About the stock and the takeover. About...my part in it. About all the disgusting things she'd planned to do to discredit you in his eyes."

"What?" Shock robbed his words. "Is...is Theseus okay? *Thee mou,* Maria! What would that accomplish except jeopardize his health? The last thing he needs just when he is finally recuperating is to learn that you—"

"That I betrayed him. That I betrayed everything he has always stood for." All the hesitation was gone from her face. "That I treated you so horribly."

"You didn't. You...only ever showed me kindness." He walked away, unable to look into her eyes. Unable to stop the dam within him from bursting. "Theseus brought me home, yes, but you welcomed me with open arms. You encouraged me when I thought I would never leave behind my dirty roots. You...gave me everything, Maria. More than I had a right to."

"But I didn't love you like I should love a son. When he told me that day that he wanted to raise you, that he had decided it, in true arrogant Theseus fashion—" laughter burst through the tears running down her cheeks "—that you were our son now, I promised him I would love you like one. That I would embrace you in every way. But I did not. I...was weak. I let my love for Helena blind me. She came so late into our lives...when I had given up on the idea of a child completely that I didn't see how much I was spoiling her."

"You don't need to explain."

"I do. I need to. I didn't just let Theseus down, and you down. I let myself down, too."

He felt her stand next to him, the subtle floral perfume she always wore twisting through him. His belly clenched, the scent of her enveloping him in kindness, filling him with longing. Filling him with an endless need for acceptance, for love.

His jaw clenched, a lump of emotion in his throat. "She is your daughter. I do not begrudge you your love for her. I never expected to be the same. Believe me, I understand. I...never expected more." But he hadn't been able to stop himself from wanting it anyway. From needing it.

"Oh, but it is your right to have everything, Kairos. It is your right to be loved unconditionally, not to be second to her. It is what I promised myself that day we brought you home with us. I'm sorry for forgetting that. You're everything Theseus said you would be. You are not just his. You're *my* son, too, and I am so sorry for...my actions."

"Please—"

"Will you forgive me, Kairos? Will you forgive my foolish hope in thinking that she would change, for thinking she deserved one more chance every time? Will you forgive me for not loving you as I should have?"

She was openly sobbing now, and the sight of it broke his heart.

Kairos took her in his arms and she came with a soft cry. Tears pooled in his own eyes and he held them back by sheer will. "Shh... Maria. I cannot bear to see you like this. I forgive you. Of course, I forgive you." His words rushed out of him, a jagged crack in his heart healing over.

A lightness he had never known filled his chest. "I... I've been fortunate enough to have two mothers, Maria. I never realized how fortunate I was. I... Please, calm yourself. I can't bear to see you cry. I did everything to shield you and Theseus from her. I... She's left me no other way to stop her. I never wanted anything that should have been hers. All I wanted was to make you and Theseus proud of me. All I wanted was..." He forced himself to speak the words he'd always denied himself. To acknowledge the need inside. To admit that loving Theseus and Maria had only made him stronger, not weaker, as he had always believed. "...your love."

She wiped her tears and looked at up at him with sad eyes.

"I know, Kairos. I know you did more than a flesh-and-blood brother would have done for her. I know all the allowances you made for Helena. I know that, despite all the stupid games she played with you, you've never spoken a word against her to Theseus. You took your cue from me. You gave me even more loyalty and love than you gave Theseus. I didn't realize that until he pointed out. Until he said we did have a child who loved us more than anything in the world. You don't owe her anymore.

"There's a certain freedom in letting go, isn't there? She came to see me yesterday, you know. I told her in no uncertain terms that I would be part of her crazy schemes no more. Theseus told me about the trust fund idea you set up and you've been more generous than even he would have been. So let us hope this time she will truly change, *ne*?"

Kairos simply nodded, unable to form words. Unable to staunch the love that flowed within his veins. His world already felt different, lighter, brighter. He felt as if he were a new man, as if everything was possible now.

As if he could let himself—

"What is this?" Maria said, taking the sheaf of documents he had left on the table. "Divorce proceedings? You and Valentina are separating?" Shock punctured very word. "I thought she left because she missed her brothers. She promised Theseus she would see him for Christmas. She..."

He had no idea what she'd seen in his eyes before he looked away. "She left me even before I came back here, before Theseus's heart attack."

"You said it had just been a small misunderstanding. Why did you bring her here then? Oh…to tell us that you were already taken." Her hand on his shoulder turned him. "Did she want to leave again when you'd accomplished everything?"

"No." Even then, she had willed him to understand. Even then, she had given him another chance. Then another chance. What a heartless man he was to have turned her away! What a coward! "I sent her away."

"And she went away dutifully? For some reason, that doesn't suit her. Why did you send her away?"

"It was for her own good. I… Valentina…she's like a storm that ravages everything in its path, in a good way. I… I have nothing to give her, Maria. She deserves better than a man like me."

Something sad flitted in Maria's eyes. She took his hands in hers, and the simple touch calmed the furor in his gut. But nothing could ever fill the void his wife had left in his life. In his heart.

"A more honorable, kinder man, Kairos? A man who could love her more than you already do? A man who needs her so desperately that he walks around like an empty shell?"

Something jerked in the deep crevices of his being. His denial froze on his lips. He could not lie. Not to her, and not to himself.

For he did love Valentina. With every breath in him. With every cell in his body.

He had fallen for her long before he had even understood what it meant.

"I rejected her one too many times. I starved her when all she'd needed was a kind word. I hurt her again and again until whatever she might have felt for me died. I don't know how to love her, Maria. I don't know if I can give her what she needs. I don't know if I could bear it if she...if she stopped loving me. She would destroy me then."

Maria enfolded her arms around him. It was a mother's embrace, something he had longed for for so long, something he had needed for so long. The fear and anguish he had been fighting for weeks flooded him.

"Oh... Kairos. Trust yourself, trust the bond between you two. And trust her love for you."

He nodded, hope unfurling within him. His wife had a generous heart. He had to trust his into her keeping. He had to take the biggest risk of his life if he wanted her.

And he did want her.

Pulling back from the hug, Maria laughed. "How about you and I make a pact? We shall be brave and beg for forgiveness from the ones we love, *ne*?"

He laughed at her suggestion, sobered at the wary glance she cast toward Theseus's bedroom. He kissed her cheek, breathing in her scent one more time. Willing her to lend him a fraction of the courage she had.

"We will be brave in love, together," he whispered.

She nodded, kissed both his cheeks. "You will not stay away for another seven years, will you, Kairos?"

"No, I won't. This is not goodbye, Maria. Valentina and I will spend Christmas here."

She nodded and hugged him again, and in her embrace, Kairos found the strength he needed.

The strength to love the woman who had stolen his heart a long time ago.

CHAPTER FOURTEEN

THE LAST THING Kairos wanted to face, when all he wanted was to see and touch Valentina, was a battalion of over-bearing, interfering, annoying Contis.

Yet when he had finally bulldozed his way into Villa De Conti on the banks of Lake Como almost three weeks later, on a crisp November evening, the family, including the patriarch Antonio, were assembled around the ornate dining table, all staring up at him, mostly with varying degrees of anger, mistrust and doubt.

Except Leandro's little girl Isabella, who instantly wrapped her arms around him for a quick hug.

"Hello, Isabella," he said returning her hug.

Sophia stared at him with searching eyes. Whatever she had seen there, she pushed her chair back and embraced him.

"I'm not going to ask you how you are," she whispered, only for his ears. "You look awful."

"You know what she's capable of," he answered in kind, not even pretending to misunderstand.

"You deserved it."

Suddenly, panic-fueled urgency filled him. "Do I have a chance, Sophia?"

She betrayed nothing. "That's for her to tell you, Kairos." She smiled fondly then. "Always calculating the odds before you take the leap, *si*? It will not work in this."

He could never understand how smart, sensible Sophia

could tolerate the charming scoundrel that was the Conti Devil, but then he still didn't understand what his vivacious wife had ever seen in him to love.

"Being married suits you," he said with a smile.

She blushed before going back to her place next to her husband.

"What the hell do you want now?" Luca growled at him from the top end of the table, sitting exactly opposite Leandro on the other side.

"I wish to speak to my wife."

"She's not here."

"You're lying. And I will beat you to a bloody pulp and mar that pretty face if you get in my way again."

Utter silence descended over the table.

"Don't you think you've hurt her enough?" Again from the crazy genius. "Not counting the fact that you endangered her by letting loose that woman on Tina."

Kairos didn't know what he was doing until he had Luca's shirt bunched in his shoulders. The fear inside him knew no bounds. "What the hell are you talking about?"

Something in his tone must have communicated itself to him, because Luca's voice softened. "Helena came to see Valentina at work and caused a huge scene. I was there thankfully, and I think Tina talked some sense into her."

"Also, Tia Tina told me she slapped that horrible woman," Izzie piped up. "Oops, I wasn't supposed to tell you guys that."

Thee mou, what had Helena done to hurt Valentina?

Luca loosened his shirt from Kairos's grip. "I honestly don't think you're right for her. All you have caused her so far is pain."

The barb stuck home but Kairos forced himself to ignore Luca. Instead he addressed Leandro, who had always been the more sensible one.

"I have been trying for three weeks to see her. To contact her. She's still my damned wife. I should have been told Helena was here. It is I who brought Valentina into her focus. I should have been—" He couldn't even get the words out.

"Tina forbade us, Kairos," Sophia added softly.

"You've no right to stop me. To block my attempts." The stunt that Luca had pulled a week ago when he had ferried Valentina away on his beastly bike while Kairos had been waiting in the front lounge made his blood boil.

Leandro sighed. "She doesn't want to see you. And I will not lose her by interfering again, just when she is back in our lives."

"I'm not asking for your interference. I'm asking you to stay out of this. She is mine—to protect and to hold on to." The ragged words escaped before he could stop them.

Every gaze looked upon him with varying degrees of shock and pity now.

Leandro's wife, Alexis, shrugged. "He has a point, Leandro. You're still protecting her."

"Have you seen the look she gets in her eyes when she thinks no one's looking at her?" Luca demanded of Alexis.

"*Si*, Luca. We have all seen it," Sophia responded, with a hand over his shoulder. "And that tells me more than anything that we should give Kairos a chance. We all make mistakes."

"Not the same one, twice," Luca added meaningfully.

"She's in the garden," Alexis added hurriedly. "And she has a guest, so maybe you should wait."

"Who?"

"Ethan King," Luca said with a wicked smile, twisting the knife a little in Kairos's gut.

Sophia sent him a warning glance. "He's been talking to her about investment opportunities in her new boutique."

Kairos had heard enough. With a muttered curse, he made his way to the garden when Izzie pointed out, "They're not in the garden anymore. I saw them going up the stairs, into her bedroom."

Valentina had barely settled in the sitting room of her suite and pulled up her website analytics with Ethan when her hand hit the glass of white wine she had poured for him.

Cursing to herself, she mopped up the wine from the sofa and was about to hand him the napkin when the door of her bedroom opened with a hard slam. It hit the wall, then swung forward until Kairos stopped its momentum.

His gaze took in her outstretched hand over Mr. King's shirt and thunder dawned in the silver gaze.

Before she could think, she guiltily snatched her hand back. And then regretted the move.

He had no rights over her. She had done nothing to be guilty about, either.

He stared at her with such naked emotion shining in his eyes that it took her a few minutes to process the surge of her own feelings. And then pathetically, once again, she landed on hope in the end.

Her heart pounded with that same eagerness that she had tried to curb since the moment she had realized he was back in Milan. That he had been trying to see her.

But she was so tired of that hope. Exhausted from the weight of it.

"I would like to speak with you," he said, almost successful in packing away all the emotion radiating from him. "In private. At length."

"I'm not free right now," she offered softly. "Ethan only has this one hour before he leaves for the States. I've been waiting for weeks for a chance to speak with him."

His gaze flew to her open laptop and then back to her.

Uncertainty and hesitation and something else flickered in his gaze. He had never looked so vulnerable.

"Take as long as you need. I will wait outside," he said and her heart slipped a little.

Over the next few minutes, she tried to corral her thoughts. But the business proposal she had put together with Sophia's help blurred. The statistics she meant to show Ethan zigzagged, her heart focused on the man waiting outside the door for her.

He had never waited for her. He had never looked at her as if his heart was in his eyes.

Sick of the turmoil in her gut, she finally apologized to Ethan and the gentleman that he was, he was nice about it and excused himself from the room.

The door had barely closed behind him when Kairos reached her.

A white shirt and black trousers hugged his powerful physique. Dark shadows circled his eyes and instead of the satisfaction she wanted to feel, all she suffered was a soft ache.

He looked so tired. She knew how hard he worked. But more than that, she knew what a toll it would have taken on him to finish what he had started with Helena and the company.

She ached to hold him, to love him, to offer him the comfort he desperately needed. But he wouldn't allow it. He needed her but he would never admit it.

"Why is it that I always have to chase you—" his nostrils flared "—and then find you with a man in some intimate situation?"

"Maybe the question you should be asking is why is it that you're always chasing me," she countered. "What is it that you do that makes me run from you in the first place?"

He flinched and she wrapped her arms around herself.

She had promised herself she wouldn't do this. She wouldn't beg. She wouldn't complain. She would want nothing from him.

But seeing him after so many weeks, she could barely breathe, barely keep herself together.

How had she forgotten how he dwarfed everything with his presence? How he took over her very breath when he was near?

"I saw the clip from the talk show. And the vlog…that was a stroke of genius."

"*Si?*"

"I knew you had it in you. I'm glad for your success, Valentina."

"I owe it to you," she said softly.

"That internship with Chiara—"

"No, it was your criticism that I was doing nothing with my life that egged me on. I wanted to prove you wrong. To show you that I could be successful, too. Only I realized how much I enjoy it. That I'm good at it. You did teach me that I could be more than the shallow, vapid Valentina, more than what the Conti genes amount to. But you also made me realize that my value as a person doesn't depend on whether I'm a success or a failure. That I'm my own person and it is your loss if you can't love me."

How many times could one's heart break?

When she tried to step back, he clasped her arm to stop her. "Don't—" he cleared his throat "—do not retreat from me, Valentina."

Her heart crawled into her throat at the rough need he couldn't hide in his voice. "Why are you here, Kairos?"

"First, please tell me Helena didn't hurt you."

"Is that why you're here? To make sure she didn't do me lasting damage? Out of guilt?" She couldn't keep the disappointment out of her voice.

"No, I didn't know until Luca told me a few minutes ago. I'm sorry, Valentina. I should have realized—"

"She didn't hurt me, Kairos. I was actually recording the vlog when she stormed into the studio at Conti Towers. I don't think even she realized how far gone she was. She ranted that you were cutting her off, that she would make you pay for it. And that she knew how to make you suffer. I couldn't take it. I slapped her so hard that my arm still hurts. It was dramatic, almost soap-opera-like, but sometimes that's what it takes, *si*?

"I told her I would tell Theseus everything she had ever done if she didn't quietly accept what you were giving her. And then she would truly be on the streets. I told her I would set my powerful brothers loose on her if she ever came near you again. If she ever hurt you again. And I think it was helpful that Luca looked exceptionally scruffy and dangerous that day—he'd been on one of his days-without-sleep composing binge, and I think for once my threats got through—"

"I love you."

"Got through to her and she…she…" Words stuck in her throat, lodged beneath her heart. Had she imagined the words? Had she… "What did you say?"

"*S'agapao*, Valentina. So much that it terrifies me. So much that I can't sleep or eat or drink."

He fell to his knees in front of her, and Tina thought she might be hallucinating. She was afraid that she was only imagining this, that it was another dream haunting her sleep…no words came.

Until he wrapped his arms around her and buried his face in her belly. So tight that she could barely breathe.

The scent of him hit her like a thunderstorm, sinking into her pores.

He was real, this was real. The arms holding her…the

soft kisses he was planting on her belly, the huffs of his breath feathering over her skin, it was all real.

He looked up then and the love shining in his eyes stole her breath all over again. "I'm crazy about you. I love your teasing smiles, your penchant for drama, your unswerving loyalty, your generous heart." His palm rested on her chest. The thud of her heart was loud enough to roar through the room. "I love your long legs, your small breasts, your perfect skin, but more than anything I love you, *agapi mou*. I love how you love me. I love that you fight so bravely for the ones you love. I love that you make me a better man, that you fill my life with so much color and drama and noise—"

She laughed at that and he laughed and then she was in his arms. Kissing him hungrily amidst sobbing. He tasted of love and acceptance and home. Palms clasping his jaw, she kissed him until she couldn't breathe anymore. But the tears refused to stop.

She knew how much he hated tears so she buried her face in his neck. The scent of him, the taste of his skin finally calmed her.

"Shh, *moru mou*. No more tears. I would rather cut out my heart then be apart from you ever again. I was a fool not to understand how much you love me. How much I already loved you. A coward to believe that you would take it away on a whim.

"I was so afraid of hurt that I didn't even realize how long I have loved you.

"I think it started the first time even. You wore an emerald green dress that bared your entire back and you had been standing amidst your admirers and when Leandro called for you, there had been such unconditional love in your eyes, such open affection... I think I was struck immediately." His words made her gasp and she fought for her breath.

They didn't come easily to him, she knew. And she loved him all the more for it.

His palm stroked up and down her back tenderly, a torrent of endearments rushing out of him amidst a million apologies.

She felt his kiss at her temple, his shallow breaths as if, just like her, he was still unsure that she was here in his arms. "Valentina?"

"*Si?*"

"I should like to hear you say it, *pethi mou*. I am dying inside with the fear that I might have pushed you away one too many times, that finally you have realized that—"

She placed her finger on his lips.

"I love you, Kairos. I always will. I love you, knowing that you are stubborn, and ruthless and reserved. But I also love you knowing that you're kind, wonderful and extremely generous when it comes to orgasms. I recently read in some magazine that very few men actually go down on a woman whereas they expect the return all the time?"

Only his wife could insert the statistics about blow jobs into the conversation while he was pouring his heart out.

Kairos laughed, picked her up and followed her down to her bed.

He tugged her to him and kissed her some more. A lot more. Hard, consuming kisses. Soft, needy kisses. Tongues and teeth, they clung to each other until the need for air forced them apart.

He stripped her clothes and his with an urgency that devoured him.

And then she was naked for him. Long, sleek limbs toned with muscle. Small pouty breasts with lush nipples. She was perfect and she was his.

She reached out her hand to him, no shadows in her eyes. Nothing but abiding love and sultry temptation. "Come to me, please. I have missed you."

"Not more than I missed you." He growled against her mouth. "I can't be slow, *pethi mou*. Not today. I... I don't want to hurt you."

"You won't, Kairos. Trust me. Trust this thing between us, *si*?"

"Si." But there was nothing he could do to stem his urgent need.

He kissed her breasts, her belly, her legs, every inch of her perfect skin. When she scratched his back, just as frantic as him, he pushed his fingers into her wet heat. As deep as she could take him.

The need riding her, her body arching off the bed when he massaged her clit, the sheen of her skin...that calmed his need.

The scent of her arousal, that she had always wanted him, that she had again chosen him to love...it calmed the furor in his blood.

He sucked on her nipples, relentlessly pushing her to the edge until she fractured around his fingers. Until tremors built and ebbed in her slender body.

And then when the edge of their hunger for each other had been taken off, when she had calmed enough to believe that he wasn't going anywhere, he sat up, pulled her into his embrace until she was straddling him and then he thrust into her snug heat.

Arms around his back, mouths glued to each other's, they made slow, lazy love. All he wanted was to be inside her. To be surrounded by her warmth. To love her for as long as there was breath in his body.

"I love you, Valentina," he whispered, before he increased his thrusts, before release claimed his soul.

Hours later, Kairos emerged from deep sleep. His hand shot out instantly searching for his wife.

When he found her, his heartbeat returned to normal.

After he had toppled them both off the edge and into exhaustion for the third time, she had snuck down to the kitchen and had assured her family that he hadn't killed her, for she had heard them outside the door, muttering and arguing,

They had devoured the cheese and fruit plate she had brought upstairs. The white wine—he had lapped it off her breasts, her tummy and her soft folds. Whatever he did, however many times release clashed through him, it wasn't enough.

He pulled her down to lie alongside him. Her back to his chest, she cozily nuzzled into him. "I'm never going to get enough of you, I'm never going to let you go," he said, unable to cover the fierceness of his tone.

"Nor will I you," she said in a low, sleep-mussed voice. "We will have a big family, maybe four, five kids...boisterous, dramatic, noisy kids like me and we will drive you up the wall."

"That sounds like paradise."

"Kairos?"

The uncertainty still in her voice gutted him. "Yes?"

"Are you still looking for a job?"

He laughed and turned her over until she was facing him. Propping himself up on an elbow, he placed a lazy kiss on her mouth. "I am. I have offers from a few MNCs to do some house cleaning but nothing I'm interested in. We can live wherever you want. Do whatever we want. I'm not in a particular hurry to return to work."

"No. I know you're busy and that's fine but I just want to spend time with you. Have those four or five kids after a couple of years maybe?"

"*Si*. I...told Maria that we would spend Christmas with them." He frowned. "I'm sorry. I should have realized that you might want to spend it with your family."

"How about New Year with the Contis instead?"

This time, she rose up and claimed him for a soft kiss. "Hopefully by then Luca and I will be able to tolerate being in the same room."

She laughed, and then sobered. "You and Maria talked?"

"She told Theseus everything."

Her tight hug said so many things words could not. He let himself bask in the warmth of it. A hundred years together and he wouldn't have enough of Valentina.

She combed her fingers through his hair and sighed. "I have a proposal for you. But you don't have to accept it."

"Sounds important," he said trying to sound encouraging.

"I would like to live in Milan for a bit, with the boutique taking off it seems like a perfect fit."

"Valentina, we can live wherever you want, as long as we're together."

"Leandro is still looking for a CEO. He's—"

"Oxhi!"

"Kairos, please listen to me. He told me you've always been the perfect candidate. He trusts you. And I think...as the Conti heiress's loving husband, it is your right."

"I never wanted to do anything that would make you doubt my love for you."

"You won't. This doesn't. *Ti amo*, Kairos, and no job you take, no woman who wants you, will change that."

Joy suffusing his very soul, Kairos said yes to his wife.

And he meant to say yes for a very long time—to everything she asked.

* * * * *

COMING SOON!

MILLS & BOON

Coming next month

THE BRIDE'S BABY OF SHAME
Caitlin Crews

"I can see you are not asleep," came a familiar voice from much too close. "It is best to stop pretending, Sophie."

It was a voice that should not have been anywhere near her, not here.

Not in Langston House where, in a few short hours, she would become the latest in a long line of unenthused countesses.

Sophie took her time turning over in her bed. And still, no matter how long she stared or blinked, she couldn't make Renzo disappear.

"What are you doing here?" she asked, her voice barely more than a whisper.

"It turns out we have more to discuss."

She didn't like the way he said that, dark and something like lethal.

And Renzo was *here*.

Right *here*, in this bedroom Sophie had been installed in as the future Countess of Langston. It was all tapestries, priceless art, and frothy antique chairs that looked too fragile to sit in.

"I don't know what you mean," she said, her lips too dry and her throat not much better.

"I think you do." Renzo stood at the foot of her bed, one hand looped around one of the posts in a lazy, easy sort of grip that did absolutely nothing to calm Sophie's nerves. "I think you came to tell me something last night but let my temper scare you off. Or perhaps it would be more accurate to say you used my temper as an excuse to keep from telling me, would it not?"

Sophie found her hands covering her belly again, there beneath her comforter. Worse, Renzo's dark gaze followed the movement, as if he could see straight through the pile of soft linen to the truth.

"I would like you to leave," she told him, fighting to keep her voice calm. "I don't know what showing up here, hours before I'm meant to marry, could possibly accomplish. Or is this a punishment?"

Renzo's lips quirked into something no sane person would call a smile. He didn't move and yet he seemed to loom there, growing larger by the second and consuming all the air in the bedchamber.

He made it hard to breathe. Or see straight.

"We will get to punishments in a moment," Renzo said. His dark amber gaze raked over her, bold and harsh. His sensual mouth, the one she'd felt on every inch of her skin and woke in the night yearning for again, flattened. His gaze bored into her, so hard and deep she was sure he left marks. "Are you with child, Sophie?"

Continue reading
THE BRIDE'S BABY OF SHAME
Caitlin Crews

Available next month
www.millsandboon.co.uk

LET'S TALK
Romance

For exclusive extracts, competitions
and special offers, find us online:

f facebook.com/millsandboon

⊙ @millsandboonuk

🐦 @millsandboon

Or get in touch on 0844 844 1351*

For all the latest titles coming soon, visit
millsandboon.co.uk/nextmonth